PRIZE STORIES 1975:
The O. Henry Awards

PRIZE STORIES 1975:

The O. Henry Awards

EDITED AND
WITH AN INTRODUCTION
BY WILLIAM ABRAHAMS

DOUBLEDAY & COMPANY, INC.
GARDEN CITY, NEW YORK
1975

CONTENTS

PUBLISHER'S NOTE

This volume is the fifty-fifth in the O. Henry Memorial Award series.

In 1918, the Society of Arts and Sciences met to vote upon a monument to the master of the short story, O. Henry. They decided that this memorial should be in the form of two prizes for the best short stories published by American authors in American magazines during the year 1919. From this beginning, the memorial developed into an annual anthology of outstanding short stories by American authors, published, with the exception of the years 1952 and 1953, by Doubleday & Company, Inc.

Blanche Colton Williams, one of the founders of the awards, was editor from 1919 to 1932; Harry Hansen from 1933 to 1940; Herschel Brickell from 1941 to 1951. The annual collection did not appear in 1952 and 1953, when the continuity of the series was interrupted by the death of Herschel Brickell. Paul Engle was editor from 1954 to 1959 with Hanson Martin coeditor in the years 1954 to 1956; Mary Stegner in 1960; Richard Poirier from 1961 to 1966, with assistance from and co-editorship with William Abrahams from 1964 to 1966. William Abrahams became editor of the series in 1967.

Doubleday also publishes *First-Prize Stories from the O. Henry Memorial Awards* in editions that are brought up to date at intervals. In 1970 Doubleday also published under Mr. Abrahams' editorship *Fifty Years of the American Short Story*, a collection of stories selected from the series.

The stories chosen for this volume were published in the period from the summer of 1973 to the summer of 1974. A list of the magazines consulted appears at the back of the book. The choice of stories and the selection of prize winners are exclusively the responsibility of the editor. Biographical material is based on information provided by the contributors and obtained from standard works of reference.

INTRODUCTION

Short stories, even as do wines, have their years: an annual collection of stories, merely by existing, bears witness to this. And even as for wines, so for the short story: there are good years and years that are less good (disappointing, shall we say?), a fact of literary life that the editor of a literary annual such as this is all too aware of, reading through the year's harvest. To be sure, the charge of the O. Henry Awards since they were first established in 1919 is simply that they be made annually to stories of outstanding quality by American authors. That there should be fifteen or seventeen such stories, even in a less than good year, among the vast number published in a variety of periodicals each year, may lead the casual reader to a falsely optimistic conclusion as to the state of the story generally.

The stories chosen for these collections are not necessarily representative of the year's production; quite often in the past they have proved to be isolated examples of excellence, rising dramatically above a prevailing level of mediocrity or worse. No, I would argue that the test of a vintage year, such as this has undoubtedly been for the American short story, is in the *general* level of quality, which this year has been several notches above the usual. Correspondingly, the culling process for the present volume has been made more difficult than usual: a reducing down from the two hundred "possibles" (an exceptionally high figure) out of the more than one thousand stories that were read to a next-to-last group of thirty-four, read and reread, from which the final eighteen, read and reread and read again, were chosen.

This year—and at the highest as well as at the general level it has been a vintage year—for the first time in the history of the O. Henry Awards two stories, Harold Brodkey's "A Story in an Almost Classical Mode" and Cynthia Ozick's "Usurpation (Other People's Stories)," are being jointly awarded First Prize. No second and third prizes are being awarded, not out of editorial indecisiveness, but because I believe that it would be invidious to single out any other stories for special recognition when so many of those included here are so evidently of outstanding quality.

Oenologists have at their disposal a platoon of logical reasons (sun, rain, climate and vines in proper conjunction) to explain a vintage year for wines. But where a vintage year for the short story is concerned, unless one claims an omniscience no one has yet been known to possess, logic falters: one can only speculate. Tentatively, then, not pontifically, I note down some reflections or speculations on the contemporary short story, based upon a year of assiduous reading, that may account for its present excellence.

First, *technical mastery*.

Admittedly, technique is not everything, but it is something, and it is worth remarking on the high degree of skill among so many of our writers of stories. Even if one questions the value of what is being done, how it is being done is seldom in question: these writers are secure in their knowledge of the effect they want to make, and they know how to achieve it. (But between the story that is technically effective and the story that transcends its technique, moving us at a deeper level of response, there is a crucial difference: the difference of art.) I am not thinking now of the mastery of a formula: to write, as though to order, what was once upon a time known as "the formula story," in one or another of its prescribed, manufactured variations. That sort of story has found its ultimate destination now in the television playlet or segment, and certain die-hard sex-oriented magazines, interestingly enough, both "media" are hedged about with taboos that virtually make a formula a necessity. Meanwhile we have arrived at a point where even the magazines of giant circulation, except those few just noted, are not aggressively seeking out the formulated story; indeed, in so far as their editors are prepared to dole out space to fiction, I've the impression that they are as likely to do so to "something different" as to "something familiar." (In these circumstances, one can't help but feel that the venerable textbooks, guidebooks and short cuts to success—even when produced by famous old hands for mail order, step-by-step writing courses— might well be consigned to the wastebasket, where the stories that have been modeled upon their advice are fairly certain to end up anyway.)

Next, *adventurousness.*

To seek out new ways of telling the story has become a concern of increasing importance among large numbers of contemporary writers, to transform according to the needs of one's own vision those elements that Tradition dictates are essential to the story—character, setting, theme and narrative—without which, Tradition would insist, there can be no story. I should add that I am not referring here to those writers who have disavowed an interest in the communicative possibilities of language at a verbal level and whose experiments thus far would seem to have greater relevance to the graphic and typographic arts than to the art of fiction.

Consider the title of Harold Brodkey's story of an adolescent boy and his mother dying of cancer: "A Story in an Almost Classical Mode." Consider, in particular, that qualifying "Almost," with its faint, bemused, inescapable ironies, for however classical or traditional the basic materials Brodkey has drawn upon—the relations of parents and children, the death of parents, the struggles of children to survive, becoming in their turn parents of children struggling to survive *their* dying—have served and will continue to serve generations of writers; these basic materials are made in his story to seem newly created, peculiar to himself, unutterably strange, and, for anyone who reads with care and sympathy, I think unforgettable.

Brodkey begins: "My protagonists are my mother's voice and the mind I had when I was thirteen." And at once Tradition, always ever so slightly missing the point of what is new, demands How can a protagonist be a "voice" (even a mother's voice) or a "mind" (even the mind of a thirteen-year-old)? The answer simply is that the author means what he says. His story is given to us with a classical severity or dignity—on a stage, so to speak, as clear of bric-a-brac as a seventeenth-century French tragedy—almost exclusively through the mother's voice and the boy's mind, but both have been realized for us by the narrator, writing years after the events he purports to describe, drawing upon memories he has dredged up and subjected to intelligent scrutiny as much (we are made to believe) for *his* benefit as to satisfy *our* curiosity. No wonder he concludes, "Make what use of this you like." He himself has already made use of it: he has written the story.

And what of the protagonist in Cynthia Ozick's "Usurpation

(Other People's Stories)," that nest of stories within stories, ever more rewarding, more tantalizing in their convolutions and metamorphoses? Who is the protagonist? Whose story *is* it?—as Tradition might be expected to ask. Is it of the narrator, an ambitious young storyteller herself, about whose "actual life" we know less than Scheherazade's? Or has Miss Ozick created a collective protagonist, all those storytellers, her predecessors and successors, with whom she seems to become entangled in this marvelous web she spins for our edification. Or is it not—yes, I think it is—storytelling itself, the storyteller's art, that is at the center of the story, its true hero/heroine? What Miss Ozick celebrates is the immemorial impulse to tell a story, the "silver crown" that like a laureate's wreath has been passed down through the centuries, although she ends, deliberately, on a note of grotesque denigration—"Then the taciturn little Canaanite idols call him, in the language of the spheres, kike"—as if to remind us that while the story may sometime become a work of art, there will always be Philistines in this world (and the next) to dismiss it as no more than a story, something of no consequence.

Finally, *a respect for language.*

Of course, it is possible to be adventurous and technically skilled, and yet be handicapped, as an artist at least, by an inability to write a prose of one's own. Successful authors suffering from this handicap are said to write in a "serviceable" style; it is also banal and lacking in character. But such epithets don't apply to the prose, in whatever style, of the contemporary short story at its best. Perhaps it is with this decisive point that I should have begun rather than ended these reflections.

It is significant, I think, that, at a time when public, official prose has sunk into a mire of platitude as dishonest in itself as the sentiments it pretends to express, writers, seemingly in reaction to the general squalor, are capable of honoring the possibilities of language, its subtleties and shadings, for expressing precisely what they mean to say. The prose in the best of their stories is of an excellence that is inseparable and indistinguishable from the excellence of the stories themselves.

I choose, as a single memorable example to quote—but the reader of this volume will discover many others in their own fashion as memorable—a paragraph from John Updike's "Nakedness," with its wonderful modulations in tone, rhythm, detail and diction:

> One morning he had walked through a mile of huckleberry and wild grape to a pond. Its rim of beach was scarcely a stride wide; only the turds and shed feathers of wild swans testified to other presences. The swans, suspended in the sun-irradiated mist upon the pond's surface, seemed gods to him, perfect and infinitely removed. Not a house, not a car, looked down from the hills of sand and scrub that enclosed the pond. Such pure emptiness under the sky seemed an opportunity it would be sacrilegious to waste. Richard took off his clothes, all; he sat on a rough warm rock. The pose of thinker palled. He stood and at the water's edge became a prophet, a Baptist; ripples of light reflected from the water onto his legs. He yearned to do something magnificent, something obscene; he stretched his arms and could not touch the sky. The sun intensified. As mist burned from the surface of the pond, the swans stirred, flapping their wings in aloof, Olympian tumult. For a second, sex dropped from him and he seemed indeed the divinely shaped center of a bowl-shaped Creation; his very skin felt beautiful—no, he felt beauty rippling upon it, as if this emptiness were loving him, licking him. Then, the next second, glancing down, he saw himself to be less than sublimely alone, for dozens of busy ruddy bodies, ticks, were crawling up through the hair of his legs, as happy in his warmth as he in that of the sun.

Prose of this quality is one of the rewards of a vintage year: we have reason to be grateful.

WILLIAM ABRAHAMS

A STORY IN AN ALMOST
CLASSICAL MODE

HAROLD BRODKEY

Harold Brodkey is the author of a collection of stories,
First Love and Other Sorrows, and a forthcoming novel.

My protagonists are my mother's voice and the mind I had when
I was thirteen.

I was supposed to have a good mind—that supposition was a
somewhat mysterious and even unlikely thing. I was physically
tough, and active, troublesome to others, in mischief or near de-
linquency at times and conceit and one thing and another (often
I was no trouble at all, however); and I composed no symphonies,
did not write poetry, or perform feats of mathematical wizardry.
No one in particular trusted my memory since each person remembered differently, or not at all, events I remembered in a way
which even in its listing of facts, of actions, was an interpretation;
someone would say, "That's impossible—it couldn't have happened like that—I don't do those things—you must be wrong."

But I did well in school and seemed to be peculiarly able
to learn what the teacher said—I never mastered a subject, though
—and there was the idiotic testimony of those peculiar witnesses,
I.Q. tests: those scores invented me.

Those scores were a decisive piece of destiny in that they affected the way people treated you and regarded you; they determined your authority; and if you spoke oddly, they argued in favor
of your sanity. But it was as easy to say and there was much evidence that I was stupid, in every way or in some ways, or as my
mother said in exasperation "in the ways that count."

I am only equivocally Harold Brodkey. I was adopted when I
was two in the month following my real mother's death, and Har-

old was a name casually chosen by Joseph Brodkey because it
sounded like Aaron, the name I'd had with my real mother. I was
told in various ways over a number of years, and I suppose it's true,
that my real father blamed me because I became ill at my mother's
death and cried and didn't trust him: I had been my mother's favorite; he kept my brother, who was older than me, and more or
less sold me to the Brodkeys for three hundred and fifty dollars
and the promise of a job in another town. I saw my brother once
a year, and he told me I was lucky to be adopted. I never told him
or anyone else what went on at the Brodkeys'.

The Brodkeys never called me Harold—Buddy was the name
they used for me. Brodkey itself is equivocal, being a corruption
of a Russian name, Bezborodko. To what extent Harold Brodkey
is a real name is something I have never been able to decide. No
decision on the matter makes me comfortable. It's the name I
ended with.

In 1943, in the middle of the Second World War, I was thirteen. Thirteen is an age that gives rise to dramas: it is a prison cell
of an age, closed off from childhood by the onset of sexual capacity
and set apart from the life one is yet to have by a remainder of
innocence. Of course, that remainder does not last long. Responsibility and Conscience, mistaken or not, come to announce that
we are to be identified from then on by what we do to other people: they free us from limitations—and from innocence—and bind
us into a new condition.

I do not think you should be required to give sympathy. In rhetoric and in the beauty of extreme feeling, we confer sympathy
always, but in most of life we do quite otherwise, and I want to
keep that perspective. The Brodkeys were a family that disasters
had pretty completely broken. My father was in his early forties
and had blood pressure so high the doctors said it was a miracle
he was alive. He listened to himself all the time, to the physiological tides in him; at any moment he could have a stroke, suffer a
blood clot, and pass into a coma: this had happened to him six
times so far; people said, "Joe Brodkey has the constitution of a
horse." He was not happy with a miracle that was so temporary.
And my mother had been operated on for cancer, breast cancer:
that is, there'd been one operation and some careful optimism,
and then a second operation and there was nothing left to remove
and no optimism at all. She was forty-five or so. My mother and

father were both dying. There was almost no end to the grossness of our circumstances. There had been money but there was no money now. We lived on handouts from relatives who could not bring themselves to visit us. I used to make jokes with my parents about what was happening, to show them I wasn't horrified, and for a while my parents were grateful for that, but then they found my jokes irritating in the light of what they were suffering, and I felt, belatedly, the cheapness of my attitude. My mother was at home, not bedridden but housebound; she said to my father such things as, "Whether you're sick or not, I have to have money, Joe; I'm not getting the best medical treatment; Joe, you're my husband: you're supposed to see to it that I have money." Joe signed himself into a Veterans Hospital where the treatment was free, so she could have what money there was and so he could get away from her. I was in ninth grade and went to Ward Junior High School.

We lived in University City, U. City, or Jew City—the population then was perhaps thirty-five percent Jewish; the percentage is higher now. St. Louis swells out like a gall on the Mississippi River. On the western edge of St. Louis, along with Clayton, Kirkwood, Normandy, Webster Groves, is U. City. The Atlantic Ocean is maybe a thousand miles away, the Pacific a greater distance. The Gulf of Mexico is perhaps seven hundred miles away, the Arctic Ocean farther. St. Louis is an island of metropolis in a sea of land. As Moscow is. But a sea of Protestant farmers. Republican small towns. A sea then of mortgaged farms.

It used to give me a crawling feeling of something profound and hidden that neither Joe nor Doris Brodkey had been born in the twentieth century. They had been born in years numerically far away from me and historically unfamiliar. We'd never gotten as far as 1898 in a history course. Joe had been born in Texas, Doris in Illinois, both in small towns. Joe spoke once or twice of unpaved streets and his mother's bitter concern about dust and her furniture, her curtains; I had the impression his mother never opened the windows in her house: there were Jewish houses sealed like that. Doris said in front of company (before she was ill), "I remember when there weren't telephones. I can remember when everybody still had horses; they made a nice sound walking in the street."

Both Joe and Doris had immigrant parents who'd made money

but hadn't become rich. Both Joe and Doris had quit college, Joe his first week or first day, Doris in her second year; both their mothers were famous for being formidable, as battle-axes; both Joe and Doris believed in being more American than anyone; both despised most Protestants (as naïvely religious, murderously competitive, and unable to have a good time) and all Catholics (as superstitious, literally crazy, and lower class). They were good-looking, small-town people, provincially glamorous, vaudeville-and-movie instructed, to some extent stunned, culturally stunned, liberated ghetto Jews loose and unprotected in the various American decades and milieus in which they lived at one time or another —I don't know that I know enough to say these things about them.

I loved my mother. But that is an evasion. I loved my mother: how much did I love Doris Marie Rubenstein? Doris Brodkey, to give her her married name. I don't think I loved her much—but I mean the *I* that was a thirteen-year-old boy and not consciously her son. All the boys I knew had two selves like that. For us there were two orders of knowledge—of things known and unknown— and two orders of persecution.

Joe and Doris had not been kind in the essential ways to me— they were perhaps too egocentric to be kind enough to anyone, even to each other. At times, I did not think they were so bad. At times, I did. My mind was largely formed by U. City; my manners derived from the six or seven mansions on a high ridge, the three or four walled and gated neighborhoods of somewhat sternly genteel houses, the neighborhoods of almost all kinds of trim, well-taken-care-of small houses, of even very small houses with sharp gables and fanciful stonework, houses a door and two windows wide with small, neat lawns; and from districts of two-family houses, streets of apartment houses—we lived in an apartment house—from rows of trees, the branches of which met over the streets, from the scattered vacant lots, the unbuilt-on fields, the woods, and the enormous and architecturally grandiose schools.

Every afternoon without stopping to talk to anyone I left school at a lope, sometimes even sprinting up Kingsland Avenue. The suspense, the depression were worst on rainy days. I kept trying to have the right feelings. What I usually managed to feel was a premature grief, a willed concern, and an amateur's desire to be of help any way I could.

It was surprising to my parents and other people that I hadn't had a nervous breakdown.

I spent hours sitting home alone with my mother. At that time no one telephoned her or came to see her. The women she had considered friends had been kind for a while, but it was wartime and my mother's situation did not command the pity it perhaps would have in peacetime. Perhaps my mother had never actually been a friend to the women who did not come to see her: my mother had been in the habit of revising her visiting list upward. But she said she'd been "close" to those other women and that they ought to show respect for her as the ex-treasurer of the Jewish Consumptive Relief Society. She wanted those women to telephone and come and be present at her tragedy. From time to time she'd make trouble: she'd call one of them and remind her how she had voted for her in this or that club election or had given her a lift downtown when she had a car and the other woman hadn't. She told the women she knew they were hardhearted and selfish and would know someday what it was to be sick and to discover what their friends were like. She said still angrier things to her sister and her own daughter (her daughter by birth was ten years older than I was) and her brothers. She had been the good-looking one and in some respects the center of her family, and her physical conceit was unaltered; she had no use for compromised admiration. She preferred nothing. She had been a passionate gameswoman, a gambler: seating herself at a game table, she had always said, "Let's play for enough to make it interesting."

People said of her that she was a screamer but actually she didn't scream very loudly; she hadn't that much physical force. What she did was get your attention; she would ask you questions in a slightly high-pitched pushy voice that almost made you laugh, but if you were drawn to listen to her, once you were attentive and showed you were, her voice would lose every attribute of sociability, it would become strained and naked of any attempt to please or be acceptable; it would be utterly appalling; and what she said would lodge in the center of your attention and be the truth you had to live with until you could persuade yourself she was crazy, that is, irresponsible and perhaps criminal in her way.

To go see my father in the hospital meant you rode buses and streetcars for three hours to get there; you rode two streetcar lines from end to end; and then at the end of the second line you took a city bus to the end of *its* line and then a gray Army bus that went through a woods to the hospital which stood beside the Mississippi. My father thought it was absurd for me to do that. He said, "I don't need anything—sickness doesn't deserve your notice—go have a good time." To force me to stop being polite, he practiced a kind of strike and would not let me make conversation; he would only say, "You ought to be outdoors." My mother said of my father, "We can't just let him die." Sometimes I thought we could. And sometimes I thought we couldn't. If it had mattered to my father more and not been so much a matter of what I thought I ought to do, it would have been different. He was generous in being willing to die alone and not make any fuss, but I would have preferred him to make a great fuss. When he wouldn't talk, I would go outside; I would stand and gaze at the racing Mississippi, at the eddies, boilings, and racings, at the currents that sometimes curled one above the other and stayed separate although they were water, and I would feel an utter contentment that anything should be that tremendous, that strong, that fierce. I liked loud music, too. I often felt I had already begun to die. I felt I could swim across the Mississippi—that was sheer megalomania: no one even fished in the shallows because of the logs in the river, the entire uprooted whirling trees that could clobber you, carry you under; you would drown. But I thought I could make it across. I wanted my father to recognize the force in me and give it his approval. But he had come to the state where he thought people and what they did and what they wanted were stupid and evil and the sooner we all died the better—in that, he was not unlike Schopenhauer or the Christian Apologists. I am arguing that there was an element of grace in his defeatism. He said that we were all fools, tricked and cheated by everything; whatever we cared about was in the end a cheat, he said. I couldn't wish him dead as he told me I should, but when I wished he'd live it seemed childish and selfish.

Sometimes my father came home for weekends—the hospital made him, I think (letting him lie in bed was letting him commit suicide), but sometimes he did it to see me, to save me from Doris. Neither Joe nor Doris liked the lights to be on; they moved around the apartment in the shadows and accused each other of being old and sick and selfish, of being irresponsible, of being ugly.

It seemed to me to be wrong to argue that I should have had a happier home and parents who weren't dying: I didn't have a happier home and parents who weren't dying; and it would have been limitlessly cruel to Joe and Doris, I thought, and emotionally unendurable for me to begin to regret my luck, or theirs. The disparity between what people said life was and what I knew it to be unnerved me at times, but I swore that nothing would ever make me say life should be anything. . . . Yet it seemed to me that I was being done in in that household, by those circumstances.

Who was I? I came from—by blood, I mean—a long line of magic-working rabbis, men supposedly able to impose and lift curses, rabbis known for their great height and temperament: they were easily infuriated, often rhapsodic men.

On the other side I was descended from supposedly a thousand years or more of Talmudic scholars—men who never worked but only studied. Their families, their children too, had to tend and support them. They were known for their inflexible contempt for humanity and their conceit; they pursued an accumulation of knowledge of the Unspeakable—that is to say, of God.

I didn't like the way they sounded either. In both lines, the children were often rebellious and ran away and nothing more was heard of them: my real father had refused to learn to read and write; he had been a semi-professional gambler, a brawler, a drunk, a prizefighter before settling down to be a junkman. He shouted when he spoke; he wasn't very clean. Only one or two in each generation had ever been Godly and carried on the rabbinical or scholarly line, the line of superiority and worth. Supposedly I was in that line. This was more important to Doris than it was to me; she was aware of it; it had meaning to her. Doris said, "If we're good and don't lie, if you pray for me, maybe God will make Joe and me well—it can't hurt to try."

We really didn't know what to do or how to act. Some people, more ardently Jewish than we were, said God was punishing Joe and Doris for not being better Jews. My real relatives said Joe and Doris were being punished for not bringing me up as a rabbi, or a Jewish scholar, a pillar of Judaism. "I don't think the Jews are the chosen people," Joe would say, "and if they are, it doesn't look as if they were chosen for anything good." He said, "What the world doesn't need is another rabbi." At school, the resident psychologist asked my classmates and me to write a short paper about our home life, and I wrote, *It is our wont to have intelligent discussions after dinner about serious issues of the day.* The psychologist congratulated Doris on running a wonderful home from her sickbed, and Doris said to me, "Thank you for what you did for me—thank you for lying." Maybe I didn't do it for her but to see what I could get away with, what I could pass as. But in a way I was sincere. Life at home was concerned with serious questions. But in a way I wasn't ever sincere. I was willing to practice any number of impostures. I never referred to Doris as my *adopted* mother, only as my mother. I had a face that leaked information. I tried to be carefully inexpressive except to show concern toward Doris and Joe. I forgave everyone everything they did. I understood that everyone had the right to do and think as they did even if it harmed me or made me hate them. I was good at games sporadically—then mediocre, then good again, depending on how I regarded myself or on the amount of strain at home. Between moments of drama, I lived inside my new adolescence, surprised that my feet were so far from my head; I rested inside a logy narcissism; I would feel, tug at, and stroke the single, quite long blond hair that grew at the point of my chin. I would look at the new muscle of my right forearm and the vein that meandered across it. It seemed to me that sights did not come to my eyes but that I hurled my sight out like a braided rope and grappled things visually to me; my sight travelled unimaginable distances, up into the universe or into some friend's motives and desires, only to collapse, with boredom, with a failure of will to see to the end, with shyness; it collapsed back inside me: I would go from the sky to inside my own chest. I had friends, good friends, but none understood me or wanted to; if I spoke about the way things were at home, or about my real father, they disbelieved me and then didn't trust me; or if I made them believe, they felt sick, and often they would treat me as someone luckless, an object of charity, and I knew myself to be better than that. So I pitied them first. And got higher grades than they did, and I condescended to them. Doris said to me a number of times, "Don't ever tell anybody what goes on in this house: they won't give you any sympathy; they don't know how—all *they* know is how to run away. . . . Take my advice and lie, say we're all happy, lie a lot if you want to have any kind of life." I did not see how it was possible for such things as curses to exist but it seemed strange I was not ill or half-crazy and my parents were: it didn't seem reasonable that anything except the collapse of their own lives had made Joe and Doris act as they did or that my adoption had been the means of introducing a curse into the Brodkeys' existences; but it seemed snotty to be certain. I didn't blame myself exactly; but there was all that pain and misery to be lived with, and it was related to me, to my life; and I couldn't help but take some responsibility for it. I don't think I was neurotic about it.

It seemed to me there were only two social states, tact and madness; and madness was selfish. I fell from a cliff face once, rode my bicycle into a truck on two occasions, was knocked out in a boxing match because I became bored and felt sorry for everyone and lowered my guard and stood there. I wanted to be brave and decent—it seemed braver to be cowardly and more decent not to add to the Brodkeys' list of disasters by having any of my own or even by making an issue of grief or discomfort, but perhaps I was not a very loving person. Perhaps I was self-concerned and a hypocrite, and the sort of person you ought to stay away from, someone like the bastard villains in Shakespeare. Perhaps I just wanted to get out with a whole skin. I thought I kept on going for Doris's and Joe's sake but possibly that was a mealymouthed excuse. I didn't know. I tended to rely on whatever audience there was; I figured if they gaped and said, "He's a really good son," I was close to human decency. I was clear in everything I did to make sure the audience understood and could make a good decision about it and me. I was safe in my own life only when there was no one to show off to.

Doris insisted I give her what money I earned. And usually I did so that I would not have to listen to her self-righteous begging and angry persuasiveness. The sums involved were small—five dollars, ten; once it was eighty-nine cents. She had, as a good-looking woman, always tested herself by seeing what she could get from people; hysteria had inflected her old habits and made them grotesque, made her grotesque. No other man was left. No one else at all was left. Not her mother, not her own daughter by blood, not her sister: they ran away from her, moved out of town, hung up if she called. Her isolation was entire except for me. When a nephew of Joe's sent me ten dollars for my birthday, Doris said,

"I need it, I'm sick, I have terrible expenses. Don't you want to give me the money? Don't you want me to have a little pleasure? I could use a subscription to a good magazine." I used to hide money from her, rolled up in socks, tucked behind photographs in picture frames, but it would always disappear. While I was at school, she would hunt it out: she was ill and housebound, as I said, and there wasn't much for her to do.

Doris never said she was my mother; she never insisted that I had to love her; she asked things of me on the grounds that I was selfish by nature and cold and cut off from human feeling and despised people too much, and she said, "Be manly—that's all I ask." She said, "I don't ask you things that aren't good for you—it's for your own good for you to be kind to me." She would yell at me, "It won't hurt you to help me! You have time for another chance!" Doris yelled, "What do you think it does to me to see you exercising in your room—when I have to die?"

I said, "I don't know. Does it bother you a lot?"

"You're a fool!" she screamed. "Don't make me wish you'd get cancer so you'd know what I'm going through!"

If I ignored her or argued with her, she became violent, and then temper and fright—even the breaths she drew—spoiled the balance of pain and morphine in her; sometimes then she would howl. If I went to her, she would scream, "Go away, don't touch me—you'll hurt me!" It was like having to stand somewhere and watch someone being eaten by wild dogs. I couldn't believe I was seeing such pain. I would stop seeing: I would stand there and be without sight; the bottom of my stomach would drop away; there is a frightening cold shock that comes when you accept the reality of someone else's pain. Twice I was sick, I threw up. But Doris used my regret at her pain as if it were love.

She would start to yell at me at times, and I would lift my arm, my hand, hold them rigidly toward her and say, "Momma, don't . . . don't . . ." She would say, "Then don't make me yell at you. Don't cause me that pain."

It seemed the meagerest imaginable human decency not to be a party to further pain for her. But the list of things she said that caused her pain grew and grew: it upset her to see high spirits in me or a long face; and a neutral look made her think I'd forgotten her predicament; she hated any reference to sports, but she also hated it if I wasn't athletic—it reflected on her if I was a Momma's boy. She hated to talk to me—I was a child—but she had no one else to talk to; that was a humiliation for her. She hated the sight of any pleasure near her, even daydreaming; she suspected that I had some notion of happiness in mind. And she hated it when anyone called me—that was evidence someone had a crush on me. She thought it would help her if I loved no one, was loved by no one, if I accepted help from no one. "How do you think it makes me feel? They don't want to help me, and I'm the one who's dying." She could not bear any mention of the future, any reference especially to my future. "DON'T YOU UNDERSTAND! I WON'T BE HERE!"

Sometimes she would apologize; she would say, "It's not me who says those things; it's the pain. It's not fair for me to have this pain: you don't know what it's like. I can't stand it, Buddy. I'm a fighter."

She said, "Why don't you know how to act so I don't lose my temper? You aggravate me and then I scream at you and it's not good for me. Why don't you understand? What's wrong with you? You're supposed to be so smart but I swear to God you don't understand anything—you're no help to me. Why don't you put yourself in my place? Why don't you coöperate with me?"

She had scorned whatever comfort—or blame—her family had offered her; she said it was incompetent; and she scorned the comfort tendered by the rabbi, who was, she said, "not a *man*—he's silly;" and she suspected the doctors of lying to her, and the treatments they gave her she thought were vile and careless and given with contempt for her. "They burned me," Doris whimpered, "they burned *me*." Her chest was coated with radium burns, with an unpliable, discolored shell. She was held within an enforced, enraged, fearful stiffness. She couldn't take a deep breath. She could only whisper. Her wingspan was so great I could not get near her. I would come home from school and she would be lying on the couch in the living room, whimpering and abject, crying with great carefulness, but angry: she would berate me in whispers: "I hate to tell you this but what you are is selfish, and it's a problem you're going to have all your life, believe me. You don't care if anyone lives or dies. No one is important to you—but you. I would rather go through what I'm going through than be like you." At two in the morning, she came into my room, turned on the ceiling light, and said, "Wake up! Help me. Buddy, wake up."

I opened my eyes. I was spread-eagled mentally, like someone half
on one side of a high fence, half on the other, but between waking and sleeping. We sometimes had to go to the hospital in the
middle of the night. The jumble of words in my head was: *emerging, urgent, murderer, emergency*. I did not call out.

She said, "Look what they've done to me. My God, look what
they've done to me." She lowered her nightgown to her waist. The
eerie colors of her carapace and the jumble of scars moved into
my consciousness like something in a movie advancing toward the
camera, filling and overspreading the screen. That gargoylish torso.
She spoke first piteously, then ragingly. Her eyes were averted,
then she fixed them on me. She was on a flight of emotion, a drug
passage, but I did not think of that: I felt her emotion like batwings, leathery and foreign, filling the room; and I felt her ani-
mosity. It was directed at me, but at moments it was not and I
was merely the only consciousness available to her to trespass
upon. She said, "I scratched myself while I slept—look, there's
blood."

She had not made me cry since I was a child; I had not let her;
nothing had ever made me scream except dreams I'd had that my
first mother was not dead but was returning. Certain figures of
speech are worn smooth but accurate: I was racked; everything
was breaking; I was about to break.

I shouted, "Stop it."

She said enraged, "Am I bothering you? Are you complaining
about me? Do you know what I'm suffering?"

I said, "No." Then I said—I couldn't think of anything sensible—"It doesn't look so bad, Momma."

She said, "What's wrong with you? Why do you talk stupidly?"
Locks of hair trailed over her face. She said, "No one wants to
touch me."

I raised my eyebrows and stuck my head forward and jerked it
in a single nod, a gesture boys used then for O.K. when they
weren't too pleased, and I climbed out of bed. My mother told me
at breakfast the next day not to mind what she had done, it had
been the drug in her that made her do what she did; the batwings
of her drug flight seemed when I stood up to fold back, to retreat
inside her: she was not so terrifying. Merely unlikable. And sickening. I put my arms around her and said, "See. I can hug you."

She let out a small scream. "You're hurting me."

"O.K., but now go back to bed, Momma. You need your sleep."

"I can't sleep, why don't you want to kill the doctor for what he's done to me . . ."

She said for weeks, whenever she was drugged, "If I was a man, I'd be willing to be hanged for killing a man who did this to a woman I loved."

She'd had five years of various illnesses and now cancer and she still wasn't dead.

I would come home from school to the shadowy house, the curtains drawn and no lights on, or perhaps one, and she would be roaming barefooted with wisps of her hair sticking out and her robe lopsided and coming open; when I stood there, flushed with hurrying, and asked, "Momma, is it worse?" or whatever, she would look at me with pinched-face insanity and it would chill me. She would shout, "What do you mean, is it worse? Don't you know yet what's happened to me? What else can it be but worse! What's wrong with you? You're more of my punishment, you're helping to kill me, do you think I'm made of iron? You come in here and want me to act like your valentine! I don't need any more of your I-don't-know-what! You're driving me crazy, do you hear me? On top of everything else, you're driving me out of my mind."

Feelings as they occur are experienced as if they were episodes in Kafka, overloaded with hints of meaning that reek of eternity and the inexplicable and that suggest your dying—always your dying—at the hands of a murderousness in events if you are not immediately soothed, if everything is not explained at once. It is your own selfishness or shamefulness, or someone else's or perhaps something in fate itself that is the murderer; or what kills is the proof that your pain is minor and is the responsibility of someone who does not care. I didn't know why I couldn't shrug off what she did and said; I didn't blame her; I even admired her when I didn't have to face her; but I did not see why these things had to happen, why she had to say these things. I think it mattered to her what I felt. That is, if I came in and said, "Hello, Momma," she would demand, "Is that all you can say? I'm in *pain*. Don't you care? My God, my God, what kind of selfish person are you? I can't stand it."

If I said, "Hello, Momma, how is your pain?" she would shriek, "You fool, I don't want to think about it! It was all right for a moment! Look what you've done—you've brought it back. . . . *I don't want to be reminded of my pain all the time!"*

She would yell, "What's wrong with you? Why don't you know how to talk to me! My God, do you think it's easy to die? Oh my God, I don't like this. I don't like what's happening to me! My luck can't be this bad." And then she would start in on me: "Why do you just stand there? Why do you just listen to me! It doesn't do me any good to have you there listening! You don't do anything to help me—what's wrong with you? You think I'm like an animal? Like a worm? You're supposed to be smart, but you don't understand anything, you're no good to me, you were never any good to me. I'd laugh at you, you're so useless to me, but it hurts me to laugh: what good are you to me? Do something for me! Put yourself in my place! Help me! Why don't you help me?"

Sometimes she would say in a horrible voice, "I'll tell you what you are—I'll tell you what everyone is! They're trash! They're all trash! My God, my God, how can my life be like this? I didn't know it would be like this. . . ."

I really did not ever speak to anyone about what went on at home, but one of the teachers at school suggested that I apply for a scholarship to Exeter, so that I could get away from the "tragedy in your home." And get a good education as well. I was secretly hopeful about going to boarding school a thousand miles away. I did not at all mind the thought that I would be poorer and less literate than the boys there. I figured I would be able to be rude and rebellious and could be hateful without upsetting my mother and I could try to get away with things.

I remember the two of us, Doris and me in the shadowy living room: I'm holding some books, some textbooks. She's wearing a short wrap-around housecoat, with a very large print of vile yellow and red flowers with green leaves on a black background. I've just told her casually I can go away to school; I put it that I would not be a burden on her anymore or get on her nerves; I told her I did not want to be a burden—I said something like that; that was my attempt at tact. She said, "All right—leave me too—you're just like all the rest. You don't love anyone, you never loved anyone. You didn't even mourn when your real mother died, you don't ever think about her—I'll tell you what you are: you're filth. Go. Get out of here. Move out of here tonight. Pack up and go. I don't need you. No one will ever need you. You're a book, a stick, you're

all booklearning, you don't know anything about people—if I
didn't teach you about people, people would laugh at you all the
time, do you hear me?"

I went into another room and I think I was sitting there or
maybe I was gathering together the ten or fifteen books I owned,
having with a kind of boy's dishonesty I suppose, taken Doris's
harangue as permission to leave her, as her saying yes in her way to
my going away, my saving myself, when she came in. She'd put on
lipstick and a hair ribbon; and her face, which had been twisted
up, was half all-right, the lines were pretty much up and down and
not crooked; and my heart began to beat sadly for myself—she was
going to try to be nice for a little while; she was going to ask me
to stay.

After that she seemed to feel I'd proved that I belonged to her;
or it had been proved I was a man she could hold near her still.
Every day, I came home from school, and Doris fluttered down
from her filthy aerie of monstrous solitude and pain: in a flurry
of dust and to the beating of leathery wings, she asked me a riddle.
Sometimes she threatened me: she'd say, "You'll die in misery too
—help me now and maybe God will be good to you." Or she'd say,
"You'll end like me if you don't help me!" She'd say it with her
face screwed up in fury. She'd say, "Why don't you put yourself
in my place and understand what I'm going through." It occurred
to me that she really didn't know what she was saying—she was
uttering words that sounded to her close to something she really
wanted to say; but what she said wasn't what she meant. Maybe
what she meant couldn't be said. Or she was being sly because
she was greedy and using bluff or a shortcut and partly it was her
own mental limitation and ineptness: that is, she couldn't say
what she hadn't thought out.

It wasn't enough that I stayed with her and did not go to Exeter. She railed at me, "You're not doing me any good—why don't
you go live in the Orphans' Home: that's where heartless people
who don't deserve to have a family belong." We both knew that I
didn't have to go to the Orphans' Home but maybe neither of us
knew what she meant when she demanded I help her. It was
queer, the daily confrontations, Doris and me not knowing what
she wanted from me or even what the riddle really was that she
was asking. She crouched there or seemed to at those moments,

in the narrow neck of time between afternoon and evening, between the metaphorical afternoon of her being consigned to death and the evening of her actual dying, and she asked me some Theban riddle while she was blurred with drugs, with rage, and I looked at her and did not know what to do.

But after a while I knew sort of what she was asking: I knew sort of what the riddle was; but I couldn't be sure. I knew it was partly she wanted me to show I loved her in some way that mattered to her, that would be useful; and it was wrong of her to ask, I knew because she was ashamed or afraid when she spoke to me and she averted her eyes, or they would be sightless, unfocussed from the morphine. In a way, pity could not make me do anything, or love. The final reasons are always dry ones, are rational and petty: I wanted to do something absolutely straightforward and finally loyal to her, something that would define my life with her in such a way that it would calm her and enable me to be confident and less ashamed in the future and more like other people. And also if I was going to live with her for a while, things had to change; I wanted to know that life for me did not have to be like *this*. Things had to be made bearable for both of us.

It doesn't sound sensible—to make her dying and my being with her bearable. But it is language and habit that make the sense odd. It was clear to me that after a process of fantastic subtraction I was all that was left to her. And for me what with one odd subtraction and another, she was the only parent I had left to me; she was my mother.

I could half see, in the chuffing, truncated kind of thought available to my thirteen-year-old intelligence that the only firm ground for starting was to be literal: she had asked me to put myself in her place. O.K. But what did that mean? How could I be a dying, middle-aged woman walking around in a housedress?

I knew I didn't know how to think; I guessed that I had the capacity—just the *capacity*—to think: that capacity was an enormous mystery to me, perhaps as a womb is to a woman. When I tried to think, I wandered in my head but not just in my head; I couldn't sit down physically and be still and think: I had to be in movement and doing something else; and my attention flittered, lit, veered, returned. Almost everyone I knew could *think* better than I could. Whenever I thought anything through, I always became a little angry because I felt I'd had to think it out to reach a point that someone better parented would have known to start with. That is, whenever I thought hard, I felt stupid and under-privileged. I greatly preferred to feel. Thinking for me was always accompanied by resentment, and was in part a defensive, a rude and challenged staring at whatever I was trying to think about; and it was done obstinately and blunderingly—and it humiliated me.

Death, death, I said to myself. I remembered Doris saying, "I don't want to be shut up in a coffin." That was fear and drama: it didn't explain anything. But it did if she wasn't dead yet: I mean I thought that maybe the question was *dying. Dying.* Going to-ward a coffin. Once when I was little I'd found a horizontal door in the grass next to a house; I had been so small the door had been very hard to lift and to lay down again because my arms were so short; when the door was open, you saw stairs, unexpected in the grass, and there was a smell of damp and it was dark below, and you went down into an orderly place, things on shelves, and the light, the noises, the day itself, the heat of the sun were far away; you were coolly melted; your skin, your name dissolved; you were turned into an openness, into being a mere listening and feeling; the stillness, the damp, the aloneness, the walls of earth, of moist, whitewashed plaster soaked you up, blurred you; you did not have to answer when anyone called you.

And when you fell from your bike, while you were falling, the way everything stopped except the knowledge that pain was com-ing. The blotting out of voices, the sudden distance of everything, the hope, the conviction almost that this was a dream, the way time drew out, was airy, and nothing was going to happen, and then everything turned to stone again; it was going to happen; the clatter of your bike crashing, your own fall; and then finally you sat up with disbelief and yet with knowledge: you saw your torn pants; you poked at the bleeding abrasions on your elbow that you had to twist your arm to see. You felt terrible but you didn't know yet, you couldn't know everything that had happened to you.

I remembered in pictures, some quite still, some full of motion, none of them rectangular; and what I meant, while it was clear enough to me at first, became liquid and foggy when I tried to es-tablish in words what it was I meant, what it was I now knew; it slid away into a feeling of childishness, of being wrong, of knowing nothing, after all.

Doris wouldn't have those feelings about dying. And my feelings were beside the point and probably wrong even for me. Then my head was blank and I was angry and despairing; but all at once my scalp and neck wrinkled with gooseflesh. I had my first thought about Doris. She wouldn't think in those pictures, and they didn't apply to her because she wouldn't ever think in pictures that way, especially about dying: dying was a fact. She was factual and pictureless.

Then after that I made what I called an equation: Doris-was-Doris. I meant that Doris was not me and she was really alive.

That made me feel sad and tired and cheated—I resented it that she was real and not me or part of me, that her death wasn't sort of a version of mine. It was going to be too much Goddamned work this way.

I went off into "thinking," into an untrained exercise of intellect. I started with x's and y's and Latin phrases. I asked myself what was a person, and, after a while, I came up with: a person is a mind, a body, and an *I*. The *I* was not in the brain, at least not in the way the mind was. The *I* is what in you most hurts other people—it makes them lonely. But the mind and body make it up to people for your *I*. The *I* was the part that was equal in all men are created equal and have the same rights to life, liberty, and the pursuit of happiness. The emotions of the *I* were very different from the emotions of the body and the mind. When all three parts of you overlapped, it was what people meant by "the heart."

Doris's heart. Doris's mind, Doris's body, Doris's *I*.

Inside a family, people have mythologically simple characters—there's the angry one, the bookish one, and so on, as if everyone was getting ready to be elevated and turned into a constellation at any moment. Notions of character were much less mythical once you got outside a family usually. Doris in her family was famous for her anger, but she had also said of herself a number of times that she had more life in her than her husband or her mother and sister and brothers and daughter. It had always made me curious. What did it mean to have more life in you? She'd never said I had much life in me, or a little. It seemed to me on reflection Doris had meant her temper. A lot of her temper came from restlessness and from seeing people and things the way she did. She'd meant she couldn't sit quietly at home or believe in things that weren't real. Or be a hypocrite. She'd meant she was a fighter; active—but she never played any sport, not any; she was the most unexercised woman I knew of: she never did housework, never went dancing anymore (I meant before she'd been sick), never swam or played tennis, never gardened or walked, never carried groceries—if she shopped she paid a delivery boy to bring the groceries home for her. She never failed to sleep at night although she complained of sleeping badly—she didn't have so much life she couldn't sleep. She dreamed a lot; she liked to have things happen, a lot every day. She liked to go places, to get dressed up, to get undressed and be slatternly: she was always acting, always busy being someone, performing in a way. Was that the life in her? She insisted on people controlling their minds and not thinking too much and she didn't approve of bodies being too active —she really was mostly interested in the *I: I like to live, I want a good life, you don't know how to live, I know what life is, I know how to live, there's a lot of life in me, I have a lot of life in me.*

I thought these things at various times; they occurred to me over a number of days. My mind wandered into and out of the subject. Preoccupied with it at times, I dropped and broke things or got off the bus at the wrong stop or stumbled on the curbstone, holding my textbooks in one hand, their spines turned upward leaning against my thigh, in the style of a sharp high school boy. Girls at school told me I was looking "a lot more mature."

Every once in a while, I would remember something: Doris saying angrily, "I pushed my brothers, I put every idea they had into their heads, I was somebody in that little town—" (In Illinois.) "People thought I was something, it was me that gave my brothers a name; that's all it takes to win an election, a name. J.J. was mayor, Mose was police commissioner—you don't think it did them some good? And I put them over. They looked *Jewish*—it was *my* looks, me and Joe, Joe was in the American Legion: believe me, that helped. And it was all my idea. Momma never wanted us to do nothing, Momma thought the Gentiles would kill us if we got to be too outstanding. She was always in Russia in her mind. I was the smartest one—Momma and my brothers weren't as smart as I was. I could always get people to do what I

wanted. Who do you think told J.J. what to wear? I taught him
how to look like a businessman so he could go into St. Louis and
people wouldn't laugh at him. I found him his wife, he owes me a
lot. But I have to give him credit, he's the only one who had
brains, he's the only one who did anything with what I told him.
If you ask me, Mose can't count to fifteen without getting a head-
ache, and Joe was not smart either. Joe was vain: when he went
bald I had to fight with him to take off his hat in the house: he did
have pretty hair: he was too blond to be a Jew. But everything
was a pose with him, he never did anything because it was smart, it
was always Joe putting his hand in his pocket and being a big
shot—believe me, a lot of women thought he was attractive. But
you couldn't talk to Joe, no one could ever talk to Joe, he wouldn't
listen, he had his own ideas—ideas! I'm the one to say it, I married
him, I made my bed—he was dumb: I had to have the brains for
both of us. But good-looking, my God. The first time I saw him I
couldn't believe it, he was so good-looking: I didn't think he was
Jewish. He was in an officer's uniform. You can imagine. I was
never photogenic but I was something to look at, myself. Joe took
one look at me and he didn't know if he was coming or going. He
cut in on me at a dance and asked me to marry him just like that
and he meant it. He meant well. I really wasn't bad-looking: people always told me everything. I was too pretty when I was young
to make it in St. Louis—older women ran things in St. Louis—you
think I didn't catch on? St. Louis is a good town for a woman
when you get older: I know what I'm talking about. I knew the
right time to move here. If Joe had been a businessman, we could
have caught up with J.J.—we had good chances, people liked me,
but Joe didn't go over, he didn't make friends with smart people,
he wouldn't take my advice. I should have been the type who could
get divorced but I never believed in divorce: it would just be the
frying pan into the fire: marriage is never easy. Listen, I'm smart:
I'd've liked to try my luck in Chicago, I've always been outstanding, I've always impressed people. . . ."

It seemed to me from what little I could remember about her
when I was little, and before Joe became ill, that she had interested the people around her. Everyone had looked at her wherever
she went and people waited for her to arrive for the excitement to
start. And they had been afraid of her too. When she was all
dressed up—and even when she wasn't—she often looked glamor-

ous and interesting: she'd worn things like a black suit with wide
lapels, very high-heeled black shoes, longish black gloves, a diamond bracelet on the outside of one glove, a fur neckpiece, fox
heads biting their tails, a tight-fitting hat with a long feather fastened to it by a red jewel, and a veil drawn over her face; and behind the veil a very red lipsticked mouth.

I hadn't as a child clearly understood what we were to each
other. She'd been so different in her moods, she hadn't ever
seemed to be one person, to be the same person for long, to be the
same person at all. When I was little, I'd been allowed to sit on
her bed and watch her get dressed—this had been a privilege
awarded me and a kind of joke and thing of affection. She'd been
a slightly dumpy, slack-skinned, nervous woman with a wried
mouth and eyes muddy with temper. She would arrange a towel
around her shoulders and bosom while she sat at a vanity table,
and then she would brush her hair; she would beat at her hair with
the brush; she would stick out her chin and brace against the force
of her brushing. What was wonderful was that as she brushed, a
faint life, like a sunrise, would creep into her face—a smoothness;
she'd be less wrinkled, less skewed in anger or impatience, in bitterness or exhaustion; a pinkness, very faint, would spread around
the line of her hair; her face would not look so ashen then. Part
of it was that her hair would begin to shine, part was that her
face would reveal an increasing, magical symmetry, part was the
life in her eyes, but she became pretty. I would stare at her reflection in the mirror. I had to keep looking at her because if I closed
my eyes or ran out of the room, the prettiness would disappear
from my head, and then I'd have to run back and look at her.
Seated at the vanity table, she'd say things that were strange to
me and grown-up (I thought) and private. "I had good coloring
when I was young but you know what they say: you don't stay
young forever." Or, "I look like a ghost." On the spur of the moment she would change the curve of her eyebrows and the shape
of her lips or use another shade of powder and of lipstick: it would
be very strained while she did it, she would be intent and bold
and willful, like a gambler. God, the hushed niceness of the looks,
the romantic, whispery, gentle niceness she would often end with.
Sometimes she tried for startlingly dramatic looks and got them
or partly got them; sometimes she failed and had to wipe her face
clean and redo her hair and start over. She would get, at this point,

if things seemed to be working, a blunt, broad, female, and sarcastic excitement, a knowing gaiety, a tough-fibered, angry pleasure and a despair that moved me. If I said, "You're pretty, Momma," she would say in the new voice of her new mood, "Do you think I'm the cat's miaow?" Sometimes she would keep repeating that but in changing, softening voices until she came to a gentle, teasing voice, one as sweet as a lullaby with agreeable and patient inner themes. She was a complete strategist. Sometimes she would sing "Yes, Sir, That's My Baby." As if she was a man and was admiring herself. Sometimes her voice would be quavering and full of half-suffocated, real pleasure, readily amorous or flirtatious. I think she was always the first to be affected by her looks.

Three times that I can think of, when I was alone at home, I sneaked a look into my mother's bureau, at her underwear . . . but also at her jewelry and handkerchiefs and sweaters: I wanted to see what was hidden. Other motives I pass over. Once, and maybe twice, I tried on a nightgown of hers and danced on the bed and saw myself in the bureau mirror. I don't remember feeling that I was like a woman in any way. I can remember moments of wanting to be one, when I was fairly young—to wear a turban and be opinionated and run everything in the house and not ever have to prove myself—but the wish wasn't sexual, so far as I know, or profound or long-lived. It was envy of women having power without having to serve apprenticeships for it. And also it was a daydream about safety and being taken care of and undoing some of the mistakes of having grown to be seven or eight years old: a woman like a little boy was a specialist in being loved.

My ignorance about women was considerable—why were women so secretive? I knew my mother and my sister faked just about absolutely everything they did with men, but why? Their temper, their good nature, their unhappiness, their happiness were almost always fake—but why? I didn't understand what the need was for all the fraud.

No man or boy was ever permitted to be outspoken near a woman. In U. City, there weren't too many docile, crushed women or girls; I didn't know any. In U. City, women sought to regulate everyone in everything; they more or less tried to supersede governmental law, instinct, tradition, to correct them and lay down new rules they insisted were the best ones. Nearly everything they wanted from us—to be polite, to sit still, to be considerate, to be protective—was like a dumb drumming of their wanting us to be like women. The rarest thing in a woman was any understanding of the male. And that wasn't asked of them. Women were highly regarded and in U. City it was considered profoundly wicked to be rude to any of them. One simply fled from them, avoided them. Their unjust claims. I mean we respected women as women, whatever they were as people.

I thought about my mother's name, Doris Marie Rubenstein Brodkey, as mine. It seemed intensely silly to be called Doris. Then one day I thought about being a woman called Doris who was all dressed up and then was being pushed head first into a keg of oil. It was unbearable. And disgusting. I thought I had imagined what it was like to be Doris dying, to be a dying woman. I woke the next day from a night's sleep having realized in my sleep I had not imagined my mother's dying at all.

She was in her forties and she had cancer and she had some twist to her character so that she drove people away. People said she had "a bad mouth"—she was cutting and shrill, demanding, she said true things in full malice. The more I thought about being her, the more masculinely I held myself: even my thoughts were baritone.

She had an odd trait of never blaming herself, and nothing anyone ever said about her affected her in a way that led her to change. She never listened to my father at all, or to her mother, or her daughter, or her friends. That simmered in my head a few days before it took another shape. I was at football practice. We were running up and down the football field lifting our knees high as we were told. I was afraid of the coach. Suddenly it occurred to me my mother was undisciplinable, ineducable and independent: she refused to be controlled by sexual pleasure, so far as I could see, or by conventional notions of what was maternal or by what people thought or by their emotional requirements. But it was a queer independence and one of the mind or of the pride: she felt it in her mind: but it wasn't what I'd call independence: she was tied to her family; she couldn't conceive of moving far away; she couldn't bear to be alone; she needed to have someone in love with her: she was independent of the claims of the person in love with her, but she needed the feelings directed at her for her to be independent of something. Time after time, after quarrels with certain friends or with her family, she would say, "I don't care, I don't need them," but she was peculiarly defenseless and *always* let people come back, even if they were just wastes of time and drains on her energy. She couldn't bear to lose anyone. She was like a creature without a shell and without claws and so on—she was rather a soft person—and she sort of with her mind or mother-wit made a shell and claws, and needed, and wanted, and pursued people, men and women, who would be part of her —of her equipment—who would care about her and outfit her and help her. She fawned on such people to get them to like her until she felt, correctly or paranoiacally, that they didn't care about her, that they had failed her; then she would assail them behind their back for practice and when the scurrility was polished she'd deliver it to their faces.

It seemed hot and airless even to begin to work on imagining what it was like to be my mother.

One thing I did not know then but half know now was that I was not independent of her. I thought then I did not love her exactly; she struck me as having no aptitude for happiness, and so there was no point in being attached to her or having a lot of feeling about her—she'd only use it against me. I knew she was no mother in any conventional sense; she herself often said as much; but the fact that she was such a terrible mother made me feel aristocratic and amused as well as tired me: I saw other mothers charging around half destroying their kids, crippling them, blinding them, and I felt protective toward my mother—this was a dry, adolescently sarcastic, helpless feeling, almost part of my sense of humor, my sense of aristocracy, if I can call it that, this being protective toward her. Also, I figured that when I was an infant someone had been kind to me: I was comparatively strong physically, and surprisingly unfrightened of things, and I gave credit for this to Doris.

But I know now I was frightened of a lot of things; I just didn't pay much attention to the fright. My ignorance, my character scared me. I could hide behind taking care of her. I leaned on the fact of having her near me; her presence, having to take care of her, supplied an answer to a lot of questions, supplied a shape. I didn't have to know who I was. Girls pushed me around a lot: there was a dim shadowy hysteria in me about that. I didn't often feel it, but I needed and resented Doris. I thought I was objective and emotionless and so on, but I wasn't: she was important to me.

I had noticed that she never blamed herself, but then I saw that she never blamed any woman much, even women she was angry with; she'd say such-and-such a woman was selfish and a lousy friend and that she never wanted to see her again but my mother really only launched diatribes against men. She had a brother who'd become rich, and she said he was ruled by his wife, that his wife kept this brother from being nice to Doris, but what Momma did was stop speaking to her brother and she went on being friends with her sister-in-law.

I couldn't see how Momma managed this presumption of sin-lessness in women. Finally I worked it out that she felt women were in an unfair situation, and had to do what they did. She never thought women were bound by honor or by any of the things men were bound by. At one point, enraptured with my daring, I wondered if my mother was basically a lesbian. But then it seemed to me she was much more afraid of women than she was of men, so maybe she was merely trying to get along with other women who were the real danger and so on.

She never forgave, never forgot anything I said to her in anger—she remembered rudenesses I'd committed when I was four years old. But she said that what *she* said didn't matter and didn't mean anything. The same with complaints; she went on and on about how grim life was and how terrible most people were but if I even so much as said that school was dull, she said, "Be a man—don't complain."

I couldn't figure out that one-sidedness: how did she expect not to irritate me, not to bore me? Then suddenly I had an inspiration which maybe had nothing to do with the truth, but I could imagine she might want to be independent of absolutely everything, even of having to be fair in the most minor way. . . .

My poor mother's freedom. She was utterly wretched, and at this point in her life she screamed most of the time rather than spoke. "I have no life. . . . Why did this happen to me. . . ." And, "My brothers are filth. . . ." And so on.

One day she was ranting about one of her brothers, "He used to be in love with me but now he won't come near me because I'm ugly and sick—" and it occurred to me she was enraged—and

amazed—to discover selfishness in anyone except her. No one had
the right to be selfish except Doris.

She remembered everything she had ever done as having been a
favor for someone. And this wasn't just madness, although I
thought so at first; it was her cold judgment of how life operated:
it was her estimate of what she was worth. Or a bluff. She thought
or hoped she was smarter and prettier and more realistic than
anyone.

To watch somebody and think about them is in a way to begin
to have the possibility of becoming them.

It seemed to me I could see certain ways we were already alike
and that I had never noticed before. I had never noticed that I
had almost no pity for what men suffered—in a war, say; I didn't
care if men got hurt, or if I hurt boys in a fight, so I was always
more comfortable with men than with women. And I caught sight
of something in me I hadn't admitted to consciousness but it was
that I judged all the time how well I was being taken care of, even
while thinking I did not ask to be taken care of at all. And she was
like that. She thought pain belonged to women; she did not like
men who suffered; she thought suffering in men was effeminate.
She didn't think men deserved help: she was a woman and too
exposed; she had to be taken care of first. I tried to imagine a conscious mind in which all this would seem sensible and obvious.

I heard a woman say, "It's easy for me to be nice—I have a husband who is good to me. . . ."

It was terrifying to contemplate the predicament hinted at in
such a speech.

I could believe a lot of what my mother was was what had been
done to her.

She said to me once, "I would have been happy married to a
gangster." I knew people did not always say what they meant:
they uttered words that seemed to make the idea in their heads
audible but often the sentence said nothing or said the opposite
to anyone outside their heads who did not know all the connections. Partly because the idea was defective, but more often because in simple egoism and folly one could say, especially if one
was a woman, "Why don't you understand me?" and never think
about the problem of having to make oneself clear. Men had to
make themselves clear in order to run businesses and to act as
judges, but in order to be clear they said less and less: they stand-

ardized their speeches. Or were tricky or—But anyway when my
mother said something it seemed easiest to take her literally because the literal meaning would cover more of her intention than
any interpretive reading would. She often became very angry with
me for taking her literally, but since no one else understood her
at all, ever, I thought my system was the best possible, and also,
by taking her literally, I could control her a little.

When she said she would have been happy with a gangster, it
was hard to know what she meant: did she need violence, did she
want a man who could be violent because of how he would act toward her, or because of the way he'd act toward other people? I
guessed she wanted someone to be tough toward the world, who
would be her fists, who would be no fool, and who, busy with his
own life, would give her a certain freedom. My mother did not
like needing anyone—"If you don't need anybody, you don't get
hurt"—but she needed people all the time. She said of my real
mother, "She was brave—she went where she wanted to go, she
would go alone, she didn't need anyone, I don't know where she
got the strength, but she could stand alone. I envied her, I
wanted to be like her. I wanted to adopt you because I thought
you would be like her."

I thought, without much confidence, that women were held
under the constraint of social custom more than men were: almost
all of *civilization* had to do with the protection and restraint of
women; but *that* seemed to be true of men too. My mother lived
a half-fantasy of being tough, she was verbally tough: a failed ad-
venturer. She wanted to have her own soul and to stand outside
the law: she thought she could be independent if only she had a
little help. My mother was willing, up to a point, to blaspheme, to
try to defraud God.

Then, more and more, it seemed to me my mother hated all
connections; even her bones did not seem to be fastened to each
other, I noticed; my mother was soft, fluid, sea-y, a sea-y creature.
What harrowed her most was the failure of her maneuvers, of her
adaptations, her lack of success. It seemed to *me* that her illness
was an experience, an act of destiny outside the whole set of things
that made up that part of life where you were a success or failure.
Will and charm and tactics could manage just so much—then you
had to believe in God or luck or both, which led you into theo-
logical corruption of a very sickening kind (I could not believe

God would help you make money). They were two different orders of experience, but my mother thought they were one. She
thought your luck as far as having looks was part of the other, even
though she said, "Anyone can be good-looking—you have to try,
you have to carry yourself right, sometimes ugly people are the
best-looking of all. . . ." She was generous enough to admit of
some women, "I was much prettier than her once but she's out-
distanced me: she knows how to dress, she's taken care of herself. . . ."

Riding on the bus I tried to imagine myself—briefly—a loose-
fleshed, loose-boned soft-looking woman like my mother with her
coarse ambitiousness and soulful public manner (when she wasn't
being shrill) and the exigent fear of defeat that went with what
she was. . . . I did it sort of absently, almost half-drowsing, I
thought it was so, well, dull, or unilluminating. But suddenly I
experienced an extraordinary vertigo, and a feeling of nausea, and
I stopped quickly.

I didn't know if I'd felt sick because I was doing something I
shouldn't do—I mean I started with that notion, and it was only
a day or so later I thought maybe the nausea had gone with imagining defeat. So far as I knew, I did not mind defeat—defeat hurt
but it offered an excuse for being indulgent and sexual and so on.

I didn't even conceive of total defeat. Being a hobo would be
a fate, getting meningitis and dying, being a homosexual, a drunk,
a lifelong shoe salesman would be a fate, maybe even amusing.
None of that really frightened me. I wondered if it was the war
that had done this to me or if I'd been cheated out of a certain
middle-classness. Maybe it was that in never having been given
much by Doris I'd come not to expect much in general, or maybe
I just didn't fear failure properly, or it had to do with being masculine.

So I had to *imagine* what it would be like to really hate failure.
I worked out a stupid idea that Doris needed family, social position, charm, looks, clothes, or she couldn't begin to have adven-
tures; something that didn't require those things was not a real
adventure. She maybe needed those things as someone might need
a hearing aid or glasses or a tractor or a car: a woman deprived of
them was deaf, blind, reduced to trudging hopelessly along.

I was not obsessed with understanding my mother; I worked on
this when I had the time.

I sometimes imagined myself in combat conditions, I tried to imagine myself undergoing humiliations, deprivations. It was a matter of pride not to run away from painful thoughts.

I knew my mother had never made an imaginative leap into my life or into any man's life; she'd said so: "I know nothing about being a boy. . . ." She'd said to my father, "I know nothing about being a man. . . ." She did not like movies that were about men. She never asked me to tell her about myself. Perhaps she was defiant because Jewish women were supposed to be respectful toward men—I couldn't handle that thought—but it seemed to me *very* clear she was interested only in her own fate as a woman. She thought everyone dealt in ruses, in subterfuge, but that she did it best. Her world bewildered me. I assumed she did not love me. I did not know to what extent I loved her. I saw that my insensitivity to her, as long as she behaved the way she did, was the only thing that made it possible for me to be halfway decent to her. If I reacted to her directly, I would become a major figure in the drama, and it would become clear she was a terrible pain in the neck, a child, and a fool. She thought if I became sensitive to her I would be struck with admiration for her in what she was going through, as once men had fallen in love with her at first sight. But I knew that would not happen. The depth of pain she suffered did not make her beautiful, could not make her beautiful: what she did, how she acted was the only thing that could make her beautiful. Maybe once sheer physical glory had made her redoubtable but I figured she'd had to work on her looks. There was nothing you could be without effort except catatonic. If I became sensitive to her and she was careless of me, I would not care if she died.

Obviously, between her and me there were two different minds and sensibilities and kinds of judgment operating: she wanted to control my mind—but without taking responsibility for it. She wanted to ascribe not a general value but a specifically masculine value to my being sympathetic toward her pain. It seemed to me she did not have that right because she had not carried out any specifically feminine side to our relationship, to any bargain. I mean she was working a swindle. She was also trying to help me. She wanted her condition considered a heroic, serious event, but I had nearly died twice in my childhood, and both times she had said, "Be brave." She had experienced no discomfort, only "aggravation" when I'd been ill—"I'm not good at illness," she'd said. You couldn't hold the past against people, but on the other hand what other contract did you have with anyone except that past?

My mother did not expect gentleness from people on the whole, but when she was desperate she wept because there was no gentleness in anyone near her. She preferred to go to Catholic hospitals when she was ill because of the nuns: they forgave her over and over. She lied to them and told them she would convert, and then she took it back and said God would punish her if she stopped being Jewish. She screamed and railed at people but the nuns always forgave her. "They're good—they understand women," she said. She whispered, "I'm a terrible person but they don't mind."

She said she could not bear it when people came near her and thought of themselves.

I did not do anything merely in order to be good to her. I decided to fiddle around with being—with being a little taken advantage of. I did it as a profanation, as a gesture of contempt for the suburb and toward people who pitied Doris; I did it as an exercise in doing something illicit and foul, as an exercise in risk-taking and general perversity. I figured, well, what the hell, why not do it, what did I have to lose? I was probably already wrecked and I'd probably be killed in the war besides.

I trained myself to listen to her talk about how she felt; I didn't wince or lose my appetite when she went on and on about what she was going through. Actually I was losing weight and having nightmares, but I'd get up in the middle of the night and do push-ups so I'd sleep and look healthy the next day. I wanted her to know I accepted what she went through as "normal."

She could of course describe only with limited skill, thank God, her pain.

"I have a burning—it begins here—" Her eyes would fill with tears "—and then it goes to *here!*" And she would start to tremble. "I want to kill everybody," she would whisper, "I become a terrible person—" (She'd been terrible before, though.) "I don't know what to do. Why is this happening to me?"

She said, "If I believed in Heaven, if I thought I could go there and see my father and my sister Sarah—they were always good to me—I wouldn't be so afraid." She said, "It always seemed to me the good died young but I wasn't good and I'm dying young."

I was much too shy to imagine myself a woman physically, in exact detail, cleft and breasted.

My mother's room had a wallpaper of roses, large roses, six or seven inches across, set quite close together. One day, sitting with her in a chair by her bed, it occurred to me she could not bear any situation in which she could not cheat. What she said was "I don't know what good morphine is! It doesn't help enough—I can't get away with anything." She may have meant *from* anything but I took her meaning the other thing. She also said, "If I pray it doesn't help, the pain doesn't stop."

"Do you believe in God, Momma?"

"I don't know—why doesn't He help me?"

"You're supposed to praise Him whether you're in pain or not."

"That's unfair."

"Well, we're not supposed to judge *Him*."

"I don't want a God like that," she said.

"If you believed what the Catholics believed, you could pray to the Virgin Mary."

"No woman made this world. I couldn't pray to a woman."

Much of her restlessness and agony came from comparing what the movies said life was and death was and what pain was for women with what she actually had to confront in her life. She didn't think movies lied—like many liars, she saw truth everywhere.

One day I was listening to her and I grew sad. She said angrily, "Why are you looking sad?"

I said, "Out of sympathy."

She said, "I don't want that kind of sympathy—I want to be cheered up." It was much worse, much more hysterical and shrill, than I'm showing.

"How do you want to be cheered up?"

"I don't know—you're so smart: you figure it out." But if I tried to cheer her up she'd say, "You're talking like a fool."

The Golden Rule seemed to me inadequate; she wanted something given to her that had nothing to do with what I wished for myself.

I finally caught on; she yearned for a certain kind of high-flown, movie dialogue: "Mother, is the pain *any* better today?" "No. . . . No! I can't bear it." "Didn't the nurse come today and give you the morphine shots?" I would say, sounding like a doctor, calm, fatherly. "Don't mention the morphine! I don't want to think about the morphine!" she would say like a rebellious girl or flirtatious woman.

She liked it if I pretended to be floored by her bravery whether she was being brave or not. Often she made herself up for these scenes. Doris could not bear to be just another patient for her doctors and nurses and could not bear her relative unimportance to them. My father had minded that too. But Doris plotted; she kept my report card face up on her bed when the doctor came; one day she told me to stay home from school and to cry when I let the doctor in. I said I couldn't cry. She became enraged.

It was her notion that people were good for their own pleasure or out of stupidity and were then used by people who were capable of extorting love: love was based on physical beauty, accident, and hardness of soul; that is to say, hardness of soul aroused love in other people.

It was a perfectly good set of notions, I suppose, but I have never noticed that women thought more clearly than men.

One day I decided just to do it finally, to sit down and actually imagine myself being her, middle-aged, disfigured, and so on.

I bicycled to some woods at the edge of town—a woods cut down since—walked and carried my bicycle through the trees, until I came to a glade I knew about where there was a tiny stream between mudbanks that were in spots mossy. Enough kids used the glade that the undergrowth had been worn away in the center and the ground was mud, moist, smooth, quivering, lightly streaked with colors. As woods went, that one was threadbare, but I thought it very fine.

I'd cut my classes.

I leaned my bicycle against a tree and I sat on the moss. I'd asked Doris's sister things about what Doris was going through and the nearly senseless answers I'd gotten had unnerved me; the casual way people expressed things so that they did not tell you anything or care or ever in words admit to what they knew really bothered me. Perhaps they didn't admit it to themselves. Doris had a niece who was very intelligent and talkative but she didn't like me: it wasn't anything personal, but in the family there were assignments, and she'd been assigned to my sister; and my sister hated me, and out of politeness to my sister this cousin did not show any liking for me. She was rigorous in this (until one day she had a quarrel with my sister, and after that she was medium friendly to me). This particular cousin was outspoken and talked about things like menstruation and desiring boys, but she would not talk to me, although she was polite about not talking to me. So I didn't know if Doris was going through menopause while she was dying of cancer or not. I didn't know if one cancelled the other out or not.

I don't think I made it clear to myself what I was doing. I did and I didn't know, I was definite and yet I crept up on it. Sitting in the glade, I thought it was all right and not upsetting to imagine oneself a young pretty girl especially if you didn't do it in detail but it seemed really foul to imagine oneself a middle-aged *woman*. It would be easiest to imagine being a very old woman, a witch, or a rude dowager—that was even sort of funny. But to think of myself as a middle-aged woman seemed to be filthy.

I wondered if I thought middle-aged women sacrosanct, or monstrous, or disgusting, or too pathetic or what. It seemed a great transgression, a trespass to think so ill of them, although a lot of boys that I knew laughed at and scorned middle-aged women, married women and teachers both. Simply contemplating the fact, the phenomenon of middle-aged women, I seemed to myself to have entered on obscenity.

Well, then, I ought just to take them for granted and avert my eyes. But then I could not imagine what it was to be Doris or what she was going through.

All at once I did imagine myself a girl, a girl my own age; it was a flicker, a very peculiar feat—clearly I was scared to death of doing any of this. But I did it a couple of times without really pausing to experience what it was I was as a girl: I just performed the feat, I flickered into it and out again. Then, carried away by confidence, I did pause and was a girl for a second but it was so obliterating, so shocking that I couldn't stand it. I was sickened. The feeling of obliteration or castration or whatever it was was unsettling as hell.

I had more than once imagined having breasts. Other boys and I had discussed what it must be like to have breasts: we'd imitated the way girls walked; we'd put books inside our shirts to simulate the weight of breasts. But I had not imagined breasts as part of a whole physical reality. Now suddenly—almost with a kind of excitement, well, with a dry excitement as in writing out an answer to an essay question on a test, working out an outline, a structure, seeing a thing take shape—I suddenly saw how shy I'd been about the physical thing, and with what seemed to me incredible daring (and feeling unclean, coated with uncleanliness), I imagined my hips as being my shoulders: I hardly used my hips for anything; and my shoulders, which were sort of the weighty center of most of my movements and of my strength, as being my hips. I began to feel very hot; I was flushed—and humiliated. Then after a moment's thought, going almost blind with embarrassment—and sweat—I put my behind on my chest. Then I whacked my thing off quickly and I moved my hole to my crotch. I felt it would be hard to stand up, to walk, to bestir myself; I felt sheathed in embarrassment, impropriety, in transgressions that did not stay still but floated out like veils; every part of me was sexual and jutted out one way or another. I really was infinitely ashamed—there was no part of me that wasn't *dirty*, that wouldn't interfere with someone else's thoughts and suggest things. I seemed bound up, packaged, tied in this, and in extra flesh. To live required infinite shamelessness if I was like this. I was suddenly very bad-tempered. . . . (Possibly I was remembering dreams I'd had, ideas I'd had in dreams.)

I felt terrible. I tried to giggle and make it all a joke, giggle inwardly—or snort with laughter. But I felt a kind of connected hysteria, a long chain of mild hysteria, of feeling myself to be explosive, hugely important, and yet motionless, inclined to be motionless. I suddenly thought that to say no was what my pride rested on; saying yes was sloppy and killing. All this came in a rush. I was filled with impatience and incredible defiance and a kind of self-admiration I couldn't even begin to grasp. The life in me, in her, seemed a form of madness (part of me was still masculine, obviously, part of my consciousness) and maddened and mad with pleasure and also unpleasantly ashamed or stubborn. I really did feel beyond the rules, borne over the channels laid down by rules: I floated over *everything*. And there was a terrible fear-excitement thing; I was afraid-and-not-afraid; vulnerable and yet emboldened by being *dirty* and not earthbound—it was like a joke, a peculiar kind of exalted joke, a tremendous, breathless joke, one hysterical and sickening but too good for me to let go of.

I began to shake.

I had only the vaguest idea of female physical weakness—women controlled so much of the world I was familiar with, so much of University City; but all at once, almost dizzyingly, almost like a monkey, I saw—I saw *connections* everywhere, routes, methods (also things to disapprove of, and things to be enthusiastic about): I was filled with a kind of animal politics. But I was afraid of having my arms and legs broken. When I was a man, I saw only a few logical positions and routes and resting places, but as a woman I saw routes everywhere, emotional ways to get things, lies, displays of myself: it was dazzling. I saw a thousand emotional strings attached to a thousand party favors. I felt a dreadful disgust for logic —logic seemed crippling and useless, unreal; and I had the most extraordinary sense of danger: it almost made me laugh: and I had a sort of immodest pride and a kind of anguished ambition and a weird determination not to be put in danger. . . . I was filled and fascinated by a sense of myself. Physical reality was a sieve which I passed through as I willed, when my luck was good. (I had read a number of books about women: "Gone with the Wind," "Pride and Prejudice," "Madame Bovary.")

Then I saw why, maybe, Doris was a terrible person—it was her attempt at freedom. Her willfulness was all toward being free; now she was ill and caught. Briefly, I felt I understood Doris a little, only a little, for the first time. I felt I understood part of the stormy thing in her, and the thing where her pains blocked out the world and her obstinate selfishness and the feeling of having a face. I did not have entire confidence in my penetration, but still I admired my sympathy for her, but dully, almost boredly—with an open mouth, half-wondering what to think about next—when suddenly, without warning, I really imagined myself her, Doris, middle-aged, disfigured, with loose skin, my voice different from what it had been—my voice was not that of a young woman. My mouth hurt with the pressure of my bitterness: my mouth was scalded. (In my own life, when I was unhappy, it was my *eyes* that hurt; my vision would hurt me: people would look like monsters to me and would seem to have evil glances, as if black cats inhabited their eyes.) It was almost as if there was steam somewhere in my throat; really, I burned with the pressure of angry words, with a truth I wasn't willing to modify, a truth meant to be wholly destructive to the errors and selfishness of others. To their complacency. I imagined all of it—not being liked by my family anymore, my husband hating me, being forsaken by my mother and sister. By my friends. As myself, as someone young, I could bear a good deal; but it takes energy to feel depressed, and when I imagined myself to be Doris, when I was Doris, I hadn't the energy anymore to die; too many things had gone wrong; I was too angry to die; I felt too much; there was no end to what I felt—I could do nothing but scream.

I didn't know if I was faking all or any of this. What does imagination consist of? I was thirteen and perhaps a superficial person. There was no guarantee I felt deeply or that I possessed any human grace at all. The trees around me, the tiny creek (like an endless parade of silvery snakes of varying thinnesses rustling over pebbles), the solitude suggested to me a gravity, a decency, a balance in life that was perhaps only the reflection of my Middle Western ignorance, or idealism. It is hard to know. But as long as I held onto the power to pity her, even while I imagined myself to be her, I did not, in my deepest self, suffer what I imagined her suffering. With what I would consider the equivalent confidence and folly of a boy playing at chemistry in the basement, I held up a mental snapshot of what I had in the second before half-experienced in imagining myself to be Doris: it was a condition of mind, of terror and bitterness and hate and a trying to win out still, all churning in me, and it was evil in that it was without bounds, without any fixity or finality, and suggested an infinite nausea—I was deeply afraid of nausea. It was a condition of mind, a sickening, lightless turmoil, unbearably foul, staled; and even to imagine it without going crazy myself or bursting into tears or yelling with horror, not to live it but just to conceive of it without going through those things was somehow unclean. But with nearly infinite coldness, a coldness that was a form of love in me, I held the thought. The mind's power to penetrate these realities is not distinguishable from the mind's power merely to imagine it is penetrating reality. My father had twice contemptuously called me the Boy Scout. Did Doris live much of the time in that foulness? I thought there was no end to her wretchedness, no end —I was thirteen—to the uselessness of her misery.

The thing about being a bad person, the thing about being free and a little cheap and not letting yourself be owned by other people at all, by their emotions, was that then you had to succeed, at everything you did, all the time: failure became an agony. And there was no alternative to that agony when it began except to become a good person. Not a saint, nothing extreme. It was just that if I imagined myself a middle-aged woman like Doris with both my breasts cut off and my husband dying, hating me while he died, turning his back on me and saying all the years he'd spent with me were foul, and with myself as selfish and hungry for triumph still, I was deprived of all justice, of all success, and my pain and terror were then so great that I would of course be insane.

Which magnified the agony.

Clearly—it seemed obvious to me as I sat there and reasoned about these things—unselfishness lessened such pain if only in the way it moved you outside your own nervous system. Generosity emptied you of any feeling of poverty anyway. I knew that from my own experience. Extended generosity predisposed you to die; death didn't seem so foul; you were already without a lot of eagerness about yourself; you were quieted.

I bicycled home, to bear the news to Momma, to tell her what I'd found out.

I was adolescent, that is I was half-formed, a sketch of a man. I told Doris unselfishness and generosity and concern for others would ease most pain, even her pain; it would make her feel better.

God, how she screamed.

She said that I came from filthy people and what I was was more filth, that I came from the scum of the earth and was more scum. Each thing she said struck her with its aptness and truth and inspired her and goaded her to greater anger. She threw an ashtray at me. She ordered me out of the house: "Sleep in the streets, sleep in the *gutter,* where you belong!" Her temper astounded me. Where did she get the strength for such temper when she was so ill? I did not fight back. My forbearance or patience or politeness or whatever it was upset her still more. I didn't catch on to this until in the middle of calling me names ("—you little bastard, you hate everybody, you're disgusting, I can't stand you, you little son of a bitch—" "Momma . . . Come on, now, Momma . . .") she screamed, "Why do you do things and make me ashamed?"

It was a revelation. It meant my *selfishness* would calm her. At first I said, "Do you really want me to go? You'll be alone here." I

was partly sarcastic, laughing at her in that way, and then I began
muttering, or saying with stubborn authority that I would not
leave, I wanted my comfort considered, I wanted her to worry
about my life. She said, huffing and gasping but less yellow and
pinched and extreme, "You're a spoiled brat." I mean she was
calmed to some extent; she was reduced to being incensed from
being insane. But she screamed still. And I kept on too: I did not
care what grounds she used—it could be on the grounds of my
selfishness—but I was really stubborn: I was determined that she
try being a good woman. I remember being so tense at my presumption that I kept thinking something physical in me would
fail, would burst through my skin—my nerves, or my blood, my
heart, everything was pounding, or my brain, but anyway that
particular fight ended sort of in a draw, with Doris insulted and
exhausted, appalled at what I'd said. At the stupidity. But with
me adamant. I couldn't have stopped myself actually.

After that, with my shoulders hunched and my eyes on the
ground or occasionally wide open and innocent for inspection
and fixed on her—I referred to her always as brave and generous. I
dealt with her as if she was the most generous woman imaginable,
as if she had been only good to me all my life. I referred to her
kindness, her bravery, her selflessness. She said I was crazy. I suppose certain accusations, certain demands, were the natural
habitat of her mind. At one point she even telephoned the junior-
high-school principal to complain I was crazy. He wouldn't listen
to her. I went right on behaving as if I remembered sacrifice after
sacrifice she had made for me. She was enraged, then irritated,
then desperate, then bored, then nonplussed, and the nonsense of
it depressed her: she felt alone and misunderstood: she did not
want me to be idealistic about her; she wanted me to be a companion to her, for her. But she stopped screaming at me.

I don't know if she saw through me or not. I don't think I consciously remembered over the weeks that this went on what had
started all this or its history; continued acts develop their own at-
mosphere; that I sincerely wanted a home of a certain kind for us
was all that it seemed to be about after a while. That I had to protect myself. When she gave in, it was at first that she indulged the
male of the family, the fool, the boy who was less realistic than
she was. Then to conceal her defeat, she made it seem she couldn't
bear to disillusion me. Also, while she more or less said that she

hadn't the energy to do what I expected of her, she must have realized it took energy to fight me. She may have said to herself—as I said to myself before I imagined myself to be her—Why not? I think too my faith seduced her, my authority: I was so sure of myself. And besides, the other didn't work anymore.

Of course it was a swindle all the way: she could no longer ask things of me so freely, so without thought of what it would do to me. She became resigned, and then after a while she became less sad—she even showed a wried amusement. She almost became good-tempered. She was generous to some extent with everyone or I was hurt. She reconciled with her mother and her daughter, with her brothers and her sister, with the neighbors sometimes at my insistence—even with my advice—but after a while she did it on her own in her own way. It seemed to me it was obvious that considering all the factors, she was much kinder to us than any of us were, or could be, to her, so that no matter what bargain she thought she was negotiating, she really was unselfish now. The bargain was not in her favor. She practiced a polite death or whatever, a sheltering politeness, which wasn't always phony, and a forgiveness of circumstances that was partly calculated to win friends: she comforted everyone who came near her, sometimes cornily; but still it was comfort. I was a little awed by her; she was maybe awed and instructed by herself; she took over the—the *role* —and my opinions were something she asked but she had her own life. Her own predicament. She still denounced people behind their backs but briefly, and she gloated now and then: when her rich brother died suddenly, she said with a gently melancholy satisfaction, "Who would have thought I could outlast J.J.?" She showed a shakily calm and remarkable daily courage; she made herself, although she was a dying woman, into a woman who was good company. She put together a whole new set of friends. Those friends loved her actually, they looked up to her, they admired her. She often boasted, "I have many, many very good friends who have stuck by me." But they were all new friends— none of her old friends came back. Young people always liked her now and envied me. What was so moving was her dying woman's gaiety—it was so unexpected and so unforced, a kind of amusement with things. Sometimes when no one was around she would yell at me that she was in pain all the time and that I was a fool to believe the act she put on. But after a certain point, that stopped too. She said, "I want to be an encouragement—I want you to remember me as someone who was a help to you." Do you see? After a certain time she was never again hysterical when I was there. Never. She was setting me an example. She was good to me in a way possible to her, the way she thought she, Doris, ought to be to me. But she was always Doris, no matter how kind she was. If at any time restlessness showed in me or if I was unhappy even about something very minor at school she would be upset; I had to have no feelings at all or stay within a narrow range for her comfort; she said often, "I know I'm unfair but wait until I die—can't you bear with me?" When I stayed out sometimes because I had to, because I was going crazy, when I came home she would say pleadingly, "Don't ask too much of me, Buddy." She would sit there, on the couch in the living room, having waited fully dressed for me to come home, and she would say that.

All right, her happiness rested on me. Her sister and one brother and her daughter told me I couldn't go to college, I couldn't leave Doris, it would be a crime. Her cancer was in remission; she had never gotten on so well with her own family (she was patient with them now), I owed it to her to stay. I am trying to establish what she gained and what she lost. Her family often said to me bullyingly, without affection, or admiration, "Her life is in your hands." I hadn't intended this. Doris said they were jealous of me. I wanted to go to college; I wanted to use my mind and all that: I was willing for Doris's life to be in her mother's and sister's hands. I was modest about what I meant to Doris—does that mean I didn't love her?

The high school, when I refused to apply to Harvard, asked me why and then someone went to see Doris, and Doris went into her bedroom and locked the door and refused to eat until I agreed to go away to college. To leave her. And she made her family and her doctor ask me to go (they pounded on her door but she wouldn't eat until they did what she told them). Doris's sister Ida came and shouted through the bedroom door at her and then said to me in a cutting, angry voice, blaming me, that Doris was killing herself. This was when I was sixteen.

I said I wasn't that important. My modesty stymied Ida.

That sacrifice, if it was that, was either the first or second thing Doris had ever done for me. But perhaps she did it for herself, to strengthen her hand for some Last Judgment. Perhaps she was glad to be rid of me. I only lost my nerve once, in accepting it from her, this gift. I was lying on my bed—it was evening in early spring and I should have been doing Physics—and I was thinking about college, Harvard, about a place, the Yard, that I'd never seen, grass and paths and a wall around it, and buildings and trees, an enclosed park for young people. The thought took me to a pitch of anticipation and longing and readiness unlike anything I'd felt in years; all at once it was unendurable that I had that and Doris had nothing—had what she had. It was terrible to think how Doris was cheated in terms of what she could see ahead of her. I felt I'd tricked her in some way. Not that that was wrong but she was too nice, now that she was cheated, for me to— I don't know what. I suppose I was out of control. Clumsy, even lumbering, I blundered into her room and without warning or explanation began to say I was sorry and that I'd better back out of going to Harvard. She breathed in the loud, nervous way of a woman concerned about herself, but then she got herself in hand and said in the detached, slightly ironic voice, gentle, convivial, and conspiratorial that she used at that time, a Middle Western voice, "Sorry for what? What is it? Buddy, you have nothing to be sorry for."

I'd never brought up in conversation with her matters that had to do with feelings of mine that were unclear or difficult: what good would it have done? She would not have made the effort to understand; she did not know how; she would only have felt lousy and been upset. I was silenced by a long tradition of lying to her and being lucid. I could at this time only say over and over that I was sorry—I couldn't try to explain any of it to her.

She said, "You're being silly. I think you're too close to me, Buddy. I don't want you to grow up to be a mother's boy."

I said, "What will you do when I go away?"

"You think I can't manage? You don't know much about me. Don't be so conceited where you're concerned." (But I'd put that idea into the air.) She said, "I can manage very well, believe me." I expressed disbelief by the way I stared at her. She said, "Go into my top bureau drawer. Look under the handkerchiefs."

There was a bottle there. I held it up. "What is it?"

"My morphine."

"You hide it?"

"I know how boys like to try things . . ."

"You hide it from *me?*"

"I don't want you to be tempted—I know you're often under a strain."

"Momma, I wouldn't take your *morphine.*"

"But I don't use it much anymore. Haven't you noticed I'm clearer lately? I don't let myself use it, Buddy—look at the date on the bottle: it's lasted over a year. The doctor can't believe I'm so reformed; he'll ask me to marry him yet. Just sometimes I take it on a rainy day. Or at night. I thought you knew I wasn't using morphine anymore."

I hadn't noticed. I hadn't been keeping track. I didn't like to be too aware of her.

She could have had another bottle hidden; there was a nurse who came twice a week and who could, and I think did, give Doris injections of morphine. I didn't want to investigate. Or know. I just wanted to go on experiencing the release of having her care about me. Worry about me. She said, "You've been a help to me. You've done more than your share. You know what they say—out of the mouths of babes. I'll be honest with you: I'd like to be young again, I'd like to have my health back. But I'm not unhappy. I even think I'm happy now. Believe me, Buddy, the pain is less for me than it was."

At Harvard, I began to forget her. But at times I felt arrogant because of what she and I had done; I'd managed to do more than many of my professors could. I'd done more than many of them would try. I knew more than they did about some things.

Often I felt I was guilty of possessing an overspecialized maturity. At times I felt called upon to defend Doris by believing the great world to which Harvard was a kind of crooked door was worthless in its cruelty and its misuse of its inhabitants and Doris was more important than any of it. Than what I had come to Harvard for. But I didn't go home.

And Doris wanted me to enter that great world: the only parts of my letters she really enjoyed were about things like my meeting a girl whose mother was a billionairess. By the standards of this new world I was sentimental and easily gulled and Doris was shrill. I did not want to see beyond a present folly or escape from one or be corrected or remember anything. Otherwise, the shadow of

Doris lay everywhere. I began to forget her even while she was alive.

The daughter of the billionairess was, in addition to everything else, a really admirable and intelligent girl. But I didn't trust her. One night she confessed various approaches she followed for winning the affection of boys. If you don't want to be silly and overly frail, you have to be immune and heartless to the fine-drawn, drawn-out, infinitely ludicrous, workable plots that women engage in. The delicacy and density of those plots. But I wasn't confident and I ran away from that girl. It seemed to me my whole life was sad. It was very hard to bear to see that in the worldly frame of Harvard Doris was, even in her relative nobility, unimportant. I had never been conscious before of the limitations of her intelligence. She had asked me to send her money and I did, my freshman year. I had a scholarship and I worked. It wasn't any longer that she was jealous of my life but she wanted me to show I cared about her still. She had changed her manner just before I left her; she had become like a German-Jewish matron of the sort who has a son at Harvard. And her letters were foolish, almost illiterate. It was too much for me, the costliness of loyalty, the pursuit of meanings, and everything savage from the past, half-forgotten or summarized (and unreal) or lost in memory already. How beautiful I thought the ordinary was. I did not go home to live with her and she did not ask me to, when, after three years of remission, and three months after my leaving her, her cancer recurred.

How can I even guess at what she gained, what she lost?

I spent the summer with her. I had a job and stayed home with her in the evenings. My manner unnerved her a bit. I was as agreeable as I knew how to be; I tried to be as Middle Western as before. When company came, Doris would ask me to stay only for a little while and then to excuse myself and leave: "People pay too much attention to you, and I like a little attention for myself."

The Christmas after that, I travelled out to be with her, fell ill and was in a delirium for most of two weeks. Doris was curiously patient, not reproachful that I'd been ill, not worried, and when we spoke it was with a curious peace, and caution too, as if we were the only two adults in the world. She said for the first time, "I love you, Buddy."

In May I was called to her bedside because she was about to die. Her family had gathered and they stood aside, or else Doris had told them to leave us alone; perhaps they recognized my prior right to her; they had never been able to get along with her, they had only loved her. Doris said, "I was waiting for you. It's awful. Mose comes in here and complains about his health and carries on about me and doesn't hear me ask for water, and Ida cries and says it's terrible for her, Ida was never any good at a deathbed— and your sister comes in here and says, 'Have a little nap,' and when I close my eyes she runs to the dresser and looks at things: she's afraid I left it all to you; she already took my compact and she uses it in front of me. I wasn't a good mother but she doesn't have to rub it in. She thinks I'm dead already. Her feelings are hurt. How is college? What I'd like to hear about is the rich people you've met. . . ."

When I started to speak, she cut in: "I was afraid you wouldn't get here in time. I didn't want to interrupt your studies and I was afraid I waited too long. I didn't let them give me a morphine shot today. I want to talk to you with a clear head. The pain is not good, Buddy, but I don't want to be drugged when we talk. I've been thinking what I would say to you. I've been thinking about it all week. I like talking to you. Listen, I want to say this first: I appreciate what you did for me, Buddy."

"I didn't do anything special for you." I did not remember clearly—I had put it out of my mind . . . I did not want any responsibility for Doris.

"Buddy, you were good to me," she said.

"Well, Momma, you were good to *me*." I was too shy, too collegiate, too anxious to praise her, too rattled by the emergency, by the thought she was dying to say anything else. I thought it would be best for us to go on to the end, as we had gone on for so long. For so many years I'd calmed and guided her this way: it was an old device. I assumed I couldn't be honest with her now. I had no notion that dying had educated her. I was eighteen, a young man who had a number of voices, who was subject to his own angers, to a sense of isolation that made him unwilling to use his gifts. In Cambridge, people I knew applied adjectives to me in the melodramatic way of college sophomores: interesting, immature, bad-tempered. There were people who were in love with me.

I was intensely unhappy and knew a great deal of it I owed to Doris.

Doris said, "I've been waiting for you. I missed you, Buddy. Listen, I'm not as strong as I was. I can't put on too good a show—if I make faces or noises, don't get upset and run for the nurse: let me talk: you make things too easy for me. Now listen, don't get mad at me but you have to promise me you'll finish college—you tend to run away from things. You're lazy, Buddy. Promise me: I have to make you promise—I want to be a good mother—will wonders never cease?"

"You always were a good mother."

"Oh, Buddy, I was terrible."

"No, Momma. No, you weren't." But I think she wanted companionship, not consolation; I guessed wrong on that last occasion. She said, "We don't have to be polite to each other now—Buddy, will you say you forgive me?"

She thought I was happy and strong, that I'd survived my childhood. I wanted her to think that. So far as I knew I didn't blame her, not for anything; but not-blaming someone is very unlike forgiving them: if I was to forgive her it meant I had first to remember. I would have collapsed sobbing on her bed and cried out, God, it was so awful, so awful, why did those things have to happen, oh God, it was so awful. . . .

I don't know if I was cruel or not. I told her I wasn't being polite, that I had nothing to forgive her for: "You were a good mother."

She said, "Buddy, you helped me—I can bear the pain."

"Momma!" I refused to understand. "You did it all yourself. You were always better than you thought."

Each breath she took was like a seesaw noisily grinding aloft, descending. Her life was held in a saucer on that seesaw. I have no gift for bearing human pain. I kept thinking, I can accept this, I can do this without getting hysterical.

"It was always easier for me than you thought, Mother; you never hurt me much; you always thought you were worse than you were. A lot of what you blame yourself for was always imaginary —you were better to me than anyone else was—at least, you lived."

"Buddy, I can face the truth, I know what I did."

"I don't know what you did."

And she even forgave me that. She said, "I understand. You

don't want to face things now. Maybe it's better not to bring it up."

"Do what you like, Momma. I'll understand sooner or later." She said, "Kiss me, Buddy. Am I very ugly?"

"No, Momma."

"You always thought I was pretty. Listen, at the end, Buddy, I tried. I loved you. I'm ready to die, I'm only alive because I wanted to talk to you, I wanted that to be the last thing—do you understand, I want you to know now how much I think of you."

"Momma—"

"I'm going to die soon, I'm very bad, Buddy. Listen: I don't want you to grieve for me. You've done your share already. I want you to have a good time. I want you to enjoy yourself." Then she said, "I can't be what you want; I don't want to upset you; just say you forgive me."

"I will if you give me your forgiveness, Momma."

"My forgiveness? Oh Buddy. I bet you're good with girls. What a liar you are. And I always thought I was a liar. I forgive you, Buddy. Don't you know what you did for me? You made it so the pain was less."

"Momma, I didn't do anything."

"Isn't it funny what people are ashamed of?" She was silent for a small second; then she said, "Do you forgive me?"

"I forgive you, Momma, but there's nothing to forgive you for. If it wasn't for you I'd be dead."

"That was a long time ago, you were still a baby then. Oh. Run now and get the nurse. I don't think I can stand the pain now. Tell her I want my shot."

After the nurse had gone, Doris said, "Buddy, I went in a wheelchair to the ward where people had cancer and were frightened, and I tried to help them—I thought you would be proud of me."

For a moment, I remembered something. *"Momma, I was a stupid boy."*

"Hold my hand while I fall asleep, Buddy. I don't know I think Harvard is such a good place—you don't face things as well as you used to. Buddy, I'm tired of it all. I don't like my family much. Is it terrible to say I don't think they're nice people? In the end you and my father were the only ones. I wish you could have known him. I loved you best. Don't let it go to your head. You never thought you were conceited but you were—that's always the part of the story you leave out—and how you like to domineer over people. It's a miracle no one's killed you yet. It's terrible to be sorry for things. Buddy, do you know why that is, why is it terrible to be sorry? I don't know why things happened the way they did. I kept thinking as I lay here it would be interesting if I understood things now and I could tell you—I know how you like to know things. Buddy, I promised your mother you would remember her —promise me you'll think well of her. She was your real mother and she loved you too. Buddy?"

"Yes."

"Find someone to love. Find someone to be good to you." Then she said, "I love you, Buddy. . . . I'm sorry."

She seemed to sleep. Then her breathing grew rough. I thought I ought to go get the doctor but then I sat down again and stared at the ceiling. I was afraid my feeling for her or some flow of regret in me or anything in me she might as a woman feel as a thread requiring her attention would interfere with her death. So I said to myself, You can die, Momma; it's all right; I don't want you to live anymore. From time to time, in her sleep, in her dying, she shouted, "Haven't I suffered enough?" and "Buddy, are you still there? Don't have anything to do with those terrible people!" Then she came to and said, "Am I shouting things? . . . I thought so. I don't want you to go away but when you're this close I don't feel right."

"Do you want me to go into the hall?"

"No. Don't leave me. But don't sit too close to me, don't look at me. Just stay near. . . . I want you here."

"All right, Momma."

I listened to her breathing grow irregular. I said to myself, Die, Momma. On this breath. I don't want you to live anymore. Her breath changed again. It began to be very loud, rackety. I began to count her breaths. I counted fifteen and then neither her breath nor her actual voice was ever heard again.

After she died, I had a nervous breakdown. I couldn't believe I missed her that much. I'd loved her at the end, loved her again, loved and admired her, loved her greatly; of course, by that time, she did not ask that the love I felt express itself in sacrificing myself for her. I loved her while I enjoyed an increasing freedom from

her but still I needed her; and, as I said, I had a nervous breakdown when she died. After a while, I got over it.

I don't know all that I gained or lost, either. I know I was never
to be certain I was masculine to the proper degree again. I always
thought I knew what women felt.

Make what use of this you like.

USURPATION

(Other People's Stories)

CYNTHIA OZICK

Cynthia Ozick is the author of *Trust*, a novel (New American Library); and *The Pagan Rabbi and Other Stories* (Knopf), nominated for a 1972 National Book Award. She has also published essays, poetry, criticism, reviews, and translations in numerous periodicals and anthologies, and has been the recipient of several prizes, including the Award for Literature of the American Academy of Arts and Letters. Her home is in New Rochelle, New York.

Occasionally a writer will encounter a story that is his, yet is not his. I mean, by the way, a writer of *stories*, not one of these intelligences that analyze society and culture, but the sort of ignorant and acquisitive being who moons after magical tales. Such a creature knows very little: how to tie a shoelace, when to go to the store for bread, and the exact stab of a story that belongs to him, and to him only. But sometimes it happens that somebody else has written the story first. It is like being robbed of clothes you do not yet own. There you sit, in the rapt hall, seeing the usurper on the stage caressing the manuscript that, in its deepest turning, was meant to be yours. He is a transvestite, he is wearing your own hat and underwear. It seems unjust. There is no way to prevent him.

You may wonder that I speak of a hall rather than a book. The story I refer to has not yet been published in a book, and the fact is I heard it read aloud. It was read by the author himself. I had a seat in the back of the hall, with a much younger person pressing the chair-arms on either side of me, but by the third paragraph

I was blind and saw nothing. By the fifth paragraph I recognized my story—knew it to be mine, that is, with the same indispensable familiarity I have for this round-flanked left-side molar my tongue admires. I think of it, in all that waste and rubble amid gold dental crowns, as my pearl.

The story was about a crown—a mythical one, made of silver. I do not remember its title. Perhaps it was simply called "The Magic Crown." In any event, you will soon read it in its famous author's new collection. He is, you may be sure, very famous, so famous that it was startling to see he was a real man. He wore a conventional suit and tie, a conventional haircut and conventional eyeglasses. His whitening mustache made him look conventionally distinguished. He was not at all as I had expected him to be—small and astonished, like his heroes.

This time the hero was a teacher. In the story he was always called "the teacher," as if how one lives is what one is.

> The teacher's father is in the hospital, a terminal case. There is no hope. In an advertisement the teacher reads about a wonder-curer, a rabbi who can work miracles. Though a rational fellow and a devout skeptic, in desperation he visits the rabbi and learns that a cure can be effected by the construction of a magical silver crown, which costs nearly five hundred dollars. After it is made the rabbi will give it a special blessing and the sick man will recover. The teacher pays and in a vision sees a glowing replica of the marvelous crown. But afterward he realizes that he has been mesmerized.
>
> Furiously he returns to the rabbi's worn-out flat to demand his money. Now the rabbi is dressed like a rich dandy. "I telephoned the hospital and my father is still sick." The rabbi chides him—he must give the crown time to work. The teacher insists that the crown he paid for be produced. "It cannot be seen," says the rabbi, "it must be believed in, or the blessing will not work."
>
> The teacher and the rabbi argue bitterly. The rabbi calls for faith, the teacher for his stolen money. In the heart of the struggle the teacher confesses with a terrible cry that he has really always hated his father anyway. The next day the father dies.

With a single half-archaic word the famous writer pressed out the last of the sick man's breath: he "expired."

Forgive me for boring you with plot-summary. I know there is nothing more tedious, and despise it myself. A rabbi whose face I have not made you see, a teacher whose voice remains a shadowy moan: how can I burn the inside of your eyes with these? But it is not my story, and therefore not my responsibility. I did not invent any of it.

From the platform the famous writer explained that the story was a gift, he too had not invented it. He took it from an account in a newspaper—which one he would not tell: he sweated over fear of libel. Cheats and fakes always hunt themselves up in stories, sniffing out twists, insults, distortions, transfigurations, all the drek of the imagination. Whatever's made up they grab, thick as lawyers against the silky figurative. Still, he swore it really happened, just like that—a crook with his crooked wife, calling himself rabbi, preying on gullible people, among them educated men, graduate students even; finally they arrested the fraud and put him in jail.

Instantly, the famous writer said, at the smell of the word "jail," he knew the story to be his.

This news came to me with a pang. The silver crown given away free, and where was I?—I who am pocked with newspaper-sickness, and hunch night after night (it pleases me to read the morning papers after midnight) catatonically fixed on shipping lists, death columns, lost wallets, maimings, muggings, explosions, hijackings, bombs, while the unwashed dishes sough thinly all around.

It has never occurred to me to write about a teacher; and as for rabbis, I can make up my own craftily enough. You may ask, then, what precisely in this story attracted me. And not simply attracted: seized me by the lung and declared itself my offspring—a changeling in search of its natural mother. Do not mistake me: had I only had access to a newspaper that crucial night (the *Post*, the *News*, the *Manchester Guardian*, *St. Louis Post-Dispatch*, *Boston Herald-Traveler*, ah, which, which? and where was I? in a bar? never; buying birth control pills in the drug store? I am a believer in fertility; reading, God forbid, a *book?*), my own story would have been less logically decisive. Perhaps the sick father would have recovered. Perhaps the teacher would not have confessed to hating his father. I might have caused the silver crown to astonish even the rabbi himself. Who knows what I might have sucked out of those swindlers! The point is I would have fingered out the magical parts.

Magic—I admit it—is what I lust after. And not ordinary magic, which is what one expects of pagan peoples; their religions declare it. After all, half the world asserts that once upon a time God became a man, and moreover that whenever a priest in sacral ceremony wills it, that same God-man can climb into a little flat piece of unleavened bread. For most people nowadays it is only the *idea* of a piece of bread turning into God—but is that any better? As for me, I am drawn not to the symbol, but to the absolute magic act. I am drawn to what is forbidden.

Forbidden. The terrible Hebrew word for it freezes the tongue —*asur:* Jewish magic. Trembling, we have heard in Deuteronomy the No that applies to any slightest sniff of occult disclosure: how mighty is Moses, peering down the centuries into the endlessness of this allure! Astrologists, wizards and witches: *asur.* The Jews have no magic. For us bread may not tumble into body. Wine is wine, death is death.

And yet with what prowess we have crept down the centuries after amulets, and hidden countings of letters, and the silver crown that heals: so it is after all nothing to marvel at that my own, my beloved, subject should be the preternatural—everything anti-Moses, all things blazing with their own wonder. I long to be one of the ordinary peoples, to give up our agnostic God whom even the word "faith" insults, who cannot be imagined in any form, whom the very hope of imagining offends, who is without body and cannot enter body . . . oh, why can we not have a magic God like other peoples?

Some day I will take courage and throw over being a Jew, and then I will make a little god, a silver godlet, in the shape of a crown, which will stop death, resurrect fathers and uncles; out of its royal points gardens will burst. —That story! Mine! Stolen! I considered: was it possible to leap up on the stage with a living match and burn the manuscript on the spot, freeing the crown out of the finished tale, restoring it once more to a public account in the *Times?* But no. Fire, even the little humble wobble of a match, is too powerful a magic in such a place, among such gleaming herds. A conflagration of souls out of lust for a story! I feared so terrible a spell. All the same, he would own a carbon copy, or a photographic copy: such a man is meticulous about the storage-matter of his brain. A typewriter is a volcano. Who can stop print?

If I owned a silver godlet right now I would say: Almighty small

Crown, annihilate that story; return, return the stuff of it to me.

A peculiar incident. Just as the famous writer came to the last word—"expired"—I saw the face of a goat. It was thin, white, blurry-eyed; a scraggly fur beard hung from its chin. Attached to the beard was a transparent voice, a voice like a whiteness—but I ought to explain how I came just then to be exposed to it. I was leaning against the wall of that place. The fading hiss of "expired" had all at once fevered me; I jumped from my seat between the two young people. Their perspiration had dampened the chair-arms, and the chill of their sweat, combined with the hotness of my greed for this magic story which could not be mine, turned my flesh to a sort of vapor. I rose like a heated gas, feeling insubstantial, and went to press my head against the cold side wall along the aisle. My brain was all gas, it shuddered with envy. Expired! How I wished to write a story containing that unholy sound! How I wished it was I who had come upon the silver crown . . . I must have looked like an usher, or in some fashion a factotum of the theater, with my skull drilled into the wall that way.

In any case I was taken for an official: as someone in authority who lolls on the job.

The goat-face blew a breath deep into my throat.

"I have stories. I want to give him stories."

"*What* do you want?"

"Him. Arrange it, can't you? In the intermission, what d'you say?"

I pulled away; the goat hopped after me.

"How? When?" said the goat. "Where?" His little beard had a tremor. "If he isn't available here and now, tell me his mailing address. I need criticism, advice, I need help—"

We become what we are thought to be; I became a factotum.

I said pompously, "You should be ashamed to pursue the famous. Does he know you?"

"Not exactly. I'm a cousin—"

"*His* cousin?"

"No. That rabbi's wife. She's an old lady, my mother's uncle was her father. We live in the same neighborhood."

"What rabbi?"

"The one in the papers. The one he swiped the story from."

"That doesn't oblige him to read you. You expect too much," I said. "The public has no right to a writer's private mind. Help from high places doesn't come like manna. His time is precious, he has better things to do." All this, by the way, was quotation. A famous writer—not this one—to whom I myself sent a story had once stung me with these words; so I knew how to use them.

"Did he say you could speak for him?" sneered the goat. "Fame doesn't cow me. Even the famous bleed."

"Only when pricked by the likes of you," I retorted. "Have you been published?"

"I'm still young."

"Poets before you died first and published afterward. Keats was twenty-six, Shelley twenty-nine, Rimbaud—"

"I'm like these, I'll live forever."

"Arrogant!"

"Let the famous call me that, not you."

"At least I'm published," I protested; so my disguise fell. He saw I was nothing so important as an usher, only another unknown writer in the audience.

"Do *you* know him?" he asked.

"He spoke to me once at a cocktail party."

"Would he remember your name?"

"Certainly," I lied. The goat had speared my dignity.

"Then take only one story."

"Leave the poor man alone."

"*You* take it. Read it. If you like it—look, only if you like it!— give it to him for me."

"He won't help you."

"Why do you think everyone is like you?" he accused—but he seemed all at once submerged, as if I had hurt him. He shook out a vast envelope, pulled out his manuscript, and spitefully began erasing something. Opaque little tears clustered on his eyelashes. Either he was weeping or he was afflicted with pus. "Why do you think I don't deserve some attention?"

"Not of the great."

"Then let me at least have yours," he said.

The real usher just then came like a broom. Back! Back! Quiet! Don't disturb the reading! Before I knew it I had been swept into my seat. The goat was gone, and I was clutching the manuscript.

The fool had erased his name.

That night I read the thing. You will ask why. The newspaper was thin, the manuscript fat. It smelled of stable: a sort of fecal stink. But I soon discovered it was only the glue he had used to piece together parts of corrected pages. An amateur job.

If you are looking for magic now, do not. This was no work to marvel at. The prose was not bad, but not good either. There are young men who write as if the language were an endless bolt of yard goods—you snip off as much as you need for the length of fiction you require: one turn of the loom after another, everything of the same smoothness, the texture catches you up nowhere.

I have said "fiction." It was not clear to me whether this was fiction or not. The title suggested it was: "A Story of Youth and Homage." But the narrative was purposefully inconclusive. Moreover, the episodes could be interpreted on several "levels." Plainly it was not just a story, but meant something much more, and even that "much more" itself meant much more. This alone soured me; such techniques are learned in those hollowed-out tombstones called Classes in Writing. In my notion of these things, if you want to tell a story you tell it. I am against all these masks and tricks of metaphor and fable. That is why I am attracted to magical tales: they mean what they say; in them miracles are not symbols, they are conditional probabilities.

The goat's story was realistic enough, though self-conscious. In perfectly ordinary, mainly trite, English it pretended to be incoherent. That, as you know, is the fashion.

I see you are about to put these pages down, in fear of another plot-summary. I beg you to wait. Trust me a little. I will get through it as painlessly as possible—I promise to abbreviate everything. Or, if I turn out to be long-winded, at least to be interesting. Besides, you can see what risks I am taking. I am unfamiliar with the laws governing plagiarism, and here I am, brazenly giving away stories that are not rightfully mine. Perhaps one day the goat's story will be published and acclaimed. Or perhaps not: in either case he will recognize his plot as I am about to tell it to you, and what furies will beat in him! What if, by the time *this* story is published, at this very moment while you are reading it, I am on my back in some filthy municipal dungeon? Surely so deep a sacrifice should engage your forgiveness.

Then let us proceed to the goat's plot:

> An American student at a yeshiva in Jerusalem is unable to concentrate. He is haunted by worldly desires; in reality he has come to Jerusalem not for Torah but out of ambition. Though young

and unpublished, he already fancies himself to be a writer worthy of attention. Then why not the attention of the very greatest?

It happens that there lives in Jerusalem a writer who one day will win the most immense literary prize on the planet. At the time of the story he is already an old man heavy with fame, though of a rather parochial nature; he has not yet been to Stockholm—it is perhaps two years before the Nobel Prize turns him into a mythical figure. ["Turns him into a mythical figure" is an excellent example of the goat's prose, by the way.] But the student is prescient, and fame is fame. He composes a postcard:

> There are only two religious
> writers in the world. You are
> one and I am the other. I will
> come to visit you.

It is true that the old man is religious. He wears a skullcap, he threads his tales with strands of the holy phrases. And he cannot send anyone away from his door. So when the student appears, the old writer invites him in for a glass of tea, though homage fatigues him; he would rather nap.

The student confesses that his own ambitiousness has brought him to the writer's feet: he too would wish one day to be revered as the writer himself is revered.

—I wish, says the old writer, I had been like you in my youth. I never had the courage to look into the face of anyone I admired, and I admired so many! But they were all too remote; I was very shy. I wish now I had gone to see them, as you have come to see me.

—Whom did you admire most? asks the student. In reality he has no curiosity about this or anything else of the kind, but he recognizes that such a question is vital to the machinery of praise. And though he has never read a word the old man has written, he can smell all around him, even in the old man's trousers, the smell of fame.

—The Rambam, answers the old man. —Him I admired more than anyone.

—Maimonides? exclaims the student. —But how could you visit Maimonides?

—Even in my youth, the old man assents, the Rambam had already been dead for several hundred years. But even if he had not been dead, I would have been too shy to go and see him. For a shy young man it is relieving to admire someone who is dead.

—Then to become like you, the student says meditatively, it is necessary to be shy?

—Oh yes, says the old man. —It is necessary to be shy. The truest ambition is hidden in shyness. All ambitiousness is hidden. If you want to usurp my place you must not show it, or I will only hang on to it all the more tightly. You must always walk with your head down. You must be a true *ba'al ga'avah*.

—A *ba'al ga'avah?* cries the student. —But you contradict yourself! Aren't we told that the *ba'al ga'avah* is the man whom God most despises? The self-righteous self-idolator? It's written that him alone God will cause to perish. Sooner than a murderer!

It is plain that the young man is in good command of the sources; not for nothing is he a student at the yeshiva. But he is perplexed, rattled. —How can I be like you if you tell me to be a *ba'al ga'avah?* And why would you tell me to be such a thing?

—The *ba'al ga'avah*, explains the writer, is a supplanter: the man whose arrogance is godlike, whose pride is like a tower. He is the one who most subtly turns his gaze downward to the ground, never looking at what he covets. I myself was never cunning enough to be a genuine *ba'al ga'avah*; I was always too timid for it. It was never necessary for me to feign shyness, I was naturally like that. But you are not. So you must invent a way to become a genuine *ba'al ga'avah*, so audacious and yet so ingenious that you will fool God and will live.

The student is impatient. —How does God come into this? We're talking only of ambition.

—Of course. Of *serious* ambition, however. You recall: "All that is not Torah is levity." This is the truth to be found at the end of every incident, even this one. —You see, the old man continues, my place can easily be taken. A blink, and it's yours. I will not watch over it if I forget that someone is after it. But you must make me forget.

—How? asks the student, growing cold with greed.

—By never coming here again.

—It's a joke!

—And then I will forget you. I will forget to watch over my place.

And then, when I least look for it to happen, you will come and steal it. You will be so quiet, so shy, so ingenious, so audacious, I will never suspect you.

—A nasty joke! You want to get rid of me! It's mockery, you forget what it is to be young. In old age everything is easier, nothing burns inside you.

But meanwhile, inside the student's lungs, and within the veins of his wrists, a cold fog shivers.

—Nothing burns? Yes; true. At the moment, for instance, I covet nothing more lusty than my little twilight nap. I always have it right now.

—They say (the student is as cold now as a frozen path, all his veins are paths of ice), they say you're going to win the Nobel Prize! For literature!

—When I nap I sleep dreamlessly. I don't dream of such things. Come, let me help you cease to covet.

—It's hard for me to keep my head down! I'm young, I want what you have, I want to be like you!

Here I will interrupt the goat's story to apologize. I would not be candid if I did not confess that I am rewriting it; I am almost making it my own, and that will never do for an act of plagiarism. I don't mean only that I have set it more or less in order, and taken out the murk. That is only by the way. But, by sticking to what one said and what the other answered, I have broken my promise; already I have begun to bore you. Boring! Oh, the goat's story was boring! Philosophic stories make excellent lullabies.

So, going on with my own version (I hate stories with ideas hidden in them), I will spring out of paraphrase and invent what the old man does.

Right after saying "Let me help you cease to covet," he gets up and, with fuzzy sleepy steps, half-limps to a table covered by a cloth that falls to the floor. He separates the parts of the cloth, and now the darkness underneath the table takes him like a tent. In he crawls, the flaps cling, his rump makes a bulge. He calls out two words in Hebrew: *ohel shalom!* and backs out, carrying with him a large black box. It looks like a lady's hat box.

"An admirer gave me this. Only not an admirer of our own

time. A predecessor. I had it from Tchernikhovsky. The poet. I presume you know his work?"

"A little," says the student. He begins to wish he had boned up before coming.

"Tchernikhovsky was already dead when he brought me this," the old man explains. "One night I was alone, sitting right there—where you are now. I was reading Tchernikhovsky's most famous poem, the one to the god Apollo. And quite suddenly there was Tchernikhovsky. He disappointed me. He was a completely traditional ghost, you could see right through him to the wall behind. This of course made it difficult to study his features. The wall behind—you can observe for yourself—held a bookcase, so where his nose appeared to be I could read only the title of a Tractate of the Mishnah. A ghost can be seen mainly in outline, unfortunately, something like an artist's charcoal sketch, only instead of the blackness of charcoal, it is the narrow brilliance of a very fine white light. But what he carried was palpable, even heavy—this box. I was not at all terror-stricken, I can't tell you why. Instead I was bemused by the kind of picture he made against the wall—'modern,' I would have called it then, but probably there are new words for that sort of thing now. It reminded me a little of a collage: one kind of material superimposed on another kind which is utterly different. One order of creation laid upon another. Metal on tissue. Wood on hide. In this case it was a three-dimensional weight superimposed on a line—the line, or luminous congeries of lines, being Tchernikhovsky's hands, ghost hands holding a real box."

The student stares at the box. He waits like a coat eager to be shrunk.

"The fact is," continues the old writer, "I have never opened it. Not that I'm not as inquisitive as the next mortal. Perhaps more so. But it wasn't necessary. There is something about the presence of an apparition which satisfies all curiosity forever—the deeper as well as the more superficial sort. For one thing, a ghost will tell you everything, and all at once. A ghost may *look* artistic, but there is no finesse to it, nothing indirect or calculated, nothing suggesting *raffinement*. It is as if everything gossamer had gone simply into the stuff of it. The rest is all grossness. Or else Tchernikhovsky himself, even when alive and writing, had a certain clumsiness. This is what I myself believe. All that pantheism and earth-worship! That pursuit of the old gods of Canaan! He thickened his tongue with clay. All pantheists are fools. Likewise trinitarians and gnostics of every kind. How can a piece of creation be its own Creator?

"Still, his voice had rather a pretty sound. To describe it is to be obliged to ask you to recall the sound of prattle: a baby's purr, only shaped into nearly normal cognitive speech. A most pleasing combination. He told me that he was reading me closely in Eden and approved of my stories. He had, he assured me, a number of favorites, but best of all he liked a quite short tale—no more than a notebook sketch, really—about why the Messiah will not come.

"In this story the Messiah is ready to come. He enters a synagogue and prepares to appear at the very moment he hears the congregation recite the 'I believe.' He stands there and listens, waiting to make himself visible on the last syllable of the verse 'I believe in the coming of the Messiah, and even if he tarry I will await his coming every day.' He leans against the Ark and listens, listens and leans—all the time he is straining his ears. The fact is he can hear nothing: the congregation buzzes with its own talk—hats, mufflers, business, wives, appointments, rain, lessons, the past, next week . . . the prayer is obscured, all its syllables are drowned in everydayness, and the Messiah retreats; he has not heard himself summoned.

"This, Tchernikhovsky's ghost told me, was my best story. I was at once suspicious. His baby-voice hinted at ironies, I caught a tendril of sarcasm. It was clear to me that what he liked about this story was mainly its climactic stroke: that the Messiah is prevented from coming. I had written to lament the tarrying of the Messiah; Tchernikhovsky, it seemed, took satisfaction exactly in what I mourned. 'Look here,' he tinkled at me—imagine a crow linked to a delicious little gurgle, and the whole sense of it belligerent as a prizefighter and coarse as an old waiter—'now that I'm dead, a good quarter-century of deadness under my dust, I've concluded that I'm entirely willing to have you assume my eminence. For one thing, I've been to Sweden, pulled strings with some deceased but still influential Academicians, and arranged for you to get the Nobel Prize in a year or two. Which is beyond what I ever got for myself. But I'm aware this won't interest you as much as a piece of eternity right here in Jerusalem, so I'm here to

tell you you can have it. You can'—he had a babyish way of repeating things—'assume my eminence.'

"You see what I mean about grossness. I admit I was equally
coarse. I answered speedily and to the point. I refused.

"'I understand you,' he said. 'You don't suppose I'm pious
enough, or not pious in the right way. I don't meet your yeshiva
standards. Naturally not. You know I used to be a doctor, I was
attracted to biology, which is to say to dust. Not spiritual enough
for you! My Zionism wasn't of the soul, it was made of real dirt.
What I'm offering you is something tangible. Have some common
sense and take it. It will do for you what the Nobel Prize can't.
Open the box and put on whatever's inside. Wear it for one full
minute and the thing will be accomplished.' "

"For God's sake, what *was* it?" shrieks the student, shriveling
into his blue city-boy shirt. With a tie: and in Jerusalem! (The
student is an absurdity, a crudity. But of course I've got to have
him; he's left over from the goat's story, what else am I to do?)

"Inside the box," replies the old writer, "was the most literal-
minded thing in the world. From a ghost I expected as much.
The whole idea of a ghost is a literal-minded conception. I've
used ghosts in my own stories, naturally, but they've always had
a real possibility, by which I mean an ideal possibility: Elijah, the
True Messiah . . ."

"For God's sake, the box!"

"The box. Take it. I give it to you."

"What's in it?"

"See for yourself."

"Tell me first. Tchernikhovsky told *you.*"

"That's a fair remark. It contains a crown."

"What kind of crown?"

"Made of silver, I believe."

"*Real* silver?"

"I've never looked on it, I've explained this. I *refused* it."

"Then why give it to me?"

"Because it's meant for that. When a writer wishes to usurp the
place and power of another writer, he simply puts it on. I've explained this already."

"But if I wear it I'll become like Tchernikhovsky—"

"No, no, like me. Like me. It confers the place and power of
the giver. And it's what you want, true? To be like me?"

"But this isn't what you advised a moment ago. *Then* you said to become arrogant, a *ba'al ga'avah*, and to conceal it with shyness—"

(Quite so. A muddle in the plot. That was the goat's story, and it had no silver crown in it. I am still stuck with these leftovers that cause seams and cracks in my own version. I will have to mend all this somehow. Be patient. I will manage it. Pray that I don't bungle it.)

"Exactly," says the old writer. "That's the usual way. But if you aren't able to feign shyness, what is necessary is a short cut. I warned you it would demand audacity and ingenuity. What I did not dare to do, you must have the courage for. What I turned down you can raise up. I offer you the crown. You will see what a short cut it is. Wear it and immediately you become a *ba'al ga'avah*. Still, I haven't yet told you how I managed to get rid of Tchernikhovsky's ghost. Open the box, put on the crown, and I'll tell you."

The student obeys. He lifts the box onto the table. It seems light enough, then he opens it, and at the first thrust of his hand into its interior it disintegrates, flakes off into dust, is blown off at a breath, consumed by the first alien molecule of air, like something very ancient removed from the deepest clay tomb and unable to withstand the corrosive stroke of light.

But there, in the revealed belly of the vanished box, is the crown.

It appears to be made of silver, but it is heavier than any earthly silver—it is heavy, heavy, heavy, dense as a meteorite. Puffing and struggling, the student tries to raise it up to his head. He cannot. He cannot lift even a corner of it. It is weighty as a pyramid.

"It won't budge."

"It will after you pay for it."

"You didn't say anything about payment!"

"You're right. I forgot. But you don't pay in money. You pay in a promise. You have to promise that if you decide you don't want the crown you'll take it off immediately. Otherwise it's yours forever."

"I promise."

"Good. Then put it on."

And now lightly, lightly, oh so easily as if he lifted a straw hat, the student elevates the crown and sets it on his head.

"There. You are like me. Now go away."

And oh so lightly, lightly, as easily as if the crown were a cargo of helium, the student skips through Jerusalem. He runs! He runs into a bus, a joggling mob crushed together, everyone recognizes him, even the driver: he is praised, honored, young women put out their hands to touch his collar, they pluck at his pants, his fly unzips and he zips it up again, oh fame! He gets off the bus and runs to his yeshiva. Crowds on the sidewalk, clapping. So this is what it feels like! He flies into the yeshiva like a king. Formerly no one blinked at him, the born Jerusalemites scarcely spoke to him, but now! It is plain they have all read him. He hears a babble of titles, plots, characters, remote yet familiar—look, he thinks, the crown has supplied me with a ready-made bibliography. He reaches up to his head to touch it: a flash of cold. Cold, cold, it is the coldest silver on the planet, a coldness that stabs through into his brain. Frost encases his brain, inside his steaming skull he hears more titles, more plots, names of characters, scholars, wives, lovers, ghosts, children, beggars, villages, candlesticks—what a load he carries, what inventions, what a teeming and a boiling, stories, stories, stories! His own; yet not his own. The Rosh Yeshiva comes down the stairs from his study: the Rosh Yeshiva, the Head, a bony miniaturized man grown almost entirely inward and upward into a spectacular dome, a brow shaped like the front of an academy, hollowed-out temples for porticoes, a resplendent head with round dead-end eyeglasses as denying as bottle-bottoms and curl-scribbled beard and small attachments of arms and little antlike legs thin as hairs; and the Rosh Yeshiva, who has never before let fall a syllable to this obscure tourist-pupil from America, suddenly cries out the glorious blessing reserved for finding oneself in the presence of a sage: Blessed are You, O God, Imparter of wisdom to those who fear Him! And the student in his crown understands that there now cleave to his name sublime parables interpreting the divine purpose, and he despairs, he is afraid, because suppose he were obliged to write one this minute? Suppose these titles clamoring all around him are only empty pots, and he must fill them up with stories? He runs from the yeshiva, elbows out, scattering admirers and celebrants, and makes for the alley behind the kitchen—no one ever goes there, only the old cats who scavenge in the trash barrels. But behind him— crudely sepulchral footsteps, like thumps inside a bucket, he runs, he looks back, he runs, he stops—Tchernikhovsky's ghost! From the old writer's description he can identify it easily. "A mistake," chimes the ghost, a pack of bells, "it wasn't for you."

"What!" screams the student.

"Give it back."

"What!"

"The crown," pursues the baby-purr voice of Tchernikhovsky's ghost. "I never meant for that old fellow to give it away."

"He said it was all right."

"He tricked you."

"No he didn't."

"He's sly sly sly."

"He said it would make me just like him. And I am."

"No."

"Yes!"

"Then predict the future."

"In two years, the Nobel Prize for Literature!"

"For him, not for you."

"But I'm *like* him."

" 'Like' is not the same as the same. You want to be the same? Look in the window."

The student looks into the kitchen window. Inside, among cauldrons, he can see the roil of the students in their caps, spinning here and there, in the pantry, in the Passover dish closet even, past a pair of smoky vats, in search of the fled visitor who now stares and stares until his concentration alters seeing; and instead of looking behind the pane, he follows the light on its surface and beholds a reflection. An old man is also looking into the window; the student is struck by such a torn rag of a face. Strange, it cannot be Tchernikhovsky: he is all web and wraith; and anyhow a ghost has no reflection. The old man in the looking-glass window is wearing a crown. A silver crown!

"You see?" tinkles the ghost. "A trick!"

"I'm old!" howls the student.

"Feel in your pocket."

The student feels. A vial.

"See? Nitroglycerin."

"What is this, are you trying to blow me up?"

Again the small happy soaring of the infant's grunt. "I remind you that I am a physician. When you are seized by a pulling, a knocking, a burning in the chest, a throb in the elbow-crook, swallow one of these tablets. In coronary insufficiency it relaxes the artery."

"Heart failure! Will I die? Stop! I'm young!"

"With those teeth? All gums gone? That wattle? Dotard! Bag!"

The student runs; he remembers his perilous heart; he slows. The ghost thumps and chimes behind. So they walk, a procession of two, a very old man wearing a silver crown infinitely cold, in his shadow a ghost made all of lit spider-thread, giving out now and then with baby's laughter and odd coarse curses patched together from Bible phrases; together they scrape out of the alley onto the boulevard—an oblivious population there.

"My God! No one knows me. Why don't they know me here?"

"Who should know you?" says Tchernikhovsky.

"In the bus they yelled out dozens of book titles. In the streets! The Rosh Yeshiva said the blessing for seeing a sage!"

But now in the bus the passengers are indifferent; they leap for seats; they snore in cozy spots standing up, near poles; and not a word. Not a gasp, not a squeal. Not even a pull on the collar. It's all over! A crown but no king.

"It's stopped working," says the student, mournful.

"The crown? Not on your life."

"Then you're interfering with it. You're jamming it up."

"That's more like the truth."

"Why are you following me?"

"I don't like misrepresentation."

"You mean you don't like magic."

"They're the same thing."

"Go away!"

"I never do that."

"*He* got rid of you."

"Sly sly sly. He did it with a ruse. You know how? He refused the crown. He took it but he hid it away. No one ever refused it before. Usurper! Coveter! *Ba'al ga'avah!* That's what he is."

The student protests, "But he *gave* me the crown. 'Let me help you cease to covet,' that's exactly what he said, why do you call him *ba'al ga'avah?*"

"And himself? *He's* ceased to covet, is that it? That's what you think? You think he doesn't churn saliva over the Nobel Prize? Ever since I told him they were speculating about the possibility over at the Swedish Academicians' graveyard? Day and night that's all he dreams of. He loves his little naps, you know why? To sleep, perchance to dream. He imagines himself in a brand-new splendiferous bow-tie, rear end trailing tails, wearing his skullcap out of public arrogance, his old wife up there with him dressed to the hobbledorfs—in Stockholm, with the King of Sweden! That's what he sees, that's what he dreams, he can't work, he's in a fever of coveting. You think it's different when you're old?"

"I'm not old!" the student shouts. A willful splinter, he peels himself from the bus. Oh, frail, his legs are straw, the dry knees wrap close like sheaves, he feels himself pouring out, sand from a sack. Old!

Now they are in front of the writer's house. "Age makes no matter," says the ghost, "the same, the same. Ambition levels, lust is unitary. Lust you can always count on. I'm not speaking of the carnal sort. Carnality's a brevity—don't compare wind with mountains! But lust! Teetering on the edge of the coffin there's lust. After mortality there's lust, I guarantee you. In Eden there's nothing but lust." The ghost raps on the door—with all his strength, and his strength is equal to a snowflake. Silence, softness. "Bang on the thing!" he commands, self-disgusted; sometimes he forgets he is incorporeal.

The student obeys, shivering; he is so cold now his three or six teeth clatter like chinaware against a waggling plastic bridge anchored in nothing, his ribs shake in his chest, his spine vibrates without surcease. And what of his heart? Inside his pocket he clutches the vial.

The old writer opens up. His fists are in his eyes.

"We woke you, did we?" gurgles Tchernikhovsky's ghost.

"You!"

"Me," says the ghost, satisfied. "Ba'al ga'avah! Spiteful! You foisted the crown on a kid."

The old writer peers. "Where?"

The ghost sweeps the student forward. "I did him the service of giving him long life. Instantly. Why wait for a good thing?"

"I don't want it! Take it back!" the student cries, snatching at the crown on his head; but it stays on. "You said I could give it back if I don't want it any more!"

Again the old writer peers. "Ah. You keep your promise. So does the crown."

"What do you mean?"

"It promised you acclaim. But it generates this pest. Everything has its price."

"Get rid of it!"

"To get rid of the ghost you have to get rid of the crown."

"All right! Here it is! Take it back! It's yours!"

The ghost laughs like a baby at the sight of a teat. "Try and take it off then."

The student tries. He tears at the crown, he flings his head upward, backward, sideways, pulls and pulls. His fingertips flame with the ferocious cold.

"How did *you* get rid of it?" he shrieks.

"I never put it on," replies the old writer.

"No, no, I mean the ghost, how did you get rid of the ghost!"

"I was going to tell you that, remember? But you ran off."

"You sent me away. It was a trick, you never meant to tell."

The ghost scolds: "No disputes!" And orders, "Tell now."

The student writhes; twists his neck; pulls and pulls. The crown stays on.

"The crown loosens," the old writer begins, "when the ghost goes. Everything dissolves together—"

"But *how?*"

"You find someone to give the crown to. That's all. You simply pass it on. All you do is agree to give away its powers to someone who wants it. Consider it a test of your own generosity."

"Who'll want it? Nobody wants such a thing!" the student shrieks. "It's stuck! Get it off! Off!"

"*You* wanted it."

"Prig! Moralist! *Ba'al ga'avah!* Didn't I come to you for advice? Literary advice, and instead you gave me this! I wanted help! You gave me metal junk! Sneak!"

"Interesting," observes the ghost, "that I myself acquired the crown in exactly the same way. I received it from Ibn Gabirol. Via ouija board. I was skeptical about the method but discovered it to be legitimate. I consulted him about some of his verse-forms. To be specific, the problem of enjambment, which is more difficult in Hebrew than in some other languages. By way of reply he gave me the crown. Out of the blue it appeared on the board—naked, so to speak, and shining oddly, like a fish without scales. Of course there wasn't any ghost attached to the crown then. I'm the first, and you don't think I *like* having to materialize thirty minutes after someone's put it on? What I need is to be left in peace in Paradise, not this business of being on call the moment some-one—"

"Ibn Gabirol?" the old writer breaks in, panting, all attention. Ibn Gabirol! Sublime poet, envied beyond envy, sublimeness without heir, who would not covet the crown of Ibn Gabirol?

"He said *he* got it from Isaiah. The quality of ownership keeps declining apparently. That's why they have me on patrol. If some-one unworthy acquires it—well, that's where I put on my emana-tions and dig in. Come on," says the ghost, all at once sounding American, "let's go." He gives the student one of his snowflake shoves. "Where you go, I go. Where I go, you go. Now that you know the ropes, let's get out of here and find somebody who de-serves it. Give it to some goy for a change. 'The righteous among the Gentiles are as judges in Israel.' My own suggestion is Oxford, Mississippi, Faulkner, William."

"Faulkner's dead."

"He is? I ought to look him up. All right then. Someone not so fancy. Norman Mailer."

"A Jew," sneers the student.

"Can you beat that. Never mind, we'll find someone. Keep away from the rot of Europe—Kafka had it once. Maybe a black. An Indian. Spic maybe. We'll go to America and look."

Moistly the old writer plucks at the ghost. "Listen, this doesn't cancel the Prize? I still get it?"

"In two years you're in Stockholm."

"And me?" cries the student. "What about me? What happens to me?"

"You wear the crown until you get someone to take it from you. Blockhead! Dotard! Don't you *listen*?" says the ghost: his accent wobbles, he elides like a Calcuttan educated in Paris.

"No one wants it! I told you! Anyone who really needs it you'll say doesn't deserve it. If he's already famous he doesn't need it, and if he's unknown you'll think he degrades it. Like me. Not fair! There's no *way* to pass it on."

"You've got a point." The ghost considers this. "That makes sense. Logic."

"So get it off me!"

"However, again you forget lust. Lust overcomes logic."

"Stop! Off!"

"The King of Sweden," muses the old writer, "speaks no Hebrew. That will be a difficulty. I suppose I ought to begin to study Swedish."

"Off! Off!" yells the student. And tugs at his head, yanks at the crown, pulling, pulling, seizing it by the cold points. He throws himself down, wedges his legs against the writer's desk, tumbling after leverage; nothing works. Then methodically he kneels, lays his head on the floor, and methodically begins to beat the crown against the wooden floor. He jerks, tosses, taps, his white head in the brilliant crown is a wild flashing hammer; then he catches at his chest; his knuckles explode; then again he beats, beats, beats the crown down. But it stays stuck, no blow can knock it free. He beats. He heaves his head. Sparks spring from the crown, small lightnings leap. Oh, his chest, his ribs, his heart! The vial, where is the vial? His hands squirm toward his throat, his chest, his pocket. And his head beats the crown down against the floor. The old head halts, the head falls, the crown stays stuck, the heart is dead.

"Expired," says the ghost of Tchernikhovsky.

Well, that should be enough. No use making up any more of it. Why should I? It is not my story. It is not the goat's story. It is no one's story. It is a story nobody wrote, nobody wants, it has no existence. What does the notion of a *ba'al ga'avah* have to do with a silver crown? One belongs to morals, the other to magic. Stealing from two disparate tales I smashed their elements one into the other. Things must be brought together. In magic all divergences are linked and locked. The fact is I forced the crown onto the ambitious student in order to punish.

To punish? Yes. In life I am, though obscure, as generous and reasonable as those whom wide glory has sweetened; earlier you saw how generously and reasonably I dealt with the goat. So I am used to being taken for everyone's support, confidante, and consolation—it did not surprise me, propped there against that wall in the dark, when the goat begged me to read his story. Why should he not? My triumph is that, in my unrenown, everyone trusts me not to lie. But I always lie. Only on paper I do not lie. On paper I punish, I am malignant.

For instance: I killed off the student to punish him for arrogance. But it is really the goat I am punishing. It is an excellent thing to punish him. Did he not make his hero a student at the yeshiva, did he not make him call himself "religious"? But what is that? What is it to be "religious"? Is religion any different from magic? Whoever intends to separate them ends in proving them to be the same.

The goat was a *ba'al ga'avah!* I understood that only a *ba'al ga'avah* would dare to write about "religion."

So I punished him for it. How? By transmuting piety into magic.

Then—and I require you to accept this with the suddenness I myself experienced it: *as if by magic*—again I was drawn to look into the goat's story; and found, on the next-to-last page, an address. He had rubbed out (I have already mentioned this) his name; but here was a street and a number:

18 Herzl Street
Brooklyn, N.Y.

A street fashioned—so to speak—after the Messiah. Here I will halt you once more to ask you to take no notice of the implications of the goat's address. It is an aside worthy of the goat himself. It is he, not I, who would grab you by the sleeve here and now in order to explain exactly who Theodore Herzl was—oh, how I despise writers who will stop a story dead for the sake of showing off! Do you care whether or not Maimonides (supposing you had ever heard of that lofty saint) tells us that the messianic age will be recognizable simply by the resumption of Jewish political independence? Does it count if, by that definition, the Messiah turns out to be none other than a Viennese journalist of the last century? Doubtless Herzl was regarded by his contemporaries as a *ba'al ga'avah* for brazening out, in a modern moment, a Hebrew principality. And who is more of a *ba'al ga'avah* than the one who usurps the Messiah's own job? Take Isaiah—was not Isaiah a *ba'al ga'avah* when he declared against observance—"I hate your feasts and your new moons"—and in the voice, no less, of the Creator Himself?

But thank God I have no taste for these notions. Already you have seen how earnestly my mind is turned toward hatred of metaphysical speculation. Practical action is my whole concern, and I have nothing but contempt for significant allusions, nuances, buried effects.

Therefore you will not be astonished at what I next undertook to do. I went—ha!—to the street of the Messiah to find the goat.

It was a place where there had been conflagrations. Rubble tentatively stood: brick on brick, about to fall. One remaining configuration of wall, complete with windows but no panes. The sidewalk underfoot stirred with crumbs, as of sugar grinding: mortar reduced to sand. A desert flushed over tumbled yards. Lintels and doors burned out, foundations squared like pebbles on a beach: in this spot once there had been cellars, stoops, houses. The smell of burned wood wandered. A civilization of mounds—who had lived here? Jews. There were no buildings left. A rectangular stucco fragment—of what? synagogue maybe— squatted in a space. There was no Number 18—only bad air, light flying in the gape and gash where the fires had driven down brick, mortar, wood, mothers, fathers, children pressing library cards inside their pockets—gone, finished.

And immediately—as if by magic—the goat!

"You!" I hooted, exactly as, in the story that never was, the old writer had cried it to Tchernikhovsky's shade.

"You've read my stuff," he said, gratified. "I knew you could find me easy if you wanted to. All you had to do was want to."

"Where do you live?"

"Number 18. I knew you'd want to."

"There isn't any 18."

He pointed. "It's what's left of the shul. No plumbing, but it still has a good kitchen in the back. I'm what you call a squatter, you don't mind?"

"Why should I mind?"

"Because I stole the idea from a book. It's this story about a writer who lives in an old tenement with his typewriter and the tenement's about to be torn down—"

The famous author who had written about the magic crown had written that story too; I reflected how some filch their fiction from life, others filch their lives from fiction. What people call inspiration is only pilferage. "You're not living in a tenement," I corrected, "you're living in a synagogue."

"What used to be. It's a hole now, a sort of cave. The Ark is left though, you want to see the Ark?"

I followed him through shards. There was no front door.

"What happened to this neighborhood?" I said.

"The Jews went away."

"Who came instead?"

"Fire."

The curtain of the Ark dangled in charred shreds. I peered inside the orifice which had once closeted the Scrolls: all blackness there, and the clear sacrificial smell of things that have been burned.

"See?" he said. "The stove works. It's the old wood-burning kind. For years they didn't use it here, it just sat. And now—resurrection." Ah: the clear sacrificial smell was potatoes baking.

"Don't you have a job?"

"I write, I'm a writer. And no rent to pay anyhow."

"How do you drink?"

"You mean *what*." He held up a full bottle of Schapiro's kosher wine. "They left a whole case intact."

"But you can't wash, you can't even use the toilet."

"I pee and do my duty in the yard. Nobody cares. This is freedom, lady."

"Dirt," I said.

"What's dirt to Peter is freedom to Paul. Did you like my story? Sit."

There was actually a chair, but it had a typewriter on it. The goat did not remove it.

"How do you take a bath?" I persisted.

"Sometimes I go to my cousin's. I told you. The rabbi's wife."

"The rabbi from this synagogue?"

"No, he's moved to Woodhaven Boulevard. That's Queens. All the Jews from here went to Queens, did you know that?"

"*What* rabbi's wife?" I blew out, exasperated.

"I *told* you. The one with the crown. The one they wrote about in the papers. The one *he* lifted the idea of that story from. A rip-off that was, my cousin ought to sue."

Then I remembered. "All stories are rip-offs," I said. "Shakespeare stole his plots. Dostoyevski dug them out of the newspaper. Everybody steals. The Decameron's stolen. Whatever looks like invention is theft."

"Great," he said, "that's what I need. Literary talk."

"What did you mean, you knew I would want to come? —Believe me, I didn't come for literary talk."

"You bet. You came because of my cousin. You came because of the crown."

I was amazed: instantly it coursed in on me that this was true. I had come because of the crown; I was in pursuit of the crown.

I said: "I don't care about the crown. I'm interested in the rabbi himself. The crown-blesser. What I care about is the psychology of the thing."

This word—"psychology"—made him cackle. "He's in jail, I thought you knew that. They got him for fraud."

"Does his wife still have any crowns around?"

"One."

"Here's your story," I said, handing it over. "Next time leave your name in. You don't have to obliterate it, rely on the world for that."

The pus on his eyelids glittered. "Alex will obliterate the world, not vice versa."

"How? By bombing it with stories? The first anonymous obliteration. The Flood without a by-line," I said. "At least everything God wrote was publishable. Alex what?"

"Goldflusser."

"You're a liar."

"Silbertsig."

"Cut it out."

"Kupferman. Bleifischer. Bettler. Kenigman."

"All that's mockery. If your name's a secret—"

"I'm lying low, hiding out, they're after me because I helped with the crowns."

I speculated, "You're the one who made them."

"No. She did that."

"Who?"

"My cousin. The rabbi's wife. She crocheted them. What he did was go buy the form—you get it from a costume loft, stainless steel. She used to make these little pointed sort of *gloves* for it, to protect it, see, and the shine would glimmer through, and then the customer would get to keep the crown-cover, as a sort of guarantee—"

"My God," I said, "what's all that about, why didn't *she* go to jail?"

"Crocheting isn't a crime."

"And you?" I said. "What did you do in all that?"

"Get customers. Fraudulent solicitation, that's a crime."

He took the typewriter off the chair and sat down. The wisp of beard wavered. "Didn't you like my story?" he accused. The pages were pressed with an urgency between his legs.

"No. It's all fake. It doesn't matter if you've been to Jerusalem. You've got the slant of the place all wrong. It doesn't matter about the yeshiva either. It doesn't matter if you really went to see some old geezer over there, you didn't get anything right. It's a terrible story."

"Where do you come off with that stuff?" he burst out. "Have *you* been to Jerusalem? Have *you* seen the inside of a yeshiva?"

"No."

"So!"

"I can tell when everything's fake," I said. "What I mean by fake is raw. When no one's ever used it before, it's something new under the sun, a whole new combination, that's bad. A real story is whatever you can predict, it has to be familiar, anyhow you have to know how it's going to come out, no exotic new material, no unexpected flights—"

He rushed out at me: "What you want is to bore people!"

"I'm a very boring writer," I admitted; out of politeness I kept from him how much his story, and even my own paraphrase of it, had already bored me. "But in *principle* I'm right. The only good part in the whole thing was explaining about the *ba'al ga'avah*. People hate to read foreign words, but at least it's ancient wisdom. Old, old stuff."

Then I told him how I had redesigned his story to include a ghost.

He opened the door of the stove and threw his manuscript in among the black-skinned potatoes.

"Why did you do that?"

"To show you I'm no *ba'al ga'avah*. I'm humble enough to burn up what somebody doesn't like."

I said suspiciously, "You've got other copies."

"Sure. Other potatoes too."

"Look," I said, riding malice, "it took me two hours to find this place, I have to go to the yard."

"You want to take a leak? Come over to my cousin's. It's not far. My cousin's lived in this neighborhood sixty years."

Furiously I went after him. He was a crook leading me to the house of crooks. We walked through barrenness and canker, a ruined city, store-windows painted black, one or two curtained by gypsies, some boarded, barred, barbed, old newspapers rolling in the gutter, the sidewalks speckled with viscous blotch. Overhead a smell like kerosene, the breath of tenements. The cousin's toilet stank as if no one had flushed it in half a century; it had one of those tanks high up, attached to the ceiling, a perpetual drip running down the pull chain. The sink was in the kitchen. There was no soap; I washed my hands with Ajax powder while the goat explained me to his cousin.

"She's interested in the crown," he said.

"Out of business," said the cousin.

"Maybe for her."

"Not doing business, that's all. For nobody whatsoever."

"I'm not interested in buying one," I said, "just in finding out."

"Crowns is against the law."

"For healing," the goat argued, "not for showing. She knows the man who wrote that story. You remember about that guy, I told you, this famous writer who took—"

"Who took! Too much fame," said the cousin, "is why Saul sits in jail. Before newspapers and stories we were left in peace, we helped people peacefully." She condemned me with an oil-surfaced eye, the colorless slick of the ripening cataract. "My husband, a holy man, him they put in jail. Him! A whole year, twelve months! A man like that! Brains, a saint—"

"But he fooled people," I said.

"In helping is no fooling. Out, lady. You had to pee, you peed. You needed a public facility, very good, now out. I don't look for extra customers for my toilet bowl."

"Goodbye," I said to the goat.

"You think there's hope for me?"

"Quit writing about ideas. Stay out of the yeshiva, watch out for religion. Don't make up stories about famous writers."

"Listen," he said—his nose was speckled with pustules of lust, his nostrils gaped—"you didn't like that one, I'll give you another. I've got plenty more, I've got a crateful."

"What are you talking," said the cousin.

"She knows writers," he said, "in person. She knows how to get things published."

I protested, "I can hardly get published myself—"

"You published something?" said the cousin.

"A few things, not much."

"Alex, bring Saul's box."

"That's not the kind of stuff," the goat said.

"Definitely. About expression I'm not so concerned like you. What isn't so regular, anyone with a desire and a pencil can fix it."

The goat remonstrated, "What Saul has is something else, it's not *writing*—"

"With connections," said the cousin, "nothing is something else, everything is writing. Lady, in one box I got my husband's entire holy life work. The entire theory of healing and making the dead ones come back for a personal appearance. We sent maybe to twenty printing houses, nothing doing. You got connections, I'll show you something."

"Print," I reminded her, "is what you said got the rabbi in trouble."

"Newspapers. Lies. False fame. Everything with a twist. You call him rabbi, who made from him a rabbi? The entire world says rabbi, so let it be rabbi. There he sits in jail, a holy man what did nothing his whole life to harm. Whatever a person asked for, this was what he gave. Whatever you wanted to call him, this was what he became. Alex! Take out Saul's box, it's in the bottom of the dresser with the crown."

"The crown?" I said.

"The crown is nothing. What's something is Saul's brain. Alex!"

The goat shut his nostrils. He gave a snicker and disappeared. Through the kitchen doorway I glimpsed a sagging bed and heard a drawer grind open.

He came back lugging a carton with a picture of tomato cans on it. On top of it lay the crown. It was gloved in a green pattern of peephole diamonds.

"Here," said the cousin, "is Saul's ideas. Listen, that famous writer what went to steal from the papers—a fool. If he could steal what's in Saul's brain what would he need a newspaper? Read!" She dipped a fist into a hiss of sheets and foamed up a sheaf of them. "You'll see, the world will rush to put in print.

The judge at the trial—I said to him, look in Saul's box, you'll see the truth, no fraud. If they would read Saul's papers, not only would he not sit in jail, the judge with hair growing from his ears they would throw out!"

I looked at the goat; he was not laughing. He reached out and put the crown on my head.

It felt lighter than I imagined. It was easy to forget you were wearing it.

I read:

Why does menkind not get what they wish for? This is an easy solution. He is used to No. Always No. So it comes he is afraid to ask.

"The power of positive thinking," I said. "A philosopher."

"No, no," the cousin intervened, "not a philosopher, what do philosophers know to heal, to make real shadows from the dead?"

Through thinning threads of beard the goat said, "not a philosopher."

I read:

Everything depends what you ask. Even you're not afraid to ask, plain asking is not sufficient. If you ask in a voice, there got to be an ear to listen in. The ear of Ha-shem, King of the Universe. (His Name we don't use it every minute like a shoelace.) A Jew don't go asking Ha-shem for inside information, for what reason He did this, what ideas He got on that, how come He let happen such-and-such a pogrom, why a good person loved by one and all dies with cancer, and a lousy bastard he's rotten to his partner and cheats and plays the numbers, this fellow lives to 120. With questions like this don't expect no replies, Ha-shem don't waste breath on trash from fleas. Ha-shem says, My secrets are My secrets, I command you what you got to do, the rest you leave to Me. This is no news that He don't reveal His deepest business. From that territory you get what you deserve, silence.

"What are you up to?" said the goat.
"Silence."
"Ssh!" said the cousin. "Alex, so let her read in peace!"

For us, not one word. He shuts up, His mouth is locked. So how come G–d conversed in history with Adam, with Abraham, with Moses? All right, you can argue that Moses and Abraham was worth it to G–d to listen to, what they said Ha-shem wanted to hear. After all they fed Him back His own ideas. An examination, and already they knew the answers. Smart guys, in the whole history of menkind no one else like these couple of guys. But with Adam, new and naked with no clothes on, just when the whole world was born, was Adam different from me and you? What did Adam know? Even right from wrong he didn't know yet. And still G–d thought, to Adam it's worthwhile to say a few words, I'm not wasting my breath. So what was so particular about Adam that he got Ha-shem's attention, and as regards me and you He don't blink an eye? Adam is better than me and you? We don't go around like a nudist colony, between good and lousy we already know what's what, with or without apples. To me and you G–d should also talk!

"You're following?" the cousin urged. "You see what's in Saul's brain? A whole box full like this, and sits in jail!"

But when it comes wishes, when it comes dreams, who says No? Who says Ha-shem stops talking? Wishes, dreams, imaginations —like fishes in the head. Ha-shem put in Joseph's head two good dreams, were they lies? The truth and nothing but the truth! Q.E.D. To Adam Ha-shem spoke one way, and when He finishes with Moses he talks another way. In a dream, in a wish. That *apikoros* Sigmund Freud, he also figured this out. Whomever says Sigmund Freud stinks from sex, they're mistaken. A wish is the voice, a dream is the voice, an imagination is the voice, all is the voice of Ha-shem the Creator. Naturally a voice is a biological thing, who says No? Whatsoever happens inside the human is a biological thing.

"What are you up to?" the goat asked again.

"Biology."

"Don't laugh. A man walked in here shaking all over, he walked out O.K., I saw it myself."

The cousin said mournfully, "A healer."

"I wrote a terrific story about that guy, I figured what he had was cystic fibrosis, I can show you—"

"There isn't any market for medical stories," I said.

"This was a miracle story."

"There are no miracles."

"That's right!" said the cousin. She dug down again into the box. "One time only, instead of plain writing down, Saul made up a story on this subject exactly. On a yellow piece paper. Aha, here. Alex, read aloud."

The goat read:

One night in the middle of dim stars Ha-shem said, No more miracles! An end with miracles, I already did enough, from now on nothing.

So a king makes an altar and bows down. "O Ha-shem, King of the Universe, I got a bad war on my hands and I'm taking a beating. Make a miracle and save the whole country." Nothing doing, no miracle.

Good, says Ha-shem, this is how it's going to be from now on.

So along comes the Germans, in the camp they got a father and a little son maybe twelve years old. And the son is on the list to be gassed tomorrow. So the father runs around to find a German to bribe, G—d knows what he's got to bribe him with, maybe his wife's diamond ring that he hid somewhere and they didn't take it away yet. And he fixes up the whole thing, tomorrow he'll bring the diamond to the German and they'll take the boy off the list and they won't kill him. They'll slip in some other boy instead and who will know the difference?

Well, so that could be the end, but it isn't. All day after everything's fixed up, the father is thinking and thinking, and in the middle of the night he goes to an old rabbi that's in the camp also, and he tells the rabbi he's going to save his little son.

And the rabbi says, "So why come to me? You made your decision already." The father says, "Yes, but they'll put another boy in his place." The rabbi says, "Instead of Isaac, Abraham put a ram. And that was for G—d. You put another child, and for what? To feed Moloch." The father asks, "What is the law on this?" "The law is, Don't kill."

The next day the father don't bring the bribe. And his eyes don't never see his beloved little child again. Well, so that could be the end, but it isn't. Ha-shem looks at what's happening, here is a man what didn't save his own boy so he wouldn't be responsible with killing someone else. Ha-shem says to Himself, I made a miracle anyhow. I blew in one man so much power of My commandments that his own flesh and blood he lets go to Moloch, so long he shouldn't kill. That I created even one such person like this is a very great miracle, and I didn't even notice I was doing it. So now positively no more.

And after this the destruction continues, no interruptions. Not only the son is gassed, but also the father, and also the boy what they would have put in his place. And also and also and also, until millions of bones of alsos goes up in smoke. About miracles Ha-shem don't change his mind except by accident. So the question menkind has to ask their conscience is this: If the father wasn't such a good commandment-keeper that it's actually a miracle to find a man like this left in the world, what could happen instead? And if only one single miracle could slip through before G–d notices it, which one? Suppose this father didn't use up the one miracle, suppose the miracle is that G–d will stop the murderers altogether, suppose! Instead: nothing doing, the father on account of one kid eats up the one miracle that's lying around loose. For the sake of one life, the whole world is lost.

But on this subject, what's written in our holy books? What the sages got to say? The sages say different: If you save one life only, it's like the whole world is saved. So which is true? Naturally, whatever's written is what's true. What does this prove? It proves that if you talk miracle, that's when everything becomes false. Men and women! Remember! No stories from miracles! No stories and no belief!

"You see?" said the cousin. "Here you have Saul's theories exactly. Whoever says miracles, whoever says magic, tells a lie. On account of a lie a holy man sits in a cage."

"And the crown?" I asked.

She ignored this. "You'll help to publish. You'll give to the right people, you'll give to connections—"

"But why? Why do you need this?"

"What's valuable you give away, you don't keep it for yourself. Listen, is the Bible a secret? The whole world takes from it. Is Talmud a secret? Whatever's a lie should be a secret, not what's holy and true!"

I appealed to the goat. He was licking his fingertips. "I can't digest any of this—"

"You haven't had a look at Saul," he said, "that's why."

The cousin said meanly, "I saw you put on her the crown."

"She wants it."

"The crown is nothing."

"She wants it."

"Then show her Saul."

"You mean in prison?" I said.

"In the bedroom on the night table."

The goat fled. This time he returned carrying a small gilded tin frame. In it was a snapshot of another bearded man.

"Look closely."

But instead of examining the photograph, I all at once wanted to study the goat's cousin. She was one of those tiny twig-thin old women who seem to enlarge the more you get used to their voices. It was as if her whine and her whirr were a pump, and pumped her up; she was now easily as tall as I (though I am myself not very tall) and expanding curiously. She was wearing a checked nylon housedress and white socks in slippers, above which bulged purplish varicose nodules. Her eyes were terribly magnified by metal-rimmed lenses, and looked out at me with the vengefulness of a pair of greased platters. I was astonished to see that a chromium crown had buried itself among the strings of her wandering hairs: having been too often dyed ebony, they were slipping out of their follicles and onto her collarbone. She had an exaggerated widow's peak and was elsewhere a little bit bald.

The goat too wore a crown.

"I thought there was only one left," I objected.

"Look at Saul, you'll see the only one."

The man in the picture wore a silver crown. I recognized him, though the light was shut off in him and the space of his flesh was clearly filled.

"Who is this?" I said.

"Saul."

"But I've seen him!"

"That's right," the cousin said.

"Because you wanted to," said the goat.

"The ghost I put in your story," I reminded him, "this is what it looked like."

The cousin breathed. "You published that story?"

"It's not even written down."

"Whose ghost was it?" asked the goat.

"Tchernikhovsky's. The Hebrew poet. A *ba'al ga'avah*. He wrote a poem called 'Before the Statue of Apollo.' In the last line God is bound with leather thongs."

"Who binds him?"

"The Jews. With their phylacteries. I want to read more," I said.

The two of them gave me the box. The little picture they set on the kitchen table, and they stood over me in their twinkling crowns while I splashed my hands through the false rabbi's stories. Some were already browning at the margins, in ink turned violet, some were on lined school paper, written with a ball-point pen. About a third were in Yiddish; there was even a thin notebook all in Russian; but most were pressed out in pencil in an immigrant's English on all kinds of odd loose sheets, the insides of old New Year greeting cards, the backs of cashiers' tapes from the supermarket, in one instance the ripped-out leather womb of an old wallet.

Saul's ideas were:

sorcery, which he denied.
levitation, which he doubted.
magic, which he sneered at.
miracles, which he denounced.
healing, which he said belonged in hospitals.
instant cures, which he said were fancies and delusions.
the return of deceased loved ones, which he said were wishful hallucinations.
the return of dead enemies, which ditto.
plural gods, which he disputed.
demons, which he derided.
amulets, which he disparaged and repudiated.
Satan, from which hypothesis he scathingly dissented.

He ridiculed everything. He was a rationalist.

"It's amazing," I said, "that he looks just like Tchernikhovsky."

"What does Tchernikhovsky look like?" one of the two crowned ones asked me; I was no longer sure which.

"I don't know, how should I know? Once I saw his picture in an anthology of translations, but I don't remember it. Why are there so many crowns in this room? What's the point of these crowns?"

Then I found the paper on crowns:

You take a real piece mineral, what kings wear. You put it on, you become like a king. What you wish, you get. But what you get you shouldn't believe in unless it's real. How do you know when something's real? If it lasts. How long? This depends. If you wish for a Pyramid, it should last as long like a regular Pyramid lasts. If you wish for long life, it should last as long like your own grandfather. If you wish for a Magic Crown, it should last as long like the brain what it rests on.

I interrupted myself: "Why doesn't he wish himself out of prison? Why didn't he wish himself out of getting sentenced?"
"He lets things take their course."
Then I found the paper on things taking their course:

From my own knowledge I knew a fellow what loved a woman, Beylinke, and she died. So he looked and looked for a twin to this Beylinke, and it's no use, such a woman don't exist. Instead he married a different type altogether, and he made her change her name to Beylinke and make love on the left side, like the real Beylinke. And if he called Beylinke! and she forgot to answer (her name was Ethel) he gave her a good knock on the back, and one day he knocked hard into the kidney and she got a growth and she died. And all he got from his forcing was a lonesome life.

Everything is according to destiny, you can't change nothing. Not that anybody can know what happens before it happens, not even Ha-shem knows which dog will bite which cat next week in Persia.

"Enough," said one of the two in the crowns. "You read and you took enough. You ate enough and you drank enough from this juice. Now you got to pay."
"To pay?"
"The payment is, to say thank you what we showed you everything, you take and you publish."
"Publishing isn't the same as Paradise."
"For some of us it is," said one.
"She knows from Paradise!" scoffed the other.
They thrust the false rabbi's face into my face.
"It isn't English, it isn't even coherent, it's inconsistent, it's crazy, nothing hangs together, nobody in his right mind would—"
"Connections you got."
"No."
"That famous writer."
"A stranger."
"Then somebody else."
"There's no one. I can't make magic—"
"*Ba'al ga'avah!* You're better than Saul? Smarter? Cleverer?

You got better ideas? You, a nothing, they print, and he sits in a box?"

"I looked up one of your stories. It stank, lady. The one called 'Usurpation.' Half of it's swiped, you ought to get sued. You don't know when to stop. You swipe other people's stories and you go on and on, on and on, I fell asleep over it. Boring! Long-winded!"

The mass of sheets pitched into my lap. My fingers flashed upward: there was the crown, with its crocheted cover, its blunted points. Little threads had gotten tangled in my hair. If I tugged the roots would shriek. Tchernikhovsky's paper eyes looked frightened. Crevices opened on either side of his nose and from the left nostril the gray bone of his skull poked out, a cheekbone like a pointer.

"I don't have better ideas," I said. "I'm not interested in ideas, I don't care about ideas. I hate ideas. I only care about stories."

"Then take Saul's stories!"

"Trash. Justice and mercy. He tells you how to live, what to do, the way to think. Righteousness fables, morality tales. Didactic stuff. Rabbinical trash," I said. "What I mean is *stories*. Even you," I said to the goat, "wanting to write about writers! Morality, mortality! You people eat yourself up with morality and mortality!"

"What else should a person eat?"

Just then I began to feel the weight of the crown. It pressed unerringly into the secret tunnels of my brain. A pain like a grief leaped up behind my eyes, up through the temples, up, up, into the marrow of the crown. Every point of it was a spear, a nail. The crown was no different from the bone of my head. The false rabbi Tchernikhovsky tore himself from the tin prison of his frame and sped to the ceiling as if gassed. He had bluish teeth and goblin's wings made of brown leather. Except for the collar and cravat that showed in the photograph, below his beard he was naked. His testicles were leathery. His eyeballs were glass, like a doll's. He was solid as a doll; I was not so lightheaded as to mistake him for an apparition. His voice was as spindly as a harpsichord: "Choose!"

"Between what and what?"

"The Creator or the creature. God or god. The Name of Names or Apollo."

"Apollo," I said on the instant.

"Good," he tinkled, "blessings," he praised me, "flowings and flowings, streams, brooks, lakes, waters out of waters."

Stories came from me then, births and births of tellings, narratives and suspenses, turning-points and palaces, foam of the sea, mermen sewing, dragons pullulating out of quicksilver, my mouth was a box, my ears flowed, they gushed legends and tales, none of them of my own making, all of them acquired, borrowed, given, taken, inherited, stolen, plagiarized, usurped, chronicles and sagas invented at the beginning of the world by the offspring of giants copulating with the daughters of men. A king broke out of the shell of my left eye and a queen from the right one, the box of my belly lifted its scarred lid to let out frogs and swans, my womb was cleft and stories burst free of their balls of blood. Stories choked the kitchen, crept up the toilet tank, replenished the bedroom, knocked off the goat's crown, knocked off the cousin's crown, my own crown in its coat contended with the vines and tangles of my hair, the false rabbi's beard had turned into strips of leather, into whips, the whips struck at my crown, it slid to my forehead, the whips curled round my arm, the crown sliced the flesh of my forehead.

At last it fell off.

The cousin cried out her husband's name.

"Alex," I called to the goat: the name of a conqueror, Aristotle's pupil, the arrogant god-man.

In the hollow streets which the Jews had left behind there were scorched absences, apparitions, usurpers. Someone had broken the glass of the kosher butcher's abandoned window and thrown in a pig's head, with anatomical tubes still dripping from the neck.

When we enter Paradise there will be a cage for story-writers, who will be taught as follows:

All that is not Law is levity.

But we have not yet ascended. The famous writer has not. The goat has not. The false rabbi has not; he sits out his year. A vanity press is going to bring out his papers. The bill for editing, printing, and binding will be $1,847.45. The goat's cousin will pay for it from a purse in the bottom bowel of the night table.

The goat inhabits the deserted synagogue, drinking wine, littering the yard with his turds. Occasionally he attends a public reading. Many lusts live in his chin-hairs, like lice.

Only Tchernikhovsky and the shy old writer of Jerusalem have ascended. The old writer of Jerusalem is a fiction; murmuring psalms, he snacks on leviathan and polishes his Prize with the cuff of his sleeve. Tchernikhovsky eats nude at the table of the nude gods, clean-shaven now, his limbs radiant, his youth restored, his sex splendidly erect, the discs of his white ears sparkling, a convivial fellow; he eats without self-restraint from the celestial menu, and when the Sabbath comes (the Sabbath of Sabbaths, which flowers every seven centuries in the perpetual Sabbath of Eden), as usual he avoids the congregation of the faithful before the Footstool and the Throne. Then the taciturn little Canaanite idols call him, in the language of the spheres, kike.

VERLIE I SAY UNTO YOU

ALICE ADAMS

Alice Adams grew up in Chapel Hill, North Carolina, and since then has lived mainly in San Francisco. This is her fifth appearance in the O. Henry Prize Stories. Her second novel, *Families and Survivors*, was published by Alfred A. Knopf in January 1975.

Every morning of all the years of the thirties, at around seven, Verlie Jones begins her long and laborious walk to the Todds' house, two miles uphill. She works for the Todds—their maid. Her own house, where she lives with her four small children, is a slatted floorless cabin, in a grove of enormous sheltering oaks. It is just down a rutted road from the bending highway, and that steep small road is the first thing she has to climb, starting out early in the morning. Arrived at the highway she stops and sighs, and looks around and then starts out. Walking steadily but not in any hurry, beside the winding white concrete.

First there are fields of broomstraw on either side of the road, stretching back to the woods, thick, clustered dark pines and cedars, trees whose lower limbs are cluttered with underbrush. Then the land gradually rises until on one side there is a steep red clay bank, going up to the woods; on the other side a wide cornfield, rich furrows dotted over in spring with tiny wild flowers, all colors—in the winter dry and rutted, sometimes frosted over, frost as shiny as splintered glass.

Then the creek. Before she comes to the small concrete bridge, she can see the heavier growth at the edge of the fields, green, edging the water. On the creek's steep banks, below the bridge, are huge peeling poplars, ghostly, old. She stands there looking down at the water (the bridge is halfway to the Todds'). The water is thick and swollen, rushing, full of twigs and leaf trash and swirling logs in the spring. Trickling and almost dried out when summer is over, in the early fall.

Past the bridge is the filling station, where they sell loaves of bread and cookies and soap, along with the gas and things for cars. Always there are men sitting around at the station, white men in overalls, dusty and dried out. Sometimes they nod to Verlie. "Morning, Verlie. Going to be any hot day?"

Occasionally, maybe a couple of times a year, a chain gang will be along there, working on the road. The colored men chained together, in their dirty, wide-striped uniforms, working with their picks. And the thin, mean guard (a white man) with his rifle, watching them. Looking quickly, briefly at Verlie as she passes. She looks everywhere but there, as her heart falls down to her stomach and turns upside down. All kinds of fears grab at her, all together: she is afraid of the guard and of those men (their heavy eyes) and also a chain gang is one of the places where her deserting husband, Horace, might well be, and she never wants to see Horace again. Not anywhere.

After the filling station some houses start. Small box houses, sitting up high on brick stilts. And the other side of the highway red clay roads lead back into the hills, to the woods. To the fields of country with no roads at all, where sometimes Mr. Todd goes to hunt rabbits, and where at other times, in summer, the children, Avery and Devlin Todd, take lunches and stay all day.

From a certain bend in the highway Verlie can see the Todds' house, but she rarely bothers to look anymore. She sighs and shifts her weight before starting up the steep, white, graveled road, and then the road to the right that swings around to the back of the house, to the back door that leads into the kitchen.

There on the back porch she has her own small bathroom, that Mr. Todd put in for her. There is a mirror and some nails to hang her things on, and a flush toilet, ordered from Montgomery Ward, that still works. No washbasin, but she can wash her hands in the kitchen sink.

She hangs up her cardigan sweater in her bathroom and takes an apron off a nail. She goes into the kitchen to start everyone's breakfast.

They all eat separate. First Avery, who likes oatmeal and then soft-boiled eggs; then Mr. Todd (oatmeal and scrambled eggs and bacon and coffee); Devlin (toast and peanut butter and jam); and Mrs. Todd (tea and toast).

Verlie sighs, and puts the water on.

Verlie has always been with the Todds; that is how they put it to their friends. "Verlie has always been with us." Of course, that is not true. Actually she came to them about ten years before, when Avery was a baby. What they meant was that they did not know much about her life before them, and also (a more important meaning) they cannot imagine their life without her. They say, "We couldn't get along without Verlie," but it is unlikely that any of them (except possibly Jessica, with her mournful, exacerbated, and extreme intelligence) realizes the full truth of the remark. And, laughingly, one of them will add, "No one else could put up with us." Another truth, or perhaps only a partial truth: in those days, there and then, most maids put up with a lot, and possibly Verlie suffers no more than most.

She does get more money than most maids, thirteen dollars a week (most get along on ten or eleven). And she gets to go home before dinner, around six (she first leaves the meal all fixed for them), since they—since Mr. Todd likes to have a lot of drinks and then eat late.

Every third Sunday she gets off to go to church.

None of them is stupid enough to say that she is like a member of the family.

Tom Todd, that handsome, guiltily faithless husband, troubled professor (the 10 percent salary cuts of the Depression; his history of abandoned projects—the book on Shelley, the innumerable articles)—Tom was the one who asked Verlie about her name.

"You know, it's like in the Bible. Verlie I say unto you."

Tom felt that he successfully concealed his amusement at that, and later it makes a marvelous story, especially in academic circles, in those days when funny-maid stories are standard social fare. In fact people (white people) are somewhat competitive as to who has heard or known the most comical colored person, comical meaning outrageously-childlishly ignorant. Tom's story always goes over well.

In her summer sneakers, shorts, and little shirt, Avery comes into the dining room, a small, dark-haired girl carrying a big book. Since she has learned to read (her mother taught her, when she was no bigger than a minute) she reads all the time, curled up in big chairs in the living room or in her own room, in the bed. At the breakfast table.

"Good morning, Verlie."

"Morning. How you?"

"Fine, thank you. Going to be hot today?"

"Well, I reckon so."

Avery drinks her orange juice, and then Verlie takes out the glass and brings in her bowl of hot oatmeal. Avery reads the thick book while she eats. Verlie takes out the oatmeal bowl and brings in the soft-boiled eggs and a glass of milk.

"You drink your milk, now hear?"

Verlie is about four times the size of Avery and many more times than that her age. (But Verlie can't read.)

Verlie is an exceptionally handsome woman, big and tall and strong, with big bright eyes and smooth yellow skin over high cheekbones. A wide curving mouth, and strong white teeth.

Once there was a bad time between Avery and Verlie: Avery was playing with some children down the road, and it got to be suppertime. Jessica sent Verlie down to get Avery, who didn't want to come home. "Blah blah blah blah!" she yelled at Verlie—who, unaccountably, turned and walked away.

The next person Avery saw was furious Jessica, arms akimbo. "How are you, how *could* you? Verlie, who's loved you all your life? How could you be so cruel, calling her black?"

"I didn't—I said blah. I never said black. Where is she?"

"Gone home. Very hurt."

Jessica remained stiff and unforgiving (she had problems of her own); but the next morning Avery ran down into the kitchen at the first sound of Verlie. "Verlie, I said blah blah—I didn't say black."

And Verlie smiled, and it was all over. For good.

Tom Todd comes into the dining room, carrying the newspaper. "Good morning, Avery. Morning, Verlie. Well, it doesn't look like a day for getting out our umbrellas, does it now?"

That is the way he talks.

"Avery, please put your book away. Who knows, we might have an absolutely fascinating conversation."

She gives him a small sad smile and closes her book. "Pass the cream?"

"With the greatest of pleasure."

"Thanks."

But despite the intense and often painful complications of his character, Tom's relationship with Verlie is perhaps the simplest in that family. Within their rigidly defined roles they are even fond of each other. Verlie thinks he talks funny, but not much more so than most men—white men. He runs around with women (she knows that from his handkerchiefs, the lipstick stains that he couldn't have bothered to hide from her) but not as much as Horace did. He bosses his wife and children but he doesn't hit them. He acts as Verlie expects a man to act, and perhaps a little better.

And from Tom's point of view Verlie behaves like a Negro maid. She is somewhat lazy; she does as little cleaning as she can. She laughs at his jokes. She sometimes sneaks drinks from his liquor closet. He does not, of course, think of Verlie as a woman —a woman in the sense of sexual possibility; in fact he once sincerely (astoundingly) remarked that he could not imagine a sexual impulse toward a colored person.

Devlin comes in next. A small and frightened boy, afraid of Verlie. Once as he stood up in his bath she touched his tiny penis and laughed and said, "This here's going to grow to something nice and big." He was terrified: what would he do with something big, down there?

He mutters good morning to his father and sister and to Verlie.

Then Jessica. Mrs. Todd. "Good morning, everyone. Morning, Verlie. My, doesn't it look like a lovely spring day?"

She sighs, as no one answers.

The end of breakfast. Verlie clears the table, washes up, as those four people separate.

There is a Negro man who also (sometimes) works for the Todds, named Clifton. Yard work: raking leaves in the fall, building a fence around the garbage cans, and then a dog kennel, then a playhouse for the children.

When Verlie saw Clifton the first time he came into the yard (a man who had walked a long way, looking for work), what she thought was: Lord, I never saw no man so beautiful. Her second thought was: he sick.

Clifton is bronze-colored. Reddish. Shining. Not brown like most colored (or yellow, as Verlie is). His eyes are big and brown, but dragged downward with his inside sickness. And his sadness: he is a lonesome man, almost out of luck.

"Whatever do you suppose they talk about?" Tom Todd says to Jessica, who has come into his study to help him with the index of his book, an hour or so after breakfast. They can hear the slow, quiet sounds of Verlie's voice, with Clifton's, from the kitchen.

"Us, maybe?" Jessica makes this light, attempting a joke, but she really wonders if in fact she and Tom are their subject. Her own communication with Verlie is so mystifyingly nonverbal that she sometimes suspects Verlie of secret (and accurate) appraisals, as though Verlie knows her in ways that no one else does, herself included. At other times she thinks that Verlie is just plain stubborn.

From the window come spring breaths of blossom and grasses and leaves. Of spring earth. Aging, plump Jessica deeply sighs.

Tom says, "I very much doubt that, my dear. Incredibly fascinating though we be."

In near total despair Jessica says, "Sometimes I think I just don't have the feeling for an index."

The telephone rings. Tom and Jessica look at each other, and then Verlie's face comes to the study door. "It's for you, Mr. Todd. A long distance."

Clifton has had a bad life; it almost seems cursed. The same sickness one spring down in Mississippi carried off his wife and three poor little children, and after that everything got even worse: every job that he got came apart like a bunch of sticks in his hands. Folks all said that they had no money to pay. He even made deliveries for a bootlegger, knocking on back doors at night, but the man got arrested and sent to jail before Clifton got any money.

He likes working for the Todds, and at the few other jobs

around town that Mrs. Todd finds for him. But he doesn't feel good. Sometimes he thinks he has some kind of sickness.

He looks anxiously at Verlie as he says this last, as though he, like Jessica, believes that she can see inside him.

"You nervous," Verlie says. "You be all right, come summertime." But she can't look at him as she says this.

They are standing in the small apple orchard where Verlie's clotheslines are. She has been hanging out the sheets. They billow, shuddering in the lively restive air of early spring.

Clifton suddenly takes hold of her face, and turns it around to his. He presses his mouth and his body to hers, standing there. Something deep inside Verlie heats up and makes her almost melt.

"Verlie!"

It is Avery, suddenly coming up on them, so that they cumbersomely step apart.

"Verlie, my father wants you." Avery runs away almost before she has stopped speaking.

Clifton asks, "You reckon we ought to tell her not to tell?"

"No, she's not going to tell."

Verlie is right, but it is a scene that Avery thinks about. Of course, she has seen other grown-ups kissing: her father and Irene Macomber or someone after a party. But Verlie and Clifton looked different; for one thing they were more absorbed. It took them a long time to hear her voice.

Tom is desperately questioning Jessica. "How in God's name will I tell her?" he asks.

Verlie's husband, Horace, is dead. He died in a Memphis hospital, after a knife fight, having first told a doctor the name of the people and the town where his wife worked.

"I could tell her," Jessica forces herself to say, and for a few minutes they look at each other, with this suggestion lying between them. But they both know, with some dark and intimate Southern knowledge, that Tom will have to be the one to tell her. And alone: it would not even "do" for Jessica to stay on in the room, although neither of them could have explained these certainties.

Having been clearly (and kindly) told by Tom what has happened in Memphis, Verlie then asks, "You sure? You sure it's Horace, not any other man?"

Why couldn't he have let Jessica tell her, or at least have let her

stay in the room? Tom is uncomfortable; it wildly occurs to him
to offer Verlie a drink (to offer Verlie a drink?). He mumbles,
"Yes, I'm afraid there's no doubt at all." He adds, in his more reasonable, professorial voice, "You see, another man wouldn't have
said Verlie Jones, who works for the Todd family, in Hilton."

Incredibly, a smile breaks out on Verlie's face. ("For a minute
I actually thought she was going to *laugh*," Tom later says to Jessica.)

Verlie says, "I reckon that's right. Couldn't be no other man."
And then she says, "Lunch about ready now," and she goes back
into the kitchen.

Jessica has been hovering in the dining room, pushing at the
arrangement of violets and cowslips in a silver bowl. She follows
Verlie into the kitchen; she says, "Verlie, I'm terribly sorry. Verlie,
wouldn't you like to go on home? Take the afternoon off. I could
drive you . . ."

"No'm. No thank you. I'd liefer get on with the ironing."

And so, with a stiff and unreadable face, opaque dark brown
eyes, Verlie serves their lunch.

What could they know, what could any of them know about a
man like Horace? Had any of them seen her scars? Knife scars and
beating scars, and worse things he had done without leaving any
scars. All the times he forced her, when he was so hurting and
quick, and she was sick or just plain exhausted. The girls she always knew he had. The mean tricks he played on little kids, his
kids. The dollars of hers that he stole to get drunk on.

She had always thought Horace was too mean to die, and as she
cleans up the lunch dishes and starts to sprinkle the dry sheets
for ironing, she still wonders: *is* Horace dead?

She tries to imagine an open casket, full of Horace, dead. His
finicky little moustache and his long, strong fingers folded together
on his chest. But the casket floats off into the recesses of her mind
and what she sees is Horace, alive and terrifying.

A familiar dry smell tells her that she has scorched a sheet, and
tears begin to roll slowly down her face.

"When I went into the kitchen to see how she was, she was
standing there with tears rolling down her face," Jessica reports to

Tom—and then is appalled at what she hears as satisfaction in her own voice.

"I find that hardly surprising," Tom says, with a questioning raise of his eyebrows.

Aware that she has lost his attention, Jessica goes on. (Where *is* he—with whom?) "I just meant, it seems awful to feel a sort of relief when she cries. As though I thought that's what she ought to do. Maybe she didn't really care for Horace. He hasn't been around for years, after all." (As usual she is making things worse: it is apparent that Tom can barely listen.)

She says, "I think I'll take the index cards back to my desk," and she manages not to cry.

Picking up the sheets to take upstairs to the linen closet, Verlie decides that she won't tell Clifton about Horace; dimly she thinks that if she tells anyone, especially Clifton, it won't be true: Horace, alive, will be waiting for her at her house, as almost every night she is afraid that he will be.

Sitting at her desk, unseeingly Jessica looks out across the deep valley, where the creek winds down toward the sea, to the further hills that are bright green with spring. Despair slowly fills her blood so that it seems heavy in her veins, and thick, and there is a heavy pressure in her head.

And she dreams for a moment, as she has sometimes before, of a friend to whom she could say, "I can't stand anything about my life. My husband either is untrue to me or would like to be—constantly. It comes to the same thing, didn't St. Paul say that? My daughter's eyes are beginning to go cold against me, and my son is terrified of everyone. Of me." But there is no one to whom she could say a word of this; she is known among her friends for dignity and restraint. (Only sometimes her mind explodes, and she breaks out screaming—at Tom, at one of her children, once at Verlie—leaving them all sick and shocked, especially herself sick and shocked, and further apart than ever.)

Now Verlie comes through the room with an armful of fresh, folded sheets, and for an instant, looking at her, Jessica has the thought that Verlie could be that friend, that listener. That Verlie could understand.

She dismisses the impulse almost as quickly as it came.

Lately she has spent a lot of time remembering college, those distant happy years, among friends. Her successes of that time. The two years when she directed the Greek play, on May Day weekend (really better than being in the May Court). Her senior year, elected president of the secret honor society. (And the springs of wisteria, heavily flowering, scented, lavender and white, the heavy vines everywhere.)

From those college days she still has two friends, to whom she writes, and visits at rarer intervals. Elizabeth, who is visibly happily married to handsome and successful Dabney Stuart (although he is, to Jessica, a shocking racial bigot). And Mary John James, who teaches Latin in a girls' school, in Richmond—who has never married. Neither of them could be her imagined friend (any more than Verlie could).

Not wanting to see Jessica's sad eyes again (the sorrow in that woman's face! the mourning!), Verlie puts the sheets in the linen closet and goes down the back stairs. She is halfway down, walking slow, when she feels a sudden coolness in her blood, as though from a breeze. She stops, she listens to nothing, and then she is flooded with the certain knowledge that Horace is dead, is at that very moment laid away in Memphis (wherever Memphis is). Standing there alone, by the halfway window that looks out to the giant rhododendron, she begins to smile, peacefully and slowly —an interior, pervasive smile.

Then she goes on down the stairs, through the dining room and into the kitchen.

Clifton is there.

Her smile changes; her face becomes brighter and more animated, although she doesn't say anything—not quite trusting herself not to say everything, as she has promised herself.

"You looking perky," Clifton says, by way of a question. He is standing at the sink with a drink of water.

Her smile broadens, and she lies. "Thinking about the social at the church. Just studying if or not I ought to go."

"You do right to go," he says. And then, "You be surprise, you find me there?"

(They have never arranged any meeting before, much less in another place, at night; they have always pretended that they were in the same place in the yard or orchard by accident.)

She laughs. "You never find the way."

He grins at her, his face brighter than any face that she has ever seen. "I be there," he says to her.

A long, hot summer, extending into fall. A hot October, and then there is sudden cold. Splinters of frost on the red clay erosions, in the fields. Ice in the shallow edges of the creek.

For Verlie it has been the happiest summer of her life, but no one of the Todds has remarked on this, nor been consciously aware of unusual feelings, near at hand. They all have preoccupations of their own.

Clifton has been working for the Macombers, friends and neighbors of the Todds, and it is Irene Macomber who telephones to tell Jessica the sad news that he had a kind of seizure (a hemorrhage) and that when they finally got him to the Negro hospital (twelve miles away) it was too late, and he died.

Depressing news, on that dark November day. Jessica supposes that the first thing is to tell Verlie (after all, she and Clifton were friends, and Verlie might know of relatives).

She is not prepared for Verlie's reaction.

A wail—"Aieeeee"—that goes on and on, from Verlie's wide mouth, and her wide, wild eyes. "Aieee—"

Then it stops abruptly, as Verlie claps her hands over her mouth, and bends over and blindly reaches for a chair, her rocker. She pulls herself toward the chair, she falls into it, she bends over double and begins to cough, deep and wrackingly.

Poor, shocked Jessica has no notion what to do. To go over to Verlie and embrace her, to press her own sorrowing face to Verlie's face? To creep shyly and sadly from the room?

This last is what she does—is all, perhaps, that she is able to do.

"You know," says Tom Todd (seriously) to Irene Macomber, in one of their rare lapses from the steady demands of unconsummated love, "I believe those two people had a real affection for each other."

Verlie is sick for a week and more after that, with what is called "misery in the chest" (no one mentions her heart).

Thinking to amuse her children (she is clearly at a loss without Verlie, and she knows this), Jessica takes them for a long walk, on the hard, narrow, white roads that lead up into the hills, the heavy, thick, dark woods of fall, smelling of leaves and earth and wood-smoke. But a melancholy mood settles over them all; it is cold and the children are tired, and Jessica finds that she is thinking of Verlie and Clifton. (Is it possible that they were lovers? She uncomfortably shrugs off this possibility.)

Dark comes early, and there is a raw, red sunset at the black edge of the horizon, as finally they reach home.

Verlie comes back the next day, to everyone's relief. But there is a grayish tinge to the color of her skin that does not go away.

But on that rare spring day months earlier (the day Horace is dead and laid away in Memphis) Verlie walks the miles home with an exceptional lightness of heart, smiling to herself at all the colors of the bright new flowers, and at the smells of spring, the promises.

ARE YOU A DOCTOR?

RAYMOND CARVER

Raymond Carver was born in Clatskanie, Oregon, and grew up in Yakima, Washington. His stories have appeared in *Esquire, Harper's Bazaar, The Iowa Review,* and other magazines. He has published two books of poetry, *Near Klamath* and *Winter Insomnia.* He received a National Endowment for the Arts Grant in 1970 and the Joseph Henry Jackson Award in 1971, and was a Wallace Stegner Creative Writing Fellow at Stanford in 1972–73. He has been a visiting lecturer at the University of California at Santa Cruz and Berkeley and at the University of Iowa Writers' Workshop, and is currently teaching at the University of California at Santa Barbara.

FOR GORDON LISH

In slippers, pajamas, and robe, he hurried out of the study when the telephone began to ring. Since it was past ten, he assumed it was his wife. She called—late like this, after a few drinks—each night she was out of town. She was a buyer, and all this week she had been away on business.

"Hello, dear. Hello," he said again.

"Who is this?" a woman asked.

"Well, who is this? What number do you want?"

"Just a minute," the woman said. "It's 273-8063."

"That's my number," he said. "How did you get it?"

"I don't know. It was written down on a piece of paper when I got in from work," the woman said.

"Who wrote it down?"

"I don't know for sure. The baby sitter, I guess. It must be her."

"Didn't you ask her?" he said.

"No. She doesn't have a phone either, or I'd call."

"Well, I don't know how she got it," he said, "but it's my telephone number, and it's unlisted. I'd appreciate it if you'd just toss it away. Hello? Did you hear me?"

"Yes, I heard," the woman said.

"Is there anything else then?" he said. "It's late and I'm busy." He hadn't meant to be curt, but one couldn't take chances. He sat down on the chair by the telephone and said, "I didn't mean to be short. I only meant that it's late, and I'll admit I'm concerned how you happen to have my number." He pulled off his slipper and began massaging his foot, waiting.

"I don't know either," she said. "I told you I just found the number written down, no note or anything. I'll ask Annette—that's the sitter—when I see her tomorrow. I didn't mean to disturb you. I only just now found the note. I've been in the kitchen ever since I came in from work."

"It's all right," he said. "Forget it. Just throw it away or something and forget it. There's no problem, so don't worry." He moved the receiver from one ear to the other.

"You sound like a nice man," the woman said.

"Do I? Well, that's nice of you to say." He knew he should hang up now, but it was good to hear a voice, even his own, in the quiet room.

"Oh, yes," she said. "I can tell."

He let go his foot.

"What's your name, if you don't mind my asking?" she said.

"My name is Arnold," he said.

"And what's your first name?" she said.

He hesitated. "Arnold is my first name."

"Oh, forgive me," she said. "Arnold is your *first* name? And your second name, Arnold? What's your second name?"

"I really must hang up," he said.

"Arnold, for goodness sake, I'm Clara Holt. Now your name is Mr. Arnold what?"

"Arnold Breit," he said, and then quickly added, "Clara Holt. That's nice. But I really think I should hang up now, Miss Holt. I'm expecting a call."

"I'm sorry, Arnold, I didn't mean to take up your time," she said.

"That's all right," he said. "It's been nice talking to you."

"You're kind to say that, Arnold."

"Will you hold the phone a minute?" he said. "I have to check on something." He went into the study for a cigar, took a minute lighting it with the desk lighter, then removed his glasses and looked at himself in the mirror over the fireplace. When he returned to the telephone he was half afraid she might be off the line.

"Hello."

"Hello, Arnold," she said.

"I thought you might have hung up."

"Oh no," she said.

"About your having my number," he said. "Nothing to worry over, I don't suppose. Just throw it away, I suppose."

"I will, Arnold," she said.

"Well, I must say good-by then."

"Yes, of course," she said. "I'll say good night now."

He heard her draw breath.

"I know I'm imposing, Arnold, but do you think we could meet somewhere we could talk? Just for a few minutes?"

"I'm afraid that's impossible," he said.

"Just for a minute, Arnold. My finding your number and everything. I feel, I feel strongly about this, Arnold."

"I'm an old man," he said.

"Oh, you're not," she said.

He let it go at that.

"Could we meet somewhere, Arnold?" Then: "You see, I haven't told you everything. There's something else."

"What do you mean?" he said. "What is this exactly? Hello?"

She had hung up.

When he was preparing for bed, his wife called, somewhat intoxicated he could tell, and they chatted for a while, but he said nothing about the other call. Later, as he was turning the covers down, the telephone rang again.

He picked up the receiver. "Hello! Arnold Breit speaking."

"Arnold, I'm sorry we got cut off. As I was saying, I think it's important we meet."

The next afternoon as he put the key into the lock, he could hear the telephone ringing. He put his brief case down and, still in his hat, coat, and gloves, hurried over to the end table and picked up the receiver.

"Arnold, I'm sorry to bother you again," the woman said. "But you must come to my house tonight around nine or nine-thirty. Can you do that much for me, Arnold?"

His heart moved when he heard her use his name. "I couldn't do that," he said.

"Please, Arnold," she said. "It's important or I wouldn't be asking. I can't leave the house tonight, because my daughter is sick with a cold. Cheryl is sick, and now I'm afraid for the boy."

"And your husband?" He waited.

"I'm not married," she said. "You will come, won't you?"

"I can't promise," he said.

"I implore you to come," she said. Then she gave him the address and hung up.

" 'I implore you to come,' " he repeated, still holding the receiver. He slowly took off his gloves and then his coat. He felt he had to be careful. He went to wash up. When he looked in the bathroom mirror he discovered the hat. It was then that he made the decision to go to see her, and he took off his hat and glasses and began to soap his face. Then he checked his nails.

"You're sure this is the right street?" he asked the driver.

"This is the street and there's the house," the driver said.

"Keep going," he said. "Let me out at the end of the block."

He paid the driver. Lights from the upstairs windows illuminated the balconies, and he could see planters sitting on the balustrades, here and there a piece of lawn furniture. At one balcony a large man in a sweater leaned on his arms over the railing and watched him walk toward the door.

He pushed the button under C. Holt. The buzzer sounded, and he quickly stepped to the door and entered. He climbed the stairs slowly, stopping to rest briefly at each landing. He remembered the hotel in Luxembourg, the five flights he and his wife had climbed so many years ago. He felt a sudden pain in his side, imagined heart trouble, and imagined his legs folding under him and a loud fall to the bottom of the stairs. He took out his handkerchief and wiped his forehead, then removed his glasses and began wiping the lenses, waiting for his heart to quiet.

He looked down the hall. For an apartment house of this size, it seemed unusually quiet. He stopped at her door, removed his hat, and knocked lightly. The door opened a crack to reveal a plump little girl in pajamas.

"Are you Arnold Breit?" she said.

"Yes, I am," he said. "Is your mother home?"

"She said for you to come in. She said she went to the drugstore for some cough syrup and aspirin."

He shut the door behind him. "What is your name? Your mother told me, but I forgot."

When the girl said nothing, he tried again.

"Cheryl," she said. "C-h-e-r-y-l."

"Yes, now I remember. Well, I was close, you must admit."

She sat on a hassock across the room and looked at him.

"So you're sick, are you?" he said.

She shook her head.

"Not sick?"

"No," she said.

He looked around. The room was lighted by a brass floor lamp that had a large ashtray and a magazine rack affixed to the pole. A television set stood against the far wall. It was on with the volume down. A narrow hall next to the kitchen led to the back of the apartment. The furnace was up, the air close with a medicinal smell. A number of hairpins and rollers lay on the coffee table. A pink bathrobe hung over the back of a couch.

He looked at the child again, then raised his eyes toward the kitchen and the glass doors that gave off the kitchen onto the balcony. The doors stood slightly ajar, and a little chill went through him as he recalled the large man in the sweater.

"Mama went out for a minute," the child said, as if suddenly waking up.

He leaned forward on his toes, hat in hand, and stared at her. "I think I'd better go," he said.

A key turned in the lock, the door swung open, and a small, pale, freckled woman of about thirty entered carrying a paper sack.

"Arnold? I'm glad to see you." She glanced at him quickly, uneasily, and shook her head gently from side to side as she walked out to the kitchen with the sack. He heard a cupboard door shut. The child sat on the hassock and watched him. He leaned his weight first on one leg and then the other, then placed the hat on his head and removed it with the same gesture as the woman reappeared.

"Are you a doctor?" she asked suddenly.

"No," he said startled. "No, I am not."

"Cheryl is sick, you see. I thought I'd ask. Why didn't you take the man's coat?" she said, turning to the child. "Please forgive her. We're not used to company."

He was embarrassed. "I can't stay," he said. "I really shouldn't have come."

"Please sit down," she said. "We can't talk like this. Let me give her some medicine first. Then we can talk."

"I really must go," he said. "From the tone of your voice, I thought there was something urgent. But I really must go." He looked down at his hands and was aware he had been gesturing feebly.

"I'll put on tea water," he heard her say, as if she hadn't been listening. "Then I'll give Cheryl her medicine, and then we can talk."

She took the child by the shoulders and steered her into the kitchen. He saw the woman pick up a spoon, open a bottle of something after scanning the label, and pour out two doses.

"Now you say good night to Mr. Breit, honey, and go to your room."

He nodded to the child and then followed the woman to the kitchen. He did not take the chair she indicated, but instead one that let him face the balcony, the bedroom hall, and the small living room. "Do you mind if I smoke a cigar?" he asked.

"I don't mind," she said. "I don't think it will bother me, Arnold. Please do."

He decided against it. He put his hands on his knees, leaned forward, and gave his face a serious expression. "This is still very much of a mystery to me," he said. "It's quite out of the ordinary, I assure you."

"I understand, Arnold," she said. "You'd probably like to hear the story of how I got your number?"

"I would indeed," he said.

They sat across from each other waiting for the water to boil. He could hear the television. He looked around the kitchen and then out toward the balcony again. The water began to bubble.

"You were going to tell me about the number," he said.

"What, Arnold? I'm sorry," she said.

He cleared his throat. "Tell me how you acquired my number," he said.

"I checked with Annette. The baby sitter—but of course you know that. Anyway, she told me the phone rang while she was here and it was somebody wanting me. They left a number to call, and it was your number she took down. That's all I know." She moved a cup around in front of her. "I'm sorry I can't tell you any more."

"Your water is boiling," he said.

She put out spoons, milk, and sugar, and poured the steaming water over tea bags.

He added sugar and stirred his tea. "You said it was urgent that I come."

"Oh that, Arnold," she said, turning away. "I don't know what made me say that. I can't imagine what I was thinking."

"Then there's nothing?" he said.

"No. I mean, yes." She shook her head. "What you said, I mean. Nothing."

"I see," he said. He went on stirring his tea. He could hear the television from down the hall.

"It's unusual," he said after a minute, almost to himself. "Quite unusual." He smiled weakly, then moved the cup to one side and touched his lips with the napkin.

"You aren't leaving?" she said.

"I must," he said. "I'm expecting a call at home."

"Not yet, Arnold."

She scraped her chair back and stood up. Her eyes were a pale green, set deep in her pale face and surrounded by what he had at first thought was dark make-up. Appalled at himself, knowing he would despise himself for it, he stood and put his arms clumsily around her waist. She let herself be kissed, fluttering and closing her eyelids briefly.

"It's late," he said, letting go, turning away unsteadily. "You've been very gracious, but I must be leaving, Mrs. Holt. Thank you. Thanks for the tea."

"You will come again, won't you, Arnold?" she said.

He shook his head.

She followed him to the door, where he held out his hand. He could still hear the television from the hall. It seemed louder, as if the volume had been turned up. He remembered the other child then, the boy. Where was he? She took his hand, raised it quickly to her lips.

"You mustn't forget me, Arnold."

"I won't," he said. "Clara. Clara Holt."

"I'm glad you came tonight," she said. "We had a good talk." She picked at something, a hair, a thread, on his suit collar. "I'm very glad you came, and I feel certain you'll come again." He looked at her carefully, but she was staring past him now as if she were trying to remember something. "Now—good night, Arnold," she said, and with that she shut the door, almost catching his overcoat.

"Strange," he said, as he started down the stairs. He took a long breath as he reached the sidewalk, paused a minute to look back at the building. But he was unable to determine which balcony was hers. The large man moved slightly against the railing and continued looking down at him. He began walking, hands deep in his coat pockets.

When he reached home, the telephone was ringing. He stood very quietly in the middle of the room holding the key between his fingers until the ringing stopped. Then, carefully, tenderly, he put a hand against his chest and felt, through the layers of clothes, his beating heart. After a time he made his way into the bedroom.

Almost immediately the telephone began to ring, and this time he answered it. "Arnold. Arnold Breit speaking," he said.

"Arnold? My, aren't we formal tonight?" his wife said, her voice strong, teasing. "I've been calling since nine. Out living it up, Arnold?"

He remained silent and considered her voice.

"Are you there, Arnold?" she said. "You don't sound like yourself."

RAMONA BY THE SEA

SUSANNAH McCORKLE

Susannah McCorkle was born in Berkeley, California, and as a child lived in various parts of the United States and South America before returning to Berkeley to study at the University of California in 1963. Since her graduation, in 1968, she has lived in Mexico City, Rome, Paris, and presently London, where she began her singing career in 1972. While singing professionally, she has continued to write, working on short stories, radio plays, and children's stories.

Ramona was the last passenger off the plane at the Jewel Beach City Airport. As she made her way down the escalator, she looked over at the fence and saw her mother, a pretty blonde woman dressed in dark slacks and a Mexican peasant blouse, who was smiling and waving at her with both hands.

"Monie! You look wonderful!" her mother cried, as she did whenever Ramona arrived from anywhere by plane—her public greeting. She examined her daughter, a fat girl with long, dirty hair, who was wearing sunglasses even though it was ten o'clock at night—a walking thundercloud. "Is this overnight case all you brought with you? I thought you were going to stay at least two weeks."

"I only have one other dress that fits me any more," Ramona answered gloomily. Standing beside her mother, she felt slow and clumsy and was sure that anyone who glanced quickly at the two of them would think that Ramona, in her shapeless cotton print dress, was the older of the two. As they moved through the terminal she was annoyed that her mother took her arm, as if they were good friends.

"You *have* gained weight, darling. You looked wonderful last

Christmas when you got back from Europe. What happened this semester?"

"I don't know. I just seem to eat all the time. To avoid doing other things, I guess."

"You see? That's probably the very thing that's making you unhappy! I'll help you diet while you're here. Charlene Wakowiak, a new friend from my comparative psychologies course, put me on to Con-gel-lac food substitute. It's a grayish powder you have to get by prescription. You mix it with water, and it gives you all your vitamin and mineral requirements for the day and keeps you from feeling hungry. It doesn't taste like much, I'm afraid, but it does wonders."

They arrived at the car, an enormous powder blue station wagon. Ramona's mother skillfully maneuvered out of the parking space, down the aisles, onto the highway. They rode for a while without speaking until Ramona's mother broke the silence.

"Jeannie's taken up playing the guitar. All we hear around the house is folk music records now, so I hope you like Jane Baez."

"I *could* correct you and say her name is Joan Baez, but with your memory for names you'd just call her Jane again, if not Frances or Louise Baez, so I guess I won't waste time correcting you," Ramona said. She felt a little better now that she had said something hostile. She slumped down in the seat, watching out her window for the only sight that interested her in Jewel Beach City: a two-block-long string of bail-bondsmen's offices, the only businesses in the city that had hand-painted (not electric) signs. She did not know this town well; she had left for a year of study in France at the same time her family had moved here, and since her return she had visited them only once. Southern California offended her newly developed esthetic sensibilities.

Her mother drove very fast now, and Ramona watched the city fly by: movie houses, supermarkets with spectacular revolving neon signs (theatre marquees starring Golden Grapefruit Special and Hamburger 49¢ a lb.), wide, flat, well-lit streets, hotels, motels, people with empty faces cruising around in huge, wasteful cars.

"Now keep your eyes peeled, Monie, there's something I want you to see," her mother said. In the darkness her short, fluffy blonde hair shone like a halo around her face; at forty-three she was still a cute girl. "It's on your side, in the middle of this next block. There! Did you see it?"

"Yes," said Ramona, twisting around to look back down the road. "A motel named Ramona-By-The-Sea."

"Isn't that a kick? Jeannie discovered it one day coming back from the Coral Village Bay Shopping Center."

"I'm flunking out, Mother," said Ramona.

"Oh, Christ," her mother said. "You said you thought you'd finish this year."

"It's just as well anyway. I have to get out of Berkeley. I think I'm losing my mind."

"Monie, try not to melodramatize. You've already dropped out twice. Why don't you just finish and get it over with? I thought that's what we agreed on when we had our Christmas talk."

"They tear-gas us now, did you read about that? We even had city-wide curfews, just like in the old war movies. One night at eight-fifteen I saw a squad car screech up in front of a hippie who was walking home from the laundromat, and four cops jumped out and pounced on him and emptied his laundry bag all over the sidewalk to check for guns and bombs. But they only found socks and underpants and a couple of towels he'd stolen from the Y." Ramona laughed in a high, unnatural giggle, and her mother glanced over at her quickly.

"Yes, we saw some of those street demonstrations on TV. But that's all blown over by now, hasn't it? What about this flunking out business? Didn't you finish the semester? Didn't you take exams? You've *never* flunked an exam."

"I can't read and I can't write."

"What?"

"I can't read any more. I can't make my head understand the words in the books. Also I can't write because my fingers forget how to make the pen form the letters of the words of the ideas that I'm supposed to get after I finish reading all the books that I can't read."

"But you've always been such a good student! Just this summer session and one more semester to go, darling!"

"Can't."

"Well, take *two* more semesters then."

"Sorry, madam, it's out of our hands! Her mind won't mind her!"

"Monie, calm down now, I mean it! When we get to the house, just be . . . don't mention any of this to your father, all right? He's already a little upset about the Faculty Peace Committee trying to force him to sign some anti-war petition."

Ramona rolled down her window and sang out into the street, "The Faculty Peace Committee is a bunch of Commie, pinko, dupe agitators!"

"Monie, you aren't funny! Stop shouting."

Ramona sank back down into the seat, her knees as high as her head. "The Faculty Peace Committee makes him nervous because he knows that ten years ago he would have been a founding member, but now he's turned into an old Orange County reactionary."

"Don't talk to him about politics, all right? Or about school—yours or his—it makes him tense when you ask him how he teaches his classes; he feels challenged. Just act normal when we get home. Don't talk to him about anything."

When they walked into the house they found Ramona's father and sister watching television in the living room, stretched out on two day-beds with several sleeping cats. "Hiya, Moan," her sister said, raising her head briefly.

Her father, an inherently courteous man, immediately stood up to greet her.

"Hello, Mona," he said, wondering if he should kiss her on the cheek. He seemed to be scrutinizing her complexion, and she stared back defiantly. "Glad to have you here with us for a while," he said. He decided it best not to kiss her after all and lay down on the couch again, very carefully, so as not to disturb the cats.

"Have you got Harold's movie on?" asked Ramona's mother. "Monie, you *have* to see Harold. He wears big, shiny suits and loud ties, and he's so proud of his old used cars! He fascinates me, he's so happy. He was best during our first year here, then something bad happened, you could see it happening, his commercials just didn't have the same zing. He lost a lot of weight, his suits got all baggy-looking. Then he was off completely for a while. Maybe it was a lawsuit? Or bankruptcy? But I like to think it was more romantic, that his wife left him or something. Then a few months ago he came back on, better than ever. A new wife?"

Ramona watched Harold "Olie" Olsen, a balding, blond man with a dazzling smile, who introduced the *real* stars of the Southland Motor Haven Midnite Movie, a long row of used cars with four-figure numbers scribbled on the windshields. He patted and stroked them as if they were prize-winning racehorses; he turned on their radios, heaters, and windshield wipers all at the same time, gunned their motors, slammed their doors and kicked their tires fiercely to show that they could withstand even the most savage treatment by their masters.

The movie bored her, and she sat on the floor, waiting to see Harold Olsen again. She reflected that her mother always knew when something was really funny, although she did not always know when something was really sad. She looked at her father: *he* was sad, a slight, handsome man, asleep now, still wearing his glasses, his hand gently resting on the stomach of a purring cat.

The morning came much too soon but at least, Ramona thought, at least she was not waking up again in her apartment in Berkeley to a roomful of open books and mimeographed lists of term papers and examination dates. At least she was not faced with another day of classes: mass lectures with some professor's tiny head bobbing up and down behind the lectern, his voice amplified to Wizard of Oz proportions, booming out over the auditorium to five hundred students who read newspapers and ate candy bars. But then the small intimate honors seminars were even worse, with the professor, some poor little man sweating away in his striped seersucker jacket, so obviously begrudging every second spent away from his research. Up close the eyes were small, apprehensive. Why? Were they all so afraid that a college senior—someone *young*, with so many other chances ahead—might carelessly ruin their lifelong projects by scooping them on the true significance of Dante's gardens or Proust's teacake?

She lay in bed in her father's cramped study and tried to guess what time it was by the intensity of the sun's rays through the wooden shutters. Ten-thirty, she thought, maybe eleven. Her father would have gone off to teach his morning classes. Jeannie would be at school, and her mother, with a little luck, would be out shopping. There might still be some of last night's apple pie in the refrigerator.

In the kitchen she found her mother, fully made up and dressed in a bright blue kimono, sitting at the bar smoking and pretending to read the newspaper. Lying in wait. "Well, good morning!

You must have been tired!" she said. "Have some coffee, I just made a pot."

"Do you still make it that same way, boiling it? Maybe I'll have that instant espresso instead, if there's any around."

"Oh, Monie, you never used to be such a pill about my coffee. You and your delicate Europeanized palate."

Ramona found the coffee behind an unopened package of cookies, which she thought she might eat later if her mother went away.

"Why don't we go to the movies tonight, you and I?" her mother said, studying the entertainment page. "Bill won't ever go any more—either they bore him or they upset him too much." She looked up and saw that her daughter still had last night's grim, ugly fat-girl expression on her face, even though Ramona was certainly not ugly, and only temporarily fat. "Monie . . . would you like a Dexedrine?" she asked softly.

"Oh God, are you back on those again?"

"Yes I am and I don't want to bicker about it. I stopped for a while after you took that biology course and made such a big stink, but I didn't have one single bad effect you said I would. I'm not addicted, I just feel happier and more interested in life if I take them. And anyway, I only take half of one a day, sometimes just a quarter if I'm already feeling pretty happy when I wake up. Even your father takes them now during his lows, and you know how he used to hate pills."

"At breakfast. Like vitamin pills."

"Speaking of taking pills that may be hazardous et cetera, you aren't by any chance taking those birth control pills, are you? Is that why you've gained all this weight?"

Ramona lied without hesitation. "No."

"*That's* good! You know the effect they had on *me*. It was *nightmarish*, like being pregnant all over again. Aunt Mary had the same symptoms. I think the women in our family must already have their full quota of female hormones—it isn't a good idea to just toss in more."

Ramona smeared two pieces of toast with butter and jam and began to read the front page.

"That's starting your diet off with a bang. Look, Monie . . . is there anything you want to talk about but are embarrassed? I think you know what I mean. Any love troubles?"

"No," said Ramona, not looking up. She did not consider this a lie, since her relationship with Louis Lustig had nothing to do with love. She stared at the newspaper. By now he would have discovered she was gone.

She had met him at a party in Berkeley at the beginning of the semester. They had sat in a corner and talked for hours: he told her that he was new in town, a graduate student, twenty-four years old, that his wife had just left him, that he was desperately depressed and saw a famous San Francisco psychiatrist three times a week. Ramona listened sympathetically; he was very handsome. He called her the next day to invite her out to dinner. They began to see each other often. He told her that he was very glad to know her since she seemed like such an exceptional person. She supposed he was also pleased by the fact that she seemed to have no one else; he could call her at the last minute and ask her to lunch or dinner so he wouldn't have to eat alone. He often apologized for his lack of vitality and explained that he was going through a very difficult period but was sure he would soon be his old self again. She started taking the pill as soon as she met him. As it turned out, he was impotent, but he loved having breakfast in bed.

He had been embarrassed but not surprised by his failure, and suggested she might try walking around the bedroom naked in spike heels for a little while to see if that would help. She thought he was joking, and told him that no one had worn spike heels for years and she didn't even own a pair. "My wife had some," he said wistfully. Would she let him spank her? He loved to spank a woman's naked buttocks, he said; he wouldn't use a belt or brush at first if she didn't want him to, just his bare hand. She let him try it once, but his strange laughter frightened her, and she made him stop right away. He was disappointed, even a little angry. Then he said that his real problem, recently uncovered by his psychiatrist, was not really a lack of sexual interest, but rather an inability to be aroused by a woman for whom he felt true affection. He told Ramona he appreciated her as a person and asked her if she would mind just being his friend and going out with him, but not having sex, for a while at least.

Her mother was watching her read, waiting for a more complete answer. Ramona studied her across the bar. Her eyes were china blue and had been painstakingly painted in front of an elaborate theatrical make-up mirror that could simulate three kinds of light. Ramona imagined how those adorable blue eyes would fill with shock and tears of vicarious pain if she told her about Louis. How could she talk to this doll-faced woman about her entanglement with a suicidal sexual deviate from Boston who prowled the Berkeley campus disguised as a first-year graduate student in romance philology?

Since the truth was too brutal for a virgin bride and faithful wife of twenty-five years, Ramona said, "No love troubles, Mother. Far from it."

"Well, I didn't *think* you were unhappy because of some boy! You wouldn't have gained so much weight if you'd been in love!" Ramona closed her eyes to shut out her mother's smug little smile. But she hadn't finished yet: "Darling, you mustn't be embarrassed to come to me if some day you *do* want to talk about having intercourse with the man you want to marry."

The weather had suddenly turned cloudy and cold, and Ramona found herself alone on the beach.

"Of course I'll still be your friend, Lou. You can count on me. You know that." Why had she said that to him? After the first month he was no longer attractive to her in any way. When she thought of him now, she thought of panicky phone calls in the middle of the night: "Ramona! Oh, thank God you're home! It's so good to hear your voice. I was lying here just staring at the walls and I got to feeling so desperate!" She saw his weak, handsome face across the table in a dozen good restaurants—he had money and the restaurants were always the finest; this was to be her compensation, she supposed—as he described in detail his last session with the famous psychiatrist. And, worst of all, she remembered how she had felt as she listened to his descriptions of easy conquests and subsequent humiliations with girls he picked up on campus, for as he explained to Ramona, even though he thought he loved her, he had to keep searching for someone with whom he could succeed sexually—the psychiatrist, too, felt that was important. Sometimes he would even drop by in his Porsche for an encouraging word before he went out on a date with someone else. "Oh, Ramona, you're so wonderful, you're the only real friend I have . . . whenever I feel I can't go on, I think of you. I don't know what I'd do without you." She wanted to give a lot

of energy and attention to a man, and since she couldn't find anyone else, she gave it to him, not because she loved him, but simply
because he could accept all she had and still need more. His de-
pendence on her made her feel strong, useful, important; she was
a woman helping a good man who was down. And then these last
weeks she had suddenly found herself growing weaker instead of
stronger. But by then it was already too late; he had told her so
many times that he would kill himself if she abandoned him that
she was convinced he really would. If she had never met Louis, she
wondered now, or if she had had enough sense to realize sooner
that reaching out to him was like walking into quicksand, would
she still feel driven to the edge at this moment? For she really was
at the edge now, and when she closed her eyes and looked over it,
she saw jagged, dark rocks and heard the sound of her own terrified screams.

She realized that she was crying again. Tears accumulated steadily in her eyes these days, then dropped of their own weight, like
water from a leaky faucet. When her eyes had dried, she sat up
and looked through her books. She had brought some of them
along, hoping that once away from Berkeley she would be able to
study again. In January she had really thought she could finish college in a year, but now she saw that she would never graduate. She
could hardly even force herself to go on campus. She could not
bear to carry books, to walk through milling crowds between
classes, to sit in a classroom. Settled uncomfortably behind a desk,
she stared at the backs of necks and listened to the droning voice
and fought off overpowering impulses to scream aloud or to run
up to the front of the room, seize the lecturer by his thin shoulders
and shake him until his glasses fell off and he began to cry. She
was sure a professor would burst into tears if shaken hard.

After the first three weeks she'd stopped attending classes,
stopped trying to read, stopped seeing her friends from her dormitory days—they hadn't been to Europe, and there was nothing
to talk to them about. What had she done then? She tried to remember the events of even a single day, but the entire semester
swam in her mind: she saw herself eating, shopping in supermarkets at night, sleeping in the sun on the campus when she
should have been in class, walking with Louis, eating with him,
eating without him, talking to him on the telephone. During finals
week she had shut herself up in her apartment with her textbooks

and empty tablets of blue-lined paper, but she'd kept falling asleep at her desk, to be awakened a moment or an hour or half a day later by her own guilt or by the telephone: Louis calling to tell her he wanted to die.

She took all her books out of her beach bag. She slept.

When she returned at six o'clock, the house was vibrating with music from Jeannie's room.

In the kitchen her mother opened the oven and basted a roast. She had walked to the beach that afternoon to see what Ramona was doing, perhaps try to talk to her some more. But when she caught sight of her, lying there like a corpse, she had thought it better to leave her alone.

"How about a movie tonight?" she said. "You choose. It doesn't matter if it's far or not—I actually enjoy driving on the freeways now. I can go anywhere if I just study the map awhile first."

Her father came home: he looked tired. Dinner was served on the woodtone formica counter that separated the living room and kitchen. A brief and silent meal that was scheduled just before the six-thirty news broadcast.

The program began with a film clip of the action in Vietnam. Ramona had not watched television all year, and she was stunned by the battle scenes filmed like highlights from a championship football game. Bombs exploded; men ran for their lives.

"You all sit around and watch the War on TV every night?" she asked.

"They don't show it every single night. They show other things, too," her mother said.

The report concluded with the box score of deaths and casualties for both sides. "What's so casual about a casualty?" Ramona asked. But no one seemed to have heard her, and after a moment she wondered if she had spoken aloud after all.

Next came some shots of the rioting in New Jersey. Dark, graceful, teenage boys ran like deer from the gunfire of gas-masked policemen, and when that scene was abruptly interrupted by Mrs. Max Pagan of Ontario, Maryland, recounting her experiences with *Tide* the Washday Miracle, Ramona's mother said, "Well, we'd better start, Monie. It's a long drive."

As they were sailing along the freeway, Ramona thought she'd try to increase her mother's awareness of the critical situation in contemporary America. "Well, we deserve these riots," she said.

"What riots?"

"The Negro riots—I mean Black. You have to say capital B. Black now, did you know that? Negro is like Colored used to be. Everything exploded that year I was away. I felt it right away when I got back, even in Berkeley, which is supposed to be such a paradise of integration. A Black guy got shot down on Telegraph Avenue last month. You can't walk alone after dark any more, too much hate. And you should have seen my hair six months ago."

"Huh?"

"Last January I went to this little beauty shop down in West Berkeley because someone had told me it was cheap. There was only one hairdresser, a Black girl about my age, not very pretty, overweight, with bad skin. I remember thinking she was a lot like me. I told her I didn't want my hair much shorter, just the split ends trimmed off, and then I showed her the way they had done it in Paris, how they had piled it all up on top of my head first and then taken it down a section at a time and cut it. And she said, 'Hunh. Must be nice to go to Paris to get your hair done.' And I laughed and said I hadn't gone to Paris just to get my hair done, I had been studying there. Then she gathered all my hair in her hand, picked up those long scissors, and with one big whack she cut it all off. I had to go around with a scarf over it for months. I remember her eyes looking at me in the mirror after she had done it, and I realized I was Whitey to her and that was how she was getting back at us all."

"God, that must have been awful! Couldn't you brush it back and put it up somehow with your switch?"

Ramona decided there was no point in continuing.

"But you know, speaking of haircuts, I did like yours a lot better when it was short. Remember when you had a pixie in the ninth grade?" Her mother wondered why the conversation had suddenly died. She tried once again. "Are you still doing politics at school this year?"

Ramona sighed heavily and thought: My mother thinks we "do politics" as a hobby, an extracurricular activity, in the same way she and her friends danced among potted palms at the Claremont Hotel or painted a fire engine blue and yellow during Big Game Week twenty-five years ago.

"No."

"Why not? I remember how stirred up you were about that Free

Speech Movement in your sophomore year. You gave Bill that book about Karl Marx at Christmas, and—"

"I tried going for a while at the beginning of the semester, but I just don't have patience any more with the people at meetings. They all seem so *young*. And they talk and write their pamphlets in this stupid jargon I can't stand: 'To significantly reorder our priorities plus which foster a relevant and a—in a very real sense of the word—meaningful dialogue.' And then there are all these splinter groups now, it isn't the way it was when it first started, thousands of people working together. Now there are kids who go to peace marches just to find a new lay and kids who sit around smoking pot and swooning over acid rock and kids who study how to make bombs and kids who—"

"Wait, did that sign say Santa Monica Freeway?"

"I don't know."

"Uh-oh. Well, we'll just have to gamble. I *think* it comes after this mayonnaise billboard."

When they were safely on the new freeway Ramona's mother said, "Did you vote? Or did that seem too stupid to you, too?"

"Oh, I voted, I voted. I cast my ballot for the first time in my life, and that night I turned on the radio and heard that Bobby Kennedy had just been shot. Martin Luther King was killed a few weeks before, remember? The radio announcer was talking from the hotel kitchen where Kennedy lay dying. I remember he said, 'The incredible thing is that something like this is no longer incredible.'"

"It's a bad time now, Monie, nobody's denying it any more, except the government. It's times like these when you need a family, some hostages to fate to anchor you. I know you don't think of us as your family any more, if you ever did. But you need somebody to go home to every day so you don't just feel you're falling in space. You really shouldn't live alone; I think it depresses you. Why don't you get a roommate to share your apartment. But you know, darling, the best thing would be for you to get married. It would solve so many of your problems."

"Oh, yeah? *C'est intéressant, ça.* Who do I marry?"

"College is the ideal place—"

"To find a husband, right? All us bright, healthy young people from similar social backgrounds. While I'm hanging around in the knotty-pine snack bar waiting to be swept off my feet by some kid in a sweatshirt and basketball sneakers, what am I supposed to do about this lousy country that kills everybody in it a little bit more every day?"

"You just have to do what you can."

"What are you and Father doing?"

"What are *you* doing?"

"Well, I lie around in my apartment and cry a lot."

"Look, Monie, just quit treating us like elected representatives of Apathetic Americans Associated, will you please? It's about as fair as the bum haircut that beautician gave you just because you were a white college girl."

Her mother had chanced upon a truth she herself had somehow overlooked. Ramona examined the smooth profile of the woman who drove so capably beside her, a pretty, popular woman who charmed supermarket checkers and gas station attendants by treating them like real men and who was on the mailing lists of Another Mother for Peace and the A.C.L.U. fund-raising cocktail party circuit.

"I'm sorry," she said.

"No one can take on the whole world. You have to do what you can in your own corner."

"What if you don't have a corner?"

"Then you have to find one, or make one. You can't live alone out in the open."

They looked at each other and were almost close.

Every day, all day long, she lay on a striped towel on the sand, flat on her stomach with her head cradled in her arms. She was much worse now; she did not even talk to anyone any more. It amazed her that she had brought all her books to Jewel Beach City. Had she really thought as recently as a week ago that after a few days on the beach she might be able to bring herself back to life after all? Sometimes her body was suffused with quiet despair. She felt as heavy as the Los Angeles smog and thought she would never again find reason to move from her deathbed on the beach. Other times panic kicked at her insides like a struggling fetus, and she was frantic and hysterical, weak with fear. She cried: she blacked out into sleep. Once she was startled awake by a whining voice—which she recognized after a moment as her own—crying out for help. She thought of walking out to sea, but she was too tired to lift herself up. She wished the waves would roll in and carry her away.

She could imagine dying, but she could not imagine killing herself. "I am not going to think in Louis Lustig clichés!" she told herself. "I'll stick it out for another year or two at least, see what happens." She was not brave enough, or else she was too brave, to carry through a final act. "Maybe it won't happen. I'm dangling, but I haven't fallen off yet. I still haven't said there's a bomb planted in the back yard, anyway."

A bomb in the back yard. Another semester break, January of her sophomore year. They had been living in another city then, a better city and a better house, big, with two floors and an attic and a basement and a garden in the back, a real house, not a fussy little beach bungalow—and her father taught history at a good university that everyone had heard of, not some junior college. Her mother met her at the airport. "Be careful around your father," she said. "He's very tired these days." But her father had not seemed tired at all; on the contrary, he was active and energetic and he talked incessantly—lecturing at every opportunity, pontificating, ordering them all around, boasting of his superior knowledge of world history and of the many important books he was planning to write. He told them that he was also considering going back to college to get a Ph.D. in either nuclear physics or linguistics. "The college years are the best years of all," he told Ramona. "You're so lucky. I'd love to be a student again." Ramona could not bear to be around him and spent every moment she could outside the house or locked in her room. "Ramona! You're hiding from me!" he hissed at her once in a dark hallway.

Then one morning he ran into the house and informed them that there was a bomb in the garden and they must evacuate immediately. Ramona had been making pancakes. "Ramona, put that down! Didn't you understand me? I said there's a bomb in the yard! Someone's trying to destroy us—I've been expecting something like this for a long time! Now I want you women to go over to the Gareys' where you'll be safe, and I'll call the police and wait for them to come." Ramona started to refuse, but her mother's eyes begged her to go. She turned off the stove and started for the back door. "Ramona! You're barefoot! Here, take my slippers!" He took off his slippers and socks. She would never forget how his feet had looked, soft and puffy, the only part of him that showed his age. "Take these and put them on, I said! And go out the front door, not the back! The slightest movement might set off that bomb!"

She and her mother had waited behind the Gareys' house and watched the police car pull up, then leave five minutes later. They returned to find him getting dressed in his best suit. "I have to take Jean out of school today," he said. "I have a feeling they might try to kidnap her." But he could not find the car keys; her mother had hidden them. To distract him Ramona quickly asked him about a paper she was writing on the French Revolution, and he talked at her for hours, citing references that supported his theories and dashing off a long bibliography of works pertaining to the topic. "You see how much I know? You see? They ask me why I haven't published any books! Hell, I could write a book on any subject! I could write a hundred books a year if I wanted to!"

Then late that evening Ramona had been awakened by a knock on her door. "Come in," she said. Her father opened the door and came in carrying two red sweaters. He was smiling, but his eyes were unfocused. "Would you come to the dining room, please, Ramona? I've prepared the dining room table for a conference."

"What?"

"Come downstairs now! I am your father and the head of this household!" She followed him to the dining room. The table was bare.

"Actually I haven't prepared it yet, that was a little white lie, but I will prepare it now," he said. "Go into the kitchen. Steady now, girl, steady on."

She went into the kitchen and waited. "Close your eyes now, don't watch me, girl, don't watch me. Steady on, just keep steady and calm," he crooned softly as he worked. She heard him moving around, lifting heavy things and putting them on the table, pushing chairs. "Steady now, steady. Almost ready."

At last he called her into the dining room. She was crying, but he did not notice. The table was decorated with two large potted plants, the soup tureen, a number of empty candle holders, and a globe. He had left only two chairs at the table, each with a red sweater carefully draped over the back.

"Sit down," he said. "Watch the spinning map, watch it now."

He spun the globe, beating it with his hand each time around. "I know you want to get away from us—far, far away. When you see my fingers touch the land where you want to be, stop my hand. I will send you there. I will send you wherever you want to go."

Ramona sobbed aloud and quickly clapped her hand over her mouth.

"Steady, now, steady on," he said, spinning the globe again and again, "I know you want to leave us, just say where, say where, say where." Ramona jumped up, raced to her room and locked the door. She heard his slow heavy steps on the stairs, coming after her.

"Ramona, please talk to me."

"No!"

"Ramona Ramona Ramona Ramón," he chanted like a child fascinated with a new word. "Ramonaramonaramonaramona—"

"Stop it!" she shrieked, covering her ears.

Quiet. Had he gone away?

"Ramona, please talk to me. I'll sit here outside your door. I won't come into your room."

"No!"

He spoke very softly. She went over to the door to listen.

"They always close the doors," he said. It sounded as if he were talking to himself. Ramona heard him knock gently but insistently on her door near the floor. The tapping grew slower, then stopped. "I'm not a failure," he said. "I'm only a failure in terms of the standards I've set for myself. I really wouldn't trade places with anyone else in the world."

"Father?"

"It's all right now, baby, just keep steady, keep the lid on, keep calm. It's that red robe you're wearing; that's why we can't talk. Red's the Stanford color, and we're from Berkeley, blue and gold, our sturdy golden bear." He hummed a tune, then sang the words. " 'Our sturdy golden bear/is watching from the sky/Looks down upon our colors there/and guards us from his lai-ai-air . . .' "

"Father?" She was kneeling on the other side of the door.

" 'Our banner blue and gold/the symbol of the bold . . .' "

"Please stop singing."

"You don't like my singing?"

"Please . . . stop."

"'Means fight for Cal-i-for-nye-ay'. . . . You know something, Ramona?"

"What?"

"If you keep your harp strings tuned too tight for too long, someday you wind up with a busted harp."

"Is your harp busted now?"

"I'm going now. Don't be afraid of me any more. I'll wake your mother up, she'll take me. You come along, too, all right? Then she won't have to ride back alone. She doesn't like to be alone. She doesn't know how."

He sat in the back seat, still singing college songs, as they drove him to the hospital.

"I could let go, too," she said aloud, covering her flabby legs with sand. "I've started to let go already, it won't be long now. Someone else will have to worry about me."

At sunset she walked the half block back to the house, ate dinner, watched television, and allowed herself to be taken to the movies in the big car that was like a ship.

The morning of the fifth day she went to the beach and lay down, but she could not concentrate; there were other people there, noisy people. She lay very still, trying to listen to the fighting inside her, but she heard only the conversation of the fraternity boys who had settled near her on the sand.

"You mean that big redhead, the sociology major? Listen, not only is she a lousy lay, but her skin's all striated!" Then their voices dropped; she heard the whispered words "fat-assed pig" and knew they were talking about her. She gathered up her towel and beach-bag and left.

The front door was open to let in the sunlight, and as Ramona approached the house, she heard her mother talking on the telephone: ". . . so damn unhappy. She's always been kind of a gloomy, nervous kid, but I've never seen her this blue, and so cranky! She can't even watch television without getting enraged. And then these crying jags all the time, Charlene! Did Marlene or Darlene do that when they were Monie's age? . . . . That's what I thought, too, but she says it isn't love troubles."

Ramona spoke from the doorway, "Shall I go away until you're

finished, or should I stick around? If you and Charlene plan to
use me as your class project, I might be of some help to you."

Without turning from the bar her mother said into the telephone, "Well, Sunshine herself just walked in. I'll see you tomorrow in class, Charlene." She hung up. "You're back so soon today.
Someone called you from Berkeley. Loomis something. Here, I
wrote it down. Loomis Lustwig."

"Louis. So he found out where I am. What did you tell him?"

"I said you weren't at home. He said could you call him right
away collect, you know the number."

Ramona made herself two sandwiches and sat down at the bar.

"Ramona, I've been thinking. I realize you feel upset about
politics and that sort of thing, too, but I think probably your real
problem is that you just need to find the right boy. If only you'd
fall in love, you'd stop thinking about yourself so much. But you're
so damn critical! Now *I* think you'd have better luck with men if
you were more tolerant of their faults. After all, you have faults,
too. This Loomis boy, for example, sounded perfectly nice on the
phone, and he's obviously interested, calling you long distance.
. . . You know, Monie, I've thought for some time that you ideal-
ize your father too much. It's called an Electra complex, and until
you—"

"You can skip the Broadway Freud, Mother."

"Stop laughing at me!"

"Can I cry at you then?"

"You act just like him! Neither of you will ever be happy! I
know you both think I'm dumb! You just love to make fun of
me! Well, I wish I were dumb enough not to realize how dumb you
think I am! I'm sorry I don't have the brains to understand all this
spiritual anguish you two put yourselves through all the time!"

Ramona went back to the beach.

Ramona's mother had proposed a variety of daytime excursions
during the week: the Dismo Beach Aquaworld-International mati-
nee, lunch at a friend's house in Loma Hermosa Annex, and a trip
to a distant shopping center. Ramona had refused to go anywhere
but the beach in the daytime and the movies at night. But Saturday morning was sunny and warm, and Ramona's beach was
crowded with junior college students and weekend swimmers. She
could not bear to have people so close around her, and she went

back to the house and sat around reading magazines and eating for a while. Finally she accepted her mother's invitation to go shopping at a large discount store in a neighboring suburb.

"I have to buy a new pressure cooker," her mother said, "and I thought I might get you something for your apartment, maybe an electric frying pan. If that seems too wasteful, you could pretend to accept it graciously and then give it to some needy family in Berkeley, how about that?"

Ramona conceded her a smile.

"You've never been to this store before, have you?" her mother said, passing three cars in a row as they raced along the freeway. She wore a bright yellow sundress and was exceedingly cheerful: it seemed to her important to get Ramona out among people, a step toward getting her back to Berkeley and college. "It's really amazing the bargains you can find," she said. "They have the best-known brand names, all at marked-down prices. I really should go there more often, but it's kind of a humiliating place to shop. Every time you buy something, the clerks staple the bag shut right away, and there are all these fat store-policemen hanging around to see if you shoplift anything, and those funny curved mirrors that make you look like a dwarf. And if you go in carrying packages, you have to check them before—Look! There it is, up ahead."

"What? You mean that great big rainbow arch in the sky over that metal building? That's it?"

"Yes. Strange-looking, isn't it?"

Ramona laughed and laughed. Her mother was glad to hear her laugh; she looked over at her with a tentative little smile, waiting for the joke to be shared.

"It looks like Saint Peter's Basilica!" Ramona said, still laughing. "That huge embracing arch, like Bernini's arc of columns, welcoming the faithful to the church! 'Give my your tired, your poor, your huddled masses yearning to save a buck on a toaster, the wretched refuse of your teeming shore . . .'"

"Monie, I'm sick and tired of this! I've seen pictures of Saint Peter's and this store does *not* look like Saint Peter's! Now just quit acting so crazy!"

"Don't you see it? A whole new trend in Southland architecture! A supermarket built to look like the Colosseum! A shopping center. Versailles Village! No shoplifting problems in the Hall of Mirrors! And with all those groovy geometrical gardens out back the customers would flock in from as far as the Sundown City Retirement Colony for Oldsters!"

"Monie, you've been back from Europe for six months. When are you going to reacclimate yourself? This isn't as tasteful and beautiful as Europe with its magnificent buildings and bad heating and plumbing. It's just poor, vulgar, convenient Southern California."

They cruised up and down the lanes of the parking lot, searching for a vacant space. "Now we have to remember just where we parked. God, I hope the rows are numbered. If there's one thing I hate, it's not being able to find the car."

As they walked toward the store Ramona's gaze moved from the immense fluorescent arch down to the corrugated metal building that reflected the bright sun, and came to rest on the people buzzing around the entrance with their supermarket shopping carts full of sealed packages.

"I can't go in there," she said. "I'll wait in the car."

"Monie!"

"Go buy your pressure cooker!" Ramona howled, and she ran blindly for the car, forgetting it was locked. Her mother ran after her, grabbed her shoulder and spun her around.

"I know you hate it here, Monie! I know you think our life here is disgusting! I don't say it's the best life human beings can live, I only say it's better than your father being in that hospital in the loony ward, making leather belts and doing experiments with window plants! Nobody ever ordered you to love Jewel Beach City! Just don't work so hard to kill it for the rest of us, all right?"

"I'm unbearable, I know it," Ramona said. "I can't even stand to be with myself. I'm sorry, I'm sorry. I'll go back to Berkeley tomorrow."

"Don't go back yet if you really want to stay. It just . . . it doesn't seem to be doing you any good to be here, and it doesn't do us any good either. Monie, for Christ's sake don't let what happened to him happen to you! You're thinking about it, I can tell. If you can still think about whether it's going to happen or not, you can still stop it!"

"Every way I look it's so awful! There's nothing I want to go to, only things I want to get away from! I can't move in any direction!"

"Yes you can, you can! You have to!"

Ramona had stopped sobbing by the time they reached the edge of the congested parking lot, and as they waited for the traffic to clear, she sat up and said weakly, "Your pressure cooker."

Her mother clicked on the left turn signal. "To tell you the truth, I didn't much want to go in there either. I hate that place."

When they arrived home, Ramona telephoned the airport to reserve a seat on the flight to Berkeley the next day. Her mother stood very still at the sink listening to the call and did not move again until Ramona had hung up.

"Well, so you've decided," she said.

"Yes."

"You'll be able to study better there, and it'll be easier for you to diet in your own apartment, without a lot of goodies in the refrigerator to tempt you."

"Yes."

It was a warm night. All the doors and windows were open, and it seemed to Ramona that even the tight little house relaxed in relief at the prospect of her departure. After dinner Jeannie went out to a party, and the three of them lay in the living room watching television and playing with the cats.

Harold Olsen was in top form: at one point he even climbed up on the roof of a 1957 Impala to show what a solid car it was. "Not even a two-hundred-eleven pound bruiser like me can make a dent in this baby," he chuckled.

"You tell 'em, Harold!" Ramona's mother said.

"You must have called him and requested a special show for my last night in the Greater Los Angeles area," Ramona said. "Either that or his new wife gave him a Dexedrine at breakfast."

"He isn't bad, but his movies put me to sleep," said Ramona's father. "Maybe we should just turn it off for a while and play cards. We haven't played cards for a long time." It was the longest statement he had made since Ramona's arrival.

They were playing hearts when Jeannie came home. She went to her room and her mother, still holding her fan of cards, stood in her doorway, plying her with questions about the party. She answered in monosyllables and finally succeeded in closing her door, shutting in her secrets. Ramona gazed at the strip of light from under her little sister's door. She remembered herself at sixteen, when she, too, had felt safest and happiest of all in her bedroom with the door locked against a family which would not leave her alone. But now being alone in a room was more horrifying to her than walking in an American city in the middle of the night.

On Sunday afternoon, an hour before Ramona's plane was due to leave, she had still not come back from the beach.

"I'll go call her," her mother said. "I know where she always sits. She must have fallen asleep."

But Ramona was not lying in her usual place, nor was she anywhere along the ocean front as far as the eye could see. Her mother shaded her eyes with her hand and scanned the beach up and down long after she was certain that Ramona was not there. She remembered the scene in the Rainbo-Save parking lot and tears ran down her cheeks. "Well, she's gone now, too," she said to herself.

When Ramona came home, the house was unlocked but empty. She took a shower, dressed, packed her plaid bag, and sat in the living room to wait. At last the door burst open and the three of them stood there staring at her.

"Monie! My God!" her mother cried. Her father slipped his arm around her shoulder to comfort her. Jeannie went into her room and closed the door.

"Where were you?" her father asked. "We went out looking for you."

"I got tired of lying there, so I walked all the way down to that motel named Ramona-By-The-Sea and back again."

"I guess I'd better drive you to the airport now or you'll miss your plane," he said. "Your mother better stay home this time. She's a little out of commission. You had her worried."

On the way to the airport she and her father did not speak, but they were not ill at ease. It was conversation, not silence, that was awkward between them. As they pulled into the parking lot he asked her about her future plans but did not wait for an answer. "I know how you squirm when I give you advice, but I'd like to see you push on through as fast as possible and then go right ahead for your Ph.D. If you work hard, you could be a top scholar in any field, do original research, be publishing by the time you're twenty-five or thirty. How did you make out this last semester, by the way?"

"I . . . haven't got my grades yet."

A smiling employee at the confirmation desk informed her that there would be a fifteen minute delay. She turned to look across the waiting room at her father, who sat on a yellow plastic couch. What could she safely talk to him about for fifteen minutes?

"I don't want to leave you before your plane takes off," he said. "We can play cards." She wondered if he, too, was afraid of spending a quarter of an hour together. "I'll buy a new deck here. We can always use another deck of cards."

Between hands of gin rummy he said, "Oh—I almost forgot. A young man named Louis Lustig called today from Berkeley. When I told him you were going back this evening, he very kindly offered to pick you up at the airport, so you won't have to struggle getting home on the bus. He seemed very glad you were coming back."

Later, on the plane, she opened the plaid bag to take out a book and found the new deck of cards. Her father must have tucked them in at the last moment as a little present for her. He had always been a very thoughtful man.

ANGEL

EVE SHELNUTT

After a childhood spent in the South, California, New York, and Florida, Eve Shelnutt attended five colleges before receiving a B.A. from the University of Cincinnati. She received an M.F.A. from the University of North Carolina at Greensboro, where she studied fiction with Fred Chappell under a Randall Jarrell fellowship. Her first short story won a *Mademoiselle* College Fiction Award, and other stories have appeared in *The Virginia Quarterly, The Greensboro Review, Descant,* and other magazines. She has completed a collection of short stories and a collection of poems and is now writing a novel while teaching creative writing and journalism at Western Michigan University in Kalamazoo.

It is a long ride up the mountains. The car is too small, as any car would be, because the mother and the cousin are larger than usual women. It is not *grotesque* cargo. Simply: these two women are oversized enough to be burdensome in a way not easily dismissed, as when a person sniffs an odor he can't place, and suddenly, the nose is all the face remembers of itself.

Then, there's the daughter, in the back with a dress-box.

Inside the box is a dress, almost like another person—compact.

Lois, the mother, and Helen, the cousin, have been fussing over the dress for weeks. The second daughter, the person who is related because they know where to find her, and how her handwriting is, and what color her favorite underwear, is supposed to wear the dress for her recital in the afternoon. If they don't get the chiffon dress to the little college-room in time, she will have to wear a borrowed dress. Then, she would be less related. Already she is distant. Her distance is why they hurry to her. They must get the dress, which they have, on her, whom they haven't.

Of the daughter inside the car—she has thought too much. They don't like her because she thinks. She should hibernate; they need time off. As it is, they keep their eyes on the curves ahead, like beasts taking courage from the feel of muscles inside.

She: she imagines the father they won't speak of is on the car carrier, windfilled. Up there, what does he think of her, quick! before dust fills his mouth? "Never*mind*," he answers. So she settles for the possible: he wouldn't miss the recital. He, in some way, claims this other daughter more than they. He and she are lost together. Claire, her name is, a bell-sound. Yet, this trio in the car will suit him up when he dies and someone calls (for he has *their* address, not the other way around.) Still, they might not know his size; they might have to wire his sister and ask.

And on the chiffon dress, it is the hem which they can't get straight. *His* are the owl-eyes. The whole head moves to a sight. He never over-ate.

Half-way, they stop at an Inn where fish oil is in the air, in the threads of the gingham curtains, in the fibers of the floor, and on the chrome napkin holder. They order fish.

"Amaze me," the daughter says, and she sits opposite to watch.

Really, they have ceased to look at one another when she says something, and this cessation makes her both more distant and more close, or a combination of the two, as in films when the long shot fades to the close-up shot.

Now she sees the down on the cousin's face. Helen is next to the window; sunlight is coming over her left shoulder and onto her left cheek where a thousand tiny hairs cover the acne scars. The same down is on her lip-line and on her arms and, presumably, between her thighs. A soft yellow fur. She looks broader than she is, and nowhere does her dress stick flat on her skin, as if the fur held up the cloth. To go with this yellow, she wears oranges and browns. She puts ketchup on her fish, and her large fingers turn the hush puppies into the red on the plate.

"Pass the salt," they say to each other. They are very much at home here. This is where they stop on each trip to the other daughter, and now the owner of the Inn knows where they are headed.

The mother chews with one hand near her mouth. There are defects on all their bodies. But none of these defects are physical so much as rhythmical—the mother's hand is *arrested* at the mouth

when the mouth chews, because once the mother had embarrass-
ing tooth-trouble, and the palm which sought to hush the crack-
ing sound the jaw made (a hollow nothing-crack with the open
and shut) failed. And now the mouth condemns the hand by making it stay where it shouldn't when the rest of the body has moved
on. And because the father left Lois, her stomach feels too large.
She is continuously pressing down on it. When she stands, she
feels her ribcage first, as if to locate the last, and missing, rib.

And they are fat, not very fat, but when they sit, their legs sprawl
from the weight, and they are always trying to find a place to lie
down for rests. Their feet are skinny, more like hands. They like
to eat, since, afterwards, the smoking tastes better, and when
they smoke, it is the longest part of the meal, with coffee, until the
taste of grease is gone, and the taste of smoke is more like it was
when they began to smoke. When they smoke in the car, they first
take out the thermos of coffee and pour themselves amounts almost measured, and then they light up. Now they pass each other
a last shared cigarette. Its filter has two colors of lipstick because
this cigarette is the final thing to do in the Inn, after the trip to
the bathroom and the stretching behind the chairs to pull the
muscles long before bending them short inside the car again.

"Oh my God," Lois says, "Look at the time!"

Pauline *knows* this isn't their lives. *She* is small, and when she
is younger and first beginning to notice how the body can tell on
a person, she imagines her very smallness will save her. She stands
on the top of her dressing table, turns backwards, and looks at
her face from between the backs of her knees, just to see how a
face like hers might look upside down and backwards. She imagines, then, nothing will surprise her, not even a tiny mole such
as the father grew after thirty-five years, on his left side and just
above the pajama-line, a mole minty-brown and white-flecked.

And there is less of herself to police, not more than five feet and
three and one-quarter inches. When Helen and Lois turn to look
back at the possum dead on the road, so newly dead his blood
marks the tires and the tires mark the road, they hardly see her,
in the middle, between the backs of Helen, who never drives, and
Lois, who drives. Too, she is quiet, like a string. Nothing moves inside her she doesn't know about. She would leave her address with
anyone, her size sewn in any coat, her letters tied in blue ribbons,

and everything she has owned laid out on the bed, on the white coverlet, as in wedding rituals and deaths.

What she thinks of the father: is that *when* he dies, it will be like a setting of sterling, burnt mellow with polish, light and dark, the head like a soup spoon laid across the upper part of a butter dish. Then she will come, a promise. And pull all the pieces into a bundle, and wrap it in navy-blue velvet, and put it very carefully back into the mahogany box. The rest of them will laugh, as at a great party where no one knows how to behave when the formal setting is laid.

"What if a tire blows?" the mother asks the cousin.

"I would hitch-hike," the cousin answers.

"You!" the mother laughs. "Light me up one."

When Helen moves, it is slowly, always. She's had three children, who surprise her. She doesn't like to stay home with them. She comes by bus to Lois' house where the child is not really a child and where the piano takes up so much of the living room she fits in with her slow movements. She has yet to break an ashtray. In a way, she is trying to catch up with her children—she pores over the picture album, of Lois and Lois' two girls, and the father —pictured in every kind of light with one hand on the car door and one hand at his necktie. In the album, Lois is last seen holding the girls when the girls are waist-high to Lois, and then, the girls begin to hate the camera; they look at it as if it were a man spying.

Pauline, herself, takes the album out secretly, and on Sundays, when Helen and Lois are in church, she shades the pictures with a lead pencil, very lightly but over and over, at intervals. She leaves his face bright, because she forgets, almost, how it was.

How it was when he brought gifts: he *smiled*, into the money (I was sixteen, myself, he says, before *I* got the goods), and the money showing so that he begins to miss certain other sights around the house that Pauline doesn't miss.

"What I thought of you then . . ." is how she wants to begin now, at this age, maybe over coffee at Howard Johnson's, since he thinks of Howard Johnson's as the place to eat, and she hasn't been able to tell him otherwise, about the color aqua.

He comes in without knocking, barely able to see over the presents, with little, important boxes from jewelry shops sticking from his pockets. "Nevermind your hair," he says to Lois. "*Look*." He doesn't see the cracks in her lips, or the gray right behind the face-skin, or the fat unless he pinches her fanny.

He thinks the pale-blue satin gown from Atlanta or New York, with its rhinestone trim from the neck to the floor, and its fringed sash, looks *fine*.

Lois, of course, puts on the satin robe, and sometime later, when he can't be found, as if he had forgotten his manners, she puts the robe on again, to hang herself in, up high, on the chandelier, and Pauline knows it will be something like this to tell him about the robe. It is a *picture:* the neck has creased because the head is to one side, and the neck is swollen, and the hand tucks just inside the rope for breathing space, and it is swollen, and the ankles sticking out from the satin robe are swollen. And the voice is froggish. "*Well*, HELP!"

He doesn't notice, either, how they smell—from what they eat and don't get to eat. He brings the present of a crate of oranges, a crate of grapefruit, tins of liver pate, and boxes of crackers, and cans of oysters, and cans of ham, and a brown mustard, and many kinds of cheese, and sometimes wine, and they eat on the floor, around the presents and his suitcase where something forgotten, some littler present, might be found; and truly, he doesn't notice.

Lois stops the car so fast, it's as if a tire *has* blown, and they are off the pavement into the gravel before Pauline sees the apple stand. But Helen has seen it, maybe miles ahead, or smelled it, and she's got change jingling. She hops out, fast for her, and says, "Peck, red ones," and "Here," and then they eat, three each until the two mouths must taste acid, and the two stomachs must churn. In the car is the smell of apple juice, fine little sprays which catch some light, and fall, and the smell of smoke caught in sunlight, and their Prince Charles perfume, cologne, or powder.

Claire's room, in past-time, smells of the big blue box, on her side of the room, by the bed and under the window, and with no electricity when the bill's not paid, if Pauline wants to see what's new in the box, she sees it in this window-light—pictures from magazines: ladies, lovely ladies with fine hair, and long fingernails, and pink toes, and fine blond hair like Claire's when it is clean, and, sometimes, men standing behind these ladies, darker, with sunglasses in their hands, or wine glasses, or flowers. Or clippings about how to make a curl, or how to pull out the hair over the lip or the eyes. Or drawings of stomachs in which parts of babies are penciled in lighter colors, looking like tadpoles, some with tails and some without. And lists, in Claire's fancy writing:

> "Be kind.
> Be kind regardless.
> Smile at least once a day, to help face muscles.
> Read less; think more.
> Imagine FUTURE.
> Gain five pounds in the legs.
> Learn to play the piano."

In the bottom of the box are two dried apples, studded with cloves and decorated with blue ribbon. And old candy-wrappers, and bobbie pins and lipsticks, a box of Brazil nuts, unopened.

They don't talk, Claire and Pauline. Pauline, in the past, is afraid to talk to her, and Claire doesn't talk to anyone. But Claire leaves the top of the box open. It is the only mystery in the house, and the house is so small there is nowhere to be on days when it rains but in the room with the box, and nowhere to be when Claire is taking wash-ups but in the room, alone with the box.

"She *lies*," Lois says. "You know she lies—he isn't *fat*, no fatter than me, and you know I wouldn't marry a fat man, not after *him*, Oh God, he was a sexy man. He ruined me, you know that?"

Helen chews on a red nail; she nods.

And it's true: Pauline lies, telling her version when she knows it isn't anything like theirs, feisty-Pauline, who gets Claire the piano by forging Claire's handwriting and making up a new sixteenth-birthday list with "PIANO" first, and second, and third, when Claire can't even imagine a real-live piano. But then, when it's crowded out two stuffed chairs and the bookcaseful of encyclopedias Lois traded for the second-hand piano, and Claire practices what she knew already and the tiny, tiny lessons just made her remember, Lois says, "Look! She has got the longest, the absolute longest fingers. And yellow hair, I swear it's yellow, and she's so skinny! What's that you're playing, dear?"

"I don't know, I don't know."

"God," says Helen, "the hair, I mean she *looks* different."

It will happen, in future-time, that Claire and Pauline will go shopping together, when Claire has gotten married and had two beautiful children, one of each kind to make it explicit, and because Claire likes to, they will go into the ugly stores with bright lights and look at material and patterns and pots and pans, together, only, for a long time, Pauline won't like what Claire picks up to look at; she won't like that it's cheap stuff. Claire won't buy, Pauline right next to her elbow, looking on like a cat.

Lois and Helen will almost cry, saying, "How *could* she! She had what must have been the best figure God put on any one girl, and look! Fat, fat, the arms, even!" They will say, "Look how she moves, like she doesn't know she's fat, not that fat yet, but how *could* she is what I want to know."

And Pauline will first get more and more sleepy-looking in the face, the figure curved in and out, the eyes the only part absolutely awake, and she first believes one side of her face is growing bigger than the other side, because: of how things are.

One time, at a big party, a man will look at her, studying, and later, at night, when the houseguests are supposed to be asleep, this man will knock on her door, and when she goes to see who it is, he will have on a raincoat, and he will say, "Come on, I have something to tell you," and, half-asleep, Pauline will follow him outside, in a drizzle, holding her nightgown close, and shivering, and when they are far from the house, this man will throw her on the ground and put his hands on her breasts, and when she is looking up at him, this time with eyes which seem stopped, he will take off his raincoat and show her he is naked and means to go into her, otherwise why is he so big?

What she will know is he was almost right, because, after she screams and runs, she knows he was just a little off, no words, no introduction to himself, or to her but what he got looking at her feline-like and tense, both. So Pauline's shoulders will start to let loose, and the neck will move more easily, and she will begin to imagine herself keeping a box which is filled with how-to-do clippings.

And she will notice Claire isn't fat like Helen and Lois—it is a bouncy fatness; she sings a lot and still plays, to the children. So they will go shopping, and this time, when Claire says, "You know how little money he gives me, don't you think these would look nice on the stove?" Pauline will say they really would. They will become almost sister-like, and when they put the mother away, they will divide what was in the house evenly, and not once mention that they hate all the odds and ends. In fact, they won't say anything at all that is a lie or a truth. And Pauline will read

Dr. Zhivago twice, trying to see why it is Claire's favorite book.

And in the future, when the recital is over, Helen and Lois will come back and lie on the sectional sofa with their legs up, and smoke, and their feet will be almost touching, their heads at opposite ends on the sofa so they can look at each other while they talk, and they will say, "My God, I am so tired, these things just wear you out."

But what do *they* know? is what Pauline asks.

Then, they get to the little college town, and go right to the dormitory, and up to the third floor, and into the room, and hug Claire two or three times, squashing her, and look around the room and see the bedspread with the lilac-colored leaves and fuchsia flowers is still on the single bed, and the roommate they never liked who has one hand, a stub so that it seems just curved under so they think of her as sneaky, they will notice she is still the roommate, and that the other girl they don't like with the short haircut and jeans is still popping her head in the room, this time to see how Claire is coming right before her concert.

"Will you look at that figure, will you?" says the girl with the short haircut, from the doorway.

There is the last of the sunlight in the room, on Claire's hair and making her cotton panties and bra look especially white.

"I have simply got to lie down," Lois says, from the bed where she is watching Claire take out the dress. "I am *bushed.*"

"Yeah," answers Helen, "let her get dressed."

Pauline now wants something to eat, before the music, but there isn't time. She bites her lip and helps lift the dress over, and pull the long hair out of the neckline. She tries to keep the long skirt moving, flowing, instead of hanging down straight.

"It's pretty, Momma," says Claire. "I like it, I really do, and thank you." And, before the mirror, she fluffs out her hair, and smiles at herself: a picture. She leans over to Pauline and asks, "Isn't the hem crooked? Why couldn't they get it straight?" not meanly, curious.

"I don't know," Pauline whispers back, "the material, the material sags after it's made, I don't know for sure. I'm sorry, but don't say."

"No." She turns, she twirls out in the room, and they all clap and laugh, and Claire keeps turning until she is dizzy, and laughs, and then they have to hurry her over, across the street and into a building, and they leave her rubbing her fingers, a frightened look on her face, the head nodding as they call, Lois and Helen together, "Do good, sugar."

Helen and Lois will get up together, in the middle of a piece by Chopin, and go out for a cigarette.

But now, in present-time, Claire walks in, not slowly—gracefully, with her shoulders back, and her head up but not looking out at the people seated below, the lights shining on the dress which she swishes with her hands so that it is never still. Then she sits and turns to the audience and smiles quickly, but Pauline sees the eyes don't really see; they are remembering, and then the fingers begin to flex. It gets very quiet, and Claire bows her head, and she plays: beautiful, and beautifully.

ART HISTORY

ANN ARENSBERG

Ann Arensberg was born in Pittsburgh, Pennsylvania, but lived most of her childhood in Havana, Cuba. She holds a B.A. in art history from Radcliffe College and a master's degree in French literature from Harvard, and has spent the past six years as an editor in book publishing. At present, she is working on a novel.

On one of the empty weekends in late spring, when Philip Roth-schild had taken wife and children to the Berkshire Mountains, Ferry Morgan began her votive collection of Italian Loves. With a decisiveness that was rare on these Saturdays and Sundays, she made a ten o'clock start from her attic studio on Louisburg Square.

The place was still sparsely furnished after her two-month's tenancy. She had abandoned career-girl housekeeping when she left her Cambridge roommates for a more inspired solitude. One ruthless afternoon she scrapped all fuchsia feather dusters, travel posters of the Grand Canal, enough yellow enamel mugs and plates for twelve, and every item made of papier-mâché, bamboo or beaten tin, and manufactured in Mexico, Hong Kong, or the Grecian Isles. Never again would she cohabit with objects or persons which had no beauty or portent. She knew from her studies that art was the result of painful calculation: with luck and care, she would begin building a significant life from the outside in. Yet on the walk down to the Charles Street antique shops she still spun out her most pleasurable daydream: that on returning, her poor garret would be changed, like Sara Crewe's, into a magical lair, with Persian rugging and tropical flowers, by the hand of a respectful turbanned emissary of her father, so long believed dead in the Anglo-Indian Wars.

The May-morning sun slanted pale onto the sidewalk, creating no glare to block Ferry's view of the shop-fronts. She hurried past windows of Queen Anne and Chippendale—tidy museum-like displays—seeking more extravagant clutter, some baroque rebuttal to Beacon Hill. Two blocks and two centuries back down the street, she stopped still. Beyond a French Renaissance armoire and a chateau-sized tapestry featuring lutenists in doublets and ladies in nothing at all, there flashed a glimmer of golden winglets, sprouting from the shoulders of a golden boy-baby revolving gently, in slow-motion, fixed in flight by the finest of metal wires, which were visible only, and then regretfully, at second glance.

The Collector's Muse is also a winged creature, but it has talons for gripping and a beak for piercing. The impulse that rooted Ferry was no benign attraction: a sharp acquisitive focus tightened her chest and shallowed her breathing; her scalp felt light and lifted inches above her skull. Her mind emptied, until the inside of her head was a large glowing space, a grand storied hall, with friezes of frisking putti and garlanded cherubs; with cupids, blindfolded, in corner niches; with flights of amorini frescoed on the ceiling—a vast gallery of boy-loves, marble, bronze and gilt wood; languid or mischievous; reclining, sitting, standing; drawing arrows from quivers, or fitting arrow to bow to launch the mortal thrust. A collection dedicated to Philip, her mentor, her lover and her Doge.

The glow expired, the vision scaled down to apartment size, and Ferry could see that cherubs are humorous, domesticable beings, impudent reminders that love is sudden and the heart outruns it, talismanic reinforcements of a still unconscious sense of irony.

Ferry's acknowledged amulet was a legacy from Aunt Molly Morgan. It enabled her to read manuscripts three days a week instead of five for a publisher of beautiful letters housed in a mansion on Tremont Street. Her office looked out through an oeil-de-boeuf onto the treetops of the Common. This lucky money also allowed her the odd whim, and she carried her pagan angel away in a wrinkled brown grocery-bag, torn quickly through by his right fist and left wing-tip. Her toothbrush was six months old and cottony, and the half-bottle of milk in the icebox was sour, but she passed the druggist's and the grocer's without a qualm, stopping only at an art supplier's, who sold her a sable brush and enough gold paint to touch up the few chips in the cupid's gessoed wooden hide.

Cupids may or may not lack genitalia, though they belong exclusively to the male sex. This one was fancy in front, not plain, a fact she had not taken stock of until she unbagged him. She spread newspapers on the kitchen floor against paint dribbles, laid him down on his side, and went to work.

Even for this ten-minute job of conservation, Ferry had taken the precaution of stripping down to her camisole and pants. Philip was so deft of hand and eye that he had cleaned his own Anonimo di Arrezzo panel in full Savile Row regalia, suited and vested and tied, and showing an astonishing length of French cuff, which remained unsullied through the entire virtuoso performance. Ferry had been allowed access to the Bradford University restoration lab because she was Philip's tutee, and writing a paper proving that the Anonymous painter was none other than the young Lorentino. She had witnessed Philip's feat a year ago in December, and could never smell acetone or varnish without losing her balance all over again.

Nail polish remover is thirty percent acetone, and the only paint solvent Ferry could find. She had knelt in a splatter of gold, and began wiping the clumsy knee with a wet cottonball. The rank liquid, with its cinnamon after-smell, stung her nostrils, and, shortly, her tear-ducts. Ferry was a messy crier; her crying spells could be measured in pints. Tears took her utterly by surprise, like a shove from behind in an angry crowd. She sat unconsciously kneading the wads of newspaper around her, the way cats weaned too early pull at their owners' cloth laps. Having no elemental vanity to muster against the assault, she lost her gay rococo looks and wept roughly and stridently, like the victim of a physical accident. She had also been known to drool.

Shock-waves of tears bring on biliousness, and Ferry had no desire to be sick in the midst of a more exalted suffering. Up she stumbled, and got herself into the windowless bathroom, turning on the right hand tap at full force. The first palmful of cold water turned tepid on her burning face, but she splashed again, until she forced down the spasms, and shuddered, once, to a full halt. Looking up into the mirror, she passed immediately into the realm of histrionics, brought her fists up to her blotched cheeks, flung back her hair, widened her swollen eyes, and unfurrowed her brow. She was two people again, actor and onlooker, not a wretched, imbecilic primitive, but an intelligence with some hold over her pain.

Without Philip every Friday to Monday, Ferry had contrived a state of partial anesthesia, but even at her best she carried herself like a full vase of water placed on an unsteady pedestal. To stave off unworthy lapses, she set herself exercises in self-expression. Left over from her grade-school repertoire were a Schubert impromptu and several Chopin nocturnes. At eleven and twelve the fingerwork had been too difficult for her, and she had herded the pieces into her memory by force of empathy alone. Now she worked an hour a day at refining them, on Aunt Molly's miniature baby grand piano. Aunt Molly had played Chopin vaguely, with the tempi all awry. She had also left tearstains on the collected poems of Coventry Patmore. Aunt Molly's sensibility was like an unweeded garden, and watching her aesthetic vaporings had had a fine cautionary effect on Ferry. She learned not to play more than an hour, by the full of the moon, or at twilight, because these indulgences brought on outbursts located only slightly lower on the Richter scale than the acetone-incident.

Since Ferry's weekends contained forty-eight hours, three hours spent at the piano left forty-five more unaccounted for; but waiting for Philip was a kind of novitiate. He was eighteen years her senior in feeling and in learning. From throwaway comments in his lectures or conversations, she had compiled a reading list that spanned Plotinus and Baron Corvo. Still, nine hours a weekend passed in devotional studies tallied at thirty-six unoccupied sixty-minute intervals, and by Sunday afternoon she was a mindless knot of expectation and anxiety, grasping at the most ignominious tranquilizers—detective stories, home pedicures, and Oreo cookies. Why was the Life-force equated to the conjunction of men and women, when love was clearly depleting her storehouse of red corpuscles? When the lover's flattering gaze is withdrawn, the princess turns back into a white sow.

Beauty slept one hundred years before her Prince braved the thorn bushes. Ferry's Philip rang her doorbell at four p.m., looking rumpled and bleak.

"We've taken sleeping pills, darling. In the middle of the Yorkshire pudding. It's all right, Mrs. Wintersteen is with the children."

"Come on, Philip, she's not . . . ?"

"Hardly."

In stress or anguish Philip's a's became very Mayfair. He had overcome a stammer as an adolescent by watching Leslie Howard movies. Ferry wished, inappropriately, that she had not buttoned her shirtfront up to the neck.

"But how can you be here?" she asked.

"She'll be out for twenty-four hours. I simply fled." He took her hand and pressed it to his cheek.

"Where can I hide, except with you?"

She met his heavy-lidded hazel eyes and began to feel some localized adult tremors. She remembered a mistress was for comfort, and led him to the gondola chaise by the fireplace.

"I'll get your whisky. You be still now. No thinking."

He let his head fall hard against the back-rest, stretched his legs out full, and dropped one arm over the sofa-edge onto the rug, where the hand rested, wrist cocked and palm cupped, like a mendicant's. He had beautiful men's legs, Ferry thought, calves of the shape termed "imperious" in Regency beaux, and trim ankles, sockless in narrow oxblood moccasins.

In the kitchen she tossed her limp hair into more enticing dishevelment, then came back and knelt by his side, placing the fingers of his down-flung hand, one by one, around the chilly glass.

"Philip, you can't stay. If it's stomach pumps or hospitals, they'll call you at home . . ."

"This is number four, darling. Threateners don't finish it—God is not so kind."

"But there must be . . . I mean, why?"

"I am accused of preventing her career on the musical stage. Alexandra's birth changed her voice quality."

Ferry frowned, in spite of herself; curiosity and self-interest grappled hand to hand with her sense of fitness. She had a long perspective on his callousness, however, and she could vindicate him between one breath and the next.

In the small Bradford art department, Philip was known as an epic womanizer. Ferry's sophomore imagination, fed on King Arthur's legend decoratively debased by Ariosto, half-expected, on entering her tutor's office for the first time, to see the pale, French-knotted heads of his victims mounted like trophies on the walls— the fourth-year graduate student who had lost thirty pounds in two weeks; the Burne-Jones brunette who had gone utterly mute during her orals; the second-year Maenad who had locked herself inside the museum after closing, and scored, hacked and gashed his mahogany knee-hole desk, not with a jeweled stiletto, but the eternally handy Swiss Army knife.

Roland, Tristram and Lancelot had been men of violence transmogrified into gentler lovers. Of an age to relish both obverse and reverse of the courtly tradition, Ferry elevated Philip to their annals, and collected rumors like a budding archivist. But never once in four college years had his feats been attributed to anything more than a superior hormonal endowment, and an uncanny resemblance to Francis the First as painted by Clouet (the Elder).

The truth ennobled him. While they were still making do with off-turnpike road-houses at odd hours, he had told her that his wife was a secret alcoholic, making light of his eleven-year vigil at exhibition openings and tenured-faculty dinners. He knew the limits of Kate's ebullience to the millilitre. His job was easiest in houses with pianos. She gave sparkling renditions of "Mimi" and "Mountain Greenery"; at the first notes of "Little Girl Blue" he carted her home.

So the mocking droop of his mouth was the mask of anxiety, not the complacency of the sexual scorekeeper. Ferry was glad, that once, that the Wintersteen fortune made a buffer to his discreet misery. Her swordsman was a closet chevalier. And when she learned, later in the meal, that out of sheer fondness for his three Burmese cats he underwent a painful weekly course of allergy shots, she felt that she could see clear through to his soul.

Now, as she urged a soft pillow behind his back, so he could raise his glass to his mouth with minimal effort, she felt that seeing him so dismantled and undone was a gift to her, a privilege freighted with responsibilities. Her awe increased as the four horizontal lines in his forehead deepened to red ridges, showing a fine and previously undetectable diagonal slash that would have been a field day for an interested phrenologist. Soundless drops ran from the corners of his eyes, and noiseless sobs racked his chest. So this was how men wept—no retching or hiccupping, no drizzling from the nose, no clawing of cheeks or wringing of hands, no wailing with its infinite modulations from whimper to shriek. Thus Philip, when the London Intelligence Office was blitzed by German fire, watching his comrade blasted thirty feet across the room and broken to death against the granite wall. Thus

Roland, marooned at Roncevaux, blaring his grief out through his horn before the end.

Ferry took his bourbon, which was sloshing precariously, and set it down behind her on the brick hearth. Both his hands were free now, and Philip whipped them up to cover his face—a useless enterprise, since there it lay, in jagged shards, upon the rug. The Japanese code of honor is deadly serious, and Ferry wondered in panic if she was an experienced enough restorer to mend his image. The Western reaction to loss of face is schoolboy embarrassment, an anti-erotic reflex if there ever was one. His power over her might square him with himself and the world, and she knew she could find a way to bring him to dominance.

She slid next to him on the chaise, pulled his hands down, and began wiping his wet cheeks with her own dry ones. She kissed his closed eyes softly until the lids stopped trembling, and pressed her lips to the center of his forehead.

"That's where your third eye should be, my beauty, my fox-prince," she murmured, supporting his head delicately and firmly, until he opened his arms and pulled her down onto his chest.

All very well that he had sighed out that she could raise the dead, darling; that he had touched her flushed cheeks and said, for a lover's sally, that it was a good thing she had no date to keep, since even the most obtuse bystander could tell what she'd been doing. Jewish puritans have a short memory for sexual exaltation, and here he was, already on his feet and into the bathroom, scrubbing rather too vigorously at the lower half of his face and his tenderest organ, then closing the door and keeping both faucets running loud, in case he should be suspected of urination.

Ferry preferred to doze and play after love, to laugh and spoon and let languor run its course, as if the bed were hung between time and space like a hammock; until it was time to make big cups of tea with honey and lemon, and sip them slowly, and make elaborate leisurely plans about where to go for supper.

Philip emerged, already modest from waist to ankle. He began looking for the shirt he had flung off twenty-five minutes earlier, found it draped over one of the ball-topped iron fire-dogs, and shook it crisply to get the worst of the wrinkles out.

"Your phone's started to ring in your head, hasn't it," said Ferry,

upending what he called her Tanagra posteriors as she groped under the bed to retrieve his shoes.

He sat down heavily on the rose velvet slipper chair.

"I have to be back at my post, darling."

"Extend your perfect feet, please," she said, kneeling in front
of him and sliding his moccasins back on in two deft gestures,
without scuffing his heels.

"My movements may not be my own the next few days, sweetheart."

"Of course not," said Ferry, "how could they be?"

"We were dining in public at the Ritz Tuesday night," said
Philip.

"Well, if we can't," answered Ferry, "just call me."

He took her hand and kissed the palm.

"You're still wearing your necklace."

"Don't," she said. "I'm going back to bed. Go out by yourself;
I don't like seeing the door close."

Ferry clapped her hands over her ears; a secondary reflex shut
her eyes tight. She stood there, blind, deaf, and bare, counting
slowly in a whisper, until she was sure she wouldn't hear the click
of the latch.

She opened her eyes and held her breath. She heard silence and
the dripping of a tap. The clock on the bureau read 6:30, and her
bedtime was midnight if she wanted to sleep the night through.
She realized she was shivering and pulled Cousin Chris's old flannel pajamas out of the second drawer. The pajamas had faded red
horses' heads on them, a rip at the shoulder seam, and a proper
boy's fly. They were a talisman from her eleventh year, when she
and Chris had sworn blood brotherhood by rubbing their cut
wrists together; when she had gone two whole months at camp
without washing her hair; when she had locked herself all night in
the root cellar, hunkering like an Indian brave on fire-watch, after
her mother had explained that she had finally become a woman.

"What happens now?" yowled Ferry at the bedpost. "What
should I do—" —she grabbed it—"kill myself?" Both fists clamped
tight around its neck, and shook and shook, and the joints creaked,
the slats rattled, the headboard swayed, and the pounding in her
head nearly drowned out the doorbell, which had rung once, diffi-
dently, and then again, with a firmer touch.

Ferry stopped dead. Released from their strangler's grip, her knuckles ached and her palms smarted. "Coming!" she called, and sounded normal even to herself. She got Chris's pajamas on, helter-skelter and inside out, and ran to look through the peep-hole in the front door.

All that was visible of Lally Morrison was a profile section of her furry upper lip and the tip of her nose. Lally had been Ferry's college roommate, and the one friend left over from Sudbury Academy. She lived with her parents on Walnut Street, and never wasted precious message units when she could stride the two blocks down to Louisburg Square instead. Lally habitually ran several paces ahead of her energies, hacking her days into uneven sections like a butcher with a meat cleaver. Her generosities out-paced her, too. When she wasn't wheeling book-wagons at Trow-bridge Hospital, or saving old Tea Wharf and the golden eagle, she worried vociferously about Ferry, who appreciated the din, since it muffled her own thoughts.

Ferry opened the door.

"Hi Lals; what's up?"

All five feet nine inches of Lally bent down, pressed her right ear to Ferry's left cheek, then walked back to the kitchen and pulled open the refrigerator.

Ferry followed her, feeling weak, and addressed her blue tweed back.

"Lally, what's that you're carrying? What are you doing? Watch out! the freezer's jammed; I hate defrosting the ice-box!"

Lally was already re-stacking packages of frozen spinach in neat piles.

"Is this all you ever eat? Mummy baked bread this aft, and we thought you ought to have some."

"That's terribly nice," said Ferry, "but why freeze it?"

"You have a whole package of English muffins left," said Lally, "I hope they're not too ancient."

"They're not," said Ferry. "Come on out of there, unless I can get you a ginger-ale."

"Nope," said Lally, "I can't stay. I really came to remind you about Pookie Bayard's shower."

This announcement caused Ferry's voice to career to a whine.

"But Lal, I barely know her! She was a class behind us. For Christ's sake, Lally, she was head of Clean-Up!"

Lally turned around and faced Ferry from her full height.

"I should have known. You've got those strained patches under your eyes. Was he just here?"

Ferry sat down on a three-legged stool.

"What kind of shower is it?" she capitulated, "kitchen or linen?"

"Kitchen," said Lally. "Nick's putting himself through law school and they won't have any money. I'll pick you up tomorrow at four."

Ferry hitched her pajama-bottoms up at the waist and followed Lally to the door.

"Have a nice hot soak," said Lally, and paused. "Do you wear those funny things around him?"

For this inconsistency Ferry gave her friend's shoulder a kindly squeeze.

"I'm fine, Lally, I really am. You sleep well too."

Surveying her Lally-free apartment, Ferry felt a lift of relief at the idea of being alone and unembattled. For a moment her loneliness seemed like a windfall, and her only task to devise ingenious ways of squandering it. Then she remembered that it comprised the debit side of the ledger of her accounts with Philip, and she began to hear the random scrabbling of her thoughts, like mice in a laboratory maze, and realized that the telephone had been dead for the hour and a half since his departure.

Ferry pulled off the receiver—the first political act of her love-affair—and ran to find a pillow, which did not stifle the little beeps of admonition. She called out *Philip!* once, as if he were only in the next room; then *Philip*, just above a whisper, as if she expected no answer at all. She remembered the telephone, unyoked, and put back the receiver to re-open the telepathic circuit.

"Philip!" Her tone was peremptory; "*Philip!*" one note higher; and she flung out both arms, reaching to him. Why couldn't he hear? Was his head so obtuse with worry, with comatose wives, seminar reports, and vomiting cats? Her internal monitor played back the emptiness of her gestures and the pathos of her sorrowful open mouth. Her dry eyes flooded. "My heart's all gone," she forced through sobs, "my heart's all gone." And in fact, it felt as if she had used it up, her prodigal organ, that it was becoming a cinder, a dead star—anti-magnetic, ancient, and cold. "She had so much to give," whispered her sympathetic mourners, "she simply burnt herself out."

Self-pity is a ready homeopathic balm; but the burning sensation, as if the stomach cavity were filled with hot lead, is called anxiety, and knows no palliative but the hardening of the heart. Ferry had a solid working relation with anxiety. Anxiety was not unlike her Cousin Chris, who had played on her fears half the summers of her childhood, giving her a dissected pregnant black snake as a birthday surprise, uncaging his parakeet in her bedroom, taking her out in a canoe and jumping overboard with the paddle. He had hunted her into a stupid, pin-point wariness, with reflexes only for retreat, like an animal that has lost its feral pride. Then she learned to take his dares and set him some of her own, to ride bareback her first time on a horse, to stay in the attic two hours after sunset, to swim in the river that was infested with snapping turtles. But she had abdicated her tomboy prowess, and now the only worthy challenges were amorous ones. If she did not act, she would be reduced to pulling the feathers one by one out of her down pillow until the bedroom looked like a Santa Claus paperweight upended, as she had done the night Philip never came to her after his curriculum meeting.

If she allowed her imagination free rein, she would run smack into the embrace of her oldest enemy. In college, her mother had sent her clippings from *Mademoiselle* and the Yale *Journal of Psychiatric Medicine*, about the nature and cure of pathological jealousy. Ferry knew all the theories: that jealousy came from a debased self-image; that it was an unresolved Electra complex; that it was, even, inverted homosexuality. But why was it painted green? Green was rest, and new leafage, and the color of her own eyes; it was the color of nausea and blackout.

She began remembering a colloquium on the function of art history in a liberal education: Philip was debating Anton Kane, of the Physics Department. They were already seated, shuffling notecards on their laps, when she came in and took one of the last places in the rear. There was a third empty chair on the stage, unaccounted for on the program. The two men glanced, stage-left, into the wings, and stood up at courtly attention. Ferry had forgotten her glasses, so all she could see of the entering third panelist was a bright red dress and raven-black hair. Professor Kane announced her as Linda Tavonian, an instructor in Philosophy and a delegate from the Graduate Students Self-Government Association.

The empty chair was next to Philip's and Miss Tavonian sat down, crossed her ankles, and leaned over to shake hands with the two male speakers. Ferry's eyesight had unblurred enough to see that Miss Tavonian looked straight at Philip, then lowered her eyes; that she had the ankles of a Derby winner; and that Philip's necktie was the same bright coral as her sheath dress.

Ferry's heart rioted. Her ears stopped up. None of her senses was operative but her vision. She was as numb and focused as a camera on a tripod, recording every tilt of heads, every shifting of limbs, every whispered aside during Kane's address; weighing the evidence for pre-colloquium collusion; studying their blocking like a director watching a rival's production of the same play. Philip didn't know she was in the audience; but lovers are psychic, so she concentrated on reaching him. He gave no answering sign; he never raised his head to scan the back of the hall. His heedlessness confirmed all her suspicions.

Ninety minutes later—by Ferry's time more than the years she had lived—the lights went up. Miss Tavonian walked down the steps to make her departure through the auditorium. She stopped five rows in front of Ferry to hail a friend. One of her eyes was badly off-center, and her skin was daubed with a blemish-cover several shades darker than her complexion. Ferry darted out of the hall like a felon. It had taken her twelve hours to sleep off her shame.

Three minutes to dress, one minute to take the four long flights downstairs, and Ferry was out the door and into a taxi. Cambridge was fifteen minutes away, and her mind was empty as a drum until the driver slowed down on Brattle and started to make the turn onto Stonington Street. She came to her senses and stopped the cab. Stonington Place was an elegant blind alley, and the noise of the motor might give her away before she was ready.

Her readiness was exalting but unreal. Like Pandora, she had no plans, only strong purposes. Twelve Stonington Place, pseudo-Tudor swagged in English ivy, did not look like a house of grief. All three stories glared with light, and the blinds were up. The phonograph was playing, and not softly, Mozart's concerto written for the hunting horn. Ferry hugged her arms against a chill in the air, and found that the sweater she was wearing had holes in both elbows.

An atavistic impulse humped her spine, and she moved low to the ground, chin up and arms loose, over the tulip-border and just under the ledge of the living room window. She kept down until she reached the corner of the window-frame, and raised up to peer inside.

Sultanic in a magenta dressing-gown, Philip was lying on the davenport, a study in brocade on brocade. Settled deep into the wing-chairs flanking the couch were his two prize graduate students. Ferry could tell Marvyn Frankel by his goatee, and Bunny Herrick by the gauzy sleeves of her trade-mark peasant blouse. Bunny was doing pantomimic things with her Gainsborough hands, and Philip's eyes were narrow, like the cat's on the rug. Suddenly Marvyn bent over and began hauling on one of Bunny's high-heeled pumps, panting and grimacing as if the shoe wouldn't come unstuck, acting out, apparently, the reverse of the Handsome Prince's search for the real Cinderella. He tugged too recklessly, got the end of one four-inch spike in the palm of his hand, and pitched backward into the wing-chair, flailing his wrist. Bunny unshod herself, slapped the bad shoe and wagged a reproving finger at it, and Philip laughed and laughed, with a generous display of gums and canines. Ferry's chest throbbed, and she realized she had forgotten to breathe during the entire dumb-show. Up the back of her neck crept a peculiar tingle, which registered, a second later, as plain, liberating embarrassment.

Down she stooped, and skittered across the six feet of new lawn to the tulip-patch. The ground was still firm, but spite and mischief were upon her, and she rooted in the packed soil until she came up with a solid clump, bulb and all, and hurled it left-handed, from a catcher's crouch, against the pane.

Then she scrambled onto her feet and tore out of there, nearly bent over double, calculating her safety by the height of every window-ledge she passed. She flew, she streaked, she performed prodigies of speed in that dwarfish position, until she tripped over a cobble where Stonington Place curved into asphalted Stonington Street, and subsided into a crab-wise lope, gleeful as Caliban before his Master caught him sowing nettles among the primroses. She was still shivering with laughter as she reached the streetlights, where the brights from a passing car caught her full in the eyes and blinded her.

When she could focus again she began to burrow in her trouser pockets for the fare home. Her fingers wouldn't close around the coins, and she realized they were hurting her. In irritation she peered at her hands. She saw her nails, torn to the quick and black with dirt and bloody, and the pain started in earnest.

Ferry woke up stunned and charged with meaning, like a princess who has had a ruby implanted in her forehead. She was afraid that the feeling would go away, so she began to practice her exercises for living in the present tense. When she swung her legs over the side of the bed she concentrated on the deep tufting of the carpet and its firm accommodation to the arches of her feet as she stood up. As she moved, without hurrying, to the kitchen, she could sense the efficient play of her thigh and calf muscles and the counter-balancing swing of her arms. Under such heightened focus, her gestures as she arranged the tea-tray became balletic; the china cup came to rest in its saucer almost soundlessly, with no clatter. She poured boiling water in a slow arc into the tea-pot, and in the arm holding the heavy iron kettle there was no strain in bicep, extensors or wrist. Equilibrium is just this coincident deployment of muscular and psychic energy, so she could carry the tray to the coffee-table like a celebrant, and the spoon never rocked on its bowl, the plate never slid, and the lid sat steady on top of the Willow pot.

What reached her nostrils was a waft of jasmine flowers, but the tea was scalding, and the first sip burnt her tongue and seared her throat going down. It was a homely accident, but she went rigid, not with pain, but humiliation. On the inside of her left wrist was a round pink welt of scar tissue. She felt it, and it was still live to the touch.

In the throes of conscience after a lingering lunch, Philip had driven them fifteen miles to Sandy Pond Reservoir the autumn before. Ferry had not yet taken her own apartment, and the great lovers of song and story do not check into third-class motels. Over Philip's car radio came Guarini's guitar concerto, which plucks also at the impatient senses.

But a New England fall, before it blazes into red and yellow, is a dusty-green reverie that harbors no Panic presence. The reservoir waters were gray from storing up the chill of the late September nights, and the sky was heavy with low-flying cloudbanks. Philip made a ground-cover of his wartime trenchcoat, and they leaned shoulder to shoulder gazing out over the pond, sad sheep in a Puritan pastoral.

"Poor orphaned us," said Ferry, "if we sit long enough the leaves will cover us up and keep us from freezing when it snows."

"We have a lot, my Ferry," he reproached her, "most people never have this much."

"As you like," she answered, a little shortly, still untamed by the melancholy landscape.

He brought out his box of blond English cigarettes, and cupped his hands against the breeze to light one. He turned to face her. His eyes were bloodshot and his mouth was thin. He pulled her left arm to his chest. She held his gaze and let her lips part and her head loll back, very slightly, inviting the supreme embrace that might ensue.

There came a sudden ache at the inside of her left forearm, which is not the prescribed locus of grown-up love. Another instant and the ache was a searing throb. She looked at its source just as Philip drew away the lit end of his Player. On her tender flesh the webbing of pale-blue veins was broken by a fiery circular pox.

"Until I can give you stronger sensations," said Philip.

She could not move, from sacredness, or shock.

The memory was trance-deep, and she came awake to find she had been gripping her wrist so hard that the puckered scar had turned virulent red again. Little dutiful reflexes lured her to her feet—tea things to wash, sheets to change, a present for Pookie Bayard. What present? Meatgrinder to inspire a Women's Page headline: Law Student's Wife Wizard With Left-Overs? Foot-high peppermill for her first fettucine Alfredo? Pook 'n' Nick playing poor for three years—Ferry rebelled at the smug benighted sham. She had a fiendish extravagant thought. The gift was right here in the apartment, but almost unwrappable. She could wind it in sheets of crackly white tissue paper, until it looked like a sinister wasps'-nest. She had no paper, no tape, and not much time, but her day was launched.

Lally had arranged to meet Ferry down in the Square.

"You're one of those five-minute-late people; I've been noticing," greeted Lally.

"Of course I'm late," said Ferry. "I'd rather be shot in the foot."

"Keep a happy face on, please; we'll be out of there by six."
Then, eyeing Ferry's armful, "You know perfectly well we keep a
closet full of boxes!"

"It isn't for you," said Ferry, "don't be governessy."

Mrs. Cornish, Pookie's future mother-in-law, opened the door.
Past her egg-yellow pageboy bob Ferry could see one end of a table—planks on sawhorses, damasked—where the shower-gifts were
accumulating. Pookie came up behind Mrs. Cornish; her eyes were
startled from being the center of attention. Her nickname was not
her fault any more than her real name (which was Josephine), but
she wore them both apologetically, as if she were making a perpetual social gaffe.

Cheekbone to cheekbone greetings all around—Alma Cornish
had a Viennese mother, and refused to learn that kisses, in Boston,
were kept for members of the immediate tribe, not extending to
second cousins.

"Who was that delicious gent walking you down Brattle Street,
Ferry?" said Mrs. Cornish, who would have been arch in an air-
raid shelter.

Ferry was spared by the arrival of Anstiss Lodge, Mrs. Everett
P., whom Alma Cornish enfolded with little cries.

It was punch, not tea, served in two cut-crystal birdbaths in the
dining-room. Banks of forsythia beyond the French windows cast
a yellow gleam through the glass. Candles had been lit on the
sideboard, though it was still early, and the air was spiced with
Lady Baltimore cake, just baked, and Mrs. Cornish's beeswax and
lemon-oil recipe for furniture polish. So much care and gracious-
ness tightened Ferry's throat, and made her wonder again why
settling down and belonging seemed as arduous as vows of chastity or silence. By now she had erred and strayed too far, and it
was only when this world of Chippendale and monogrammed
soaps disclosed its surprising edge of beauty that she felt cut off
from grace. For the moment she passed—a stranger ape unde-
tected, the one unblushing pair of cheeks at the communion rail.
What danger did she run in this assembly of sparrows? What dis-
grace on any scale, except that of being the last girl chosen at
dancing class? She was only a closet pariah, and Philip was not
Trotsky in exile, just her married lover who happened to be a Jew.

Her ruminations had not stymied her social reflexes. She found
she had been smiling and ladling punch for the Sudbury Yearbook

Board—Jane Bourne, Elf Howland, and Daphne Piper. Subliminally it had penetrated that they were clubbing together to buy Pookie a dishwashing machine.

"She won't mind an i.o.u.," said Daphne, "I mean she wouldn't, would she?"

"We have to write down a particular brand," said Jane, "or they have to be rinsed first."

"Look at Lally's mother's; all she uses it for is a sterilizer," said Elf.

"Kitchen-Aid," said Ferry, who was conscious again and fully camouflaged, "some models do pots."

The hum of female voices rose higher. Twenty girls and matrons were magnetized one by one and two by two, through the living-room and back into the well-like, two-storied foyer, attracted to the white damask altar and its cascade of satiny boxes, all green and gold and silver, and two stand-out shocking pinks. Propped up at the center was the Yearbook Board's promissory note, inside a creamy vellum envelope inscribed in Elf Howland's outsize cursive script. The presentation was about to begin.

Mrs. Cornish steered Pookie, walking duckfooted from stage-fright, toward the table. The bride-elect never chooses the packages herself, lest the donors take obscure offense at her order of selection. Lally stood by to do the honors, which was merciful, since she would have no scruples, in the interests of pace, at snatching an obdurate knot out of Pookie's awkward fingers.

She had no qualms, in the interests of drama, at tunneling deep in the glittering hoard—boxes tipping and skidding from her zeal —blind to an offering from the Grande Maison de Linge, indifferent to a crested coffer from Hubble and Pell.

Transfigured by malice, she rooted even deeper, working the unsteady boxes like a sleight-of-hand artist working a full deck of cards. In a moment of pure charisma she thrust both arms, up to the elbows, into the center, and brought forth Ferry's crackly paper hive. The whole violated heap lurched, shuddered, and caved in, packages colliding with a volley of clicks, settling slowly into layers after the tremor.

Lally raised the shape high for the eyes of the back row. It was coming unshrouded, shredding, leper-like, in her grip. Eighteen scalps prickled, and eighteen napes. Something very like scandal was afoot.

Ferry flashed beams of hate at Lally's head; she gouged Lally's eyes; she skewered her excited nostrils. Pookie faltered a half-step forward, or was pushed. Her arms hung dead at her sides.

"I'm insanely curious," said Lally, thrusting the package onto Pookie's bosom.

Still no reflexes showed in Pookie's arms, so Lally picked up one inert hand and applied it flat against the nursing cocoon. The fingers splayed wildly, then held on; the other hand rose normally, and began tearing.

Pookie tore evenly, conquering dread by sheer doggedness. In the hush the ripping paper was as loud as toast being chewed in front of strangers. One, two, three, sheets of tissue, lacy eyeleted strips of it, floated down around Pookie's ankles like discarded lingerie. Another sheet uncoiled. Now the cocoon was shadowy inside.

A golden fist punched its way out, followed by its doll-sized sparring mate. A knee fought through, Anstiss shrieked (the original eeeek), and Pookie keened, "I can't hold it, Lally, I can't hold it!"

Ferry lost patience. She pushed her way to ringside and caught the package sheer inches from the floor. She unswaddled it in three strokes, right there on the rug, while Mrs. Cornish planted herself square in the center of the front row, flinging her arms out to hold back the craning girls, like a policeman at the scene of a hit and run accident.

In his white tissue manger lay the boy-cherub, the chandelier-beams playing over his pouting mouth and his shell-shaped curls. Pookie forgot her shyness and crouched down beside Ferry.

"Oh, he's a valentine!" she glowed, holding him up for her friends to see. Smiles broke out on face after face, like lights strung on a staggered circuit. Delight trilled through the room, and Anstiss herself started the applause. Pookie held him at the waist and made him mime bow after bow. Every girl whistled and cheered and stamped, and linked arms in tomboy solidarity; and it was like the great day when Sudbury took the hockey cup from Walnut Hill, when they wore red bloomers and shinguards and high sneakers, and knew their strength, as amazons and kin.

RAGTIME

E. L. DOCTOROW

E. L. Doctorow was born in 1931 in New York City
and was educated at Kenyon College and Columbia
University. His earlier novels are *Welcome to Hard
Times* and *Big as Life*, and his most recent novel is
The Book of Daniel. Formerly editor-in-chief of a
New York publishing house, he was most recently
writer-in-residence at the University of California at
Irvine. He lives in Westchester County with his wife
and three children.

I live in a house that was built in 1906. It is a great ugly three-story
house with dormers, bay windows, and a screened porch. When
it was new the shingles were brown and striped awnings shaded
the windows. Teddy Roosevelt was president. Women were
stouter then. They visited the fleet carrying white parasols. Everyone wore white in summer. There was a lot of sexual fainting.
There were no Negroes. There were no immigrants. On Sunday
afternoon, after dinner, Mother and Father would go upstairs together and close their bedroom door. Grandfather fell asleep on
the divan in the parlor. The little boy in the sailor blouse sat on
the screened porch and waved away the flies. Down at the bottom
of the hill Mother's Younger Brother boarded the streetcar and
rode to the end of the line. This was an empty field of tall marsh
grasses. The air was salt. Mother's Younger Brother in his white
linen suit and boater rolled his trousers and walked barefoot in
the salt marshes. Seabirds started and flew up. This was the time
in our history when Winslow Homer was doing his painting. A
certain light was still available along the eastern seaboard. Homer
painted the light. It gave the sea a heavy dull menace and shone
coldly on the rocks and shoals of the New England coast. There

were unexplained shipwrecks and brave towline rescues. Odd
things went on in lighthouses and in shacks nestled in the wild
beach plum. Across America sex and death were barely distinguishable. Runaway women died in the rigors of ecstasy. Stories were
hushed up and reporters paid off by rich families. One read between the lines of the journals and gazettes. In New York City
the papers were full of the shooting of the famous architect Stanford White by Harry K. Thaw, eccentric scion of a coke and railroad fortune. Harry K. Thaw was the husband of Evelyn Nesbit,
the celebrated beauty who had once been Stanford White's mistress. The shooting took place in the roof garden of the Madison
Square Garden on 26th Street, a spectacular block-long building
of yellow brick and terra-cotta that White himself had designed
in the Sevillian style. It was the opening night of a revue entitled
Mamzelle Champagne, and as the chorus sang and danced the eccentric scion, wearing on this summer night a straw boater and
heavy black coat, pulled out a pistol and shot the famous architect
three times in the head. On the roof. There were screams. Evelyn
fainted. She had been a well-known artist's model at the age of 15.
Her underclothes were white. Her husband habitually whipped
her. She happened once to meet Emma Goldman, the revolution-
ary. Goldman lashed her with her tongue. Apparently there *were*
Negroes. There *were* immigrants. And though the newspapers
called the shooting the Crime of the Century, Goldman knew it
was only 1906 and there were 94 years to go.

At this time in history Jacob Riis, a tireless newspaper reporter
and reformer, wrote about the need of housing for the poor. They
lived too many to a room. There was no sanitation. The streets
reeked of shit. Children died of mild colds or slight rashes. Children died on beds made from two kitchen chairs pushed together.
They died on floors. Many people believed that filth and starva-
tion and disease were what the immigrant got for his moral de-
generacy. But Riis believed in air shafts. Air shafts, light and air,
would bring health. He went around climbing dark stairs and
knocking on doors and taking flash photos of indigent families in
their dwellings. He held up the flash pan and put his head under
the hood and a picture exploded. After he left, the family, not daring to move, remained in the position in which they had been
photographed. They waited for life to change. They waited for

their transformation. Riis made color maps of Manhattan's ethnic populations. Dull gray was for Jews, their favorite color, he said. Red was for the swarthy Italian. Blue for the thrifty German. Black for the African. Green for the Irishman. And yellow for the cat-clean Chinaman, a cat also in his traits of cruel cunning and savage fury when aroused. Add dashes of color for Finns, Arabs, Greeks, and so on, and you have a crazy quilt, Riis cried, a crazy quilt of humanity!

One day Riis decided to interview Stanford White, the eminent architect. He wanted to ask White if he'd ever designed housing for the poor. He wanted his ideas on public housing, on air shafts, on light. He found White down at the docks looking at arriving shipments of architectural furnishings. Riis marveled at what was coming out of the holds of the ships: whole facades of Florentine palaces and Athenian atria, stone by marked stone; paintings, statuary, tapestries, carved and painted ceilings in crates, tiled patios, marble fountains, marble stairs and balustrades, parqueted floors and silk wall panels; cannon, pennants, suits of armor, crossbows and other ancient weaponry; beds, armoires, chaises, refectory tables, sideboards, harpsichords; barrels of glassware, silver, gold plate, porcelain and china; boxes of church ornaments, boxes of rare books, snuffboxes. White, a robust burly man with reddish brush-cut hair turning gray, went about smacking the backs of the handlers with his rolled-up umbrella. Careful you fools! he shouted. Riis had wanted to ask him his questions. Housing for the poor was Riis's story. But he had a vision of the dismantling of Europe, the uncluttering of ancient lands, the birth of a new aesthetic in European art and architecture. He himself was a Dane.

That evening White went to the opening night of *Mamzelle Champagne* at the roof garden at Madison Square. This was early in the month of June and by the end of the month a serious heat wave had begun to kill infants all over the slums. The tenements glowed like furnaces and the tenants had no water to drink. The sink at the bottom of the stairs was dry. Fathers raced through the streets looking for ice. Tammany Hall had been destroyed by reformers but the hustlers on the ward still cornered the ice supply and sold little chips of it at exorbitant prices. Pillows were placed on the sidewalks. Families slept on stoops and in doorways. Horses collapsed and died in the streets. The Department of Sanitation sent drays around the city to drag away horses that had died. But it was not an efficient service. Horses exploded in the heat. Their exposed intestines heaved with rats. And up through the slum alleys, through the gray clothes hanging listlessly on lines strung across air shafts, rose the smell of fried fish.

The death of Stanford White caused Evelyn Nesbit to revise her daily appointment book. She had now to devote herself to the rehearsal of the testimony she would give in her husband's forthcoming trial. She had not only to deal with Thaw in her almost daily visits to the Tombs, the city jail where he was kept, but with his lawyers, of whom there were several, with his mother, a regal Pittsburgh dowager who despised her, and with her own mother, whose greediest dreams of connived wealth she had surpassed. The press followed her every move. She tried to live quietly in a small residential hotel. She tried not to think how Stanford White looked with his face shot away. She had not been surprised by the shooting. She took her meals in her rooms. She rehearsed her lines. She retired early believing that sleep would improve her skin tone. She was bored. She ordered clothes from her dressmaker. The key to the defense of Harry K. Thaw would be that he had become temporarily deranged by the story she had told him about her ruination at the age of 15. At the time she was an artist's model and aspiring actress. Stanford White had invited her to his apartments in the tower of Madison Square Garden and offered her champagne. The champagne was drugged. When she woke up the following morning the effulgence of White's manhood lay over her thighs like a baker's glaze.

But it was going to be difficult to persuade a jury that Harry K. Thaw became deranged only upon the telling of that tale. He was a violent man who all his life had created incidents in restaurants. He drove cars up sidewalks. He was suicidal and had once consumed an entire bottle of laudanum. He had a habit of clenching his fists and beating them against his temples. He was imperious, possessive, and insanely jealous. Before they were married he had concocted a scheme whereby Evelyn was to sign an affidavit accusing Stanford White of beating her. She refused and told White about it. Harry's next move was to take her to Europe where he could have her without worrying if White was to have his turn when he was through. Her mother went along as chaperone. They

sailed on the *Kronzprincessin Cecile*. In Southampton Harry paid
off Evelyn's mother and took Evelyn alone to the Continent.
Eventually they arrived at an ancient mountain castle in Austria
that Harry had rented—the Schloss Katzenstein. Their first night
in the schloss, he pulled off her robe, threw her across the bed, and
applied a dog whip to her buttocks and the backs of her thighs.
Her shrieks echoed down the corridors and stone stairwells. The
German servants in their quarters listened, grew flushed, opened
bottles of goldwasser, and copulated. Shocking red welts disfigured
Evelyn's flesh. She cried and whimpered all night. In the morning Harry returned to her room, this time with a razor strop. She
was bedridden for weeks. During her convalescence he brought
her stereopticon slides of the Black Forest and the Austrian Alps.
He was gentle when he made love to her and mindful of the tender
places. Nevertheless she decided their relationship had gone beyond its tacit understanding. She demanded to be sent home. She
sailed back to America alone on the *Carmania*, her mother having
long since returned. When she reached New York she immediately
went to see Stanford White and told him what had happened.
She showed him the traces of a laceration across the flesh of the
inside of her right thigh. Oh my, oh my, Stanford White said. He
kissed the spot. She showed him a tiny yellow and purple discolora-
tion on the face of her left buttock where it curved toward the
cleft. How awful, Stanford White said. He kissed the spot. The
following morning he sent her to a lawyer who prepared an affidavit as to what happened in the Schloss Katzenstein. Evelyn
signed the affidavit. Now darling, when Harry comes home you
show him that, Stanny White said, smiling broadly. She followed
his instructions. Harry K. Thaw read the affidavit, turned pale,
and immediately proposed marriage. She had only been in the
chorus but she had done as well as any of the Floradora girls.

And now Harry, in jail, was on public display. His cell was on
Murderer's Row, the top tier of the cavernous Tombs. Each eve-
ning the guards brought him the papers so that he could follow
his favorite team, the Pittsburgh Nationals, and their star Honus
Wagner. Only when he had read about the ball games would he
read about himself. He went through every paper—the *World*, the
Tribune, the *Times*, the *Evening Post*, the *Journal*, the *Herald*.
When he finished reading a paper he would fold it up, stand at

the bars, and flip it over the rail of the cellblock promenade so that
it came apart, fluttering in pieces six stories down through the central vault, or well, around which the cellblock tiers were arranged.
His behavior fascinated the guards. It was seldom they had people of this class. Thaw was not really fond of the jail fare so they
brought in his meals from Delmonico's. He liked to feel clean so
they passed along a change of clothes delivered each morning to
the jail doors by his valet. He disliked Negroes so they made sure
no Negro prisoner was lodged near his cell. Thaw was not un-
mindful of the guards' kindnesses. He showed his gratitude not
discreetly but with impeccable style, crumpling and tossing $20
bills at his feet and telling them what swine they were as they
stooped to retrieve the money. They were very happy. Reporters
asked their views when they left the Tombs at the end of a shift.
And each afternoon when Evelyn arrived looking crisp in her high-
collared shirtwaist and pleated linen skirt, the husband and wife
would be permitted to stroll back and forth across the Bridge of
Sighs, the iron catwalk that connected the Tombs with the Criminal Courts building. Thaw walked with a dipping, pigeon-toed
gait, as someone with brain damage. He had the wide mouth and
doll eyes of a Victorian closet queen. Sometimes they saw him
gesticulate wildly while Evelyn stood with her head bowed, her
face in shadow under her hat. Sometimes he would ask for use of
the consultation room. The guard whose station was just outside
the consultation room door with its small porthole window
claimed that Thaw sometimes cried and sometimes he held Evelyn's hand. Sometimes he paced back and forth and beat his fists
against his temples while she gazed through the barred window.
Once he demanded proof of her devotion and it turned out nothing else would do but a fellatio. Abutted by Thaw's belly Evelyn's
broad-brimmed hat with its topping of dried flowers in tulle slowly
tore away from her coiffure. Afterward he brushed the sawdust
from the front of her skirt and gave her some bills from his money
clip.

Evelyn told reporters who met her outside the Tombs that her
husband Harry K. Thaw was innocent. His trial will prove my husband Harry K. Thaw is innocent, she said one day stepping into
the electric hansom provided her by her august mother-in-law.
The chauffeur closed the door. In the privacy of the car she wept.
She knew better than anyone how innocent Harry was. She had

agreed to testify in his behalf for the sum of $200,000. And her price for a divorce was going to be even higher. She ran her fingertips over the car upholstery. Her tears dried. A strange bitter exaltation suffused her, a cold victory grin of the heart. She had grown up playing in the streets of a Pennsylvania coal town. She was the Gaudens statue Stanny White had put at the top of the tower of Madison Square Garden, a glorious bronze nude Diana standing on her toes, her face in the skies.

Coincidentally this was the time in our history when the morose novelist Theodore Dreiser was suffering terribly from the bad reviews and negligible sales of his first book, *Sister Carrie*. Dreiser was out of work, broke, and too ashamed to see anyone. He rented a furnished room in Brooklyn and went to live there. He took to sitting on a wooden chair in the middle of the room. One day he decided his chair was facing in the wrong direction. Raising his weight from the chair, he lifted it with his two hands and turned it to the right, to align it properly. For a moment he thought the chair was aligned, but then he decided it was not. So he moved it another turn to the right. He tried sitting in the chair now but it still felt peculiar. He turned it again. Eventually he made a complete circle and still he could not find the proper alignment for the chair. The light faded on the dirty window of the furnished room. Through the night Dreiser turned his chair in circles seeking the proper alignment.

But the impending Thaw trial was not the only excitement down at the Tombs. Two of the guards in their spare time had fashioned new leg-irons that they claimed were better than the standard equipment. To prove it, they challenged Harry Houdini himself to put them to the test. At this time Houdini, the escape artist, was a headliner in the top vaudeville circuits. Houdini always filled the house but never with the likes of a Stanford White or a Harry K. Thaw. His audiences were poor people—peddlers, hod carriers, policemen, children. His life was absurd. He went all over the world accepting all kinds of bondage and escaping. He was roped to a chair. He escaped. He was chained to a ladder. He escaped. He was handcuffed, his legs were put in irons, he was tied up in a straitjacket and put in a locked cabinet. He escaped. He escaped from bank vaults, nailed-up barrels, sewn mailbags; he escaped from a zinc-lined Knabe piano case, a giant football, a galvanized iron boiler, a roll-top desk, a sausage skin. His escapes were mystifying because he never damaged or appeared to unlock what he escaped from. The screen was pulled away and there he stood disheveled but triumphant beside the inviolate container that was supposed to have contained him. He waved to the crowd. He escaped from a sealed milk can filled with water. He escaped from a Siberian exile van. From a Chinese torture crucifix. From a Hamburg penitentiary. From an English prison ship. From a Boston jail. He was chained to automobile tires, waterwheels, cannon, and he escaped. He dove manacled from a bridge into the Mississippi, the Seine, the Mersey, and came up waving. He hung upside down and straitjacketed from cranes, biplanes, and the tops of buildings. He was dropped into the ocean padlocked in a diving suit fully weighted and not connected to an air supply, and he escaped. He was buried alive in a grave and could not escape, and had to be rescued. Hurriedly they dug him out. The earth is too heavy, he said gasping. His nails bled. Soil fell from his eyes. He was drained of color and couldn't stand. His wife wept. His assistant threw up. Houdini wheezed and sputtered. He coughed blood. They cleaned him off and took him back to the hotel. Today, nearly 50 years since his death, the audience for escapes is even larger.

The great magician arrived one morning at the office of the warden of the Tombs and was photographed shaking the hand of the warden and standing between the two smiling guards with his arms around their shoulders. He traded quips with reporters. He gave out lots of free tickets. He held the leg-irons under the light and examined them carefully. He accepted the challenge. He would escape from the irons at the following night's performance at the Keith Hippodrome. With the press crowded around, Houdini now proposed his own challenge: that then and there he be stripped and locked in a cell and his clothing placed outside the cell: and if everyone would then leave he would contrive to escape from the cell and appear fully dressed in the warden's office within five minutes. The warden demurred. Houdini professed astonishment. After all he, Houdini, had accepted the guards' challenge without hesitation: was the warden not confident of his own jail? The reporters took Houdini's side. Knowing what the newspapers could do with his refusal to go along with the stunt, the warden gave in. He believed in fact his cells were secure. The walls of his office were pale green. Photographs of his wife and his mother stood on his desk. A humidor with cigars and a decanter of Irish whiskey stood on a table behind his desk. He picked up his new phone and holding the shaft in one hand and the earpiece with the other he looked significantly at the reporters.

A while later Houdini was led, stark naked, up the six flights of stairs to Murderer's Row on the top tier of the jail. There were fewer inhabitants on this tier and the cells were believed to be escape proof. The guards locked Houdini in an empty cell. They placed his clothing in a neat pile on the promenade outside the cell, beyond his reach. Then the guards and the accompanying reporters withdrew and, as they agreed, went back to the warden's office. Houdini carried in various places on his person small steel wires and bits of spring steel. This time he ran his palm along the sole of his foot and extracted from a slot in the callous of his left heel a strip of metal about a quarter inch wide and one and a half inches long. From his thick hair he withdrew a piece of stiff wire that he fitted around the strip of metal as a handle. He stuck his hand through the bars, inserted the makeshift key in the lock, and twisted it slowly clockwise. The cell door swung open. At that moment Houdini realized that across the vault of gloom the cell directly opposite was lighted and occupied. A prisoner sat there staring at him. The prisoner had a broad flat face with a porcine nose, a wide mouth, and eyes that seemed unnaturally bright and large. He had coarse hair combed back from an oddly crescent hairline. Houdini, a vaudevillian, thought of the face of a ventriloquist's dummy. The prisoner was sitting at a table laid with linen and service. On the table were the remains of a large meal. An empty bottle of champagne was stuck upside down in a cooler. The iron cot was covered with a quilted spread and throw pillows. A regency armoire stood against the stone wall. The ceiling fixture had been ornamented with a Tiffany lampshade. Houdini could not help staring. The prisoner's cell glowed like a stage in the perpetual dusk of the cavernous prison. The prisoner stood up and waved, a stately gesture, and his wide mouth offered the trace of a smile. Quickly Houdini began to dress. He put on his briefs, his trousers, his socks and garters and shoes. Across the well the prisoner began to undress. Houdini put on his undershirt, his shirt, his collar. He tied his tie and set the stickpin. He snapped his suspenders in place and pulled on his jacket. The prisoner was now as naked as Houdini had been. The prisoner came up to the front of his cell and raising his arms in a shockingly obscene manner he thrust his hips forward and flapped his penis between the bars. Houdini rushed down the promenade, fumblingly unlocked the cellblock door, and closed it behind him.

Houdini was to tell no one of this strange confrontation. He went through the celebrations of his jailhouse feat in an uncharacteristically quiet, even subdued, manner. Not even the lines at the box office following the stories in the evening papers could cheer him up. Escaping from the leg-irons in two minutes gave him no pleasure at all. Days passed before he realized that the grotesque mimic on Murderer's Row had to have been the killer Harry K. Thaw. People who did not respond to his art profoundly distressed Houdini. He had come to realize they were invariably of the upper classes. Always they broke through the pretense of his life and made him feel foolish. Houdini had high inchoate ambition and every development in technology made him restless. On the shabby confines of a stage he could create wonder and awe. Meanwhile men were beginning to take planes into the air, or race automobiles that went 60 miles an hour. A man like Roosevelt had run at the Spanish on San Juan Hill and now sent a fleet of white battleships steaming around the world, battleships as white as his teeth. The wealthy knew what was important. They looked on him as a child or a fool. Yet his self-imposed training, his dedication to the perfection of what he did, reflected an American ideal. He kept himself as trim as an athlete. He did not smoke or drink. Pound for pound he was as strong as any man he had ever run up against. He could tighten his stomach muscles and with a smile invite anyone at all to punch him there as hard as they liked. He was immensely muscular and agile and professionally courageous. Yet to the wealthy all this was nothing.

New in Houdini's act was an escape in which he released himself from an office safe and then opened the safe to reveal, handcuffed, the assistant who had been onstage a moment before. It was a great success. One evening after the performance Houdini's manager told him of being called by Mrs. Stuyvesant Fish of 78th Street, who wanted to book Houdini for a private party. Mrs. Fish was one of the 400. She was famous for her wit. Once she had given a ball at which everyone had to talk baby talk. Mrs. Fish was throwing a commemorative ball in honor of her friend the late Stanford White, the architect of her home. He had designed her home in the style of a doge's palace. A doge was the chief magistrate in the republic of Genoa or Venice. I won't have nothing to do with those people, Houdini told his manager. Dutifully the manager reported to Mrs. Fish that Houdini was not available. She doubled the fee. The ball was held on a Monday evening. It was the first big event of the new season. At about 9 o'clock Houdini drove up in a hired Pierce-Arrow. He was accompanied by his manager and his assistant. Behind the car was a truck carrying Houdini's equipment. The entourage was shown to the trade entrance.

Unknown to Houdini, Mrs. Stuyvesant Fish had also engaged for the evening the entire sideshow of the Barnum and Bailey circus. She liked to shock fuddy-duddies. He was led into some sort of waiting room where he found himself encircled by a mob of freaks all of whom had heard of him and wanted to touch him. Creatures with scaled iridescent skins and hands attached to their shoulders, midgets with the voices of telephones, Siamese twin sisters who leaned in opposite directions, a man who lifted weights from iron rings permanently attached to his breasts. Houdini removed his cape and his top hat and his white gloves and handed them to his assistant. He slumped in a chair. His grips were waiting for instructions. The freaks yattered at him.

But the room itself was very beautiful, with carved wood ceilings and Flemish tapestries of Actaeon being torn apart by dogs.

Early in his career Houdini had worked in a small circus in western Pennsylvania. He recalled his loyalties now in order to regain his composure. One of the midgets, a woman, separated herself from the rest and got everyone to step back a few paces. She turned out to be the eminent Lavinia Warren, the widow of General Tom Thumb, the most famous midget of all. Lavinia Warren Thumb was dressed in a magnificent gown supplied by Mrs. Fish: it was supposed to be a joke on Mrs. Fish's nemesis, Mrs. William Astor, who had worn the identical design the previous spring. Lavinia Thumb was coiffed in the Astor manner and wore glittering copies of the Astor jewels. She was nearly 70 years old and carried herself with dignity. Upon her wedding 50 years before, she and Colonel Thumb had been received in the White House by the Lincolns.

Houdini wanted to cry. Lavinia was no longer working in the circus but she had come down to New York from her home in Bridgeport, a clapboard house with escalloped bargeboards and a widow's walk, which cost something to maintain. That was why she had taken this evening's job. She lived in Bridgeport to be near the grave of her husband who had died many years before and was commemorated in stone atop a monumental column in Mountain Grove Cemetery. Lavinia was two feet tall. She came to Houdini's knees. Her voice had deepened with age and she now spoke in the tones of a normal 20-year-old girl. She had sparkling blue eyes, silver white hair, and the finest of wrinkles on her clear white skin. Houdini was reminded of his mother. Come on kid, do a couple of numbers for us, Lavinia said.

Houdini entertained the circus folk with sleight of hand and some simple tricks. He put a billiard ball in his mouth, closed his mouth, opened it, and the billiard ball was gone. He closed his mouth and opened it again and removed the billiard ball. He stuck an ordinary sewing needle into his cheek and pulled it through the inner side. He opened his hand and produced a live chick. He withdrew from his ear a stream of colored silk. The freaks were delighted. They applauded and laughed. When he felt he had discharged his responsibilities, Houdini rose and told his manager he would not perform for Mrs. Stuyvesant Fish. There were remonstrations. Houdini stormed out the door. Crystal light dazzled his eyes. He was in the grand ballroom of the doge's palace. A string orchestra played from a balcony. Great pale red drapes framed the clerestory windows and 400 people were waltzing on a marble floor. Shading his eyes, he saw bearing down on him Mrs. Fish herself, a clutch of jeweled feathers rising from her piled hair, ropes of pearl swinging pendulously from her neck, a witticism forming on her lips like the bubbles of an epileptic.

Despite such experiences Houdini never developed what we think of as a political consciousness. He could not reason from his own hurt feelings. To the end he would be almost totally unaware of the design of his career, the great map of revolution laid out by his life. He was a Jew. His real name was Ehrich Weiss. He was passionately in love with his ancient mother whom he had installed in his brownstone home on West 113th Street. In fact, Sigmund Freud had just arrived in America to give a series of lectures at Clark University in Worcester, Massachusetts, and so Houdini

was destined to be, with Al Jolson, the last of the great shameless
mother lovers, a 19th-century movement that included such men
as Poe, John Brown, Lincoln, and James McNeill Whistler. Of
course Freud's immediate reception in America was not auspi-
cious. A few professional alienists understood his importance, but
to most of the public he appeared as some kind of German sexolo-
gist, an exponent of free love who used big words to talk about
dirty things. At least a decade would have to pass before Freud
would have his revenge and see his ideas begin to destroy sex in
America forever.

Freud arrived in New York on the Lloyd liner *George Washington*. He was accompanied by his disciples Jung and Ferenczi, both
some years his junior. They were met at the dock by two more
younger Freudians, Drs. Ernest Jones and A. A. Brill. The entire
party dined at Hammerstein's Roof Garden. There were potted
palms. A piano violin duo played Liszt's "Hungarian Rhapsody."
Everyone talked around Freud, glancing at him continuously to
gauge his mood. He ate cup custard. Brill and Jones undertook to
play hosts for the visit. In the days following they showed Freud
Central Park, the Metropolitan Museum, and Chinatown. Cat-
like Chinamen gazed at them out of dark shops. There were glass
cabinets filled with litchi nuts. The party went to one of the silent
films so popular in stores and nickelodeons around the city. White
smoke rose from the barrels of rifles and men wearing lipstick and
rouge fell backward clutching their chests. At least, Freud thought,
it is silent. What oppressed him about the New World was its
noise. The terrible clatter of horses and wagons, the clanking and
screeching of streetcars, the horns of automobiles. At the wheel
of an open Marmon, Brill drove the Freudians around Manhattan.
At one point, on Fifth Avenue, Freud felt as if he was being observed; raising his eyes, he found some children staring down at
him from the top of a double-decker bus.

Brill drove the party down to the Lower East Side with its Yiddish theaters and pushcarts and elevated trains. The fearsome elevated rumbled past the windows of tenements in which people
were expected to live. The windows shook, the very buildings
shook. Freud had to relieve himself and nobody seemed to be able
to tell him where a public facility could be found. They all had
to enter a dairy restaurant and order sour cream with vegetables

so that Freud could go to the bathroom. Later, back in the car, they pulled up to a corner to watch a street artist at work, an old man who with nothing but a scissors and paper made miniature silhouette portraits for a few cents. Standing for her portrait was a beautiful well-dressed woman. The excitable Ferenczi, masking his admiration for the woman's good looks, declared to his colleagues in the car his happiness at finding the ancient art of silhouette flourishing on the streets of the New World. Freud, clamping his teeth on his cigar, said nothing. The motor idled. Only Jung noticed the little girl in the pinafore standing slightly behind the young woman and holding her hand. The little girl peeked at Jung and the shaven-headed Jung, who was already disagreeing on certain crucial matters with his beloved mentor, looked through his thick steel-rimmed spectacles at the lovely child and experienced what he realized was a shock of recognition, although at the moment he could not have explained why. Brill pressed the gear pedal and the party continued on its tour. Their ultimate destination was Coney Island, a long way out of the city. They arrived in the late afternoon and immediately embarked on a tour of the three great amusement parks, beginning with Steeplechase and going on to Dreamland and finally late at night to the towers and domes, outlined in electric bulbs, of Luna Park. The dignified visitors rode the shoot-the-chutes and Freud and Jung took a boat together through the Tunnel of Love. The day came to a close only when Freud tired and had one of the fainting fits that had lately plagued him when in Jung's presence. A few days later the entire party arrived in Worcester for Freud's lectures. When the lectures were completed, Freud was persuaded to make an expedition to the great natural wonder of Niagara Falls. They arrived at the falls on an overcast day. Thousands of newly married couples stood, in pairs, watching the great cascades. Mist like an inverted rain rose from the falls. There was a high wire strung from one shore to the other and some maniac in ballet slippers and tights was walking the high wire, keeping his balance with a parasol. Freud shook his head. Later the party went to the Cave of Winds. There, at an underground footbridge, a guide motioned the others back and took Freud's elbow. Let the old fellow go first, the guide said. The great doctor, age 53, decided at this moment that he had had enough of America. With his disciples he sailed back to Germany on the *Kaiser Wilhelm der*

Grosse. He had not really gotten used to the food or the scarcity of American public facilities. He believed the trip had ruined both his stomach and his bladder. The entire population seemed to him overpowering, brash, and rude. The vulgar wholesale appropriation of European art and architecture regardless of period or country he found appalling. He sat in his quiet cozy study in Vienna, glad to be back. He said to Ernest Jones, America is a mistake, a gigantic mistake.

At the time of course not a few people on these shores were ready to agree with him. Millions of men were out of work. Those fortunate enough to have jobs were dared to form unions. Courts enjoined them, police busted their heads, their leaders were jailed, and new men took their jobs. A union was an affront to God. The laboring man would be protected and cared for not by the labor agitators, said one wealthy man, but by the Christian men whom God in His infinite wisdom had given the control of the property interests of this country. If all else failed, the troops were called out. Armories rose in every city of the country. In the coal fields a miner made $1.60 a day if he could dig three tons. He lived in the company's shacks and bought his food from the company stores. On the tobacco farms Negroes stripped tobacco leaves 13 hours a day and earned six cents an hour, man, woman, or child. Children suffered no discriminatory treatment. They were valued everywhere they were employed. They did not complain as adults tended to do. Employers liked to think of them as happy elves. If there was a problem about employing children, it had to do only with their endurance. They were more agile than adults but they tended in the later hours of the day to lose a degree of efficiency. In the canneries and mills these were the hours they were most likely to lose their fingers or have their hands mangled or their legs crushed. So they had to be counseled to stay alert. In the mines they worked as sorters of coal and sometimes were smothered in the coal chutes. So they were warned to keep their wits about them. One hundred Negroes a year were lynched. One hundred miners were burned alive. One hundred children were mutilated. There seemed to be quotas for these things. There seemed to be quotas for death by starvation. There were oil trusts and banking trusts and railroad trusts and beef trusts and steel trusts. It became fashionable to honor the poor. At palaces in New York

and Chicago people gave poverty balls. Guests came dressed in
rags and ate from tin plates and drank from chipped mugs. Ball-
rooms were decorated to look like mines with beams, iron tracks,
and miners' lamps. Theatrical scenery firms were hired to make
outdoor gardens look like dirt farms and dining rooms like cotton
mills. Guests smoked cigar butts offered to them on silver trays.
Minstrels performed in black face. One hostess invited everyone
to a stockyard ball. Guests were wrapped in long aprons and their
heads covered with white caps. They dined and danced while
hanging carcasses of bloody beef trailed around the walls on moving pulleys. Entrails spilled on the floor. The proceeds were for
charity.

OVER BY THE RIVER

William Maxwell was born in Lincoln, Illinois, and finished his growing up in Chicago. He joined the editorial
staff of *The New Yorker* in 1936 and has been there
ever since. He has published five novels, of which the
best known is *The Folded Leaf*; he has also published
a collection of stories, a family memoir, and a book for
children.

The sun rose somewhere in the middle of Queens, the exact moment of its appearance shrouded in uncertainty because of a cloud
bank. The lights on the bridges went off, and so did the red light
in the lantern of the lighthouse at the north end of Welfare Island. Seagulls settled on the water. A newspaper truck went from
building to building dropping off heavy bundles of, for the most
part, bad news, which little boys carried inside on their shoulders.
Doormen smoking a pipe and dressed for a walk in the country
came to work after a long subway ride and disappeared into the
service entrances. When they reappeared, by way of the front elevator, they had put on with their uniforms a false amiability and
were prepared for eight solid hours to make conversation about
the weather. With the morning sun on them, the apartment buildings far to the west, on Lexington Avenue, looked like an orange
mesa. The pigeons made bubbling noises in their throats as they
strutted on windowsills high above the street.

All night long, there had been plenty of time. Now suddenly
there wasn't, and this touched off a chain explosion of alarm
clocks, though in some instances the point was driven home without a sound: Time is interior to animals as well as exterior. A bare
arm with a wristwatch on it emerged from under the covers and
turned until the dial was toward the light from the windows.

"What time is it?"

"Ten after."

"It's always ten after," Iris Carrington said despairingly, and turned over in bed and shut her eyes against the light. Also against the clamor of her desk calendar: *Tuesday 11, L. 3:30 Dr. de Santillo . . . 5:30—7:30? . . . Wednesday 1:45, Mrs. McIntosh speaks on the changing status of women. 3:30 Dr. F . . . Friday 11C. Get Albertha . . . Saturday, call Mrs. Stokes. Ordering pads. L ballet 10:30. 2 Laurie to Sasha's. Remaining books due at library. Explore dentists. Supper at 5. Call Margot . . .*

Several minutes passed.

"Oh my God, I don't think I can make it," George Carrington said, and put his feet over the side of the bed, and found he could make it, after all. He could bend over and pick up his bathrobe from the floor, and put it on, and find his slippers, and close the window, and turn on the radiator valve. Each act was easier than the one before. He went back to the bed and drew the covers closer around his wife's shoulders.

Yawning, stretching, any number of people got up and started the business of the day. Turning on the shower. Dressing. Putting their hair up in plastic curlers. Squeezing toothpaste out of tubes that were all but empty. Squeezing orange juice. Separating strips of bacon.

The park keepers unlocked the big iron gates that closed the river walk off between Eighty-third and Eighty-fourth Streets. A taxi coming from Doctors Hospital was snagged by a doorman's whistle. The wind picked up the dry filth under the wheels of parked cars and blew it now this way, now that. A child got into an orange minibus and started on the long, devious ride to nursery school and social adjustment.

"Have you been a good girl?" George inquired lovingly, through the closed door of the unused extra maid's room, where the dog slept on a square of carpet. Puppy had not been a good girl. There was a puddle of urine—not on the open newspaper he had left for her, just in case, but two feet away from it, on the black-and-white plastic-tile floor. Her tail quivering with apology, she watched while he mopped the puddle up and disposed of the wet newspaper in the garbage can in the back hall. Then she followed him through the apartment to the foyer, and into the elevator when it came.

There were signs all along the river walk:

> No Dogs
> No Bicycles
> No This
> No That

He ignored them with a clear conscience. If he curbed the dog beforehand, there was no reason not to turn her loose and let her run—except that sometimes she stopped and arched her back a second time. When shouting and waving his hands didn't discourage her from moving her bowels, he took some newspaper from a trash container and cleaned up after her.

At the flagpole, he stood looking out across the river. The lights went off all the way up the airplane beacon, producing an effect of silence—as if somebody had started to say something and then decided not to. The tidal current was flowing south. He raised his head and sniffed, hoping for a breath of the sea, and smelled gasoline fumes instead.

Coming back, the dog stopped to sniff at trash baskets, at cement copings, and had to be restrained from greeting the only other person on the river walk—a grey-haired man who jogged there every morning in a gym suit and was afraid of dogs. He smiled pleasantly at George, and watched Puppy out of the corner of his eyes, so as to be ready when she leapt at his throat.

A tanker, freshly painted, all yellow and white, and flying the flag of George had no idea what country until he read the lettering on the stern, overtook him, close in to shore—so close he could see the captain talking to a sailor in the wheelhouse. To be sailing down the East River on a ship that was headed for open water . . . He waved to them and they waved back, but they didn't call out to him *Come on, if you want to,* and it was too far to jump. It came to him with the seriousness of a discovery that there was no place in the world he would not like to see. Concealed in this statement was another that he had admitted to himself for the first time only recently. There were places he would never see, experiences of the first importance that he would never have. He might die without ever having heard a nightingale.

When they stepped out of the elevator, the dog hurried off to the kitchen to see if there was something in her dish she didn't know about, and George settled down in the living room with the

Times on his lap and waited for a glass of orange juice to appear at his place at the dining-room table. The rushing sound inside the walls, as of an underground river, was Iris running her bath. The orange juice was in no hurry to get to the dining-room table. Iris had been on the phone daily with the employment agency and for the moment this was the best they could offer: twenty-seven years old, pale, with dirty blond hair, unmarried, overattached to her mother, and given to burning herself on the antiquated gas stove. She lived on tea and cigarettes. Breakfast was all the cooking she was entrusted with; Iris did the rest. Morning after morning his boiled egg was hard enough to take on a picnic. A blind man could not have made a greater hash of half a grapefruit. The coffee was indescribable. After six weeks there was a film of grease over everything in the kitchen. Round, jolly, neat, professionally trained, a marvellous cook, the mother was everything that is desirable in a servant except that, alas, she worked for somebody else. She drifted in and out of the apartment at odd hours, deluding Iris with the hope that some of her accomplishments would, if one were only patient, rub off on her daughter.

"Read," a voice said, bringing him all the way back from Outer Mongolia.

"Tonight, Cindy."

"Read! Read!"

He put the paper down and picked her up and when she had settled comfortably in his lap he began: " 'Emily was a guinea pig who loved to travel. Generally she stayed home and looked after her brother Arthur. But every so often she grew tired of cooking and mending and washing and ironing; the day would seem too dark, and the house too small, and she would have a great longing to set out into the distance. . . .' "

Looking down at the top of her head as he was reading, he felt an impulse to put his nose down and smell her hair. Born in a hurry she was. Born in one hell of a hurry, half an hour after her mother got to the hospital.

Laurie Carrington said, "What is the difference, what is the difference between a barber and a woman with several children?" Nobody answered, so she asked the question again.

"I give up," Iris said.

"Do you know, Daddy?"

"I give up too, we all give up."

"A barber . . . has razors to shave. And the woman has shavers to raise."

He looked at her over the top of his half-glasses, wondering what ancestor was responsible for that reddish-blond hair.

"That's a terribly funny one, Laurie," he said. "That's the best one yet," and his eyes reverted to the editorial page. A nagging voice inside his head informed him that a good father would be conversing intelligently with his children at the breakfast table. But about what? No intelligent subject of conversation occurred to him, perhaps because it was Iris's idea in the first place, not his.

He said, "Cindy, would you like a bacon sandwich?"

She thought, long enough for him to become immersed in the *Times* again, and then she said, "I would like a piece of bacon and a piece of toast. But not a bacon sandwich."

He dropped a slice of bread in the toaster and said, "Py-rozz-quozz-gill"—a magic word, from one of the Oz books. With a grinding noise the bread disappeared.

"Stupid Cindy," Laurie remarked, tossing her head. But Cindy wasn't fooled. Laurie used to be the baby and now she wasn't anymore. She was the oldest. And what she would have liked to be was the oldest *and* the baby. About lots of things she was very piggy. But she couldn't whistle. Try though she might, *whhih, whhih, whhih,* she couldn't. And Cindy could.

The toast emerged from the toaster and Iris said, "Not at the breakfast table, Cindy." The morning was difficult for her, clouded with amnesia, with the absence of energy, with the reluctance of her body to take on any action whatever. Straight lines curved unpleasantly, hard surfaces presented the look of softness. She saw George and the children and the dog lying at her feet under the table the way one sees rocks and trees and cottages at the seashore through the early-morning fog; just barely recognizable they were.

"Why is a church steeple—"

"My gloves," he said, standing in the front hall, with his coat on.

"They're in the drawer in the lowboy," Iris said.

"Why is a church steeple—"

"Not those," he said.

"Why is a—"

"Laurie, Daddy is talking. Look in the pocket of your chesterfield."

"I did."

"Yes, dear, why is a church steeple."

"Why is a church steeple like a maiden aunt?"

"I give up."

"Do you know, Daddy?"

"No. I've looked in every single one of my coats. They must be in my raincoat, because I can't find that either."

"Look in your closet."

"I did look there." But he went into the bedroom and looked again anyway. Then he looked all through the front-hall closet, including the mess on the top shelf.

Iris passed through the hall with her arms full of clothes for the washing machine. "Did you find your raincoat?" she asked.

"I must have left it somewhere," he said. "But where?"

He went back to the bedroom and looked in the engagement calendar on her desk, to see where they had been, and it appeared that they hadn't been anywhere.

"Where did we go when we had Albertha to babysit?"

"I don't remember."

"We had her two nights."

"Did we? I thought we only went out one night last week."

She began to make the bed. Beds—for it was not one large bed, as it appeared to be in the daytime, but twin beds placed against each other with a king-sized cotton spread covering them both. When they were first married they slept in a three-quarter bed from his bachelor apartment. In time this became a double bed, hard as a rock because of the horsehair mattress. Then it also proved to be too small. For he developed twitches. While he was falling asleep his body beside her would suddenly flail out, shaking the bed and waking her completely. Six or seven times this would happen. After which he would descend at last into a deep sleep and she would be left with insomnia. So now there were twin beds, and even then her bed registered the seismic disturbances in his, though nothing like so much.

"We went to that benefit. With Francis," she said.

"Oh . . . I think I did wear my raincoat that night. No, I wore the coat with the velvet collar."

"The cleaner's?"

"No."

"I don't see how you could have left your raincoat somewhere," she said. "I never see you in just a suit. Other men, yes, but never you."

He went into the hall and pulled open a drawer of the lowboy and took out a pair of grey gloves and drew them on. They had been his father's and they were good gloves but too small for him. His fingers had burst open the seams at the end of the fingers. Iris had mended them, but they would not stay sewed, and so he went to Brooks and bought a new pair—the pair he couldn't find.

"The Howards' dinner party?" he said.

"That was the week before. Don't worry about it," Iris said. "Cindy, what have you been doing?"—meaning hair full of snarls, teeth unbrushed, at twenty-five minutes past eight.

"It makes me feel queer not knowing where I've been," George said, and went out into the foyer and pressed the elevator button. From that moment, he was some other man. Their pictures were under his nose all day but he had stopped seeing them. He did not even remember that he had a family, until five o'clock, when he pushed his chair back from his desk, reached for his hat and coat, and came home, cheerfully unrepentant. She forgave him now because she did not want to deal with any failure, including his, until she had had her second cup of coffee. The coffee sat on the living-room mantelpiece, growing cold, while she brushed and braided Cindy's hair.

"Stand still! I'm not hurting you."

"You are too."

The arm would not go into the sweater, the leggings proved to be on backwards, one mitten was missing. And Laurie wild because she was going to be late for school.

The girls let the front door bang in spite of all that had been said on the subject, and in a moment the elevator doors opened to receive them. The quiet then was unbelievable. With the *Times* spread out on the coffee table in the living room, and holes in the Woman's Page where she had cut out recipes, she waited for her soul, which left her during the night, to return and take its place in her body. When this happened she got up suddenly and went into the bedroom and started telephoning: Bloomingdale's, Saks, the Maid-to-Order service, the children's school, the electrician, the pediatrician, the upholsterer—half the population of New York City.

Over the side of the bed Cindy went, eyes open, wide awake. In her woolly pyjamas with feet in them. Even though it was dark outside—the middle of the night—it was only half dark in the bedroom. There was a blue night-light in the wall plug by the doll's house, and a green night-light in the bathroom, beside the washbasin, and the door to the bathroom was partly open. The door to the hall was wide open and the hall light was on, but high up where it wasn't much comfort, and she had to pass the closed door of Laurie's room and the closed door to the front hall. Behind both these doors the dark was very dark, unfriendly, ready to spring out and grab her, and she would much rather have been back in her bed except it was not safe there either, so she was going for help.

When she got to the door at the end of the hall, she stood still, afraid to knock and afraid not to knock. Afraid to look behind her. Hoping the door would open by itself and it did. Her father—huge, in his pyjamas, with his hair sticking up and his face puffy with sleep. "Bad dream?" he asked.

Behind him the room was all dark except for a little light from the hall. She could see the big windows—just barely—and the great big bed, and her mother asleep under a mound of covers. And if she ran past him and got into the bed she would be safe, but it was not allowed. Only when she was sick. She turned and went back down the hall, without speaking but knowing that he would pick up his bathrobe and follow her and she didn't have to be brave anymore.

"What's Teddy doing on the floor?" he said, and pulled the covers up around her chin, and put his warm hand on her cheek. So nice to have him do this—to have him there, sitting on the edge of her bed.

"Can you tell me what you were dreaming about?"

"Tiger."

"Yes? Well that's too bad. Were you very frightened?"

"Yes."

"Was it a big tiger?"

"Yes."

"You know it was only a dream? It wasn't a real tiger. There aren't any tigers in New York City."

"In the zoo there are."

"Oh yes, but they're in cages and can't get out. Was this tiger out?"

"Yes."

"Then it couldn't have been a real tiger. Turn over and let me rub your back."

"If you rub my back I'll go to sleep."

"Good idea."

"If I go to sleep I'll dream about the tiger."

"I see. What do you want me to do?"

"Get in bed with me."

What with Teddy and Raggedy Ann and Baby Dear, and books to look at in the morning, and the big pillow and the little pillow, things were a bit crowded. He put his hand over his eyes to shut out the hall light and said, "Go to sleep," but she didn't, even though she was beginning to feel drowsy. She was afraid he was going to leave her—if not right this minute then pretty soon. He would sit up in bed and say *Are you all right now?* and she would have to say *Yes*, because that was what he wanted her to say. Sometimes she said no and they stayed a little longer, but they always went away in the end.

After a while, her eyes closed. After still another while, she felt the bed heave under her as he sat up. He got out of bed slowly and carefully and fixed the covers and put the little red chair by the bed so she wouldn't fall out. She tried to say *Don't go*, but nothing happened. The floorboards creaked under the carpeting as he crossed the room. In the doorway he turned and looked at her, one last look, and she opened her eyes wide so he would know she wasn't asleep, and he waved her a kiss, and that was the last of him, but it wasn't the last of her. Pretty soon, even though there wasn't a sound, she knew something was in the room. Hiding. It was either hiding behind the curtains or it was hiding in the toy closet or it was hiding behind the doll's house or it was behind the bathroom door or it was under the bed. But wherever it was it was being absolutely still, waiting for her to close her eyes and go to sleep. So she kept them open, even though her eyelids got heavier and heavier. She made them stay open. And when they closed she opened them again right afterward. She kept opening them as long as she could, and once she cried out *Laurie!* very loud, but in her mind only. There was no sound in the room.

The thing that was hiding didn't make any sound either, which made her think maybe it wasn't a tiger after all, because tigers have a terrible roar that they roar, but it couldn't have been anything else, for it had stripes and a tail and terrible teeth and eyes that were looking at her through the back of the little red chair. And her heart was pounding and the tiger knew this, and the only friend she had in the world was Teddy, and Teddy couldn't move, and neither could Raggy, and neither could she. But the tiger could move. He could do anything he wanted to except roar his terrible roar, because then the bedroom door would fly open and they would come running.

She looked at the tiger through the back of the little red chair, and the tiger looked at her, and finally it thrashed its tail once or twice and then went and put its head in the air-conditioner.

That isn't possible. . . . But it was. More and more of his body disappeared into the air-conditioner, and finally there was only his tail, and then only the tip of his tail, and when that was gone so was she.

The young policeman who stood all night on the corner of East End Avenue and Gracie Square, eight stories below, was at the phone box, having a conversation with the sergeant on the desk. This did not prevent him from keeping his eyes on an emaciated junkie who stood peering through the window of the drugstore, past the ice-cream bin, the revolving display of paperbacks, the plastic toys, hair sprays, hand creams, cleansing lotions, etc., at the prescription counter. The door had a grating over it but the plate-glass window did not. One good kick would do it. It would also bring the policeman running.

The policeman would have been happy to turn the junkie in, but he didn't have anything on him. Vagrancy? But suppose he had a home? And suppose it brought the Civil Liberties Union running? The policeman turned his back for a minute and when he looked again the junkie was gone, vanished, nowhere.

Though it was between three and four in the morning, people were walking their dogs in Carl Schurz Park. Amazing. Dreamlike. And the sign on the farther shore of the river that changed back and forth continually was enough to unhinge the mind: PEARL-WICK HAMPERS became BATHROOM HAMPERS, which in turn became

PEARLWICK HAMPERS, and sometimes for a fraction of a second
BATHWICK HAMPERS.

In the metal trash containers scattered here and there along
the winding paths of the park were pieces of waxed paper that had
been around food but nothing you could actually eat. The junkie
didn't go into the playground because the gates were locked and
it had a high iron fence around it. He could have managed this
easily by climbing a tree and dropping to the cement on the other
side. Small boys did it all the time. And maybe in there he would
have found something—a half-eaten Milky Way or Mounds bar
that a nursemaid had taken from a child with a finicky appetite—
but then he would have been locked in instead of out, and he knew
all there was to know about that: Sing Sing, Rikers Island, Au-
burn, Dannemora. His name is James Jackson, and he is a figure
out of a nightmare—unless you happen to know what happened
to him, the steady rain of blows about his unprotected head ever
since he was born, in which case it is human life that seems like a
nightmare. The dog walkers, supposing—correctly—that he had a
switchblade in his pocket and a certain amount of experience in
using it, chose a path that detoured around him. The wind was
out of the southeast and smelled of the sea, fifteen miles away on
the other side of Long Beach and Far Rockaway. The Hell Gate
section of the Triborough Bridge was a necklace of sickly-green
incandescent pearls. When the policeman left his post and took a
turn through the south end of the park, the junkie was sitting in-
nocently on a bench on the river walk. He was keeping the river
company.

And when the policeman got back to his post a woman in a long
red coat was going through the trash basket directly across the
street from him. She was harmless. He saw her night after night.
And in a minute she would cross over and tell him about the doctor at Bellevue who said she probably dreamed that somebody
picked the lock of her door while she was out buying coffee and
stole her mother's gold thimble.

The threads that bound the woman in the long red coat to a
particular address, to the family she had been born into, her husband's grave in the Brooklyn cemetery, and the children who never
wrote except to ask for money, had broken, and she was now free
to wander along the street, scavenging from trash containers. She
did not mind if people saw her, or feel that what she was doing

was in any way exceptional. When she found something useful or valuable, she stuffed it in her dirty canvas bag, the richer by a pair of sandals with a broken strap or a perfectly clean copy of "Sartor Resartus." What in the beginning was only an uncertainty, an uneasiness, a sense of the falsity of appearances, a suspicion that the completely friendly world she lived in was in fact secretly mocking and hostile, had proved to be true. Or rather, had become true —for it wasn't always. And meanwhile, in her mind, she was perpetually composing a statement, for her own use and understanding, that would cover this situation.

Three colored lights passed overhead, very high up and in a cluster, blinking. There were also lights strung through the park at intervals, and on East End Avenue, where taxicabs cruised up and down with their rooflights on. Nobody wanted them. As if they had never in their life shot through a red light, the taxis stopped at Eighty-third Street, and again at Eighty-fourth, and went on when the light turned green. East End Avenue was as quiet as the grave. So were the side streets.

With the first hint of morning, this beautiful quiet came to an end. Stopping and starting, making a noise like an electric toaster, a Department of Sanitation truck made its way down Eighty-fourth Street, murdering sleep. Crash. Tinkle. More grinding. Bump. Thump. Voices. A brief silence and then the whole thing started up again farther down the street. This was followed by other noises—a parked car being warmed up, a maniac in a sports car with no muffler. And then suddenly it was the policeman's turn to be gone. A squad car drove by, with the car radio playing an old Big Crosby song, and picked him up.

Biding his time, the junkie managed to slip past the service entrance of one of the apartment buildings on East End Avenue without being seen. Around in back he saw an open window on the ground floor with no bars over it. On the other hand he didn't know who or what he would find when he climbed through it, and he shouldn't have waited till morning. He stood flattened against a brick wall while a handyman took in the empty garbage cans. The sound of retreating footsteps died away. The door to the service entrance was wide open. In a matter of seconds James Jackson was in and out again, wheeling a new ten-speed Peugeot. He straddled the bicycle as if he and not the overweight insurance broker in 7E had paid good money for it, and rode off down the street.

" 'Cloudy with rain or showers . . .' Cindy, did you know you dreamt about a tiger last night?"

"Cindy dreamt about a tiger?" Iris said.

"Yes. What happened after I left?"

"Nothing."

"Congratulations. I dreamt the air-conditioner in our room broke and we couldn't get anybody to come and fix it."

"Is it broken?" Iris asked.

"I don't know. We'll have to wait till next summer to find out."

"Good morning, Laurie. Good morning, Cindy," Jimmy the daytime elevator man said cheerfully. No answer. But no rudeness intended either. They did not know they were in the elevator.

The red-haired doorman at No. 7 Gracie Square stretched out his arms and pretended he was going to capture Cindy. This happened morning after morning, and she put up with it patiently.

"Taxi!" people wailed. "*Taxi!*" But there were no taxis. Or if one came along there was somebody in it. The doorman of No. 10 stood in the middle of East End Avenue and blew his whistle at nothing. On a balcony five stories above the street, a man lying on his back with his hips in the air was being put through his morning exercises by a Swedish masseur. The tired middle-aged legs went up and down like pistons. Like pistons, the elevators rose and fell in all the buildings overlooking the park, bringing the maids and laundresses up, taking men with briefcases down. The stationery store and the cleaners were now open. So was the luncheonette.

The two little girls stopped, took each other by the hand, and looked carefully both ways before they crossed the car tunnel at No. 10. On the river walk Laurie saw an acquaintance and ran on ahead. Poor Cindy! At her back was the park—very agreeable to play in when she went there with her mother or the kindergarten class, but also frequented by rough boys with water pistols and full of bushes it could be hiding in—and on her right was the deep pit alongside No. 10; it could be down there, below the sidewalk and waiting to spring out when she came along. She did not look to see if it was there but kept well over to the other side, next to the outer railing and the river. A tug with four empty barges was nosing its way upstream. The Simpsons' cook waved to Cindy from their kitchen window, which looked out on the river walk, and Cindy waved back.

In the days when George used to take Laurie to kindergarten because she was too small to walk to school by herself, he had noticed her—a big woman with blond braids in a crown around her head. And one day he said, "Shall we wave to her and see what happens?" Sometimes her back was turned to the window and she didn't know that Cindy and Laurie were there. They did not ever think of her except when they saw her, and if they had met her face to face she would have had to do all the talking.

Laurie was waiting at the Eighty-third Street gate. "Come on," she said.

"Stupid-head," Cindy said.

They went into the school building together, ignoring the big girls in camel's-hair coats who held the door open for them. But it wasn't like Jimmy the elevator man; they knew the big girls were there.

Sitting on the floor of her cubby, with her gym sneakers under her bottom and her cheek against her green plaid coat, Cindy felt safe. But Miss Nichols kept trying to get her to come out. The sandbox, the blocks, the crayons—Cindy said no to them all, and sucked her thumb. So Miss Nichols sat down on a little chair and took Cindy on her lap.

"If there was a (   )?" Cindy asked finally.

In a soft coaxing voice Miss Nichols said, "If there was a what?" Cindy wouldn't say what.

The fire engines raced down Eighty-sixth Street, sirens shrieking and horns blowing, swung south through a red light, and came to a stop by the alarm box on the corner of East End Avenue and Gracie Square. The firemen jumped down and stood talking in the middle of the street. The hoses remained neatly folded and the ladders horizontal. It was the second false alarm that night from this same box. A county fair wouldn't have made more commotion under their windows but it had happened too often and George and Iris Carrington went on sleeping peacefully, flat on their backs, like stone figures on a medieval tomb.

In the trash basket on the corner by the park gates there was a copy of the *Daily News* which said, in big letters, "TIGER ESCAPES," but that was a different tiger; that tiger escaped from a circus in Jamestown, R.I.

"What *is* it?" Iris asked, in the flower shop. "Why are you pulling at my skirt?"

The flower-shop woman (pink-blond hair, Viennese accent) offered Cindy a green carnation, and she refused to take it. "You don't like flowers?" the woman asked, coyly, and the tiger kept on looking at Cindy from behind some big, wide rubbery green leaves. "She's shy," the flower-shop woman said.

"Not usually," Iris said. "I don't know what's got into her today."

She gave the woman some money, and the woman gave her some money and some flowers, and then she and Cindy went outside, but Cindy was afraid to look behind her. If the tiger was following them, it was better not to know. For half a block she had a tingling sensation in the center of her back, between her shoulder blades. But then, looking across the street, she saw that the tiger was not back there in the flower shop. It must have left when they did, and now it was looking at her from the round hole in a cement mixer.

The lights changed from red to green, and Iris took her hand and started to cross over.

"I want to go that way," Cindy said, holding back, until the light changed again. Since she was never allowed on the street alone, she was not really afraid of meeting the tiger all by herself. But what if some day it should walk into the elevator when Jimmy wasn't looking, and get off at their floor, and hide behind Laurie's bicycle and the scooters. And what if the front door opened and somebody came out and pressed the elevator button and the tiger got inside when they weren't looking. And what if—

"Oh, please don't hold back, Cindy! I'm late as anything!"

So, dangerous as it was, she allowed herself to be hurried along home.

Tap, tap, tap . . .
In the night this was, just after Iris and George had got to sleep.
"Oh, no!" Iris moaned.
But it was. When he opened the door, there she stood.

Tap, tap . . .
That same night, two hours later. Sound asleep but able to walk

and talk, he put on his bathrobe and followed her down the hall. Stretched out beside her, he tried to go on sleeping but he couldn't. He said, "What were you dreaming about this time?"

"Sea-things."

"What kind of seethings?"

"Sea-things under the sea."

"Things that wiggled?"

"Yes."

"Something was after you?"

"Yes."

"Too bad. Go to sleep."

Tap, tap . . .

This time as he heaved himself up, Iris said to him, "*You* lie still."

She got up and opened the door to the hall and said, "Cindy, we're tired and we need our sleep. I want you to go back to your bed and stay there."

Then they both lay awake, listening to the silence at the other end of the hall.

"I came out of the building," Iris said, "and I had three letters that Jimmy had given me, and it was raining hard, and the wind whipped them right out of my hand."

He took a sip of his drink and then said, "Did you get them?"

"I got two of them. One was from the Richards children, thanking me for the toys I sent when Lonnie was in the hospital. And one was a note from Mrs. Mills. I never did find the third. It was a small envelope, and the handwriting was Society."

"A birthday party for Cindy."

"No. It was addressed to Mr. and Mrs. George Carrington. Cocktail party, probably."

He glanced at the windows. It was already dark. Then, the eternal optimist (also remembering the time he found the button that flew off her coat and rolled under a parked car on Eighty-fifth Street): "Which way did it blow? I'll look for it tomorrow."

"Oh, there's no use. You can see by the others. They were reduced to pulp by the rain, in just that minute. And anyway, I did look, this afternoon."

In the morning, he took the Seventy-ninth Street crosstown

bus instead of the Eighty-sixth, so that he could look for the invitation that blew away. No luck. The invitation had already passed through a furnace in the Department of Sanitation building on Ninetieth Street and now, in the form of ashes, was floating down the East River on a garbage scow, on its way out to sea.

The sender, rebuffed in this first tentative effort to get to know the Carringtons better, did not try again. She had met them at a dinner party, and liked them both. She was old enough to be Iris's mother, and it puzzled her that a young woman who seemed to be well-bred and was quite lovely-looking and adored "Middlemarch" should turn out to have no manners, but she didn't brood about it. New York is full of pleasant young couples, and if one chooses to ignore your invitation the chances are another won't.

"Did you hear Laurie in the night?" Iris said.

"No. Did Laurie have a nightmare?"

"Yes. I thought you were awake."

"I don't think so."

He got up out of bed and went into the children's room and turned on the radiators so they wouldn't catch cold. Laurie was sitting up in bed reading.

"Mommy says you had a bad dream last night."

"There were three dreams," she said, in an overdistinct voice, as if she were a grown woman at a committee meeting. "The first dream was about Miss Stevenson. I dreamed she wasn't nice to me. She was like the wicked witch."

"Miss Stevenson loves you."

"And the second dream was about snakes. They were all over the floor. It was like a rug made up of snakes, and very icky, and there was a giant, and Cathy and I were against him, and he was trying to shut me in the room where the snakes were, and one of the snakes bit me, but he wasn't the kind of snake that kills you, he was just a mean snake, and so it didn't hurt. And the third dream was a happy dream. I was with Cathy and we were skating together and pulling our mommies by strings."

With his safety razor ready to begin a downward sweep, George Carrington studied the lathered face in the mirror of the medicine cabinet. He shook his head. There was a fatal flaw in his character: Nobody was ever as real to him as he was to himself. If people

knew how little he cared whether they lived or died, they wouldn't
want to have anything to do with him.

The dog moved back and forth between the two ends of the
apartment, on good terms with everybody. She was in the dining
room at mealtimes, and in the kitchen when Iris was getting dinner (when quite often something tasty fell off the edge of the
kitchen table), and she was there again just after dinner, in case
the plates were put on the floor for her to lick before they went
into the dishwasher. In the late afternoon, for an hour before it
was time for her can of beef-and-beef-byproducts, she sat with her
front paws crossed, facing the kitchen clock, a reminding statue.
After she had been fed, she went to the living room and lay down
before the unlit log fire in the fireplace and slept until bedtime.
In the morning, she followed Iris back and forth through room
after room, until Iris was dressed and ready to take her out. "Must
you nag me so?" Iris cried, but the dog was not intimidated. There
was something they were in agreement about, though only one of
them could have put it in words: It is a crime against Nature to
keep a hunting dog in the city. George sometimes gave her a slap
on her haunches when she picked up food in the gutter or lunged
at another dog. And if she jerked on her leash he jerked back,
harder. But with Iris she could do anything—she could even stand
under the canopy and refuse to go anywhere because it was
raining.

Walking by the river, below Eightieth Street, it wasn't necessary
to keep her on a leash, and while Iris went on ahead Puppy sniffed
at the godforsaken grass and weeds that grew between the cement
walk and the East River Drive. Then she overtook Iris, at full
speed, overshot the mark, and came charging back, showing her
teeth in a grin. Three or four times she did this, as a rule—with
Iris applauding and congratulating her and cheering her on. It
may be a crime against Nature to keep a hunting dog in the city,
but this one was happy anyway.

After a series of dreams in which people started out as one person and ended up another and he found that there was no provi-
sion for getting from where he was to where he wanted to go and
it grew later and later and even after the boat had left he still went
on packing his clothes and what he thought was his topcoat turned

out to belong to a friend he had not seen for seventeen years and naked strangers came and went, he woke and thought he heard a soft tapping on the bedroom door. But when he got up and opened it there was no one there.

"Was that Cindy?" Iris asked as he got back into bed.

"No. I thought I heard her, but I must have imagined it."

"I thought I heard her too," Iris said, and turned over.

At breakfast he said, "Did you have any bad dreams last night?" but Cindy was making a lake in the middle of her oatmeal and didn't answer.

"I thought I heard you tapping on our door," he said. "You didn't dream about a wolf, or a tiger, or a big black dog?"

"I don't remember," she said.

"You'll never guess what I just saw from the bedroom window," Iris said.

He put down his book.

"A police wagon drove down Eighty-fourth Street and stopped, and two policemen with guns got out and went into a building and didn't come out. And after a long while two more policemen came and *they* went into the building, and pretty soon they all came out with a big man with black hair, handcuffed. Right there on Eighty-fourth Street, two doors from the corner."

"Nice neighborhood we live in," he said.

"Daddy, Daddy, Daddy, Daddy!" came into his dreams without waking him, and what did wake him was the heaving of the other bed as Iris got up and hurried toward the bedroom door.

"It was Cindy," she said when she came back.

"Dream?" he asked.

"Yes."

"I heard her but went on dreaming myself."

"She doesn't usually cry out like that."

"Laurie used to."

Why all these dreams, he wondered, and drifted gently back to sleep, as if he already knew the answer. She turned and turned, and finally, after three-quarters of an hour, got up and filled the hot-water bottle. What for days had been merely a half-formed thought in the back of her mind was now suddenly, in the middle of the night, making her rigid with anxiety. She needed to talk, and couldn't bring herself to wake him. What she wanted to say was they were making a mistake in bringing the children up in New York City. Or even in America. There was too much that there was no way to protect them from, and the only sensible thing would be to pull up stakes now, before Laurie reached adolescence. They could sublet the apartment until the lease ran out, and take a house somewhere in the South of France, near Aix perhaps, and the children could go to a French school, and they could all go skiing in Switzerland in the winter, and Cindy could have her own horse, and they both would acquire a good French accent, and be allowed to grow up slowly, in the ordinary way, and not be jaded by one premature experience after another, before they were old enough to understand any of it.

With the warmth at her back, and the comforting feeling that she had found the hole in the net, gradually she fell asleep too.

But when she brought the matter up two days later he looked at her blankly. He did not oppose her idea but neither did he accept it, and so her hands were tied.

As usual, the fathers' part in the Christmas program had to be rehearsed beforehand. In the small practice room on the sixth floor of the school, their masculinity—their grey flannel or dark-blue pin-striped suits, their size 9, 10, 11, 11½, and 12 shoes, their gold cufflinks, the odor that emanated from their bodies and from their freshly shaved cheeks, their simple assurance, based on, among other things, the *Social Register* and the size of their income—was incongruous. They were handed sheets of music as they came in, and the room was crammed with folding chairs, all facing the ancient grand piano. With the two tall windows at their backs they were missing the snow, which was a pity. It went up, down, diagonally, and in centrifugal motion—all at once. The fact that no two of the star-shaped crystals were the same was a miracle, of course, but it was a miracle that everybody has long since grown accustomed to. The light outside the windows was cold and grey.

"Since there aren't very many of you," the music teacher said, "you'll have to make up for it by singing enthusiastically." She was young, in her late twenties, and had difficulty keeping discipline in the classroom; the girls took advantage of her good nature, and never stopped talking and gave her their complete attention. She sat down at the piano now and played the opening bars of "O come, O come, Emmanuel/And ransom captive I-i-i-zrah-el . . ."

Somebody in the second row exclaimed, "Oh God!" under his breath. The music was set too high for men's voices.

"The girls will sing the first stanza, you fathers the second—"

The door opened and two more fathers came in.

"—and all will sing the third."

With help from the piano (which they would not have downstairs in the school auditorium) they achieved an approximation of the tune, and the emphasis sometimes fell in the right place. They did their best, but the nineteenth-century words and the ninth-century plainsong did not go well together. Also, one of the fathers had a good strong clear voice, which only made the others more self-conscious and apologetic. They would have been happier without him.

The music teacher made a flip remark. They all laughed and began again. Their number was added to continually as the door opened and let in the sounds from the hall. Soon there were no more vacant chairs; the latecomers had to stand. The snow was now noticeably heavier, and the singing had more volume. Though they were at some pains to convey, by their remarks to one another and their easy laughter, that this was not an occasion to be taken seriously, nevertheless the fact that they were here was proof of the contrary: they all had offices where they should have been and salaries they were not at this moment doing anything to earn. Twenty-seven men with, at first glance, a look of sameness about them, a round, composite, youngish, unrevealing, New York face. Under closer inspection, this broke down. Not all the eyes were blue, nor were the fathers all in their middle and late thirties. The thin-faced man at the end of the second row could not have been a broker or a lawyer or in advertising. The man next to him had survived incarceration in a Nazi prison camp. There was one Negro. Here and there a head that was not thickly covered with hair. Their speaking voices varied, but not so much as they conceivably might have—no Texas drawl, for instance. And all the fingernails were clean, all the shoes were shined, all the linen was fresh.

Each time they went over the hymn it was better. They clearly needed more rehearsing, but the music teacher glanced nervously at the clock and said, "And now 'In Dulci Jubilo.'"

Those who had forgotten their Latin, or never had any, eavesdropped on those who knew how the words should be pronounced. The tune was powerful and swept everything before it, and in a flush of pleasure they finished together, on the beat, loudly, making the room echo. They had forgotten about the telephone messages piling up on their desks beside the unopened mail. They were enjoying themselves. They could have gone on singing for another hour. Instead, they had to get up and file out of the room and crowd into the elevators.

In spite of new costumes, new scenery, different music, and—naturally—a different cast, the Christmas play was always the same. Mary and Joseph proceeded to Bethlehem, where the inns were full, and found shelter in the merest suggestion of a stable. An immature angel announced to very unlikely shepherds the appearance of the Star. Wise Men came and knelt before the plastic Babe in Mary's arms. And then the finale: the Threes singing and dancing with heavenly joy.

"How did it sound?" George asked, in the crowd on the stairs.

"Fine," Iris said.

"Really? It didn't seem to me—maybe because we were under the balcony—it didn't seem as if we were making any sound at all."

"No, it was plenty loud enough. What was so nice was the two kinds of voices."

"High and low, you mean?"

"The fathers sounded like bears. Adorable."

In theory, since it was the middle of the night, it was dark, but not the total suffocating darkness of a cloudy night in the country. The city, as usual, gave off light—enough so that you could see the island in the middle of the river, and the three bridges, and the outlines of the little houses on East End Avenue and the big apartment buildings on Eighty-sixth Street, and the trees and shrubs and lampposts and comfort station in the park. Also a woman standing by the railing of the river walk.

There was no wind. The river was flowing north and the air smelled of snow, which melted the moment it touched any solid object, and became the shine on iron balustrades and on the bark of trees.

The woman had been standing there a long time, looking out over the water, when she began awkwardly to pull herself up and over the curved iron spikes that were designed, by their size and shape, to prevent people from throwing themselves into the river. In this instance they were not enough. But it took some doing. There was a long tear in the woman's coat and she was gasping for breath as she let herself go backward into space.

The sun enters Aquarius January 20th and remains until February 18th. *"An extremely good friend can today put into motion some operation that will be most helpful to your best interest, or else introduce you to some influential person. Go out socially in the evening on a grand scale. Be charming."*

The cocktail party was in a penthouse. The elevator opened directly into the foyer of the apartment. And the woman he was talking to—or rather, who was talking to him—was dressed all in shades of brown.

"I tried to get you last summer," she said, "but your wife said you were busy that day."

"Yes," he said.

"I'll try again."

"Please do," somebody said for him, using his mouth and tongue and vocal cords—because it was the last thing in the world he wanted, to drive halfway across Long Island to a lunch party. "We hardly ever go anywhere," he himself said, but too late, after the damage had been done.

His mind wandered for an instant as he took in—not the room, for he was facing the wrong way, but a small corner of it. And in that instant he lost the thread of the story she was telling him. She had taken her shoe off in a movie theater and put her purse down beside it, and the next thing he knew they refused to do anything, even after she had explained what happened and that she must get in. Who "they" were, get in where, he patiently waited to find out, while politely sharing her indignation.

"But imagine!" she exclaimed. "They said, 'How valuable was the ring?'"

He shook his head, commiserating with her.

"I suppose if it hadn't been worth a certain amount," she went on, "they wouldn't have done a thing about it."

The police, surely, he thought. Having thought at first it was the manager of the movie theatre she was talking about.

"And while they were jimmying the door open, people were

walking by, and nobody showed the slightest concern. Or interest."

So it wasn't the police. But who was it, then? He never found out, because they were joined by another woman, who smiled at him in such a way as to suggest that they knew each other. But though he searched his mind and her face—the plucked eyebrows, the reserved expression in the middle-aged eyes—and considered her tweed suit and her diamond pin and her square figure, he could not imagine who she was. Suppose somebody—suppose Iris came up and he had to introduce her?

The purse was recovered, with the valuable ring still in it, and he found himself talking about something that had occupied his thoughts lately. And in his effort to say what he meant, he failed to notice what happened to the first woman. Suddenly she was not there. Somebody must have carried her off, right in front of his unseeing eyes.

". . . but it isn't really distinguishable from what goes on in dreams," he said to the woman who seemed to know him and to assume that he knew her. "People you have known for twenty or thirty years, you suddenly discover you didn't really know how they felt about you, and in fact you don't know how anybody feels about anything—only what they *say* they feel. And suppose that isn't true at all? You decide that it is better to act as if it is true. And so does everybody else. But it is a kind of myth you are living in, wide awake, with your eyes open, in broad daylight."

He realized that the conversation had become not only personal but intimate. But it was too late to back out now.

To his surprise she seemed to understand, to have felt what he had felt. "And one chooses," she said, "between this myth and that."

"Exactly! If you live in the city and are bringing up children, you decide that this thing is not safe—and so you don't let them do it—and that thing *is* safe. When, actually, neither one is safe and everything is equally dangerous. But for the sake of convenience—"

"And also so that you won't go out of your mind," she said.

"And so you won't go out of your mind," he agreed. "Well," he said after a moment, "that makes two of us who are thinking about it."

"In one way or another, people live by myths," she said.

He racked his brain for something further to say on this or any other subject.

Glancing around at the windows, which went from floor to ceiling, the woman in the tweed suit said, "These vistas you have here."

He then looked and saw black night, with lighted buildings far below and many blocks away. "From our living room," he said, "you can see all the way to the North Pole."

"We live close to the ground," she said.

But where? Cambridge? Princeton? Philadelphia?

"In the human scale," he said. "Like London and Paris. Once, on a beautiful spring day, four of us—we'd been having lunch with a visiting Englishman who was interested in architecture—went searching for the sky. Up one street and down the next."

She smiled.

"We had to look for it, the sky is so far away in New York."

They stood nursing their drinks, and a woman came up to them who seemed to know her intimately, and the two women started talking and he turned away.

On her way into the school building, Laurie joined the flood from the school bus, and cried, "Hi, Janet . . . Hi, Connie . . . Hi, Elizabeth . . ." and seemed to be enveloped by her schoolmates, until suddenly, each girl having turned to some other girl, Laurie is left standing alone, her expression unchanged, still welcoming, but nobody having responded. If you collect reasons, this is the reason she behaved so badly at lunch, was impertinent to her mother, and hit her little sister.

He woke with a mild pain in his stomach. It was high up, like an ulcer pain, and he lay there worrying about it. When he heard the sound of shattered glass, his half-awake, over-sensible mind supplied both the explanation and the details: two men, putting a large framed picture into the trunk compartment of a parked car, had dropped it, breaking the glass. Too bad . . . And with that thought he drifted gently off to sleep.

In the morning he looked out of the bedroom window and saw three squad cars in front of the drugstore. The window of the drugstore had a big star-shaped hole in it, and several policemen were standing around looking at the broken glass on the sidewalk.

The sneeze was perfectly audible through two closed doors. He turned to Iris with a look of inquiry.

"Who sneezed? Was that you, Laurie?" she called.

"That was Cindy," Laurie said.

In principle, Iris would have liked to bring them up in a Spartan fashion, but both children caught cold easily and their colds were prolonged, and recurring, and overlapping, and endless. Whether they should or shouldn't be kept home from school took on the unsolvability of a moral dilemma—which George's worrying disposition did nothing to alleviate. The sound of a child coughing deep in the chest in the middle of the night would make him leap up out of a sound sleep.

She blamed herself when the children came down with a cold, and she blamed them. Possibly, also, the school was to blame, since the children played on the roof, twelve stories above the street, and up there the winds were often much rawer, and teachers cannot, of course, spend all their time going around buttoning up the coats of little girls who have got too hot from running.

She went and stood in the doorway of Cindy's room. "No sneezing," she said.

Sneeze, sneeze, sneeze.

"Cindy, if you are catching another cold, I'm going to shoot myself," Iris said, and gave her two baby-aspirin tablets to chew, and some Vitamin C drops, and put an extra blanket on her bed, and didn't open the window, and in the morning Cindy's nose was running.

"Shall I keep her home from school?" Iris asked, at the breakfast table.

Instead of answering, George got up and looked at the weather thermometer outside the west window of their bedroom. "Twenty-seven," he said, when he came back. But he still didn't answer her question. He was afraid to answer it, lest it be the wrong answer, and she blame him. Actually, there was no answer that was the right answer: They had tried sending Cindy to school and they had tried not sending her. This time, Iris kept her home from school—not because she thought it was going to make any difference but so the pediatrician, Dr. de Santillo, wouldn't blame her. Not that he ever said anything. And Cindy got to play with Laurie's things all morning. She played with Laurie's paper dolls until she was tired, and left them all over the floor, and then she colored in Laurie's coloring book, and Puppy chewed up one of the crayons but not one of Laurie's favorites—not the pink or the blue—and then Cindy rearranged the furniture in Laurie's doll house so it was much nicer, and then she lined up all Laurie's dolls in a row on her bed and played school. And when it was time for Laurie to come home from school she went out to the kitchen and played with the eggbeater. Laurie came in, letting the front door slam behind her, and dropped her mittens in the hall and her coat on the living-room rug and her knitted cap on top of her coat, and started for her room, and it sounded as if she had hurt herself. Iris came running. What a noise Laurie made. And stamping her foot, Cindy noted disapprovingly. And tears.

"Stop screaming and tell me what's the matter!" Iris said.

"Cindy, I hate you!" Laurie said. "I hate you, I hate you!"

Horrible old Laurie . . .

But in the morning when they first woke up it was different. She heard Laurie in the bathroom, and then she heard Laurie go back to her room. Lying in bed, Cindy couldn't suck her thumb because she couldn't breathe through her nose, so she got up and went into Laurie's room (entirely forgetting that her mother had said that in the morning she was to stay out of Laurie's room because she had a cold) and got in Laurie's bed and said, "Read, read." Laurie read her the story of "The Tinder Box," which has three dogs in it—a dog with eyes as big as saucers, and a dog with eyes as big as millwheels, and a third dog with eyes as big as the Round Tower of Copenhagen.

Tap, tap, tap on the bedroom door brought him entirely awake. "What's Laurie been reading to her?" he asked, turning over in bed. That meant it was Iris's turn to get up. While she was pulling herself together, they heard *tap, tap, tap* again. The bed heaved.

"What's Laurie been reading to you?" she asked as she and Cindy went off down the hall together. When she came back into the bedroom, the light was on and he was standing in front of his dresser, with the top drawer open, searching for Gelusil tablets.

"Trouble?" she said.

Standing in the doorway of Cindy's room, in her blue dressing gown, with her hairbrush in her hand, Iris said, "Who sneezed? Was that you, Cindy?"

"That was Laurie," Cindy said.

So after that Laurie got to stay home from school too.

"I saw Phyllis Simpson in Gristede's supermarket," Iris said. "Their cook committed suicide."

"How?"

"She threw herself in the river."

"No!"

"They think she must have done it sometime during the night, but they don't know exactly when. They just came down to breakfast and she wasn't there. They're still upset about it."

"When did it happen?"

"About a month ago. Her body was found way down the river."

"What a pity. She was a nice woman."

"You remember her?"

"Certainly. She always waved to the children when I used to walk them to school. She waved to me too, sometimes. From the kitchen window. What made her do such a thing?"

"They have no idea."

"She was a big woman," he said. "It must have been hard for her to pull herself up over that railing. It's quite high. No note or anything?"

"No."

"Terrible."

On St. Valentine's Day, the young woman who lived on tea and cigarettes and was given to burning herself on the gas stove eloped to California with her mother, and now there was no one in the kitchen. From time to time, the employment agency went through the formality of sending someone for Iris to interview—though actually it was the other way round. And either the apartment was too large or they didn't care to work for a family with children or they were not accustomed to doing the cooking as well as the other housework. Sometimes they didn't give any reason at all.

A young woman from Haiti, who didn't speak English, was willing to give the job a try. It turned out that she had never seen a carpet sweeper before, and she asked for her money at the end of the day.

Walking the dog at seven-fifteen on a winter morning, he suddenly stopped and said to himself, "Oh God, somebody's been murdered!" On the high stone stoop of one of the little houses on East End Avenue facing the park. Somebody in a long red coat. By the curve of the hip he could tell it was a woman, and with his heart racing he considered what he ought to do. From where he stood on the sidewalk he couldn't see the upper part of her body. One foot—the bare heel and the strap of her shoe—was sticking out from under the hem of the coat. If she'd been murdered, wouldn't she be sprawled out in an awkward position instead of curled up and lying on her side as though she was in bed asleep? He looked up at the house. Had they locked her out? After a scene? Or she could have come home in the middle of the night and discovered that she'd forgotten to take her key. But in that case she'd have spent the night in a hotel or with a friend. Or called an all-night locksmith.

He went up three steps without managing to see any more than he had already. The parapet offered some shelter from the wind, but even so, how could she sleep on the cold stone, with nothing over her?

"Can I help you?"

His voice sounded strange and hollow. There was no answer. The red coat did not stir. Then he saw the canvas bag crammed with the fruit of her night's scavenging, and backed down the steps.

Now it was his turn. The sore throat was gone in the morning, but it came back during the day, and when he sat down to dinner he pulled the extension out at his end and moved his mat, silver, and glass farther away from the rest of them.

"If you aren't sneezing, I don't think you need to be in Isolation Corner," Iris said, but he stayed there anyway. His colds were prolonged and made worse by his efforts to treat them; made worse still by his trying occasionally to disregard them, as he saw other people doing. In the end he went through box after box of Kleenex, his nose white with Noxzema, his eyelids inflamed, like a man in a subway poster advertising a cold remedy that, as it turned out, did not work for him. And finally he took to his bed, with a transistor radio for amusement and company. In his childhood, being sick resulted in agreeable pampering, and now that he was grown he preferred to be both parties to this pleasure. No one could make him as comfortable as he could make himself, and Iris had all but given up trying.

On a rainy Sunday afternoon in March, with every door in the school building locked and the corridors braced for the shock of Monday morning, the ancient piano demonstrated for the benefit of the empty practice room that it is one thing to fumble through the vocal line, guided by the chords that accompany it, and something else again to be genuinely musical, to know what the composer intended—the resolution of what cannot be left uncertain, the amorous flirtation of the treble and the bass, notes taking to the air like a flock of startled birds.

The faint clicking sounds given off by the telephone in the pantry meant that Iris was dialling on the extension in the master bedroom. And at last there was somebody in the Carringtons' kitchen again—a black woman in her fifties. They were low on milk, and totally out of oatmeal, canned dog food, and coffee, but the memo pad that was magnetically attached to the side of the Frigidaire was blank. Writing down things they were out of was not something she considered part of her job. When an emergency arose, she put on her coat and went to the store, just as if she were still in North Carolina.

The sheet of paper that was attached to the clipboard hanging from a nail on the side of the kitchen cupboard had the menus for lunch and dinner all written out, but they were for yesterday's lunch and dinner. And though it was only nine-thirty, Bessie already felt a mounting indignation at being kept in ignorance about what most deeply concerned her. It was an old-fashioned apartment, with big rooms and high ceilings, and the kitchen was a considerable distance from the master bedroom; nevertheless, it was just barely possible for the two women to live there. Nature had designed them for mutual tormenting, the one with an exaggerated sense of time, always hurrying to meet a deadline that did not exist anywhere but in her own fancy, and calling upon the angels or whoever is in charge of amazing grace to take notice that she had put the food on the hot tray in the dining room at precisely one minute before the moment she had been told to have dinner ready; the other with not only a hatred of planning meals but also a childish reluctance to come to the table. When the minute hand of the electric clock in the kitchen arrived at seven or seven-fifteen or whatever, Bessie went into the dining room and announced in an inaudible voice that dinner was ready. Two rooms away, George heard her by extrasensory perception and leapt to his feet, and Iris, holding out her glass to him, said, "Am I not going to have a second vermouth?"

To his amazement, on Bessie's day off, having cooked dinner and put it on the hot plate, Iris drifted away to the front of the apartment and read a magazine, fixed her hair, God knows what, until he discovered the food sitting there and begged her to come to the table.

"They said they lived in Boys Town, and I thought Jimmy let them in because he's Irish and Catholic," Iris said. "There was nothing on the list I wanted, so I subscribed to *Vogue*, to help them out. When I spoke to Jimmy about it, he said he had no idea they were selling subscriptions, and he never let solicitors get by him—not even nuns and priests. Much as he might want to. So I don't suppose it will come."

"It might," George said. "Maybe they were honest."

"He thought they were workmen because they asked for the eleventh floor. The tenants on the eleventh floor have moved out and Jimmy says the people who are moving in have a five years' lease and are spending fifty thousand dollars on the place, which they don't even *own*. But anyway, what they did was walk through the apartment and then down one floor and start ringing doorbells. The super took them down in the back elevator without asking what they were doing there, and off they went. They tried the same thing at No. 7 and the doorman threw them out."

Walking the dog before breakfast, if he went by the river walk he saw in the Simpsons' window a black-haired woman who did not wave to him or even look up when he passed. That particular section of the river walk was haunted by an act of despair that nobody had been given a chance to understand. Nothing that he could think of—cancer, thwarted love, melancholia—seemed to fit. He had only spoken to her once, when he and Iris went to a dinner party at the Simpsons' and she smiled at him as she was helping the maid clear the table between courses. If she didn't look up when he passed under her window it was as though he had been overtaken by a cloud shadow—until he forgot all about it, a few seconds later. But he could have stopped just once, and he hadn't. When the window was open he could have called out to her, even if it was only "Good morning," or "Isn't it a beautiful day?"

He could have said, *Don't do it.* . . .

Sometimes he came back by the little house on East End Avenue where he had seen the woman in the red coat. He invariably glanced up, half expecting her to be lying there on the stoop. If she wasn't there, where was she?

In the psychiatric ward of Bellevue Hospital was the answer. But not for long. She and the doctor got it straightened out about her mother's gold thimble, and he gave her a prescription and told her where to go in the building to have it filled, and hoped for the best—which, after all, is all that anybody has to hope for.

The weather thermometer blew away one stormy night and after a week or two George brought home a new one. It was round and encased in white plastic, and not meant to be screwed to the window frame but to be kept inside. It registered the temperature outside by means of a wire with what looked like a small bullet attached to the end of it. The directions said to drill a hole through the window frame, but George backed away from all that and, instead, hung the wire across the sill and closed the window on it. What the new thermometer said bore no relation to the actual temperature, and drilling the hole had a high priority on the list of things he meant to do.

There was also a racial barometer in the apartment that registered *Fair* or *Stormy*, according to whether Bessie had spent several days running in the apartment or had just come back from a weekend in her room in Harlem.

The laundress, so enormously fat that she had to maneuver her body around, as if she were the captain of an ocean liner, was a Muslim and hated all white people and most black people as well. She was never satisfied with the lunch Bessie cooked for her, and Bessie objected to having to get lunch for her, and the problem was solved temporarily by having her eat in the luncheonette across the street.

She quit. The new laundress was half the size of the old one, and sang alto in her church choir, and was good-tempered, and fussy about what she had for lunch. Bessie sometimes considered her a friend and sometimes an object of derision, because she believed in spirits.

So did Bessie, but not to the same extent or in the same way. Bessie's mother had appeared to her and her sister and brother, shortly after her death. They were quarrelling together, and her mother's head and shoulders appeared up near the ceiling, and she said they were to love one another. And sometimes when Bessie was walking along the street she felt a coolness and knew that a spirit was beside her. But the laundress said, "All right, go ahead, then, if you want to," to the empty air and, since there wasn't room for both of them, let the spirit precede her through the pantry. She even knew who the spirit was.

It was now spring on the river, and the river walk was a Chinese scroll which could be unrolled, by people who like to do things in the usual way, from right to left—starting at Gracie Square and walking north. Depicted were:
A hockey game between Loyola and St. Francis de Sales
Five boys shooting baskets on the basketball court
A seagull
An old man sitting on a bench doing columns of figures
A child drawing a track for his toy trains on the pavement with a piece of chalk
A paper drinking cup floating on the troubled surface of the water
A child in pink rompers pushing his own stroller
A woman sitting on a bench alone, with her face lifted to the sun
A Puerto Rican boy with a transistor radio
Two middle-aged women speaking German
A bored and fretful baby, too hot in his perambulator, with nothing to look at or play with, while his nurse reads
The tugboat Chicago pulling a long string of empty barges upstream
A little girl feeding her mother an apple
A helicopter
A kindergarten class, in two sections
Clouds in a blue sky
A flowering cherry tree

Seven freight cars moving imperceptibly, against the tidal current, in the wake of Herbert E. Smith

A man with a pipe in his mouth and a can of Prince Albert smoking tobacco on the bench beside him

A man sorting his possessions into two canvas bags, one of which contains a concertina

Six very small children playing in the sandpile, under the watchful eyes of their mothers or nursemaids

An oil tanker

A red-haired priest reading a pocket-size New Testament

A man scattering bread crumbs for the pigeons

The Coast Guard cutter CG 40435 turning around just north of the lighthouse and heading back towards Hell Gate Bridge

A sweeper with his bag and a ferruled stick

A little boy pointing a red plastic pistol at his father's head

A pleasure yacht

An airplane

A man and a woman speaking French

A child on a tricycle

A boy on roller skates

A reception under a striped tent on the lawn of the mayor's house

The fireboat station

The Franklin Delano Roosevelt Drive, a cinder path, a warehouse, seagulls, and so on

Who said *Happiness is the light shining on the water. The water is cold and dark and deep.* . . . .

"It's perfectly insane," George said when he met Iris coming from Gristede's with a big brown paper bag heavy as lead under each arm and relieved her of them. "Don't we still have that cart?"

"Nobody in the building uses them."

"But couldn't you?"

"No," Iris said.

"All children," Cindy said wisely, leaning against him, with her head in the hollow of his neck, "all children think their mommy and daddy are the nicest."

"And what about you? Are you satisfied?"

She gave him a hug and a kiss and said, "I think you and

Mommy are the nicest mommy and daddy in the whole world."

"And I think you are the nicest Cindy," he said, his eyes moist with tears.

They sat and rocked each other gently.

After Bessie had taken the breakfast dishes out of the dishwasher, she went into the front, dragging the vacuum cleaner, to do the children's rooms. She stood sometimes for five or ten minutes, looking down at East End Avenue—at the drugstore, the luncheonette, the rival cleaning establishments (side by side and, according to rumor, both owned by the same person), the hair-styling salon, and the branch office of the Chase Manhattan Bank. Together they made a canvas backdrop for a procession of people Bessie had never seen before, or would not recognize if she had, and so she couldn't say to herself, "There goes old Mrs. Maltby," but she looked anyway, she took it all in. The sight of other human beings nourished her mind. She read them as people read books. Pieces of toys, pieces of puzzles that she found on the floor she put on one shelf or another of the toy closet in Cindy's room, gradually introducing a disorder that Iris dealt with periodically, taking a whole day out of her life. But nobody told Bessie she was supposed to find the box the piece came out of, and it is questionable whether she could have anyway. The thickness of the lenses in her eyeglasses suggested that her eyesight was poorer than she let on.

She was an exile, far from home, among people who were not like the white people she knew and understood. She was here because down home she was getting forty dollars a week and she had her old age to think of. She and Iris alternated between irritation at one another and sudden acts of kindness. It was the situation that was at fault. Given halfway decent circumstances, men can work cheerfully and happily for other men, in offices, stores, and even factories. And so can women. But if Iris opened the cupboard or the icebox to see what they did or didn't contain, Bessie popped out of her room and said, "Did you want something?" And Iris withdrew, angry because she had been driven out of her own kitchen. In her mind, Bessie always thought of the Carringtons as "my people," but until she had taught them to think of themselves as her people her profound capacity for devotion would go unused; would not even be suspected.

You can say that life is a fountain if you want to, but what it more nearly resembles is a jack-in-the-box.

Half awake, he heard the soft whimpering that meant Iris was having a nightmare, and he shook her. "I dreamt you were having a heart attack," she said.

"Should you be dreaming that?" he said. But the dream was still too real to be joked about. They were in a public place. And he couldn't be moved. He didn't die, and she consulted with doctors. Though the dream did not progress, she could not extricate herself from it but went on and on, feeling the appropriate emotions but in a circular way. Till finally the sounds she made in her sleep brought about her deliverance.

The conversation at the other end of the hall continued steadily —not loud but enough to keep them from sleeping, and he had already spoken to the children once. So he got up and went down the hall. Laurie and Cindy were both in their bathroom, and Cindy was sitting on the toilet. "I have a stomach ache," she said.

He started to say, "You need to do bizz," and then remembered that the time before she had been sitting on the toilet doing just that.

"And I feel dizzy," Laurie said.

"I heard it," Iris said as he got back into bed.

"That's why she was so pale yesterday."

And half an hour later, when he got up again, Iris did too. To his surprise. Looking as if she had lost her last friend. So he took her in his arms.

"I hate everything," she said.

On the top shelf of his clothes closet he keeps all sorts of things —the overflow of phonograph records, and the photograph albums, which are too large for the bookcases in the living room. The snapshots show nothing but joy. Year after year of it.

On the stage of the school auditorium, girls from Class Eight, in pastel-colored costumes and holding arches of crêpe-paper flowers, made a tunnel from the front of the stage to the rear right-hand corner. The pianist took her hands from the keys, and the headmistress, in sensible navy blue, with her hair cut short like a man's, announced, "Class B becomes Class One."

Twenty very little girls in white dresses marched up on the stage two by two, holding hands.

George and Iris Carrington turned to each other and smiled, for Cindy was among them, looking proud and happy as she hurried through the tunnel of flowers and out of sight.

"Class One becomes Class Two." Another wave of little girls left their place in the audience and went up on the stage and disappeared into the wings.

"Class Two becomes Class Three."

Laurie Carrington, her red hair shining from the hairbrush, rose from her seat with the others and started up on the stage.

"It's too much!" George said, under his breath.

Class Three became Class Four, Class Four became Class Five, Class Five became Class Six, and George Carrington took a handkerchief out of his right hip pocket and wiped his eyes. It was their eagerness that undid him. Their absolute trust in the Arrangements. Class Six became Class Seven, Class Seven became Class Eight. The generations of man, growing up, growing old, dying in order to make room for more.

"Class Eight becomes Class Nine, and is now in the Upper School," the headmistress said, triumphantly. The two girls at the front ducked and went under the arches, taking their crêpe-paper flowers with them. And then the next two, and the next, and finally the audience was left applauding an empty stage.

"Come here and sit on my lap," he said, by no means sure Laurie would think it worth the trouble. But she came. Folding her onto his lap, he was aware of the length of her legs, and the difference of her body; the babyness had departed forever, and when he was affectionate with her it was always as if the moment were slightly out of focus; he felt a restraint. He worried lest it be too close to making love to her. The difference was not great, and he was not sure whether it existed at all.

"Would you like to hear a riddle?" she asked.

"All right."

"Who was the fastest runner in history?"

"I don't know," he said, smiling at her. "Who was?"

"Adam. He was the first in the human race. . . . Teeheeheeheehee, wasn't that a good one?"

Waking in the night, Cindy heard her mother and father laughing behind the closed door of their room. It was a sound she liked to hear, and she turned over and went right back to sleep.

"What was that?"
He raised his head from the pillow and listened.
"Somebody crying 'Help!'" Iris said.
He got up and went to the window. There was no one in the street except a taxi-driver brushing out the back seat of his hack. Again he heard it. Somebody being robbed. Or raped. Or murdered.

"Help . . ." Faintly this time. And not from the direction of the park. The taxi-driver did not look up at the sound, which must be coming from inside a building somewhere. With his face to the window, George waited for the sound to come again and it didn't. Nothing but silence. If he called the police, what could he say? He got back into bed and lay there, sick with horror, his knees shaking. In the morning maybe the *Daily News* would have what happened.

But he forgot to buy a *News* on his way to work, and days passed, and he no longer was sure what night it was that they heard the voice crying "Help!" and felt that he ought to go through weeks of the *News* until he found out what happened. If it was in the *News*. And if something happened.

GETTING INTO DEATH

THOMAS M. DISCH

Thomas M. Disch is best known for science fiction, including *The Genocides*, *Fun with Your New Head*,
Camp Concentration, and *334*. *Getting into Death* will
be the title of his latest collection of short stories, and
he has just finished a novel for Knopf and is midway
through another. He is also a poet (*The Right Way to
Figure Plumbing*) and an editor of anthologies. Mr.
Disch lives in New York City.

I

Like another Madame Defarge, fat Robin sat there knitting a
sweater for her dying mother, who, from her $200 a day bed, re-
garded the pudgy, industrious fingers with a complacent irony.
Just so (Cassandra fancied) might an aristocrat, at the height of
the Terror, have looked down from his tumbril, then leant across
to the pretty duchess accompanying him to the place of their exe-
cution to whisper some pleasantry. But the duchess, distraught,
could no more have caught his drift than poor dear Robin could
catch hers.

"Anyhow." Cassandra squeezed her little finger into the top of
the pack to tickle a crushed Chesterfield loose from the far corner.
"To get back to what we were saying."

"Mother. You know you shouldn't."

"It's all right so long as I don't inhale." She lit it, inhaled. "*Anyhow*. You'd think that having to deal continually with the actual
physical fact of it would make *some* difference."

Robin, apart from a simple lack of curiosity about the inner life
of undertakers, thought it extremely poor taste for her mother to
be forever harping on of all subjects this. Death (she believed),
like sex, requires circumspection: a fond unspoken understand-

ing, a few unavoidable tears, and then a stoic and polite silence. "*Mother*. Please!"

Cassandra trampled on these finer feelings. "But possibly the people who go into it as a profession have already lost most of their capacity to respond. But have *I*—that's what worries me. Maybe if I'd written poetry all along, instead of murder mysteries, I might be able to face my own death now with some dignity. I'm jaded. I've filled myself with cheap candy and now that it's dinnertime I have no appetite."

"Would you like me to bring in some poetry?" Robin asked, desperate to change the subject.

"No. Books can't help me now, can they?" Then, realizing the opportunity she'd just been offered, she backtracked. "On second thought, would you bring me *Leaves of Grass*? The boxed edition."

"Right." Robin unrove a course of stitches to where she'd skipped a beat, unrove her benign chatter back to: "Margaret sends her love, did I mention?"

"Margaret can go fuck herself."

Robin had long ago solved the problem of her mother's obscenities by refusing to hear them. "She said," she continued blandly, "that she *would* have come with me last Friday, but she didn't think you'd—Well, she thought you'd *rather* have just me. You two were never exactly pals."

"So why did she want to come here? To jeer?"

"You know why? I think Margaret feels—" She shook out the bold zigzags of heather and gold to signify, as in a Noh play, a judgment: "—guilty."

Guilty? Margaret, the second Mrs. Millar, was a cocktail pianist at the other end of the George Washington Bridge. Robert had moved on to a third wife long ago, but Robin, then in junior year of high school, had remained with her step-mother in New Jersey, for which Cassandra had never felt anything but gratitude. "Guilty?" she asked.

The Catholic chaplain was a smoothly handsome, stupid priest in the pre-Conciliar style of the 40's. Any Catholic who'd grown up believing in Bing Crosby could have died comfortably in his muscular arms, but beyond the promise of a prayer he didn't have much to offer Cassandra. He disapproved of the too ecumenical spirit that had led her to check all three possibilities on the hospital's Religious Information card, and when his Protestant counterpart arrived he committed her to the consolations of *his* religion with evident relief.

Rev. Blake lacked the sex appeal of the Catholic chaplain and was not much more articulate. But he did try. Theologically he favored a fundamentalism redolent of brimstone and redeeming blood, but the severity of his creed was moderated by the hesitance of his manner. His exhortations suggested the rote sales pitch of a youngster just cured of a speech impediment and liable at any moment to relapse. Whenever he stumbled to a halt Cassandra would ask another intelligent question about the product. Dutifully he would recite the answer. At last he came right out and asked if she was buying any.

"I'd like to. I really would. It would be such a comfort to be able to believe what you've been saying."

"Faith is a gift, Mrs. Millar, that's true. But—"

"Yes, I think I do understand the concepts. But I can't feel them —here." She placed her hand, gently, on her defective heart.

Rev. Blake bowed his head resignedly, as though he'd been told she already had a set of his company's knives, or encyclopedias.

"There *is* one thing, though. A favor you might do me. But perhaps you wouldn't care to. I mean, it's only curiosity on my part."

"Whatever I can do, Mrs. Millar." He pulled his chair closer to the bed and regarded her suspiciously.

"Could you tell me something about the other people here? The people like me—that is, the terminal cases. I'd really like to know how other people take it, especially the ones who believe. Are they mostly afraid, or regretful, or what? And how do their feelings change from day to day?"

"Dear me, Mrs. Millar, I'm afraid that would be absolutely, absolutely . . ."

"Unprofessional? I suppose it would be, a little. But it might be the instrument, you know, of leading me to Christ."

Rev. Blake assured her that he'd pray that her heart should be touched and her eyes opened, but he could not, in all conscience, act as her informer. All her hopes rested, therefore, on the Jewish chaplain, who called on her the next day.

Rabbi Yudkin proved to be the best of all possible chaplains— bright, liberal, and a natural-born gossip. Cassandra scarcely had to ply him. He was a mine of case histories. The very juiciest of these was one Mrs. Hyman in Ward "D". This woman, after a life lived unexceptionably on the surface of Scarsdale, was now suffering a death of exemplary anguish. Seedlings of cancer swarmed through her flesh, blossoming everywhere into pain. She wept for the doctors to increase her ration of morphine, screamed at her husband, abased herself to Rabbi Yudkin, denouncing herself, her family, the hospital, God. It was Tolstoyan. By comparison Cassandra scarcely seemed to be dying at all.

Cassandra Millar wrote two kinds of books: gothic romances, under the pseudonym of Cassandra Knye, and her "seriouses", the mysteries and thrillers of B. C. Millar. The gothics, which she wrote with a blithe, teasing contempt for her readers, were far and away the more successful. Eight years before, at the height of the craze for gothics, Signet had re-issued eight of the Knye books with uniform covers in murky pastels representing the same wind-blown, distressed young lady in front of a variety of dark buildings. They went through printing after printing. *Blackthorn* became a movie; *Return to Blackthorn* went to the Literary Guild; the whole saga with all five generations, its various family curses and threatened brides, became the basis of a daytime serial on ABC. Cassandra earned literally a million dollars.

By contrast B. C. Millar seemed barely to scrape along. Most of *her* books were out of print, though they had been championed by certain older critics as chief avatars of the deductive mystery. Her cleverest notions were forever being borrowed by other mystery writers, Miss Knye most notoriously, and yet she was happy if any book earned back its modest $2,000 advance. The sad fact of the matter was that for all her incidental drollnesses, for all the ingenuity of her plots, for all her vaunted irony, B. C. Millar couldn't write. Her characters were wooden, her dialogue false, her prose a solecism. As a stylist even Cassandra Knye put her to shame. Miss Knye gushed, she fluttered and cooed, but she was, however vulgarly, alive. As much could not be said for B. C. Millar.

She'd been put to sleep at her dentist's office, preparatory to a minor extraction, and woke in the hospital several hours later. She owed her life, as much as was left, to her dentist's unusual presence of mind, for at the first sign of arrest he'd placed her on the floor and performed external cardiac massage while his reception-ist, who was always so rude on the phone, applied mouth-to-mouth respiration. By the time a doctor had been called down from the next floor her heartbeat was restored.

At the hospital she had demanded to know the worst, and after only a little hemming and hawing her doctor, Alec Dotsler, told her she could expect, with the best of luck, another month. The natural flow of her blood, bottlenecked by a critical valve stenosis, would lessen until advanced hypotension produced another, and another, failure of her heart. Surgery was impossible, drugs useless. It would be painless.

She wondered if she would have been able to believe in her death more if instead of floating off on a breeze she could feel its teeth. Like natural childbirth. During her nightly bouts of insom-nia she would lie staring up at the dark ceiling and thinking stren-uously about death. *Death,* she thought. *I am dying.* As well might she have told herself she was in love, or mad. Was *this* a form of defiance? Resignation? Or only incredulity?

She tried to picture her own body decaying in the grave, all wormy and forlorn. Nothing.

She tried to think of the spaces between the stairs, of timeless-ness, and nonexistence. But such notions affected her no more than stories of the war in India.

Finally she gave up trying, and did what she had always done on nights of insomnia: she plotted new mysteries.

Except in *The Seventh Codicil,* which was a virtual textbook of testamentary law, B. C. Millar had always rather scanted wills as motives for her murders. Cassandra Knye had necessarily more to do with legacies, entails, and such, but even for her these mat-ters had been only so much gothic lumber, in a class with secret passages, mute servants, and mysterious footsteps.

But now, ah! Now she had actually to write her own. Her money would become someone else's. Her money, which she'd meant to spend on jewelry and geriatric treatments! Here was occasion for an elegy. People were no more than the compost in which dollars grew, ripened fell, and grew again.

Despite his most plausible arguments she couldn't bring herself to sign the model document her lawyer had drawn up for her. Half a million dollars to Robin? Inconceivable? Trust funds for nieces, for nephews, for second cousins she wouldn't have recognized on the street? But who or what else should she lavish herself upon? Her ex-husband? His memory evoked, at best, a lingering wistful hatred. Charities? Or some foundation, like Shaw's, to advance some freakish cause of her own?

"Couldn't I just give it *all* to the government?" she pleaded.

Mr. Saunders shook his head.

Finally she came up with a formula that satisfied both herself and him. All three-hundred-forty-nine names on her last year's Christmas card list were to receive absolutely equal shares in her estate. This would give each heir a little less than $4,000. Robin was to get, additionally, the farmhouse in Vermont and its furnishings.

Mr. Saunders called the next morning to ask: "The Lennox Hill Liquor Store?"

"Yes, they've always been very nice to me there. Cashing my checks. And every year they send me a calendar."

"Any particular person there?"

"Oh, I see what you mean. No, divide it up."

"And at Doubleday's, is it Miss Bergen, or Berger. The letter is typed over on the list."

"Who?"

"Bergen. Or Berger."

"I don't think I can remember any such creature at Doubleday's. Maybe you should call them."

"I did. There's one of each, and both are editors."

"If it's holding things up, let's give each of them a share."

The will ran to forty pages. She signed it, and Mr. Saunders and Mr. Dotsler were witnesses.

"Have you ever thought," Yudkin asked, furrowing his brow and deepening his voice from light social to medium serious, "*why* it is that most readers prefer the one kind of book—'gothics' you call them?—to the other kind that *you* prefer?"

Cassandra sighed. The chaplain was turning her life into a breakfast-time talk show on Channel 13. He had to be stopped. "Most people are stupid."

It didn't stop him. "Well, yes maybe. I'd say childish rather than stupid. Children, when they like a story, want to hear it over and over again, and we're all grown-up children. But why this—" He tapped the spine of *Clara Reeve*, Miss Knye's latest triumph. "—particular story over and over rather than what you like, the detective story?"

"What Bob used to say—Bob Millar, he was my agent before we got married—is that my detectives are never sympathetic. They're like computers. In fact one of the books I'll never write now was going to have the murder *solved* by a computer."

"Whereas the heroines in your gothics are sympathetic?"

"Have you ever *read* one of my gothics?" In a tone of voice at once aggrieved and sarcastic.

"I haven't, no, but Mrs. Hyman has read everything Cassandra Knye's ever written. The reason I brought this up, in fact, is because she asked me—"

"Mrs. Hyman!"

"Oh, I didn't tell her your real name, of course, but I noticed the book beside her bed, and naturally we spoke of it. You should have seen the expression on her face when I told her you were here in the same hospital. You're her favorite writer."

"Mrs. Hyman's?"

"As I was saying, she asked me to take this copy with me and ask you if you would sign it. Would you?" He handed her the copy of *Clara Reeve*. "You're laughing. At Mrs. Hyman? At me?"

It was a pantomime rather than real, physiological laughter. She opened the book to the flyleaf, thought a moment, and wrote: "To Mrs. Hyman, Till we meet soon, in those Gardens where the Summer never fades, please accept my heartfelt best wishes—and say a prayer for—Cassandra Knye."

Yudkin read the inscription. "Oh, she'll treasure that."

"It's not too much?"

"Too much?" he asked, as if this were a contradiction in terms. "Oh, not for her. Did I tell you what trick she's up to now, by the way? Spiritualism. Every morning a medium visits her in Ward 'D' and helps her get in touch with the other side. They've reached a spirit called Natalie, who's going to be Mrs. Hyman's guide as soon as she arrives in the spirit world."

"Does it help?"

"More than I ever seemed to. Would *you* like to try it?"

"Not yet, no. When I'm riper, perhaps." She winked to make it clear that she was joking.

II

As an aid to levelheadedness (she was soaring) Cassandra put on pantyhose, a bra, a blouse, and her tweedy authorish suit from the Tailored Woman of long long ago. Looking at herself through the dense roses (lovely roses) she felt as neat and crisp as a parenthesis. Here was the one and only Cassandra Millar, back in her clothes and immortal as ever. And high? As an elephant's eye.

Then, prudently, she returned the Baggy of grass back inside Walt Whitman (the Heritage Club boxed edition), returned the book to the little desert island of masterpieces she'd stocked in her enamel bedside cupboard. There they all were—Proust, Virgil, Cervantes, Montaigne, whole months and years of good intentions.

It didn't matter now. What mattered was being alive (high and alive). There was a passage in Ezekiel that Yudkin was forever quoting at her: *For I have no pleasure in the death of him that dieth, saith the Lord God; wherefore turn yourselves, and live ye.* Cassandra had to agree.

It just kept getting better. It passed all bounds. Something had happened to her metabolism. Grass had never done this to her before. Colors began to shift. Objects took on a beautiful but slightly scary edginess like van Gogh's furniture.

She walked a mile across the room to the window. Outside high winds rasped wisps of Persian from the edges of dreamsicle clouds that rode eastward against the current of the sunlight. The poems disintegrated, line by line, into the tense, the trembling element. A single bird flew up from the parking lot. And up! Nature.

She wanted it all.

At last she got the window open. The colder outdoor air swept in and turned her skin to Coco-Cola. She took the jacket off. Sunglasses. The shivering blouse. Rings and hairpins. Ishtar at apogee. Freedom now! She closed the window, the door, the eyes, and let her living fingers feel, falling back across the bed, her self. She peeled back the calyx of her pantyhose and headed straight for the source. Her fingers pressed past petal after petal like Fabergé bees whose wings (rose-enameled nails) whirred and beat against and bruised the delighted, anguished flower. It was everything magnificent, but even as the twenty-eighth flavor spilled and flickered over the top of the opal dam she had enough irony left (she always did) to think, Now more than *ever* seems it rich to die!

Once she'd started on this bowl of heavenly popcorn she couldn't stop, though even as Pelion was heaped on Ossa she sensed that she was missing the boat. Usually her highs had been models of goal-oriented ecstasy, cornucopias of awareness. Finally, forlornly, she looked about her tumbled bedclothes and saw—

Imagine some dumb widow who's just blown all the insurance money on a suite of shoddy furniture and a fake fur coat. Imagine her entering her living room a year later and looking in the mirror. The gilding of the stucco frame is turning brown. The so-called mink is shedding. There's no chance now to take that secretarial course. And the money's gone. What does she think? Cassandra thought so too.

So when Robin came with her old Tap, tappy-tap-tap, Tap-Tap on the door it was like the Marshall Plan coming to the rescue of a devastated Europe.

"Robin? Robin, darling! Don't come in. I mean, give me a minute."

That night, after conspiratorially flushing the hospital's loathsome chow mein down the toilet, Cassandra and Robin settled down to a feast of real Chinese food from Woh Ping and cold beer from a deli. They ate voraciously, praising the food and making toasts, once they'd slowed down a bit, to the great meals of yesteryear: the holiday dinners, picnics, and homecooked pies of the '40's; from the '50's (when the money had first started rolling in) their extravaganzas at restaurants on Robin's weekend visits into the city; crowning all these, the glories of Robin's own devising now she was grown up with a kitchen all her own—the creamed mushroom omelettes and shrimps polonaise, the sweetbreads and shortcakes, the crêpes and soufflés.

Robin began to cry.

"Robin! Darling, what is it?" (Had the fact of her death, her inevitable death, finally broached Robin's defenses?)

"I'm sorry. But it's just—so awful." She swallowed, took a sip of beer to help it down, and denied that it was anything. However, after sufficient cajoling she confessed that their talk of food had upset her. "I know other people find it offensive just to look at me. No, don't say they don't. They do. And I just can't—" She shook her head dismally. "You see, I *want* to stop. I try, but—I go a day, two days, and then it comes over me. Like another person takes control. And then afterwards I just *hate* myself. I feel so awful. I mean, physically awful." It developed, after still more tears, that Robin had tried to become a nurse, had even been accepted into a school—conditional upon her losing fifty pounds. Since her acceptance she'd put on another fifteen.

"I've never heard of anything so cruel and . . . preposterous! Why didn't you tell me before? I'm sure we could have found another school. I'm sure we still can. What you weigh, Robin, is a matter for your own. . . ." ("Conscience"? Decidedly not.) ". . . for *you* to decide."

"No, Mother, they're right. Anyhow, that's all in the past. I'm happy with the job I've got. I don't want to be a nurse. It's only coming *here* every day, and seeing all of them, seeing how they look at me. . . ."

This, though, was to be only the prelude to the whole, woeful tale. Robin was in love. The man was married. His wife was Robin's best friend (they'd met at Weight Watchers). All three of them were wretched.

Cassandra was aghast, having never imagined any other existence for Robin than this, in which she ate, played cards, knitted socks and sweaters, and paid visits to herself, who (this seemed to have been the understanding) had been the source of whatever was actual, vivid, and passionally alive in the diminished family of mother and daughter: a mistake.

III

"It really was," Yudkin said, "a beautiful death."

"Really?"

"Really. And to be perfectly honest, I was surprised."

"It was lucky you happened to be there then."

"Lucky for me perhaps. Such moments are my chief reward. Not that I can take credit for *her* good death. But just the knowledge that it's possible—that's something."

"It happened this morning?"

"A little before eight. Ward 'D' faces the river, so that the early light is direct and very intense. The explanation may be as simple as that."

"And what did she say?" Cassandra asked once again.

"The light! The light is blinding."

"It *sounds* like she may have wanted you to lower the blinds."

"But she was smiling so as she said it. A smile like—Well, I can't describe it."

For the rest of the day Cassandra felt alone and slightly panicky. She'd come to depend on Mrs. Hyman in so many little ways. Her hysteria and credulity were the foils to Cassandra's own coolness and rationality. All her anguished writhings, as Yudkin had reported them to her daily, had been an admonishment not to go off down the same steep road herself. It galled her that Mrs. Hyman, who'd actually had some hope of recovering, should beat her to the exit; it was insufferable that she should do so with such panache. *"The light!"* indeed! she thought grimly. Who did Mrs. Hyman think she was? Goethe? Little Nell?

There was nothing, next morning, in the paper. Mr. Hyman was a prominent toy manufacturer on 31st Street; surely his wife's death rated a mention in *The Times,* if only her name and age and who she was survived by. Cassandra herself was counting on four column inches, and though Mrs. Hyman couldn't have asked for as much as that, this total neglect seemed tantamount to being left unburied, out on a dungheap, like Antigone's brother.

From this it was only a short step to doubting Mrs. Hyman's existence. Once doubting, she was easily disproved. Cassandra discovered, from the aide who came in to make her bed that morning, that Ward "D" was devoted entirely to male geriatric cases. A phonecall to the admissions office cinched it.

Rabbi Yudkin was not to be blamed for having invented Mrs. Hyman (hadn't she almost demanded it of him?)—only for having allowed his audience to fall into disbelief at the high point of his tale. Her death had been too nice, too merely decorative. If only he'd baited his transcendental hook with some engaging, toothsome detail Cassandra might never have thought to doubt his story. If, for instance, towards the end Mrs. Hyman had tried to destroy her Charge-a-Plate, or got the hiccoughs, like Pope Pius XII. But to bathe her in that blinding light, to have practically sent down a ladder to her from on high! That showed a want of tact.

She had phoned down to the cashier's office, and when Yudkin called by for his afternoon chat she was ready for him.

"When is the funeral?" she asked.

"Not till Friday."

"Here? Or in Scarsdale?"

"In Scarsdale. It will probably be quite a production. Mr. Hyman seems to be in his element again, organizing things."

Cassandra beckoned Yudkin closer to her bed. "Here," she said, pressing the envelope into his hand. "I want you to do a favor for me. A little deception."

He looked doubtful.

"A wreath. I want to send her the very best wreath you can get."

"Oh. But."

"The card needn't say any more than—'With sincere sympathy, Cassandra Knye'."

"Impossible. I mean—" He looked into the envelope. "Oh, Mrs. Millar, this is far too much!"

"For a wreath? Nonsense. I called a florist and asked. And don't try and tell me they don't want flowers. I know Scarsdale."

"But—" He was caught. Either he had to admit that Mrs. Hyman had never existed, or he had to take the money.

"I would have sent the wreath myself, but then, you see, they might have been able to trace it back to *me*. I want to be the person I always love in a story—the anonymous benefactor. And I know I can count on you to preserve my pseudonym. But if there's some reason you'd rather not, I *could* get Robin to send it."

"No! No, I just questioned the—" He held up the bulging envelope.

"The propriety of it?"

"Yes. To be frank."

"But it isn't really disproportionate when you think of all I've got. Oh, say you'll do it."

Yudkin wavered, sighed, and pocketed the envelope.

"I knew you would." She leaned forward in the bed and pinched his cheek. "If you could *see* the way you're blushing!"

She'd made her pile by telling people what they seemed to want to hear—that Death is a gentleman whose kisses were tender even as he threatened rape, that one may venture out onto the terrace with him and come back to the party, like silly Clara Reeve, a bit sadder, a bit wiser, but intact. In fact, there are no survivors of that waltz, and so the heart of every one of her books had been a lie. But what of that? Her readers had wanted it, and now at last she wanted it too. For Yudkin had invented Mrs. Hyman in response to her expressed, her almost strident need, and Cassandra had been his more than willing dupe. She wanted no further knowledge of *real* people, of how they were cheated, cornered, betrayed, and themselves driven to cheat, entrap, and betray in turn. She could have killed Robin for reminding her of the processes of love—the anguish of being rejected, the guilt of rejecting, the desolations of loneliness. No, she craved fiction. "Reality," as one of her old buttons had proclaimed, "is a crutch." If this were a lie, well then, she needed what help she could get.

And so did everyone.

Yudkin had done the right thing. He'd told the lie his duty had demanded and persisted in it, even at the expense of self-respect.

Cassandra could do no less.

That same afternoon she contacted Mr. Saunders to revoke her first whimsical will and have him bring in his model document, which he did. She signed it. She wrote a rich, ripe heartthrob of a letter to Bob, telling him what, in the last analysis, a wonderful husband he'd been, and what a phenomenal lover. She sent cheery, heartbreaking little notes to all the nieces and nephews and second cousins. All these were forthright, uncomplicated plagiarisms from The Best-Loved Lies of the American People. The real test would be Robin, who, for all her prissy pieties and pretended deafnesses, was her mother's sternest audience and cruelest judge.

In the summer of '45 Bob and Cassandra and Robin and Bob's cousin Margaret Millar had all driven west in a Kaiser station wagon to see the actual country Bob had been writing about all these years. The culmination of the many misadventures of the trip came when Bob and Margaret contrived to be lost for four days in Grand Canyon National Park, leaving Cassandra with Robin, the dying Kaiser, and eight dollars. At that time Cassandra had been a haggard twenty-six, Margaret a dazzling nineteen.

Time and affluence had improved Cassandra; the same amount of time and too much liquor had made of the second Mrs. Millar a shipwreck of her former self. Conscious of their reversed fortunes and without considering that they were about to be reversed again, Margaret on her visit was abjectly complimentary. How wonderful Cassandra looked! What a lovely negligee! How lucky she was to have a private room!

"When *I* was in the hospital," she said, "I was in the general ward. With all these colored women? You can imagine what *that* was like. Hackensack! But this! This is more like a hotel room than a hospital. The furniture! Though you would think for what you're paying you'd have a room with a view to the river. Still it's not a *bad* view. In fact, it's nice."

"Would you like a cigarette?" Cassandra asked.

"I shouldn't. But thank you, I will." The knuckles of Margaret's hand were swollen, the flesh puffy, the skin coarse. To think she was still able to play the piano! "Chesterfields! You don't see many of them nowadays."

"No, you don't. Bob used to smoke Chesterfields. I must have picked it up from him."

This was the first mention of his name since Margaret had come in the door twenty minutes ago.

"Do you hear from him?" Margaret asked.

"Not often. He lives in London. And he's married again. But that's old news by now."

Margaret shrieked with laughter. "Always the gay Lothario!"

It was her chance. "Yes," she said softly, "he was that."

Margaret, who had prepared herself to unite with Cassandra in vilifying their ex-husband, was dismayed now to hear him so eloquently praised, so candidly cherished. Cassandra wanted (she said) only to remember what had been good and live and warm and tender: the laughter they had shared, the growing and deepening sense of mutual discovery, the love. But who could describe love? One could only experience it.

"You loved him too, didn't you?" she said, catching hold of Margaret's hand as soon as she'd stubbed out the cigarette. "Oh, of course you did! How could you have helped it? How could I?"

Margaret tried, gently, to pry her hand away. (It was such an ugly hand.) "But I always thought—"

"That I was jealous? Oh, at first I may have been. But how could I have gone on feeling like that after all you've done for me? You brought up Robin. You were the mother to her that I was too busy and too selfish to be."

"But wasn't I—?"

"Yes?" Cassandra let her free her hand.

"Wasn't I just as selfish, in my own way? For years I lived off the money that you and Bob sent me for Robin."

"Oh, money!" She waved her hand through a column of cigarette smoke: that's all money was. "The important thing is that you brought up Robin to be the dear, beautiful person that she is, and for that I'll always be grateful."

Margaret looked up doubtfully, but already, even with those doubts unresolved, the tears had started to her eyes. "Do you really love Robin then?"

"Love her!"

"She always wanted you to, you know. So badly."

"I guess I never knew how to express it."

"That's what I would tell her. But this last week, Mrs. Millar—" Margaret stopped short.

"Cassandra. Please."

"This last week, Cassandra, she's been so happy. She's been another person."

"Has she? I'm glad. I was so afraid that I'd have . . . passed on before I had a chance to . . . make her understand. And that's why I told her I wanted to see *you* too. I don't want to leave *any* bad feelings behind me. Oh, when I think of the time I've wasted, the love I've thrown away. You and I, Margaret—you and I!"

Margaret seemed to consider this deeply, but could do no better than meekly to echo, "You and I."

Cassandra elaborated: "We had so much in common."

"Oh, Mrs.—"

"Bob thought so too, you know. He said to me once, years and years later, that he thought we were like two twins, you and I. Not physically, of course, because you're much prettier than me, but deep down, where it counts."

By now Margaret was thoroughly raddled. Cassandra's revelations had exceeded all her capacities as a spectator. She'd lost track of who the characters were and what relationships were presumed to exist between them.

Cassandra leaned forward, to cup Margaret's rouged jowls in her fine hands. She looked lingeringly into her bleary, fuddled blue eyes and then, with a more than sisterly emphasis, kissed her mouth.

"There!" she said, returning to her pillow with a sigh. "That's what I wanted to do the moment you came in the door."

She had arrived at what she thought would have to be her last word on the subject of death, and it was as astonishing in its way as the detective's announcement, in the last chapter of the book, that *none* of the suspects was guilty.

It was just this: Death is a social experience; an exchange; not a relationship in itself, but the medium in which relationships may exist; not a friend or a lover, but the room in which all friends and lovers meet.

She reached for the Chesterfields, took one, offered the pack to Margaret, who accepted one after a tremor of hesitation. A flame flicked from the lighter, and Margaret inhaled.

Then there was a knock on the door. Tap tappy-tap-tap. Tap. Tap.

"That will be Robin," said both Mrs. Millars together.

NORWEGIANS

PATRICIA ZELVER

Patricia Zelver was born in California, and grew up in
Medford, Oregon. She attended Stanford. She has published two novels, *The Honey Bunch* and *The Happy
Family*, as well as short stories. This will be her third
appearance in the O. Henry collection. She is married
and has two sons.

This time Mr. and Mrs. Jessup just concentrated on one country
—Norway. "Norway isn't ruined by tourism, yet," Mr. Jessup said.
"Let's do Norway before it turns into a Venice."

*"The country of Norway is extremely picturesque and not yet
ruined by tourism,"* Mrs. Jessup dictated into her husband's port-
able dictating machine as she sat in the bedroom of their inn. The
tapes were mailed to Mr. Jessup's office in Evanston, typed and
Xeroxed by his secretary, and distributed to relatives, friends and
business associates. The letters were Mr. Jessup's idea. Mrs. Jessup
had done it in the Orient, too, and everyone had commented
favorably. The first time she felt shy, but now she had developed
more facility. Mr. Jessup said he thought it was good for Mrs. Jessup. Since their two sons had grown up and married he had detected a lack of purpose in her life. Recently, he had had a
physical by their family doctor. The doctor had inquired after Mrs.
Jessup; Mr. Jessup had mentioned that this was a difficult time in
a woman's life.

Mrs. Jessup told the machine about the fjords, the curious little
Lapps, the stave churches, the Viking ships, the Munch Museum
and their visit to the home of a Norwegian couple in Bergen. The
man had a connection with Mr. Jessup's firm. Sometimes Mrs.
Jessup used a little book for help, which Mr. Jessup had purchased
for her in Oslo. It was called *Facts About Norway*.

"The predominating trees in Norwegian forests, which cover

nearly one fourth of the land, are fir and pine, but birch and other deciduous trees are found even in mountainous districts," the book said.

Mrs. Jessup changed this when she talked to the machine, to make it sound more like her own style. *"Most of the trees are fir and pine,"* she told the machine, *"but there are also some birch and other deciduous trees."*

After seeing what Mr. Jessup called the "main attractions," Mr. Jessup had gone to a "simpatico" traveling agent in their Oslo hotel and told him they wished to settle down for a week in a small country village with its own industry, unconnected with the tourist trade, a place where they could rest and "walk among the people." "This," Mr. Jessup said to Mrs. Jessup, "is the way to end a trip."

"We are now in a quaint rustic inn in a small fishing village, unconnected with the tourist trade," Mrs. Jessup said to the machine, while Mr. Jessup unpacked. *"It is not a fancy resort. Far from it! Papa, at the desk; Mama, in the kitchen; the children helping out. Here we will rest and walk among the people, which is the best way to end a trip."*

After a simple lunch in the inn's sedate dining room, they went back up to their room again. Mr. Jessup always lay down for a half hour after his noon meal; the doctor had told him this was one of the best ways for men with responsibilities, such as he had, to avoid getting into trouble. Mrs. Jessup continued with her letter.

"The room in our inn looks out upon the water," she said to the machine. She spoke in a low voice so as not to disturb her husband. *"The water is grey, dotted with grey rocks. Grey rocks, grey gulls, a grey sky. An ancient lighthouse stands on the rocky promontory across the water in all its pristine glory. Picturesque—"*

She stopped, remembering she had used that word before lunch. She erased the tape and went on. *"Fishing boats, straight out of an Impressionistic painting, bob up and down beside an empty wharf."*

Mrs. Jessup glanced at Mr. Jessup; his eyes were open. "Is the water a fjord?" she asked him.

"We've seen our fjords," said Mr. Jessup with an encouraging smile. "It's more of a bay."

"Having had our fill of fjords, the water is more of a bay," said Mrs. Jessup to the machine.

When Mr. Jessup had finished his rest period, they both put on their new Norwegian sweaters. Mr. Jessup put on his Tyrolean hat, which was decorated with a perky little brush, and slung his camera bag over his shoulder. They went downstairs again. Mr. Jessup asked Papa at the desk if there was anything especially worthwhile seeing in the village. They were particularly interested in old architecture, he said.

There was a long silence. "Well, that depends," said Papa. "What I might consider worth seeing you might not consider worth seeing. People differ, you see."

"The Norwegians are not servants," said Mr. Jessup as they went out the front door for their walk. "There's no 'yes, sir; no, sir.' No bowing and scraping. No spit and polish, like the English."

"The English do a lot of polishing," Mrs. Jessup agreed, recalling the glowing silver tea sets and the shining brass hardware.

"It has to do with courage in the face of adversity," Mr. Jessup said.

"Polishing?" said Mrs. Jessup.

"Keeping up appearances, despite all," Mr. Jessup said.

"The Norwegians don't seem to polish," she said. She thought for a moment. "But Norwegians are courageous, too, aren't they?" she said.

"We know that they are," said Mr. Jessup. "Their Vikings, their Resistance, their brave battle with the sea. It's another tradition, that's all. That's why we travel. The Norwegians are a proud and independent race."

Mrs. Jessup made a note in her head of this last phrase for her letter. "Though the Norwegians do not polish like the English," she said to herself, "they are a proud and independent race."

It was a cool September afternoon. "A hint of winter in the air," said Mr. Jessup, buttoning up his sweater. They were walking through a small park. A young woman in a mini-skirt and boots sat on a bench beside a baby buggy. Mrs. Jessup, thinking of her new grandchild, hesitated for a moment beside the buggy, then

peeped inside it. Mr. Jessup, who liked to walk briskly—the doctor had told him this was the best sort of exercise for men who
spent their days at their desks—was already some paces ahead of
her. When he noticed that Mrs. Jessup was not beside him, he
stopped; he waited with a courtly patience as she admired the infant and congratulated the mother. Suddenly, Mrs. Jessup sensed
his absence. She scurried to catch up with him, as if she had been
caught day-dreaming in school. Mr. Jessup took her hand in his
and squeezed it tenderly.

There were two statues in the park. One statue, on a pedestal, was
a bronzed, bearded gentleman in a frock coat, with a watch and
chain dangling from his vest pocket; the other—made of white
stone—was a slim young girl, naked, with small, high breasts and
flowing, snakelike hair. The girl stood, proud, under the gentleman's sober gaze.

   Mr. Jessup stopped in front of the man. He studied the inscription on the base of the pedestal. "Henrik Ibsen," he said. He
glanced at the girl. "The nude was obviously done later," he told
Mrs. Jessup. "I must say, it's a curious juxtaposition."

   "Maybe somebody was playing a little joke," said Mrs. Jessup.

   "Ibsen," said Mr. Jessup, "is one of their national heroes."

   "That's what makes it funny," Mrs. Jessup said. "It wouldn't be
funny if he wasn't."

   "You don't make jokes with public money," Mr. Jessup said. "I
would guess it was just bad planning," he said.

They walked on. School was just out and the streets were alive
with children. Two large boys were tussling, while a circle of their
companions cheered them on. A tiny girl, with a mass of curly
yellow snarled hair, stuck out her tongue at Mrs. Jessup. When
Mr. Jessup wasn't looking, Mrs. Jessup stuck out her tongue at the
girl. A small boy picked up a rock and pretended he was going to
hurl it at Mr. Jessup. Mr. Jessup gave him a stern look. The boy
laughed and made an obscene gesture with his finger. Mrs. Jessup
giggled.

   "Rowdy bunch," said Mr. Jessup, taking Mrs. Jessup's arm.

   A few blocks further, they found themselves in front of a small
military installation surrounded by a stone wall. Its gate was
guarded by a young soldier with long hair hanging out from be-

neath his helmet. Mr. Jessup looked past the soldier through the open gate. "There are some interesting old buildings in there," he said to Mrs. Jessup. "I wonder if the fellow speaks English."

He went up to the guard. "We are Americans," he said.

The guard nodded solemnly.

"My wife and I would like to take a look at the old buildings in there. Would this be possible?"

"Sorry," said the guard, "it's against the rules."

At that moment, a hatless officer, wearing three stars on his epaulets, strode out of the gate; Mr. Jessup waited until he was out of earshot of the guard, and then approached him. "Excuse me, sir," he said respectfully.

The officer stopped.

"We are Americans. We are traveling in your splendid country. I happened to notice the fine old buildings in your presidio. They appear to date from medieval times."

"Yes, yes, very old," said the officer.

"I wondered if it would be possible for my wife and I to take a look at them?"

The officer pulled a billfold out of a pocket and removed a card and handed it to Mr. Jessup. "My card," he said affably. "Just tell the guard at the gate that I said you may go in."

"That's extremely generous of you, sir," Mr. Jessup said.

"My pleasure," said the officer, with a little bow of his head; then he hurried on.

Mr. Jessup looked at the card, then smiled at Mrs. Jessup. "It's usually simply a matter of approaching the right person," he said. He went up to the guard again and presented the card. The guard gave it an indifferent glance and handed it back. "Your General said we might see the old buildings," Mr. Jessup said.

"Sorry," said the guard, "it's against the rules."

Mr. Jessup's voice took on a slight edge of exasperation. "But you saw me, just this moment, talking to him!" he said.

The fellow grinned. "Yes, but you see, it's like this," he said. "The General isn't here now, is he? I'm the boss now."

"It's easy to see how the Germans took over if their privates make up all the rules," Mr. Jessup said to Mrs. Jessup as they left.

Mrs. Jessup remembered seeing a church when they had entered town. She knew Mr. Jessup liked taking photographs of churches.

She led him around another gang of loitering, noisy youths, down
a narrow street of small shops and across a plaza. "Voilà!" she said
proudly, pointing to a small yellow wooden building with a cross
on its top, surrounded by a graveyard.

"It's not a stave church, is it?" Mrs. Jessup said, a bit apologetically.

"We've seen our stave churches," said Mr. Jessup. "They resemble Siamese temples. Siam. Thailand, now. Remember?"

"Oh, yes," said Mrs. Jessup.

"Still—it has a nice simplicity." Mr. Jessup walked up the steps
and tried the door. It was locked. He backed up a few steps, un-
zipped his camera bag and began to tinker with his equipment,
measuring the light with a meter, adjusting the lens. "You stand
on the porch," he said.

Mrs. Jessup knew how long it took Mr. Jessup to set things up
properly when he took a picture; he took great pride in his photog-
raphy. She would try to look bright and alert, but her mind would
often wander. Standing on the steps of Nôtre Dame, she had
seen a dog trot by and was reminded of a dog she had loved as a
child; in front of the Taj Mahal, the warm, muggy air had taken
her back to a summer evening and a boy. She had laughed out
loud, remembering. Mr. Jessup had caught her laugh in the picture. After their trip, when they had presented their usual slide
show for their friends, there she was—laughing—and everyone had
remarked how much Mrs. Jessup seemed to be enjoying her exotic
adventure.

"I haven't had my hair done for days," she told Mr. Jessup now.
"You take the picture and I'll go for a walk in the graveyard."

Mrs. Jessup walked around the church on a path which led
through the graves. An old woman was bent over one of them,
busily pulling out weeds from around a flat stone marker. Mrs.
Jessup stood quietly in back of her and tried to make out the words
carved on the stone. They were in Norwegian, but she could read
the name and date.

Olaf Olafson

1923–1940

Olaf Olafson had been seventeen when he died, Mrs. Jessup
thought. Danny Plummer—that had been the name of her old
boyfriend—had been twenty when he was killed on Guadalcanal.

The woman looked up at Mrs. Jessup. Mrs. Jessup smiled at her shyly. "Your son?" she said, rocking an imaginary baby in her arms.

The old woman nodded. She picked up her black pocketbook, which was on the ground beside her, and stood up. She opened the bag and took out a photograph and showed it to Mrs. Jessup.

"He was very handsome," said Mrs. Jessup, hoping that by her tone and expression the old woman would understand.

The old woman put her pocketbook back upon the ground. She stood up. Her body stiffened in a mock military posture; she swung one hand to her forehead in a Nazi salute. Then she dropped her hand, put both hands around her thin neck and twisted them; her face grew contorted, her tongue hung out.

Mrs. Jessup gasped. Olaf Olafson had been hanged, she thought. Danny Plummer's body had been shattered by a mortar shell.

Mrs. Jessup took the old woman's hand and shook it. She walked slowly back around the church, wiping tears from her eyes.

Mr. Jessup was still tinkering with the camera. "I've been waiting for you," he said jovially. "I need some human interest."

Mrs. Jessup took out her comb and combed her hair and posed for him on the church steps.

"You look like you just lost your last friend," said Mr. Jessup. "Let's have a little smile. Come on, now. Say cheese."

Mrs. Jessup said "cheese," and Mr. Jessup snapped the shutter.

"That could be a good one," he said, putting his camera equipment away. "The light was perfect."

"*The people of Norway are a proud and independent race,*" Mrs. Jessup said into the machine, while Mr. Jessup took his shower before dinner. She paused. She could not write about Olaf Olafson—not in this kind of letter. It was not what people would expect. Nor did she think Mr. Jessup would approve. She had not, in fact, even told Mr. Jessup about Olaf. She was not sure why she had not told him. He was a kind and thoughtful man. He would certainly have been sympathetic.

"*Norwegians differ from the English, another proud and independent race, in that they do not spend their time polishing,*" Mrs. Jessup told the machine. "*Despite this, it is a clean country. Handsome statues adorn its plazas. Architecture, of a simple design—*"

She had never told Mr. Jessup about Danny Plummer, either.

She had told no one at all. When he died, nobody knew she had lost a lover. She was not the same person who had loved the dead boy, anyhow.

"*Architecture of a simple design—*" she repeated to the machine. She seemed to be bogging down. Perhaps it would help to look at *Facts About Norway* again. This time she talked directly from the book: "*Rich grave finds from the Viking age around 1000 A.D. show that even at that time Norwegians had a great sense of beauty, color and form, and liked to surround themselves with beautiful things.*"

Mr. Jessup came out of the shower, wrapped in a towel, all pink and steamy.

"*This afternoon,*" Mrs. Jessup was saying in her own words now, "*we went for a pleasant walk. There is a hint of winter in the air.*"

Mr. Jessup smiled at her approvingly.

Mrs. Jessup showered and put on a simple black dress and the pearls Mr. Jessup had given her for their thirtieth wedding anniversary. Mr. Jessup complimented Mrs. Jessup upon her appearance. They were about to go down for an early dinner when they heard a commotion below their window. Mrs. Jessup looked out. "Something is happening on the wharf," she said. "Another boat has come in."

"I could stand more of a stroll before eating," Mr. Jessup said.

The whole town seemed to be on the wharf; it was like a carnival. They surrounded the boat, which had just arrived; its decks were filled to the gunwales with tiny silver fish.

"It's a herring catch," said Mr. Jessup.

The fishermen were shoveling up the herring and dropping them into crates. The kids had gone wild. They swarmed over the boat, balanced on the gunwales, climbed the rigging and threw themselves recklessly into the shining, slippery catch. A few older boys, mimicking the men, were trying to help out. No one seemed to mind.

"Someone should stop those kids. These are busy men," said Mr. Jessup.

Mrs. Jessup did not answer. She was looking on in amazement.

As she looked, the same little girl she had seen in the park poked her head out of the herring; her tousled hair glistened with fish scales. She saw Mrs. Jessup and stuck out her tongue again, with a grin. Mrs. Jessup stuck out her tongue in reply.

"The Northern waters being so frigid, the local custom here is to swim in herring," Mrs. Jessup said to herself, as if she were talking to the machine. *"I felt a bit timid at first, but soon I, too, slipped off my shoes and stockings and joined the natives. The sensation is unique, one might go as far as to say 'indescribable.' I have experienced nothing like it in all my travels throughout the world."*

Maybe I'm going cuckoo, she thought, as Mr. Jessup led her back down the wharf through the noisy crowd.

It was now very cold. Mrs. Jessup shivered and put up the collar of her coat.

"Chilly?" said Mr. Jessup with concern.

"A bit," Mrs. Jessup said.

They were passing a pub next to the inn. It was crowded with people from the wharf and soldiers from the army post. Loud voices and the clinking of beer mugs came from the open door.

"A drink would warm you up," said Mr. Jessup.

They entered the pub. The tables were all filled. Two young men, noticing their predicament, beckoned the Jessups to join them.

"Thank you very much, gentlemen," said Mr. Jessup in a hearty voice as the Jessups sat down between them.

The young men spoke English; they were from Bergen; they were in the army reserve, spending two weeks here on compulsory military duty. "We are here to save our country," one of them said. They both laughed; they seemed to be a little drunk. The General the Jessups had met that morning was at a nearby table; he greeted them with a loud, "Hello, my friends!"

Everyone seemed to be enjoying himself immensely.

The second young man—an exceptionally handsome young man, thought Mrs. Jessup—spoke to them. "You are Americans?" he said.

"Tourists," Mrs. Jessup was about to say; then she remembered that Mr. Jessup did not care for that word.

"We are Americans here to see your country," Mr. Jessup said.

He signaled to a waiter. "May I offer you gentlemen two more beers?" he said.

"Thank you," said the first young man.

Mr. Jessup ordered a glass of sherry for Mrs. Jessup, and three beers.

"And what do you think of our country?" the second young man said to Mrs. Jessup.

"We think it's very beautiful. We like it very much." She looked at Mr. Jessup for confirmation, but he was busy paying the waiter for the drinks.

"Yes, we Norwegians are very fortunate," the second young man said. "I went to school in your country, by the way. I went to the University of California. Every weekend, I drove up to your Sierra to ski."

"Did you ever consider staying there?" said Mr. Jessup.

The young man laughed, as if at some secret joke. He said, "I'm a Norwegian. Perhaps if I were a Dane or a Swede I might have considered the—ah—business possibilities. But I'm a Norwegian, you see."

"It must be like belonging to a private club," Mrs. Jessup said. She felt oddly envious, as if she were standing by a window looking in at a nice party to which she had not been invited.

"Yes, yes, that's an excellent analysis," the young man said to her. His eyes, she noticed, were incredibly blue and fringed with long curly pale lashes.

"If it's so satisfactory being a Norwegian," said Mr. Jessup, "—I'm only asking out of an intellectual curiosity, you understand —how do you explain your high suicide rate?"

The young man smiled. He had a charming dimple on his left cheek; Mrs. Jessup almost had to keep herself from reaching out to touch it. The sherry, she thought, must have gone to my head.

"Perhaps you are confusing us with the Swedes," the young man was saying to Mr. Jessup. "Still, we Norwegians commit suicide now and then." He tipped his chair back, took a swallow of beer, then put the mug down. He leaned toward Mr. Jessup. "You know what they say of us Norwegians? They say, 'You only get to know a Norwegian—up to a point.'"

Mrs. Jessup wanted to ask, "At what point *don't* we get to know you?" but she was afraid that this might sound forward.

"In other words, you can't explain it," said Mr. Jessup, genially.

"Everything cannot be explained," the young man said. "Some say it's lack of sun. Others say we live, then we die, on our own, so to speak, when it suits *us*."

"I hope it suits *you* to live!" Mrs. Jessup said, with sudden feeling.

This time the young man smiled at her—a sweet, strangely compassionate smile.

"*Norwegian men have incredibly blue eyes and sweet smiles,*" Mrs. Jessup said to herself, as if she were dictating again. "*They are also extremely compassionate and understand the secret heart of woman. How do I know this? Shall we just call it my little indiscretion?*"

Oh, dear, I really must be tipsy, she thought. She put her glass down, hurriedly.

"Ready?" said Mr. Jessup to her.

Mrs. Jessup stood up.

"It was most kind of you to ask us to join you, gentlemen," said Mr. Jessup, shaking hands with both young men.

As they left, the General rose and gave them a salute. Mr. Jessup nodded briskly at him, then guided Mrs. Jessup in a different direction toward the door.

"*Norwegians,*" Mrs. Jessup said to the machine that evening after dinner, "*are very proud of their nation.*"

Mr. Jessup was already in bed, reading, but Mrs. Jessup had not yet undressed. Her memory was not as good as it used to be, and she wanted to get her impressions down before she lost them.

"There's something all over your shoes," Mr. Jessup said.

Mrs. Jessup glanced down. Her black suede traveling shoes glittered with shining dots, like sequins. She stared at them for a moment. "I think it's the herring from the wharf," she said.

"Better get them off now," Mr. Jessup said.

She got up from her chair and went to the armoire and took out her suede brush. She slipped off her shoes and brushed them carefully. The silver scales flew off and disappeared into the rug. Again, Mrs. Jessup felt the same peculiar sadness she had felt in the pub. She returned quickly to her job.

"*It could perhaps be compared to belonging to an exclusive club,*" she continued. She paused, considered for a moment, then went on. "*There is an old saying, 'You only get to know a Norwe-*

gian up to a point.'" This last sentence bothered her. She decided to play it back for Mr. Jessup.

"Sounds fine to me," Mr. Jessup said.

"But you could say it about anyone, couldn't you? Not just about Norwegians?" Mrs. Jessup said.

"I would say it applies to Norwegians very well," said Mr. Jessup. "No one would say it about you, for example, would he?"

Mrs. Jessup thought for a moment. Then she decided that Mr. Jessup was, as usual, right.

CERTAIN HARD PLACES

LINDA ARKING

Linda Arking was born and raised in Atlantic City, New
Jersey. "Certain Hard Places," her second piece of fiction, is from a cycle of stories she is presently at work
on. Other work has appeared in *The New Yorker*, *The
Atlantic*, and *Antaeus*.

This story is about something that happened in New York City
shortly after abortion had become legal but before the President
went to China. There were those two facts, and I should remember.

I'd just returned from several years abroad when I called Danny.
He was no stranger. We were students at the New School, where
we had many discussions in the cafeteria. He was advanced then,
already on his doctorate in sociology. I went to classes at night,
and in the daytime worked at Bellevue on the hospital newspaper,
which gave me topics for sociology and money for rent. He liked
me a lot then. I could tell. Still, I steered clear. He was a big guy,
usually decked out in plaid wool shirts and large corduroys—he
was too wide for jeans. He had shortish arms and legs, enormous
hands, and a powerful chest. I felt attraction, sympathy—he was
so amiable, and willing—but there was something about him that
left me uneasy. Even while I was thinking how likable he was, I'd
notice how his fingernails were bitten down to the quick, how he
swayed his whole body slowly as he talked. His complexion was
blotchy, and since he'd stay up at night reading, his eyes were
often red. But what bothered me most was the dispersion of everything, the sense of diffusion, of, well, helplessness in the way his
large features seemed to float across his face, how his head of curly
hair haplessly frizzed out around the edges. I must have been un-
sure of myself then, too.

We were both deeply interested in sociology, though I knew my commitment was not worth as much as his. I was saving from my salary to go to Europe. When I told Danny I was going, that I wanted to go to Florence and see the museums, he said he was surprised I'd choose such a classical pastime, and warned me about becoming irrelevant. Though of course I'd still exist.

I stayed three years in Europe, mostly Italy, and meanwhile heard in letters that Danny had been taken on as an instructor at a city college. I, too, made headway; I found a job teaching English with Berlitz, learned to speak good Italian, and sold two articles to American magazines. It was on the plane back that I decided to call him. I was flying home to see my parents, line up assignments, find an agent. I was enjoying the flight. Who knows, I thought, but that in these still formative years Danny, too, had pulled himself together? I was curious, and I thought something would happen.

So I called him. We arranged to meet at five in the lobby of the expanded New School, on Fifth Avenue, in the building I remembered as Lane's Department Store. I waited inside and saw him approaching the glass doors. He had on a brown shaggy sweater and dark-brown pants. He was bulky as ever, but he'd grown a beard. That and the dark clothes gave him a certain solidity. He came plunging through the revolving door. We were really glad to see each other.

In honor of our common past, we went to Ratner's, where the waiter gave us the bread basket the minute we sat down.

"Well, Margo," Danny said, looking at me from across the table and three years of absence, "I guess Europe must have fed only healthy things into you."

"Oh, right," I said, patting my thigh. "Three years of spaghetti."

"No," he said gravely. "I mean, you look more—put together, more in touch with yourself."

One thing I learned in Europe was to avoid abstractions, and to talk in anecdotes; struggling in a foreign language, I had to be concrete. So I told him a story I'd picked up somewhere. "Once in Greece," I said, "at the Academy, there was a certain door with a plaque over it inscribed 'Only Those Who Know the Secret May Enter.' Everyone looked at it, and thought about it, and knew *they* didn't know the secret, and the door stayed closed. Until one day somebody just went up to it and opened the door and walked through—that was the secret."

"That's what you learned in Greece?" Danny looked a little blank.

"No. Yes!" I really liked that story. "I learned it by, well, travelling, living in different countries, one, then another, but surviving in each of them. Self-reliance, the bird in the hand, right? You can do anything, but you've got to do."

His face cleared. He smiled. "Why, Margo," he said, "that's wonderful!" His smile kept on spreading. We both flushed, higher and higher, clasping our steamy glasses of tea. My warm friend, I thought, oh my old pal, my kinsman. I remembered his ardor for me three years ago, and I considered the moral of the story I had just finished telling.

So I suggested it. "Danny," I said, laying my hand lightly on his sleeve. "Dear, why don't we walk later to your place?"

His face went to pieces. He turned pale. He plunged forward as though his head, his big shoulders, could fall apart into my lap. He said, in a whisper, "Nothing's . . . been easy for me lately."

He'd quit the New School in protest before finishing his Ph.D., and lost the college teaching post for ridiculing the curriculum. With friends, all Ph.D. candidates, he'd formed a political consciousness-raising group, whose technique was to enroll themselves back at the city college, as freshmen, but in the sociology courses they had already taught. I said that from the outside this seemed like a dead end, but he said no, because his role in class now was to interrupt with questions exposing the professor's bias, thereby alerting the students. But still he felt stymied. His students were middle-class and easily bored, and he was ambivalent, too, about the other group members, who, he felt, were politically conscious but not personally warm.

He lived by giving math lessons—I knew he had that bent—and though he now rejected social sciences for their reliance on statistics, he found he could easily make a living tutoring New Yorkers in Boolean algebra for computers. So from one executive he could count on five hours a week, and three more teaching the new math to the six-year-old son of a psychiatrist in Queens. "For three weeks running," he said, "I'm ushered right out afterward; but the end of the month, when they pay me, they bring out fancy candy and liquor. I'm like the mailman at Christmas; they're so condescending."

He had given up the airy apartment I'd known near the New School and moved crosstown to a railroad flat on Avenue B. "Ethnically I know it's shot," he admitted, "but it's still a community. They still have real family." He got this apartment from a fellow-student, a history candidate who moved uptown when he transferred his credits to Columbia, and charged Dan four hundred and fifty dollars for his exposed-brick walls and built-in cabinets. This flat was ten feet across, forty long, and overrun with roaches, he said. He saw them the night he moved in, but he had found he could control them by spreading boric-acid powder around and by leaving the lights on.

At this point, Dan must have thought he'd told me more than he had, because he paused, waiting, with his head down, expecting me to speak, and when I didn't say anything he blurted out, "Look. All I want is to live so I feel close to people. Is that so inconceivable? Margo? But I feel so blockaded, it's stifling, a suffocation. I can't reach out; my whole environment cramps me." He lowered his eyes again and began to talk about the political group. "We're all trying to be warmer," he said. "Maybe we'll buy some land together."

An elderly waiter in a yellow jacket came over and took away our bread basket. "That's not our waiter," Danny said. "He wants to pick over our best onion rolls for that family at his own table. The poor old *pischer*—oh, Christ, let him go; seventy years old, stealing bread for his tips. That's what Yiddishness has come to on Second Avenue. To think this place was built in the days of our Socialist grandfathers." He pushed back his chair. "C'mon, let's go. This big room with its hanging mirrors is like Nebuchadnezzar's palace."

Actually, I'd always liked Ratner's and the other big Jewish restaurants—the uptown cafeterias that reminded me of ocean liners, with long curving chrome counters and fifty kinds of cold salads. Still, I knew what Danny meant. The place could make you feel alien; besides, I didn't like the prices.

Sunset reddened the storefronts on Second Avenue. I hadn't remembered it was cobbled. We crossed the street and, arm in arm, walked along, past ashcans, pushcarts, laundry hanging, past pots and frying pans on the sidewalk, baby carriages filled with groceries and babies. As in Europe, where it's poorer there is more out in the open. When we got to First, we stopped at a fruit stand blocking the corner. While Dan was buying a bag of apples, I looked at the bins of fruit. In Italy, in the marketplace, reading and pronouncing every label, I learned to spell, and to talk.

In the window of a Polish dress shop Dan spotted some embroidered blouses. "Let's go in," he said. "I gave a lesson today." He insisted on buying a blouse for me. All hand-embroidered, the lady guaranteed. When we came out, it was dark. We crossed the next street, Avenue A, and, leisurely, confiding—I told him about the language school, he told me about a boy from Georgia who lived in the flat above his—started down the block of the old immigrant flats, with rusty fire escapes all the way up the brick fronts and with families from the tenements sitting on the stoops.

"Danny," I said, "*why* do you feel so bad about your life? I mean, what's wrong, say, with that family in Queens?"

"Well," he said, "they're funny, and they all like each other, but that whole . . . *class* is so insensitive. Even as parents. I mean, when they want to yell at the kid, they pull him over to them by his hair. So long and blond, the most beautiful thing that child has, and they pull on it. It's so humiliating."

"It also hurts."

"Well, anyway."

Danny left me in front of a building on the far side of Avenue B and went upstairs to make a telephone call—either about a math lesson or the political group, I forget. And I walked ahead a little, looking in the lighted windows of the Puerto Rican stores. I wondered how long it would take me to learn Spanish. Boys passed by and made remarks, like the teen-agers in Rome, who come up to you with shoeshine on their hair and say "Nice Forum—you like?" Danny caught up with me and said, "Did you have any trouble, guys looking at you? You know why? They can see how you're dressed, how you're not from the neighborhood."

"Oh," I said. "In Italy they look just because I'm a woman."

We came to his building, which had a grey slate stoop and a black iron railing. I remarked that the hand-carved pediment over the door looked as if it was done by an Italian.

"All right," he said, pausing on the stairs. "Before, you wanted an example. Here's this skinny kid upstairs, from Georgia, only now he's so cramped, so depressed he's immobilized—the city's bleeding him white. Doesn't eat, couldn't find work, so he sold his guitar, right? I mean, it's obscene enough that he arrives in New York without any money. Now the lousy kid can't have music, either. I gave him my radio."

We went up another flight and down a narrow hallway, past walls of patterned tin, and stopped at his door. He put his key in, lifted and pushed, and the iron bar of a police lock scraped on the wooden floor inside. The electric light was on—I'd forgotten about the bugs when we were walking over here—and, leaning around his shoulder, I looked in. I expected exposed brick, but what I saw instead everywhere was books. All over. Books stretching up to the ceiling—paperbacks, hardcovers, packed in tight, crammed on shelves against the walls, and even boarding up the window. The floor was buried ankle-deep in magazines, pamphlets, catalogues, typed term papers, stacks of newspapers waiting to be read. A leather armchair for reading stood in the middle of the room, with a hassock and a side table holding a record-player. Beyond one bookcase was a strip of brick wall. A lumberjacket hung from a nail.

The place was a dump, but I walked in, sort of padding over the papers, and took off my coat.

I asked Dan to make some tea, to make us feel at home, and while he boiled water on the hot plate I walked around the front room, looking at book titles, then around the middle room, and then through to the back. "Very nice woodwork here, Dan," I called out. "But tell me, why is this bed built two feet from the ceiling?"

"Lower East Side split-level, ha, ha," he called back. "It's to make closet space underneath. I never hung the curtain."

When I returned to the front room, he'd put a record on—Heifetz, I think—and was sitting on the hassock. I sat down in the armchair. "Here's your tea," he said, handing it to me, and while I was sitting there with the glass in both my hands he leaned down and slipped my shoes off and, cupping his hands under my heels in their nylons, he gently brought both my feet up to lie across his lap. "Lean back, sip your tea," he said. "Slowly. It's hot." We listened for an hour, and then I said, "Dan," when the record-changer clicked itself off.

Looking down, he stroked my ankles. "I guess you'll need your shoes on, for walking back to the bed." Still he sat there, looking vague and unfocussed. His face began to blur to me, as though I saw him underwater, and with one thick arm dangling he reached down toward the floor. He brought up my left shoe, sniffed at the inside, and, closing his eyes, brought his face forward to sniff my outstretched foot.

My mouth fell open, but no words came out.

Shaking his head, he put the shoe down and brought up the other shoe, sniffed around inside it, and smiled, surprised and pleased, as if stirring, dreaming, in his sleep. He slipped it on my foot. "With you," he said, "I can't tell my right from my left."

"You clown," I said. "How can you stand to smell people's feet?"

He shrugged. "Yeah, well, basically I'm a homebody." He nuzzled my head as we walked together through the papers, past the walls of books. Through the ceiling I heard country-and-Western and thought, Dan's radio yet. Later, drifting off to sleep, with the ceiling one foot above me, I remember thinking, For God's sake, who wouldn't be cramped by such an environment?

I probably haven't made Danny sound too attractive. I'm sure I couldn't have explained it to any of the girls I knew, and certainly not, on the above basis, to Jane, who was married, and my most trusted friend of all, and whose Riverside Drive apartment I'd apparently deserted. Each night when I'd phone and tell her not to expect me, I'd say only that I had called an old friend and it was a four-day date. What I felt in Dan's presence wasn't a thing I could have explained on the phone. He could still give off intimations of diffuseness, yet what I felt in him now was a solid core—schmalz and humor, sure, but more; he seemed to have a basic bulk of humanity that, combined with his physical bigness, did not leave me unmoved.

"You know what I liked about you back in school?" he said. We were sitting in his car, which he never removed from its parking space on Second Avenue. We'd bought scallions from the vegetable stand to dip in a container of sour cream and eat with rolls left over from breakfast at Ratner's. "You'd give such earnest reports in sociology seminar, then once you told me you were so scared you'd stayed up all night rehearsing but, before taking the elevator up to class, for luck you'd stopped in the lobby, to find

Hannah Arendt's name in the phone book." He looked out through the windshield. "That was so vulnerable, I loved it." Then down at the open container of sour cream. "People are so much more human than they admit. You think Marx is all economics, but it's human relationships—people involved, participating, people belonging." Aroused, he sat up. "Marx's test of social activity, his whole ethical theory, was that people are happy when they feel close, when they feel they're helping each other. But that depends on society, and when the relationships are competitive you can't have community. You can't care for others if class means every step you take is at someone else's expense, if even your success comes from someone else's failure. Can such a man be your brother? I mean, *beyond* the family."

I was taken by his seriousness and shifted to face him.

"Look at this city," he went on. "You must have done some of those second-semester papers—capitalism and alienation, mass man and anomie. . . . Look at these ghetto streets. No wonder they're the only ones left with any life, with real neighborhood. You know why I moved over here from the West Side? I was cramped, all those high-rises going up around me. I'd rather live in the ghetto than be sealed inside a cubicle. Even here on Second Avenue, more high-rises going up. What's happening is so classic I could teach it backward and forward." He spread his hands. "That's why I was fired."

I wanted to hear what Danny wanted so much to say, and encouraged him to talk, and he did talk at length to me during those days—about life in the city, mass alienation, middle-class depression, isolation, disconnectedness.

Meanwhile, we were sitting inside a parked car. This fact does not escape me, but where else in the city can adults have proximity to the street while sitting to talk together about things that go on? You can't do it in restaurants; it gets too expensive. And, while Nedick's was cheaper than Ratner's, we'd have had to stand. But here in the car we could sit close by the curb, with lunch on our laps, from right on the corner, and only a glass windshield separating us from what was visible, immediate, on the street. I like to think it was because it *was* so visible that Dan found much to say, and was so moved by what he saw.

And we saw so much, so much that could be eased if only, Dan pointed out, people could know one another's pain. "I mean, doctors, right? They're the first who should care. Their whole job is to cure illness. Yet even doctors in our society learn to compete, to think of profit . . . as if patients with less money were more expendable. It's so ugly, such a corruption."

Another time, he said, looking more pained than angry, "Isn't it insane? Babies are born and lined up in identical bassinets, and if one set of parents instead of another takes you home and they happen to have thinner wallets in their pockets you will get inferior health care for the rest of your life."

He stretched across me to the glove compartment, to pull out a paperback book. A wad of parking tickets fell onto my feet. "You should read this," he said. "It's by a British surgeon in China. Radical Socialist medicine—how they respect you, they've such concern." He leafed through the pages. "God, imagine discussing medicine in terms of human relationships! And they can do that there, that's how they think, because the goal beyond medicine is to bring people closer. They made a community in this hospital, Marg, like a family." He showed me parts he'd underlined. "Collective decision-making; nurses, relatives, even orderlies make suggestions. Sometimes patients can help map their own treatment. They have question periods. Here are fellow-patients making ward rounds with the doctor. Everyone works together, everyone's learning. You're not just a dumb animal that gets an injection. It says acupuncture was revived during the Cultural Revolution. Well, know why, I think? Because it's a Socialist value that people should participate, be active and alert, comprehend their experience—in this case, the patient his operation. Whereas here, for Chrissake, you're supposed to sleep through it like through everything else. Just be passive, don't ask questions, don't bother the doctor. God, anesthesia's another form of alienation."

"Well," I said, "I know I've been away. I see your idea, but—I'm not sure about doctors. I'm not sure it *is* political. I'm not even sure it's so different in China, because—" I had to shift my legs, it was so cramped in his car.

"You're wrong," he said, leafing through the book and sighing. "We see *them* as regimented. If they saw Second Avenue, they'd think we were monsters. Look at that crazy old wino there, lying on the sidewalk. Y'know what that comes from? Treating each other like pieces of merchandise. Even someone's illness becomes another's source of profit. Except that slob can't pay, so his illness is irrelevant."

The book slid from his lap, and he leaned down and extracted it from the parking tickets on the floor. "The other day I was in Ratner's, arguing about recognition for China, and the waiter—a *worker*—said, 'Eight hundred million. Imagine if everyone buys one Bayer aspirin.' And all I said was 'That's nice. We're not even friends yet and already we're wishing them headaches.'" He placed the book on my lap. "Read it, *Ketzele*. My whole point is, if your doctor has to make a profit, he can't afford to treat you as one of the family." He looked out the window. "But how could you know? You've never had that experience."

Sitting and talking with Dan in the parked car those days was like the way Europeans talk with close friends in cafés. Cued usually by things we saw right there on the street, his observations, his comments followed no real pattern, and I find I can remember only isolated fragments. I also find I can't forget them. For example, his theory of compassion.

"I guess," he said once, "I have this theory of compassion. People think it's competition that makes you resourceful; they're wrong. It's caring. *That's* when you try harder, when you put yourself, passionately, in the other person's place; you identify so much you're desperate to help. When Che Guevara heard his mother had cancer, he was so desperate he tried to find a cure at home in the basement. In China they'll operate on paralytics. Their barefoot doctors cross mountains to reach peasants. Our doctors won't even make house calls in the city. But the Chinese, they'll move heaven and earth to help; they're Socialists, and they identify."

One afternoon, he said, "When I taught at college, I ate in the faculty dining room, and while all the food was bought for bottom prices by the city, ours was somehow nicer, better than in the students' cafeteria. And I'd sit there watching the head of my department, this élitist that already makes fifteen thousand and could afford to eat out, come in and eat better food than his own students and then go in to lecture about the Urban Poor—you know, the Puerto Rican, the black waiters who were washing his dishes. He was so odious." Dan winced. "I felt such revulsion."

Another time, he said, "My freshman year at Yale, they kept telling us how great we were, how many other guys we'd kept out.

That was supposed to make us feel good. And I was so impressed by the place—not just by the library. I was even impressed by the bathrooms, how clean they kept them for us. I thought, Gee, that's so nice, they really care about their students. . . . Only they cared about us at everyone else's expense."

And: "Never mind why, but when I was eighteen my father and I were arguing a lot, and he had me placed for a month in a psychiatric hospital. He was a doctor, he could do it. Still, it wasn't so bad: I could talk with the patients and orderlies, I worked on math problems. The worst part was I had to talk to a psychiatrist. Even so, I wanted to be honest with him, confide, and I told him how ever since I was little I'd felt, I don't know, *instinctively* that there was something beautiful, sublime, high that men envision and yearn for. And he said, 'How long have you had these feelings?' Do you see? They make everything pathological, every emotion's a symptom. They can't just relax and say, 'That's a given in human nature—people want naturally to be open, trusting, cooperative.' That's how it was for years—even social science at Yale. I'd say 'beauty,' 'courage,' and they said I was being metaphysical. Or I'd say most people are exploited, and they'd tell me I was paranoid. I felt in a desert. Reading on my own, I found the only writers who spoke unashamedly of courage, resilience, joy, who insisted *every* man's life had all these potentialities. They weren't psychiatrists, sociologists. They were Marxists. You're lucky, really; you still have that ahead of you. Read Mao, too, now that you're back—how he describes the New Man, the hope he holds out to us. In these books there's such a sense of family, community, that you and I, Margo, are just missing out on."

He said, "I'm not paranoid, you understand, but what can I think? Racism, sexism, rampant divorce, the generation gap—these divisions go together. Any Socialist knows that."

He said, "So they fired me from the college—said I'd alienated the professors. How could I do that? They were alienated to begin with. They'll always teach their own side. Their interests are so self-serving, so puny. That whole middle class—you've seen them uptown, how confused they look, how anxious about style. 'Life style'—hey, that's a new one since you left. As if the terms on which you live and die were only questions of style. Of course, the middle class is completely despiritualized; they have no values.

Values? That's what you get at Macy's. . . . It's wearying, Margo. The Chinese are so far ahead. They must feel so sorry for us."

And: "We can't even conceive what human personality could be. Look at our mothers, expressing themselves through their furniture."

And: "Still, *people*. Oh Marg, look at them out there! Part of my deal for getting out of the psychiatric hospital was to work one summer in a nursing home, and I saw, hot afternoons, all these old, these old ladies, they, well, they lie on their beds masturbating, alone, off in corners. And I had seen them downstairs, in the dining room, right, their leathery faces, how mean and nasty they could be. But even old and decrepit, there's such basic self-love; they don't question that they deserve pleasure. Human beings, it's encouraging."

And: "Marg, I can't stand it. I've so much bottled up inside me. I hear music and I want to weep; my emotions are unbearable. I can't even travel. Say I took a ship: every place it docked would have been, at one time, a colonial port. You can't ignore what went on then—the despair, the shame, the mass sense of impotence. . . . And the massive humiliation, even here, right on the street. How do the poor keep their morale up? I *don't* understand."

I believed Danny's anguish then. I still do. Talking in the car those days, he opened a new world to me. I didn't always see things as he did, but I was grateful to learn from him, and it wasn't entirely theorizing. For I learned that since moving to this side of town he had gradually lent over two thousand dollars to families in the neighborhood. Whatever else, you have to admit you don't find people like that very often.

I say "whatever else" because I also came to feel that he'd been in the city too long—that twelve years without a break was too much. For example, I am subject to spells of yawning, and when I'd yawn and then apologize he'd say, "But it's so organic." Or, once we were buying pizza from a place near Second Avenue where the pizza man was Puerto Rican, and Danny said as we left the counter, "You're lucky to live in Italy with real Italians."

"There are plenty of Italians here," I said. "More than in Naples."

"They aren't real Italians."

"They look real to me," I said.

Another time, after telling me that he hadn't spoken to his father for years, he said, "Maybe I don't need a father anyway. Trees grow all the time and they don't have fathers." I thought that was insane; how could a man confuse himself with a tree?

Dan's not the only person in New York who talks like that.

There was something else I had misgivings about: shoplifting. At first I didn't understand, because he limited it to bookstores, and when someone speaking of a book said "ripped off" I thought they meant the covers. I couldn't imagine him stealing three years ago.

Anyway, when he told me that more and more lately he had been wanting seriously to buy some land in the country, I said why not move the car and drive upstate this weekend, find an agent. I also said that expecting to be a farmer overnight was wrong, but to live idly in the city was not good, either.

So we drove upstate together. By Sunday night he'd made a few contacts, and all the way back was wondering aloud about A-frames, tool kits, and abutting acreage. I told him it didn't matter if he didn't know what he was getting into, because whatever it was, he'd learn step by step; he had to. "That's like Learning from Tachai," he said, and went on to describe the Chinese farming village in Shensi Province that had become a model for problem-solving and self-reliance. He had a book about it.

A few days later, we had to say goodbye. I took the train to Baltimore to see my parents, and then on to Washington to meet a magazine editor. Then New Haven and Boston and back to New York. After that I flew to Arizona to visit my brother and his wife. I remember calling Jane from Kennedy. "Well, yes," I said, "I'm definitely interested in Dan, but after Arizona I have to go back to Italy. I have an assignment. I even have an advance. . . . Sure, I really like him—only not for right now; I think he still has to pull himself together. I'm curious to see how he is, say, in a year."

Except that I was pregnant. I'd been pregnant three weeks. I didn't know it, though; I didn't even realize it the whole week in Arizona until the last day, when I remarked to my sister-in-law, "Strange, I'm so *tired* out here in Arizona"—meaning my two-hour afternoon naps. "Maybe it's the air." I'd also been napping every morning.

"That doesn't sound natural," she said, looking at her watch—she had to leave for work. "Maybe you're anemic. I mean, the only other people who sleep so much are women who are pregnant."

"What?" I asked, and she said it again.

"In that case," I exclaimed, "how could you tell? I mean, if it could be either, I suppose you'd have to have a blood test—"

"God, a smart girl with her eyes open would just see," she said. "Your breasts, for example, would've swelled within a week. Not to mention a skipped period." She stood up and smoothed her skirt. "And that's aside from the sleeping. Oh, don't worry. There'd be lots of signs."

There were. I just hadn't put them all together.

When she left, I moved from the sofa bed over to the ladder-back chair. I sat there, looking down at my fingers.

I lay down on the sofa bed some more to think it over. But what was there to think about? I got up and walked around, I looked in the mirror. That night I called Jane, from the wall phone in the kitchen, and what she said was "Oh baby, then you want an abortion."

Well, sure. If it was clear that I was pregnant, I was clear about that, too. Having a baby was out of the question. I didn't even need to think about it. She reminded me that abortion had been legal in New York for a year. And I was going back there anyway before Europe. I had a week, and I had the money. Finally we said good night and hung up, and I stood beside the phone in the kitchen, in the dark.

There didn't seem to be any more questions.

I went into the bathroom and turned on the faucet, and when I saw myself in the mirror, straight on like that and exposed under the lights, I realized I'd never openly pictured myself pregnant. And I thought, Now you can see, you can visualize, you can fill in the rest. More there, some more here. It's clear how it would have gone.

But it's not your last chance.

Now I knew, and that was knowledge for the future. I'd bank on it someday, and it would be as firm in my grip as this bright chrome faucet. I thought, If it already looks so lovely after only three weeks, think what it'll be like when you'll be free to enjoy the whole thing. Wait. Choose. You needn't grab at pieces. Picture the future. At least you've had a glimpse.

I knew I had to look at the situation straight on.

Because, God, it was amazing! Riding the plane East, I was awed all over again, I was openmouthed just thinking of it—carrying extra weight, and yet I felt so buoyant. With one day's knowledge I'd grown into the part. When I'd made this trip before, in the opposite direction, I was, unknowingly and effortlessly, escorting this condition to which I was party through the skies above my country—three thousand miles—greeting, seeing, meeting, busily presiding yet oblivious of the privilege, accompanying this presentation with its own insulation over which my chatter, before and after, could only roll like water off a duck's back. For all the time, every minute there . . . I thought of all the topics, the issues discussed; I counted up hotels, and editors' offices; I thought of entire cities I'd been pregnant in.

And this plane. Streaking straight through space, five hundred miles an hour, temperature-controlled. What an invention. I sat above the wing, so wide out there, and watched its slim tip catch the sun as we turned wide on our axis and the light bathed all the metal. Before us stretched the sky, that broad avenue, inviting.

I leaned back. I felt poised, I felt classic. I felt like a queen in my plush seat.

So on and on we flew, through the sunset, toward evening. A distant star came out, tiny reading lamps went on in the cabin. Outside, a rosy glow.

And time passed. And I turned my eyes in now, away from the window, and as night drew about the cabin I liked it even more than the vastness and brilliance of the sky. It was more intimate, offered more to look at. I let my eyes rest on the seat there in front of me and thought of the Italian for "tray" and "pouch" and "brochure" and "map."

And now it was dark out. And I could no longer see the wing tip. I felt I could ride up here forever, seeing things with inexhaustible curiosity and feeling. My hands folded in my lap, I turned my head to one side. The plush pricked my cheek, but that was O.K. So many customers, such variety of people. Many slept. I gazed at their faces, picturing their lives. A hostess came down the aisle with a kosher tray for the old woman by my side. I smiled, half asleep. Kosher meals on super jet planes. I was glad for the old woman. I was glad for us all. Maybe when I called Danny from Arizona and asked if he could meet me at the airport I should have told him. He'd have wanted to clean the apartment, have it ready, waiting for me.

When I saw him standing in the crowd, immense and gentle, with his great hands empty at his sides, he looked to me as if he was, well, waiting for news. He took my overnight bag from me and we sort of stood around. "How was your lesson?" I asked, knowing that he'd driven straight to the airport from Queens.

"What? Oh, right. That Muzak has me addled," he said, shaking his head. "They've got the whole airport wired." We started walking down the corridor. "Yeah, well, the kid." He sighed. "Yeah, he's pretty good for six; the kid's a satisfaction. But they paid me tonight. God, it's so boring, I just cannot empathize. Plus, they gave me a twenty." He paused. "I couldn't use the toilet."

"What?"

"I had this twenty-dollar *bill*. Sure, this flaming airport. Richest country in the world, only it doesn't think it can afford to give people free toilets."

I couldn't tell whether he was in a serious mood or joking, until he raised his arm like an orator warming up and pitched his voice higher. "I mean, talk about exploiting the human body for profit. And here, *messieurs*, we show you the ultimate in capitalism—private ownership even of the means of defecation. Which in Socialist societies is a minimal public service, one of man's basic needs when he leaves the house in the morning. Welcome to America! Finally I panhandled a dime. And the guy looked at me like I might save it up for heroin. I wanted to say, 'Mister, look, we're more alike than you think.' "

I'd forgotten how antic he could be. It was so good to walk along beside him, with him in a good mood, and I felt closer to him than I ever had before. We picked up my suitcase at the luggage chute, and then started off toward the parking lots.

"Oh wow," he said. "This air's so great I'll forget it's polluted. The Muzak got me so depressed"—he put his arm around me—"and then you came from the plane smiling at me, and now I feel —great. Oh, Margo, I can't wait to tell you—I just found out. I'm leaving the city."

I looked at him.

"I'm finally buying *land*. That's why I'm so cheerful."

We walked past row after row of parked cars in the dark. Again I wished I had told him I was pregnant when I called him. Then I remembered how we did most of our talking inside the car anyway. Dan unlocked the doors of his car and we got in, and before he turned the key in the ignition I told him.

He just sat, like the car with the motor off.

And finally I said the one thing I could think of. "I'm arranging it through Jane. But just stay with me till the abortion—all right? Because I've never been through that. I can't know what I'm heading into."

He sort of heaved around. "Well, of course I'll stick with you— my God, what did you think? That's the least . . ." I thought he was going to put his arms around me, and instead he placed his hands on the steering wheel. "Listen," he said wearily, his face toward the windshield. "Let's go get some Chinese food."

"God, sure, Dan, of course," I said. "If you're hungry."

He parked half on the sidewalk on Mott Street, and I followed him down a flight of metal stairs from the street level. At the bottom, he pushed a door, its address stencilled in red across the glass, and we squeezed into a vestibule facing a single room—square, low-ceilinged, with dark-green plaster walls.

I said, "Are you sure this is it, Dan?"

"I've been eating here two years." He ducked his head to enter. "Night dishwashers eat here, so it's open late, for workers. Look, I met the cook's son two years ago, when I researched ethnic gangs, O.K.?"

Why was he impatient?

On the way to a table he stopped to fill a glass of water at the cooler. The table was next to the wall, and narrow and long, made to be shared, with no tablecloth. Two men, speaking Chinese, sat at one end. Dan nodded as we sat down, and they nodded back.

The waiter brought two glasses of tea, and chopsticks. I asked for a fork. While Dan ordered, I sat leaning back, watching him. The waiter left and I lifted my glass of hot tea and smiled across at Dan, but he was looking past me, into empty space.

"Do you remember Tachai?" he asked suddenly.

"Oh, right—that village; self-reliance. Are you still reading about it?"

"Well, no, I was just thinking . . . about my land. Remember?" At that moment the food came.

He ate with chopsticks, his face close to the dish, and kept his eyelids lowered. His eyes looked tired. I glanced up at the wall clock. That he didn't say anything bothered me. Three hours ahead. For people here it was the middle of the night, for me only evening; that was why he was tired.

I looked around. I wondered if they had *tried* to make this place look gloomy; probably not. Only, originally it was a cellar, no escaping that. I let my eyes wander around the dark-green walls with gold-leaf-cutout zig-zag running around the top like the border of my horrible desk blotter at college. I heard laughter in the kitchen. I wondered if Dan knew the cook.

When our dishes had been cleared away, he said, "It's rotten, you having to go to a hospital. In a Socialist country it's nothing; it's like getting a tooth pulled. Those women—their own clinics; they walk in by themselves, walk out on their own. . . . How much is your abortion going to cost you?"

I took out my wallet. "I'm looking for a dime," I said. If it was really so late, I had to call Jane.

"That's O.K. They'll let you call. I'm a customer here."

"Oh, right, Marg," Jane said when I got her on the phone. "My gynecologist will see you tomorrow morning early, but stop up here first. You'll need the address on Madison . . . Uh, look, I have a question."

"What?"

"Well, I know I haven't met him or anything, I'm just curious—has he discussed finances yet?"

I walked back to the table. Dan was standing up. "Your chow mein's two-fifty," he said.

He turned away to lift my coat from the rack. Hanging from the same hook, by a string, was a pink Chinese back scratcher. He spoke toward the wall: "You know what Chinese women use these for?"

I thought he was being funny. "What?" I said.

"The same thing American women use coat hangers for."

I clutched at his sleeve—I couldn't believe it was happening. I was also afraid of him for the first time; maybe he of me, too. It took us a while to get our coats on, buttoned straight. Then heavily, side by side, we climbed the steps up to the street. Walking toward the car, we passed a Chinese grocery. Dan looked in the window. "It's wonderful how they still have these homemade cookies," he said. We got into the car and drove uptown. Walking up the stairs and down the narrow hallway to his apartment, I did what you do when you are straining to identify: I matched my steps to his, so that we moved together. Later, I undressed and climbed the ladder steps to the loft and thought, In five months I couldn't even squeeze in here. I stretched out flat on my half. He climbed up and stretched himself out on his half, five inches to my right. I looked at the ceiling and knew we'd wait separately for sleep. Lying there, staring in the dark, I wandered in my mind to other people's apartments, places I'd stayed, thinking about the way they were arranged and where I might fit in, trying to position myself mentally—my brother's out West, Jane's apartment on the upper West Side, and so on. . . . But the only place I could see myself sleeping was here beside the man I was pregnant by. It made so much sense.

In the morning I wanted to go straight uptown to Janie's, but Dan wanted breakfast at Ratner's first. "There's time," he said. "I'll drive. You won't have to go by subway."

He let me off at the restaurant and drove on, looking for a parking space. Ratner's is the same in the morning as at any other time, except that this morning it was emptier than usual. The waiters stood around like aged unemployed.

He came in, some minutes later, carrying a book. "I *offered* this, but you just ignored it. You left it in the car." He sat down and we gave our order. "Look," he began. "I was thinking all night about it—how I can help; how you ought to approach your abortion. I realize what you lack is, well, you have no framework, Marg, no context. Do you remember this book? This one about China? If you'd been reading things like this, you'd have a model, for comparison; you'd have vision and understanding. You could grasp your situation."

I looked at him.

"You can't even conceive of the treatment you'd be entitled to, how you'd be responded to in China, how glad they'd be to help you. Any Socialist country. Did you know in Belgrade an abortion costs under eight dollars? That in Poland it's free? But you—you'd probably say 'Thank you' because here it's now legal. Listen, all they've done is incorporate abortion into the existing health delivery system; they've expanded their line of merchandising, is all. And you're not even angry. You're running uptown. You should feel the same revulsion for Jane's doctor that I had for my professor. Why do you submit to élitist exploitation? I mean, why should you give up your money like that?"

Sipping his coffee, Dan said, "The fact is, you're a victim. You don't know you are exploited. Try identifying yourself as one of the oppressed. Some people take advantage. You must become aware of this."

My face must have changed. "Say," he said, "you're tired. You just sit here. I'll go get some newspapers from women's liberation. From the radical bookshop, around the corner on St. Marks. They're smart about abortion, what the issues are. Maybe they've got addresses. Sure, women's lib—you missed out on that in Europe, too."

I was wrong when I said Ratner's doesn't change in the morning; under the right conditions, it can give an impression of nightmare.

Ten minutes later he returned empty-handed and surprised; he'd been barred from the bookshop on suspicion of shoplifting. "We'll get a New York *Times* at the corner," he said. "Let's go."

The *Times* had a front-page story on abortion. He stood on the sidewalk and read the headline aloud: " 'ABORTION REFERRAL AGENCY SHUT BY NEW YORK COURTS.' See?" he said. "Some private office is closed for charging outrageous fees, but this typical élitist newspaper doesn't relate to your real needs. If this were really a people's paper, if they really wanted to help, they'd say outright —I mean, they'd voluntarily say, 'The above agency is untrustworthy, and thus we, concerned editors, suggest you go to such-and-such a place.' "

"Can we go to Jane's?" I said. "My appointment's in an hour."

Driving uptown, he said, "Does Janie have a phone?"

"What?" I said. "I don't— Sure, two extensions."

"Well, good," he said. "It's a start. I want to call the Young Lords Party. They've done amazing things in health care for the ghettos." He stopped for a light. "I just read their paper posted in the bookshop window. Up in East Harlem, in door-to-door testing with unused city-hospital equipment, they detected eight hundred positive tuberculosis cases. They've got so much initiative, I bet they could help you." I kept staring at the street, through the windshield. I didn't know what the Young Lords Party was—I'd been in Europe. I kept waiting for some expression of concern, for him to say that whatever it was we'd go through it together.

"Hi, Marg," Jane said, opening her door and drawing me in.

"Hi, Jane, this is Dan. Dan," I said, "Jane."

"Dan?" she said. "Oh, hi." Janie turned back to me. "Your appointment's pretty soon."

"Yes," said Dan, "but we'd like to use, uh, one of your phones first."

Jane looked at him a little strangely. Then she kissed me on the cheek. "Are you O.K., Marg?" she said. "I don't know. You look a bit dishevelled—like you haven't slept all night."

"Well, no," I said. "Just, this is the same dress I wore back yesterday from Arizona."

"Look, could I use your phone?" Dan asked Jane again. "I want to call up the Young Lords. I mean, it's great that you went ahead, recommending your gynecologist and all, but I think we ought to give Margo some choice. Check out free clinics. In other neighborhoods."

Jane glanced at him briefly. "Well, sure, you can use my phone, I don't mind." Then to me she said, "Hon, maybe you want to take ten minutes to, I don't know, put on some makeup for the doctor." Dan walked into the living room looking for a phone book. I walked into the bathroom. Jane followed me in and sat on the edge of the bathtub to talk.

"Marg, I just want to tell you . . . There are all kinds of ways you can approach this, right? Just keep your perspective; it only involves yourself. I mean, getting through—it's just up to the individual."

With her foot she shifted a puppy-litter box under the sink. "And boy," she said, straightening up, "you really are lucky! All last night I was thinking—a year ago and you'd really have had to do it illegally. Or suppose you were back in Europe now? Talk about the right place, the right time; people come from all over. You're not alone, you'll see. Just mention pregnancy to people and their abortion stories will start coming out from under the toaster. This is the center. Couldn't have it better—legal, the best facilities. . . ." She crossed her legs. "What a break, though. How come you always manage to land on your feet?"

I looked at Jane; she's worn her hair in bangs ever since I can remember. She stood up and put her arms around me. "Margo, jeez,
I've hardly seen you this trip. You haven't slept over once."

We came out of the bathroom. Dan was standing in the hall.
"It's no use," he said. "What the Young Lords suggested was
Bellevue. But you can't go there, not without paying; you're not
on welfare. Besides, you're from out of state." He shook his head.
"This guy at the Young Lords, though, was just so *decent*."

He said he'd drive me crosstown, and did, but he crawled so
slowly through the Park I knew I would be late. "I have to
go slow," he said. "I have too many parking tickets. . . . It was a
dumb idea anyway. What was I thinking of? You can't go to a free
clinic. I couldn't take you there; they'd only get angry. They'd *see*
that you're not poor."

I walked back to Jane's after the doctor. I didn't decide to go
there. I just worked my way back to the last place I'd come from.
That was how I thought of it. Back to the last clear place I could
remember.

When Dan called, it was past midnight. "I'm so cramped in this
phone booth," he said. "I've only got one dime, and the number's
ripped out. You can't call me back. When the operator cuts me
off, I'll really be in limbo. Still, shouldn't pick on phones; it's the
only way New Yorkers can find out the weather."

I didn't say anything.

"You know, in Cuba phones are free," he said. "That's true; people can just call up and talk to each other." There was a pause.
Then: "Marg? How are you?"

I thought of him in that glass booth about ninety blocks downtown and how there wasn't any place to put problems on the table.
"I'm O.K.," I said.

Nothing.

I said, "I didn't see you after, so . . . I walked back to Jane's."

"Did the doctor say you're pregnant?"

"Oh. That—it's inconclusive. He told me to get another lab test.
I get my choice of labs." I swallowed. "It was fifty-five dollars. But
that's because it's a first visit; the second visit costs less."

"Well, sure. They penalize you for not needing a doctor sooner."

I didn't know what to say.

"Then, I guess you won't be needing me for a week," he went

on. "Because what I was thinking was, I have to leave the city. You know, to buy that land." There was no change in his tone of voice or anything. "I mean, Margo, this is major; it could affect my whole life; it's the first thing I've felt optimistic about in years. Tomorrow I could drop your suitcase off. I'll leave it with the doorman. On my way up to the bridge. Besides, someone's depending on me—you know? The kid upstairs. I'm giving him money for land, too. He's so excited and . . . Margo? Oh, d'you have to cry? Really?" I heard him switch the receiver. "Did that doctor upset you? God, I can just imagine his condescension, the rhetoric. I— Look, why don't you come out now for Chinese food? I'll get the car, see? This is why I wanted to take you to the Young Lords; at least they would have treated you like a human being." Again he switched the receiver. "It's so awful, what you're going through. Sweetheart, if I could just touch you, if I could just reach out and . . ."

Sweetheart, he'd said. I said, "Why is it the only time you can be nice to me is on the phone?"

There was a silence, and then he said slowly, "I guess the only time I can feel close to you is when you're crying."

It didn't matter that I hung up; he'd just think I was upset. I walked back through the apartment to the bathroom and turned on the faucet; only forty-eight hours since that bathroom in Arizona, the bright chrome, my own clear sight. I bent to wash my face, I couldn't even *see,* and when, eyes streaming, I looked up, there before me was the mirror.

God, what a waste. Such stress and pullings, swellings, a whole face at cross-purposes. My face, through wet eyes, looked like a battlefield, floating, beyond recognition. I could not afford this— this dumb anarchy, turmoil coming out of confusion, because, at the end, I was drained, emptied despite all that effort on the part of my face. I looked: this wasn't activity, it was submitting to onslaught.

I just stood looking, one hand still on the faucet . . . and my eyes began to clear. I saw what to do. I mean, I suddenly felt I could see through the mirror. I would be all right again, whole and plausible, calmed, myself. Somehow I had to keep a sense of that; I had to hold that idea in my head and let it happen. There'd be the hospital to plan soon, arrangements to make, and as for Danny, he— Well, he'd already taken himself out of the picture.

Fact. So I couldn't afford him, either, not even in my mind, and it didn't matter what I thought, why he was doing this, whether I could try to understand or not. I knew he'd still exist; he just wouldn't count.

I leaned on the sink—it felt good to lean—and looked down at Janie's bath mat, soft, on the floor. In the morning I would sleep late—till noon if I needed—and in these coming days I'd eat well, go shopping, visit friends. I'd see to it that I got fresh air, lots of rest. I was pregnant, and I had to take care of myself.

As it turned out, I made the arrangements from Macy's. I'd been there two hours, wandering around and not buying anything. I used the pay phone near the elevator behind Slack Sets, third floor. For one thing, you never know you'll find a phone working in the street. Sometimes I feel I was raised in department stores.

The doctor said that the test was positive. What did I choose to do?

"But, Doctor," I said, into the receiver, "perhaps you don't remember me. I definitely said—"

"Then you want an abortion." He sounded in a hurry. "Well, the arrangements are easy. It depends on what you pay. If I perform it, four hundred dollars; that's in my hospital downtown, and you may stay for two nights."

"Oh," I said. "Is there anything less?"

"Yes, dear, there's an agency. Only, you won't have your choice of doctor. You won't meet him first, you know, or talk to him. But as you say, that's cheaper."

He gave me the name of the agency, and said I would find the number in the Yellow Pages.

"Hold on, please," said the agency voice. "I'll be right with you." I was glad it was a woman. I didn't mind waiting. "Abortions," she said. "Yes, well, here are your options. You may spend two hundred dollars, or three hundred dollars."

For the same operation?

"The difference in price," she said, "is at night. That is, you may leave the same day, but if you take a hospital bed it's a hundred dollars more. Of course, you may not leave unless you have someplace to stay—that's one of the rules."

I thought, *I have Jane.*

"Well," I said, "I guess I can sign up for the two-hundred-dollar plan—one day, no nights. For now, anyway."

"When do you want the operation? Tomorrow?"

I was taken aback. "But don't you want me to come down first? Don't you have to meet me?"

I swear I heard her smile. "Heavens no," she said. Then she told me what hospital to report to and gave me a morning appointment. I said I had traveller's checks, and she said, "No, dear, only cash."

By nine o'clock we were a dozen—girls, women, coming into the hospital lobby, looking around, taking a seat.

At nine-thirty a nurse started moving down the line, asking, "How many weeks?"

"I want the saline solution," the woman alongside said to me. "I've got three kids and I love them, but my husband, we decided no more. I'm from Chicago. I'm sixteen weeks. That's why I need the saline solution."

A Puerto Rican couple came in, walked over to the nurse. She pointed to the cashier's window. A moment later, I heard the cashier say, "I'm sorry, but you're twenty-five short. I can't let you stay without cash in advance."

You could hear everything in that lobby.

Fifteen minutes later, they were back. The man had a bankbook in his hand, and looked as if he'd been running. "For heaven's sake," the nurse said, annoyed, to the woman. "You both didn't have to leave. I mean, you could have stayed while your husband went for the money." Then, to the woman next to me, "We're not giving saline solutions today."

I got up and went to the cashier's window. When she had taken my money, she sent me to an adjoining room, where a technician took a blood sample. Finally, we were all herded into the elevator. The Puerto Rican man waved to his wife, and the doors closed, cutting off the words of the wailing voice outside: "I want the saline solution! I want the sa—"

The doctor who was giving me the physical said, "Six weeks." He looked very pleased, a discoverer.

"No," I said, looking around. I was getting a little bored. "It's only five, really."

"Oh, no," he insisted. "You're wrong. It's six."

"Six weeks ago I was in Switzerland." I wanted to cry. "You don't know who my real doctor will be?"

"For later? No, I don't."

Wearing a paper gown and carrying my clothes, I was shown to a small room with a window looking out on an air shaft, and I got into bed and fell asleep. When I woke up, it must have been noon. Hard to tell; they'd taken my watch from me downstairs. I thought I heard trays. Then I remembered: no lunch. And, somehow, finding myself in bed in the middle of the day had given me the feeling I couldn't speak English. There was no one to talk to. I looked out on a brick wall. My mind wandered sideways to what they would do to me: D and C, they said. "D and C stands for dusting and cleaning," a med student I dated once scribbled in my notebook. I was sleepy again. Oh that's bad, I thought. I shouldn't have let them give me a sedative; now the anesthesia won't work.

Some time later, a nurse came in with a Kleenex. "Wipe all cream and makeup off your face."

More time passed. Another nurse came in. "Remove your earrings," she said. "Seal them in this envelope."

The first nurse came back. She pointed to my hair. "You'll have to pin every bit of that back," she said, taking from her pocket what looked like a white gauze shower cap. It pulled on my forehead.

I must have been dozing when the third nurse came in—how huge and white she was—carrying a bowl of lather and a tiny safety razor hanging on a string around her neck.

I didn't know that they did that. I thought she was going to wash me.

After she left, I raised myself up and looked down at the sheet, that seemed to go on forever. This bed, I thought, and me with wrists no wider than a ruler . . . and nothing to hold on to. I felt white, hairless. Did I have to be alone?

Two men in white came in and then the bed was adrift, moving through the corridor like a barge through a canal. We were heading for an elevator, its gaping space, and my head was sliding toward it when a nurse called, "Wait!" She came out from her nurses' station with a dab of white cotton and a tiny colorless bottle—by this time my head was in the elevator—and, lifting the sheet, she looked down at my feet. Then we waited while she wiped a trace of polish from my toenails.

I was alone in the operating room. At Bellevue I used to hear "O.R." on the loudspeaker all the time. A nurse with a clipboard came in to check my name, and another nurse came in and started taping my left arm to a tube that led up to a bottle. The one with the clipboard said, "Do you have any questions?"

"Please," I said, "I've been wanting to ask all day, before the doctor starts—are you sure, is it sure I can get pregnant again?"

"All you women, you ask the same question," she said, writing on her chart. "Didn't you have biology in high school?"

A man in white came in. Doctor? He saw that my arm was hooked up and clasped my hand. "Hi," he said. "Everything is going to be great. My name's Lieberman. I'm from Staten Island. What's your name?"

"Margo," I said. He squeezed my hand and dropped it. Then, "I'm giving her a needle," said a voice from the other side and, terrified, I thought, Ohhhh, I forgot to tell them I already slept this morning.

Wake up. *Slap.* The face of the girl next to me. "Wake up! Wake up!" An orderly wheeled a third stretcher into the recovery room. I knew that he was only an orderly, but still I had to ask, *Is everything . . . is everything all right?* Three of us here, side by side. I'm in the middle. They're depending on me. I'm the one who has to ask, *Is everything—* Silence. Here he comes. Now he's wheeling me around the corner and into the elevator again. The ceiling was closer here; it was easier to talk. "Is everything all right?" Finally, I had said it.

A nurse came into my cubicle. I said, "I can't wake up. Can't I stay overnight? I mean, the bed's messed up anyway."

Telephone ringing. Nurse at the door. "Your telephone's ringing."

"Sweetheart." It was Janie. "Baby, oh hiya. . . . I said your friend is in the lobby. They told me you're O.K. Only, I've got my dog with me; they won't let me up. I'll meet you at eight, here, the lobby." At eight, down there, the lobby. Who will help me get dressed?

Night nurse by my side, her arms full of sheets. "You'll have to get up soon. The night administrator's come on. You'll be charged another hundred if you stay in bed past nine. I'll let you sleep till eight." And then, "You really must get up now. Here's dinner anyway. . . . You're not really sick, you know. You'll wake up when you're on the street."

From inside the elevator, I see Jane in a chair, her dog in her lap. I wish this were her living room.

I said, "Let's sit a few minutes."

"This lobby's so interesting. You just should've seen, Marg. These young girls stepping out of the elevator and these guys waiting—same jeans, same hair, only carrying flowers—and they see each other and look embarrassed, then the guy puts his arm around her and they're both so relieved. And that's how they leave together, from the lobby, wrapped up like *babies*."

Stop at the desk for a mimeographed instruction sheet to take home.

Jane said, "I've got a cab outside. Today, hon, we're ladies."

"Well, only crosstown," I said. "I'd rather try to walk up Broadway."

Walking up Broadway, I remembered how I used to tell Parisians that "Broadway" meant "boulevard." I love it up here, I thought. Sloppiest street in the city next to Avenue B. Same cigar stores, same fruit stands. A Polish embroidered-blouse shop, like the one near Ratner's. How the city reproduces: we're on the upper West Side, but the lower East is present, too, behind us, far, far behind us, on our right. I feel it in my back. And in front waves of people rising over the curb toward us. I'd like to lie down on this sidewalk—"Jane, you go ahead"—just lie here and rest, and watch, look up. That curb is like a cliff. . . . "No, dear, of course not, I'm just feeling relief." How tired I feel; with this air so soft, I could lay my head on it. My very own father had his first shop up here. How young he was then. From the lower East Side.

"One more block, doll. The couch is all made up and ready for you."

We had known each other since kindergarten.

"Jane, I cooked up real chicken soup while you were out." Days later this was. "Gave myself a little airing; walked as far as Broadway." And stood on the corner looking out at that island of old people, their benches, in the middle of the street. Where else can old friends sit talking together about things that they see? Yiddish? That's Spanish? Who hears them anyway? Mouths flapping, toothless, in the middle of traffic. "So walking home I got this barbecued chicken, out of the Merit Farms window, and I threw it in boiling water, with a bouillon cube. That's how I cured myself in Europe, whenever I had a cold."

"Look, girls, I have a question: How do I know he really operated? Don't laugh. I mean, that Dr. Lieberman was very nice and all, but maybe he got distracted—line twelve of us up and it could happen, right? I am not crazy. Look at this instruction sheet. It says amount of post-op bleeding varies. *Varies*. Me? Nothing. Besides, my breasts. I should know—exactly the same. Three days, they're still swollen."

Jane gives a shout of laughter. "Oh, Marg, what did you think —they put a hole in the bottom and all the air comes out?"

"You really are fun—"

"Now listen, where's your perspective? Look how relaxing this is, sitting in the living room with your girl friends. They've all come to visit you. What do you need that schmuck for?"

"I didn't think it'd be so soon," Danny said. We were at our front table at Ratner's. His back was to the window. He looked both bigger and more broken.

I leaned back slightly, trying to ease my shoulder into the wash of light through the glass. The sun warmed my cheek, it comforted my hair, and now in its warmth I looked around.

I was feeling, well, chastened, and yet quietly hopeful, as during the course of a long convalescence. I walked slowly these days. I took my time breathing. I felt I'd passed through some sort of surrender, having sensed that yielding might bring a kinder safety: the sense that beyond any one thing or person we are we are all in this together, you know?

Dan's face was turned. Looking closely at his cheek I was a little shocked to see small white signs of stress, like faint scars, faded, beneath the skin. I looked at him and his maze of trouble. "I didn't mention when you called last night—I'm leaving for Europe. Tomorrow."

He nodded. "Maybe that's the best thing for you." He looked down at his hands; the knuckles were red, the fingernails were bitten.

I asked about his land.

"It never happened," he said. "The kid upstairs— The radio, you know. I . . . well, I guess what I'd say fairly is that he let me down. I really have to say that. I trusted him. Oh, not just that he sold my radio. I knew that before. I mean, that I handed over my car, then his friends, the money I gave him—" He interrupted himself. "Look, that's not why I called." He reached down for a paper bag lying on a chair near him and drew out some books and put them on the table. "I bought these for you."

I saw that the book on top was about China. He took some pamphlets from the bag and placed these with the books. "Here," he said. "What I have, if— The reason you and I can talk is, we are willing to be basic. I still believe that. I know that about us. And— What I have to tell you, what I want you to realize, is that everything I said before about politics is *right*. I know how I sound. I don't care." He pushed the books aside and drew his chair closer to the table. "I know I'm out of your life now. I know what Janie's saying, your girl friends. But I don't want you to think the things I said were empty. I can't know how the hospital went. But I know how it had to go. And I know that it's political. And that because you got through it you can't now just forget it. It doesn't end with the hospital. It doesn't end with me. It isn't enough that you can get through the day. These situations are political. And yes, I dare say this, and I do, in fact, just *because* of what's happened. I'm not expressing this well. I mean, what happens in your hospital is part of what happens in this street every day. Everything's political— corporation food, grapes, that man's lettuce; you see that. And so was your friend's doctor, so was that waiter with our bread basket, and my professor, your private hospital, my real-estate agent. And so was I. With you. But just because I can be that way, too . . . I still have to understand where exploitative behavior comes from and how it gets taught and learned and repeated. I haven't understood, and I want to understand, and I'll just have to stay and figure it out, without blaming. But if only you could do that, too. . . . Please start these readings; they'll open so much. This is what I believe, Marg. It's this I can offer. I am trying to invite you; I say we are political, we're all in this together. I— Oh, Marg, the reason I insist is, the thing about an idea is: if you give it away to someone, then both people have it."

He stopped, as if he'd suddenly become aware of his own earnestness, and I slowly nodded and could feel his relief. "You know," he went on, flushed, "somehow these six weeks, you, the kid upstairs, you're the first—well, experiences I've had in two *years*. It's so difficult for me to tell things apart."

I thought, My dear God, he was scared all along.

He said, "This place reminds me of our dining room at home. I mean, it's big and it's familiar."

I said, "In Italian the word 'familiar' is from 'family'—it really means 'familial.'"

"In English, too," he said, and smiled. "It's nice." We both looked around. I noticed that there was a picture of Mr. Ratner above the register, and that there were hippies in the afternoon, in off the street, parked here—the Return of the Immigrant's Child. Boys without shoes, girls without bras—sure, why not—eating their buckwheat.

"What do you see, Dan?"

"Oh, that these old waiters speak Yiddish, while the teen-age busboys are speaking Spanish." He shook his head. "Well, anyway," he said gently, "let's check our bread basket." He drew it from the table edge to a spot midway between us and lifted the napkin and contemplated the rolls, as dark and secretive as if they'd just been unearthed. The waiter brought hot barley soup in small, handled cups, and I poured his into his bowl.

"Funny ladle," he said, embarrassed and pleased to have someone looking after him.

"There's so much," I said.

"And the rolls are warm. What are they today—crazy?" And we both ate leaning forward, grateful, present. He wished me only well—I saw that and believed it. "You know," he said, "it's not true that some people feel more than others. It's so unfeeling to think that; so arrogant. Take that kid upstairs—he feels plenty in his life, and what he feels is frustration." He put his spoon down. "That crazy kid, he really stole from me, you know? Still, who knows what's wrong with him? I mean, he's unhappy, too."

I looked at Dan and suddenly had such a sense of his wholeness. I couldn't subtract that. He was no villain. I didn't feel like his victim. What were we, then?

"For the kid, that's his struggle. And everywhere, every day, people are struggling, and that's what politics is about—the constraints on people's lives and their struggles, their constant and different struggles to overcome them. But then we become afraid, and turn on each other. And that's why I admired you for going to Europe, trying to be a writer, because writers can give courage. All that people need for understanding is to know their own story. And you could write your stories. And you don't need to take a straight Marxist line. I do, but you don't; I can see how you need, you should have, the fullest freedom. Take these books I bought you, do, but, I mean, you could probably just read all of Balzac, and Shakespeare, and there alone would be such vast humanity to draw on. . . . Tomorrow, could I drive you to Kennedy? I mean, I know you want to leave. You have so much ahead. I can understand that. But at least let me drive you. I'll fix the car—"

"Well, I was planning to go from the bus terminal on First," I said.

"I know you could. But you don't want to leave alone. Nobody does. We can talk on the way. I'd really like to, if you'd like."

"All right, then—thanks," I said, as easy as that, feeling I'd moved into the midst of great abundance, and thinking how striking it was that the only abundance lay in what was freely given, and that in making your way, in travelling through this abundance, you are constantly learning and being transformed.

And I knew also that soon I'd be in a plane again, high in the air. And I thought back over the last two months, about certain hard places where I could have tripped, had despair, have somehow gone under—and I hadn't, and Dan had, and I wondered why I was different from him, and had less fear, more resilience. Once, talking about his frustrations, his self-doubts, he said, "For God's sake, Margo, try to understand—there've been whole periods in my life that I would rather die than go through again."

I can't understand. I know that that feeling exists, I suppose I must have had it, but I can't conjure it up, not even to think about. I would never rather die; I'd rather find something else. And if I had to describe myself in this sense I would only say that for most of my life, not just these years of travelling but from the time I was four, when I saw I'd gotten taller than when I was three, and I understood, I *saw*, that my life would be years of getting taller and taller, first one year, then another, and that in this way I would come someday to match my mother—that from that time I always felt I deserved the best of everything.

THE STORY OF A SCAR

JAMES ALAN McPHERSON

James Alan McPherson was born in Savannah, Georgia,
in 1943 and grew up there. His education includes
studies at Morris Brown College, Morgan State College,
Harvard Law School, and the University of Iowa Writers' Workshop. His fiction has been published in *Atlantic Monthly*, *Playboy*, and *Ploughshares*. He is
presently at work on a novel.

Since Dr. Wayland was late and there were no recent newsmaga-
zines in the waiting room, I turned to the other patient and said:
"As a concerned person and as your brother, I ask you, without
meaning to offend, how did you get that scar on the side of your
face?"

The woman seemed insulted. Her brown eyes, which before
had been wandering vacuously about the room, narrowed suddenly
and sparked humbling reprimands at me. She took a draw on her
cigarette, puckered her lips, and blew a healthy beam of smoke toward my face. It was a mean action, deliberately irreverent and
cold. The long curving scar on the left side of her face darkened.
"I ask *you*," she said, "as a nosy person with no connections in
your family, how come your nose is all bandaged up?"

It was a fair question, considering the possible returns on its
answer. Dr. Wayland would remove the bandages as soon as he
came in. I would not be asked again. A man lacking permanence
must advertise. "An accident of passion," I told her. "I smashed it
against the headboard of my bed while engaged in the act of love."

Here she laughed, but not without intimating, through heavy,
broken chuckles, some respect for my candor and the delicate cause
of my affliction. This I could tell from the way the hardness mel-
lowed in her voice. Her appetites were whetted. She looked me up

and down, almost approvingly, and laughed some more. This was a robust woman, with firm round legs and considerable chest. I am small. She laughed her appreciation. Finally, she lifted a brown palm to her face, wiping away tears. "You *cain't* be no married man," she observed. "A wife ain't worth *that* much."

I nodded.

"I *knowed* it," she said. "The best mens don't git married. They do they fishin' in goldfish bowls."

"I am no adulterer," I cautioned her. "I find companionship wherever I can."

She quieted me by throwing out her arm in a suggestion of offended modesty. She scraped the cigarette on the white tile beneath her foot. "You don't have to tell me a thing," she said. "I know mens goin' and comin'. There ain't a-one of you I'd trust to take my grandmama to Sunday school." Here she paused, seemingly lost in some morbid reflection, her eyes wandering across the room to Dr. Wayland's frosted glass door. The solemnity of the waiting room reclaimed us. We inhaled the antiseptic fumes which wafted from the inner office. We breathed deeply together, watching the door, waiting. "Not a-one," my companion said softly, her dark eyes wet.

The scar still fascinated me. It was a wicked black mark which ran from her brow down over her left eyelid, skirting her nose but curving over and through both lips before ending almost exactly in the center of her chin. The scar was thick and black and crisscrossed with a network of old stitch patterns, as if some meticulous madman had first attempted to carve a perfect half-circle in her flesh and then decided to embellish his handiwork. It was so grotesque a mark that one had the feeling it was the art of no human hand and could be peeled off like so much soiled putty. But this was a surgeon's office and the scar was real. It was as real as the honey-blond wig she wore, as real as her purple pantsuit. I studied her approvingly. Such women have a natural leaning toward the abstract expression of themselves. Their styles have private meanings, advertise secret distillations of their souls. Subjectively, this woman was the true sister of the man who knows how to look while driving a purple Cadillac. Their figures, and their disfigurations, make meaningful statements. Such craftsmen must be approached with subtlety if they are to be deciphered. "I've never seen a scar quite like that one," I began, glancing at my watch. Any minute Dr. Wayland would arrive and take off my bandages, removing me permanently from access to her sympathies. "Do you mind talking about what happened?"

"I *knowed* you'd git back around to that," she answered, her brown eyes cruel and level with mine. "Black guys like you with them funny eyeglasses are a real trip. You got to know everything. You sit in corners and watch people." She brushed her face, then wiped her palm on the leg of her pantsuit. "I read you the minute you walk in here."

"As your brother . . ." I began.

"How can you be my brother when your mama's a man?" she said.

We both laughed.

"I was pretty once," she began, sniffing heavily. "When I was sixteen my mama's preacher was set to leave his wife and his pulpit and run off with me to Deetroit City. Even with this scar and all the weight I done put on you can still see what I had." She paused. "*Cain't* you?" she asked significantly.

I nodded quickly, looking into her big body for the miniature of what she was.

From this gesture she took assurance. "I was twenty when it happen," she went on. "I had me a good job in the Post Office, down to the Tenth Street branch. I was a sharp dresser too, and I had me my choice of mens: big ones, puny ones, old mens, married mens, even D. B. Ferris, my shift supervisor, was after me on the sly—don't let these white mens fool you. He offered to take me off the primaries and turn me on to a desk job in hand-stampin' or damaged mail. But I had my pride. I told him I rather work the facin' table, *every shift*, than put myself in his debt. I shook my finger in his face and said, 'You ain't foolin' me, with your *sly self!* I know where the *wild goose went*; and if you don't start havin' some *respect* for black women he go'n come *back!*' So then he turn red in the face and put me on the facin' table. Every shift. What could I do? You ain't got no rights in the Post Office, no matter what lies the government tries to tell you. But I was makin' good money, dressin' bad, and I didn't want to start no trouble for myself. Besides, in them days there was a bunch of good people workin' my shift: Leroy Boggs, Red Bone "Big Boy" Tyson, Freddy May."

"What about that scar?" I interrupted her tiresome ramblings. "Which one of them cut you?"

Her face flashed a wall of brown fire. "This here's *my* story!" she muttered, eyeing me up and down with suspicion. "You dudes cain't stand to hear the whole of anything. You want everything broke down in little pieces." And she waved a knowing brown finger. "That's how come you got your nose all busted up. There's some things you have to take your time about."

Again I glanced at my watch, but was careful to nod silent agreement with her wisdom.

"It was my boyfriend that caused it," she continued in a slower, more cautious tone. "And the more I look at you the more I can see you just like him. He had that same way of sittin' with his legs crossed, squeezin' his sex juices up to his brains. His name was Billy Crawford, and he worked the parcel-post window down to the Tenth Street branch. He was nine years older than me and was goin' to school nights on the G.I. Bill. I was twenty when I met him durin' lunch break down in the swing-room. He was sittin' at a table against the wall, by hisself, eatin' a cheese sandwich with his nose in a goddamn book. I didn't know any better then. I sat down by him. He look up at me and say, 'Water seeks its own level, and people do too. You are not one of the riff-raff or else you would of sit with them good-timers and bullshitters 'cross the room. Welcome to my table.' By riff-raff he meant all them other dudes and girls from the back room who believed in havin' a little fun playin' cards and such durin' lunch hour. I thought what he said was kind of funny and so I laughed. But I should of knowed better. He give me a cheese sandwich and started right off preachin' at me about the 'low-life in the back room.' Billy couldn't stand none of 'em. He hated the way they dressed, the way they talked, and the way they carried on durin' work hours. He said if all them tried to be like him and advanced themselfs the Negro wouldn't have no problems. He'd point out Eugene Wells or Red Bone or Crazy Sammy Michaels and tell me, 'People like them think they can homestead in the Post Office. They think these primaries will need human hands for another twenty years. But you just watch the Jews and Puerto Ricans that pass through here. *They* know what's goin' on. I bet you don't see none of them settin' up their beds under these tables. They tryin' to improve them-

selves and get out of here, just like me.' Then he smile and held
out his hand. 'And since I see you're a smart girl that keeps a cold
eye and some distance on these bums, welcome to the club. My
name's Billy Crawford.'

"To tell you the truth, I liked him. He was different from all
the jive-talkers and finger-poppers I knew. I liked him because he
wasn't ashamed to wear a white shirt and a black tie. I liked the
way he always knew just what he was gonna do next. I liked him
because none of the other dudes could stand him and he didn't
seem to care. On our first date he took me out to a place where
the white waiters didn't git mad when they saw us comin'. That's
the kind of style he had. He knew how to order wine with funny
names, the kind you don't never see on billboards. He held open
doors for me, told me not to order rice with gravy over it or soda
water with my meal. I didn't mind him helpin' me. He was a
funny dude in a lot of ways: his left leg was shot up in the war and
he limped sometimes, but it looked like he was struttin'. He would
stare down anybody that watched him walkin'. He told me he had
cut his wife loose after he got out of the Army, and he told me
about some of the games she had run on him. Billy didn't trust
women. He said they all was after a workin' man's money, but he
said that I was different. He said he could tell I was a God-fearin'
woman and my mama had raised me right and he was gonna improve my mind. In those days I didn't have no objections. Billy
was fond of sayin', 'You met me at the right time in your life.'

"But Red Bone, my co-worker, saw what was goin' down and
began to take a strong interest in the affair. Red was the kind of
strong-minded sister that mens just like to give in to. She was one
of them big yellow gals with red hair and a loud rap that could put
a man in his place by just soundin' on him. She liked to wade
through the mail room elbowin' dudes aside and sayin', 'You don't
wanna mess with *me*, fool! I'll *destroy* you! Anyway, you ain't
nothin' but a dirty thought I had when I was three years old!' But
if she liked you she could be warm and soft, like a mama. 'Listen,'
she kept tellin' me, 'that Billy Crawford is a potential punk. The
more I watch him the less man I see. Every time we downstairs
havin' fun I catch his eyeballs rollin' over us from behind them
goddamn books! There ain't a rhythm in his body, and the only
muscles he exercises is in his eyes.'

"That kind of talk hurt me some, especially comin' from her.

But I know it's the way of some women to badmouth a man they want for theyselves. And what woman don't want a steady man and a good provider? . . . which is what Billy was. Usually, when they start downgradin' a steady man, you can be sure they up to somethin' else besides lookin' out after you. So I told her, 'Billy don't have no bad habits.' I told her, 'He's a hard worker, he don't drink, smoke, nor run around, and he's gonna git a *college* degree.' But that didn't impress Red. I was never able to figure it out, but she had something in for Billy. Maybe it was his attitude; maybe it was the little ways he let everybody know that he was just passin' through; maybe it was because Red had broke every man she ever had and had never seen a man with no hand-holes on him. Because that Billy Crawford was a strong man. He worked the day shift, and could of been a supervisor in three or four years if he wanted to crawl a little and grease a few palms; but he did his work, quiet-like, pulled what overtime he could, and went to class three nights a week. On his day off he'd study and maybe take me out for a drink after I got off. Once or twice a week he might let me stay over at his place, but most of the time he'd take me home to my aunt Alvene's, where I was roomin' in those days, before twelve o'clock.

"To tell the truth, I didn't really miss the partyin' and the dancin' and the good-timin' until Red and some of the others started avoidin' me. Down in the swing-room durin' lunch hour, for example, they wouldn't wave for me to come over and join a card game. Or when Leroy Boggs went around to the folks on the floor of the mail room collectin' money for a party, he wouldn't even ask me to put a few dollars in the pot. He'd just smile at me in a cold way and say to somebody loud enough for me to hear, 'No, sir; ain't no way you can git quality folk to come out to a Saturday night fish fry.'

"Red squared with me when I asked her what was goin' down. She told me, 'People sayin' you been wearin' a high-hat since you started goin' with the professor. The talk is you been throwin' around big words and developin' a strut just like his. Now I don't believe these reports, being your friend and sister, but I do think you oughta watch your step. I remember what my grandmama used to tell me: "It don't make no difference how well you fox-trot if everybody else is dancin' the two-step." Besides, that Billy Crawford is a potential punk, and you gonna be one lonely girl when somebody finally turns him out. Use your mind, girl, and stop bein' silly. Everybody is watchin' you!"

"I didn't say nothin', but what Red said started me to thinkin' harder than I had ever thought before. Billy had been droppin' strong hints that we might git married after he got his degree, in two or three years. He was plannin' on being a high school teacher. But outside of being married to a teacher, what was I go'n git out of it? Even if we did git married, I was likely to be stuck right there in the Post Office with no friends. And if he didn't marry me, or if he was a punk like Red believed, then I was a real dummy for givin' up my good times and my best days for a dude that wasn't go'n do nothin' for me. I didn't make up my mind right then, but I begin to watch Billy Crawford with a different kind of eye. I'd just turn around at certain times and catch him in his routines: readin', workin', eatin', runnin' his mouth about the same things all the time. Pretty soon I didn't have to watch him to know what he was doin'. He was more regular than Monday mornings. That's when a woman begins to tip. It ain't never a decision, but somethin' in you starts to lean over and practice what you gonna say whenever another man bumps into you at the right time. Some women, especially married ones, like to tell lies to their new boyfriends; if the husband is a hard worker and a good provider, they'll tell the boyfriend that he's mean to them and ain't no good when it comes to sex; and if he's good with sex, they'll say he's a cold dude that's not concerned with the problems of the world like she is, or that they got married too young. Me, I believe in tellin' the truth: that Billy Crawford was too good for most of the women in this world, me included. He deserved better, so I started lookin' round for somebody on my own level.

"About this time a sweet-talkin' young dude was transferred to our branch from the 39th Street substation. The grapevine said it was because he was havin' woman-trouble over there and caused too many fights. I could see why. He dressed like he was settin' fashions every day; wore special-made bell-bottoms with so much flair they looked like they was starched. He wore two diamond rings on the little finger of his left hand that flashed while he was throwin' mail, and a gold tooth that sparkled all the time. His name was Teddy Johnson but they called him 'Eldorado' because that was the kind of hog he drove. He was involved in numbers and other hustles and used the Post Office job for a front. He was a strong talker, a easy walker, that dude was a *woman* stalker! I have to give him credit. He was the last *true* son of the Great McDaddy. . . ."

"Sister," I said quickly, overwhelmed suddenly by the burden of insight. "I *know* the man of whom you speak. There is no time for this gutter-patter and indirection. Please, for my sake and for your own, avoid stuffing the shoes of the small with mythic homilies. This man was a bum, a hustler and a small-time punk. He broke up your romance with Billy, then he lived off you, cheated on you, and cut you when you confronted him." So pathetic and gross seemed her elevation of the fellow that I abandoned all sense of caution. "Is your mind so *dead*," I continued in a high voice, "did his switchblade slice so *deep*, do you have so little *respect* for yourself or at least for the idea of *proportion* in this sad world that you'd sit here and *praise* this brute!?"

She lit a second cigarette. Then, dropping the match to the floor, she seemed to shudder, to struggle in contention with herself. I sat straight on the blue, plastic couch, waiting. Across the room the frosted glass door creaked, as if about to open; but when I looked, I saw no telling shadow behind it. My companion crossed her leg and held back her head, blowing two thoughtful beams of smoke from her broad nose. I watched her nervously, recognizing the evidence of past destructiveness yet fearing the imminent occurrence of more. But it was not her temper or the potential strength of her fleshy arms that I feared. Finally she sighed, her face relaxed, and she wet her lips with the tip of her tongue. "You know everything," she said in a soft tone much unlike her own. "A black mama birthed you, let you suck her titty, cleaned your dirty drawers, and you still look at us through paper and movie plots." She paused, then continued in an even softer and more controlled voice. "Would you believe me if I said that Teddy Johnson loved me, that this scar is to him what a weddin' ring is to another man? Would you believe that he was a better man than Billy?"

I nodded my firm disbelief.

She seemed to smile to herself, although the scar, when she grimaced, made the expression more like a painful frown. "Then would you believe that I was the cause of Billy Crawford goin' crazy and not gettin' his college degree?"

I nodded affirmation.

"Why?" she asked.

"Because," I answered, "from all I know already that would seem to be the most likely consequence. I would expect the man to have been destroyed by the pressures placed on him. And, although you are my sister and a woman who has already suffered greatly, I must condemn you and your roughneck friends for this destruction of a man's ambitions."

Her hardened eyes measured my face. She breathed heavily, seeming to grow larger and rounder on the red chair. "My brother," she began in an icy tone, "is as far from what you are as I am from being patient." Now her voice became deep and full, as if aided suddenly by some intricately controlled wellspring of pain. Something aristocratic and old and frighteningly wise seemed to have awakened in her face. "Now this is the way it happened," she fired at me, her eyes wide and rolling. "I want you to *write* it on whatever part of your brain that ain't already covered with pageprint. I want you to *remember* it every time you stare at a scarred-up sister on the street, and *choke* on it before you can work up spit to condemn her. I was *faithful* to that Billy Crawford. As faithful as a woman could be to a man that don't ever let up or lean back and stop worryin' about where he's gonna be ten years from last week. Life is to be *lived*, not traded on like *dollars!* . . . All that time I was goin' with him my feets itched to dance, my ears hollered to hear somethin' besides that whine in his voice, my body wanted to press up against somethin' besides that facin'-table. I was young and pretty; and what woman don't want to enjoy what she got while she got it? Look around sometime: there ain't *no mens*, young nor old, chasin' no *older womens*, no matter how pretty they *used to be!* But Billy Crawford couldn't see nothin' besides them *goddamn books* in front of his face. And what the Jews and Puerto Ricans was doin'. Whatever else Teddy Johnson was, he was a dude that knowed how to *live.* He wasn't out to *destroy* life, you can believe *that!* Sure I listened to his rap. Sure I give him the come-on. With Billy workin' right up front and watchin' everything, Teddy was the only dude on the floor that would take to me. Teddy would say, 'A girl that's got what you got needs a man that have what I have.' And that ain't all he said, *either!*

"Red Bone tried to push me closer to him, but I am not a sneaky person and didn't pay her no mind. She'd say, 'Girl, I think you and Eldorado ought to git it on. There ain't a better lookin' dude *workin'* in the Post Office. Besides, you ain't goin' *nowheres* with that professor Billy Crawford. And if *you* scared to tell him to lean up off you I'll do it *myself*, bein' as I am your sister and the one with your interest in mind.' But I said to her, 'Don't do me no favors. No matter what you think of Billy, I am no sneaky woman. I'll handle my own affairs.' Red just grin and look me straight in the eye and grin some more. I already told you she was the kind of strong-minded sister that could look right down into you. Nobody but a woman would understand what she was lookin' at.

"Now Billy wasn't no dummy durin' all this time. Though he worked the parcel-post window up front, from time to time durin' the day he'd walk back in the mail room and check out what was goin' down. Or else he'd sit back and listen to the gossip durin' lunch hour down in the swing-room. He must of seen Teddy Johnson hangin' round me, and I know he seen Teddy give me the glad-eye a few times. Billy didn't say nothin' for a long time, but one day he pointed to Teddy and told me, 'See that fellow over there? He's a bloodletter. There's some people with a talent for stoppin' bleedin' by just being around, and there's others that start it the same way. When you see that greasy smile of his you can bet it's soon gonna be a bad day for somebody, if they ain't careful. That kind of fellow's been walkin' free for too long.' He looked at me with that tight mouth and them cold brown eyes of his. He said, 'You know what I mean?' I said I didn't. He said, 'I hope you don't ever have to find out.'

"It was D. B. Ferris, my shift supervisor, that set up things. He's the same dude I told you about; the one that was gonna give me the happy-hand. We never saw much of him in the mail room, although he was kinda friendly with Red Bone. D. B. Ferris was always up on the ramps behind one of the wall-slits, checkin' out everything that went down on the floor and tryin' to catch somebody snitchin' a letter. There ain't no tellin' how much he knew about private things goin' on. About this time he up and transferred three or four of us, the ones with no seniority, to the night shift. There was me, Red, and Leroy Boggs. When Billy found out he tried to talk D. B. Ferris into keepin' me on the same shift as his, but Ferris come to me and I told him I didn't mind. And I didn't. I told him I was tired of bein' watched by him and everybody else. D. B. Ferris looked up toward the front where Billy was workin' and smiled that old smile of his. Later, when Billy asked me what I said I told him there wasn't no use tryin' to fight the government. 'That's true,' he told me—and I thought I saw some meanness in his eyes, 'but there are some other things you can fight,' he said. At that time my head was kinda light and I didn't catch what he meant.

"About my second day on the night shift Teddy Johnson began workin' overtime. He didn't need the money and didn't like to work no-how, but some nights around ten or eleven, when we clocked out for lunch and sat around in the swing-room, in would strut Teddy. Billy would be in school or at home. Usually, I'd be sittin' with Red and she'd tell me things while Teddy was walkin' over. 'Girl, it *must* be love to make a dude like Eldorado work overtime. *He* needs to work like *I* need to be a Catholic.' Then Teddy would sit down and she'd commence to play over us like her life depended on gittin' us together. She'd say, 'Let's go over to my place this mornin' when we clock out. I got some bacon and eggs and a bottle of Scotch.' Teddy would laugh and look in my eyes and say, 'Red, we don't wanna cause no trouble for this here fine young thing who I hear is engaged to a college man.' Then I'd laugh with them and look at Teddy and wouldn't say nothin' much to nobody.

"Word must of gotten back to Billy soon after that. He didn't say nothin' at first but I could see a change in his attitude. All this time I was tryin' to git up the guts to tell Billy I was thinkin' about breaking off, but I just couldn't. It wasn't that I thought he needed me; I just knew he was the kind of dude that doesn't let a girl decide when somethin' is over. Bein' as much like Billy as you are, you must understand what I'm tryin' to say. On one of my nights off, when we went out to a movie, he asked, 'What time did you get in this mornin'?' I said, 'Five-thirty, same as always.' But I was lyin'. Red and me had stopped for breakfast on the way home. Billy said, 'I called you at six-thirty this morning and your aunt Alvene said you was still out.' I told him, 'She must of been too sleepy to look in my room.' He didn't say more on the subject, but later that evenin', after the movie, he said, 'I was in the war for two years. It made me a disciplined man, and I hope I don't ever have to lose my temper.' I didn't say nothin', but the cold way he said it was like a window shade flappin' up from in front of his true nature, and I was scared.

"It was three years ago this September twenty-second that the thing happened. It was five-thirty in the mornin'. We had clocked out at four-forty-five but Red had brought a bottle of Scotch to work and we was down in the swing-room drinkin' a little with our coffee, just to relax. I'll tell you the truth: Teddy Johnson was there too. He had come down just to give us a ride home. I'll never forget that day as long as I live. Teddy was dressed in a pink, silk shirt with black ruffles on the sleeves, the kind that was so popular a few years ago. He was wearin' shiny black bell-bottoms that hugged his little hips like a second coat of skin, and looked like pure silk when he walked. He sat across from me, flashin' those diamond rings every time he poured more Scotch in our cups. Red was sittin' back with a smile on her face, watchin' us like a cat that had just ate.

"I was sittin' with my back to the door and didn't know anything until I saw something change in Red's face. I still see it in my sleep at night. Her face seemed to light up and git scared and happy at the same time. She was lookin' behind me, over my shoulder, with all the smartness in the world burnin' in her eyes. I turned around. Billy Crawford was standin' right behind me with his hands close to his sides. He wore a white shirt and a thin black tie and his mouth was tight like a little slit. He said, 'It's time for you to go home,' with that voice of his that was too cold to be called just mean. I sat there lookin' up at him. Red's voice was even colder. She said to me, 'You gonna let him order you around like that?' I didn't say nothin'. Red said to Teddy, 'Ain't *you* got something to say about this?' Teddy stood up slow and swelled out his chest. He said, 'Yeah. I got somethin' to say,' looking hard at Billy. But Billy just kept lookin' down at me. 'Let's go,' he said. 'What you got to say?' Red Bone said to Teddy. Teddy said to me, 'Why don't *you* tell the dude, baby?' But I didn't say nothin'. Billy shifted his eyes to Teddy and said, 'I got nothing against you. You ain't real, so you don't matter. You been strutting the streets too long, but that ain't my business. So keep out of this.' Then he looked down at me again. 'Let's go,' he said. I looked up at the

way his lips curled and wanted to cry and hit him at the same time.
I felt like a trigger bein' pulled. Then I heard Red sayin', 'Why
don't you go back to bed with them *goddamn books, punk!* And
leave decent folks *alone!*' For the first time Billy glanced over at
her. His mouth twitched. But then he looked down at me again.
'This here's the *last time* I'm asking,' he said. That's when I exploded and started to jump up. 'I ain't goin' *nowhere!*' I screamed.
The last plain thing I remember was tryin' to git to his face, but
it seemed to turn all bright and silvery and hot and then I couldn't
see nothin' no more.

"They told me later that he sliced me so fast there wasn't time
for nobody to act. By the time Teddy jumped across the table I
was down and he had stabbed me again in the side. Then him and
Teddy tussled over the knife while me and Red screamed and
screamed. Then Teddy went down holdin' his belly and Billy was
comin' after me again when some of the dudes from the freight-
dock ran in and grabbed him. They say it took three of them to
drag him off me, and all the time they was pullin' him away he kept
slashin' out at me with that knife. It seemed like all the walls was
screamin' and I was floatin' in water and I thought I was dead and
in hell, because I felt hot and prickly all over and I could hear
some woman's voice that might of been mine screamin' over and
over, 'You Devil! . . . You *Devil!*' "

She lit a third cigarette. She blew a relieving cloud of smoke
downward. The thin white haze billowed about her purple legs,
dissipated, and vanished. A terrifying fog of silence and sickness
crept into the small room, and there was no longer the smell of
medicine. I dared not steal a glance at my watch, although by this
time Dr. Wayland was agonizingly late. I had heard it all, and now
I waited. Finally her eyes fixed on the frosted glass door. She wet
her lips again and, in a much slower and more pained voice, said,
"This here's the third doctor I been to see. The first one stitched
me up like a turkey and left this scar. The second one refuse to
touch me." She paused and wet her lips again. "This man fixed
your nose for you," she said softly. "Do you think he could do
somethin' about this scar?"

I searched the end table next to my couch for a newsmagazine,
carefully avoiding her face. "Dr. Wayland is a skilled man," I told
her. "Whenever he's not late. I think he may be able to do something for you."

She sighed heavily and seemed to tremble. "I don't expect no miracle or nothin'," she said. "If he could just fix the part around my eye I wouldn't expect nothin' else. People say the rest don't look too bad."

I clutched a random magazine and did not answer. Nor did I look at her. The flesh around my nose began to itch and I looked toward the inner office door with the most extreme irritation building in me. At that moment it seemed a shadow began to form behind the frosted glass, signaling perhaps the approach of someone. I resolved to put aside all notions of civility and go into the office before her, as was my right. The shadow behind the door darkened, but vanished just as suddenly. And then I remembered the most important question without which the entire exchange would have been wasted. I turned to the woman, now drawn together in the red plastic chair as if struggling to sleep in a cold bed. "Sister," I said, careful to maintain a casual air. "Sister . . . what is your name?"

WITH CHE AT KITTY HAWK

RUSSELL BANKS

Russell Banks is a native of New Hampshire who now resides in Northwood Narrows. A graduate of the University of North Carolina at Chapel Hill, he teaches in the English Department of the University of New Hampshire. He has published numerous stories in magazines and anthologies including *Partisan Review, Fiction, Triquarterly, New American Review,* and *Best American Short Stories 1971.* A novel, *Family Life,* was published this winter by Avon, and a collection of short stories, *Searching for Survivors,* is scheduled for this spring from The Fiction Collective in association with Braziller. "With Che at Kitty Hawk" is from that collection.

Her first day at Kitty Hawk, she stayed at the cottage with her mother and father and explained to them why she was leaving Roger. They sat on the beach in canvas and aluminum chairs and watched the children play with shovels and buckets at the edge of the water. As if speaking into a tape recorder, the three adults stared straight ahead while they talked to one another. The sun was white, unencumbered, untouched, in a cloudless sky, burning at the center of the dark blue, circular plane.

Bored with buckets and shovels, the two little girls—daughters and granddaughters—put the toys down and moved closer to the water, to dodge the waves, tempting them, dodging again. At first laughing gaily, then slightly frightened by the noise and power of the surf whenever a wave shoved ankles and knees or, as it receded, caught them from behind, their laughter would suddenly, momentarily, turn manic, and small, brown faces would shift to grey, mouths gaping, eyes searching the beach for Mama.

"Jesus, it's like Greece, this sky and that sun!"

"All week," her father said. "It's been like this all week, Janet.
Can you believe it?" With leathery, tanned skin, boney face and
round, wrinkle-rimmed eyes, he looked like a giant sea turtle
ripped cruelly from its shell and thrown into a canvas beach chair.
He lay there, rather than sat, staring at his granddaughters, fingertips nervously drumming on knobby knees, toes digging into the
hot, white sand. "Listen, honey," he finally said, "maybe you can
give it one last chance. You've got the children to think about,
you know."

"That's what I've *done*, for God's sake, is think about those two
children! I mean, figure it out for yourself, Daddy. Are they any
better off with one parent who's reasonably sane and more or less
happy, or with two parents, both of whom are crazy and miserable
and blaming their craziness and misery on each other? Which
would *you* have preferred? For that matter, which do you think *I*
would have preferred?" Chewing her upper lip, she still did not
look at him, though she knew the difficulty her questions would
cause him, his inability to answer truthfully, and the weakness
that would not let him force her to restate or withdraw them. She
wondered about herself—Would she become idly cruel?

Her father started to stammer, then inhaled deeply (a reversed
sigh), and talked rapidly about his mother and father, reminding
himself, his wife and his daughter that at least once in his life there
had been utter success in the universal attempt to make a perfect
marriage. In the middle of his eulogy, his paean, his wife got up
from her chair, wiped clinging grains of sand from her lumpy
calves and hands, and walked back to the cottage.

"Do you want a drink, Janet?" she called over her sun-reddened
shoulder. The turquoise straps of her bathing suit were cutting
into loaves of flesh.

"God, no, Mother! It's only three o'clock!"

"Yes. What about you, Charles?"

"What? What? Oh! Yeh, fine, fine, Anne. Gin and tonic. You
know."

Silently, the mother turned and waded through the deep sand,
over the low ridge to the cottage. The daughter and the father
continued to sit in the low-slung chairs, side by side, watching the
two little girls playing. For several minutes the old man and the
young woman said nothing.

Then the man sighed loudly, and said, as if to a friendly bartender, "Jesus, what a goddam shame."

She turned slowly and looked at him. "Yes, it's a goddam shame. A shame that it took me eight years. That's all *I'm* ashamed of!" she snapped. She got up from her chair and jogged down to the water, pounding through the surf until she was waist-deep, and dove into a breaking wave, disappearing and popping up after several seconds, beyond the wave, in smooth, dark green, deep water.

She poked one hand up in the air and waved to her father. He lifted a skinny, brown arm and slowly waved back.

She was what they used to call a "good looker"—neat, trim, sexy if tanned and wearing carefully selected clothes, a fashionably casual haircut and minimal makeup (but not without makeup altogether), the kind of woman whose attractiveness to men depended greatly on the degree to which she could reveal that men were attractive to her; if, however, it turned out that, for whatever reason or length of time, actually she was not so interested in men, her boyish, physical intensity repelled them. These were occasions when she was thought a lesbian, which, on these occasions, pleased her. It would serve the bastards right, she thought.

Stalking past the bunch of teenaged boys and men in tee shirts with sleeves rolled up to show off biceps and tattoos (flat-eyed hunters waiting for the quarry and drinking cans of beer cooled in styrofoam boxes at their feet), she hurried to a place about halfway down the Fish Pier. Out at the end of the pier, the serious fishermen had gathered, fifteen or twenty of them, redfaced, white men in duck-bill caps and bright-colored, short-sleeve shirts and bermuda shorts, all of them leaning like question marks over the waisthigh wood railing, peering out and down at their lines, silently attentive.

She slipped in between two small groups of black people, men and women, and stuffing a cold, slumbering bloodworm onto the hook, leaned over the rail and flipped the tip of the rod, casting underhanded, sending the weighted hook and worm forty or fifty feet out and twenty feet down into the dark water. Slowly, she reeled the line back in, watching the people around her as she worked.

"How you doin'?" a man with an enormous head asked her. "Any bites?" He flashed a mouthful of gold-trimmed teeth.

"No. But I just got here," she said. She heard the words clicking in a hard, flat, Boston accent. She never heard her own accent, except when she happened to be speaking with blacks—no matter that they were blacks from Chicago or Brooklyn. Southern whites, strangely, only made her conscious of *their* accent, not her own. The same was true for Puerto Ricans.

The man was with two women, both of whom seemed to be older than he, and two men, also older than he. None of the others were fishing. Instead, they drank beer and ate fried chicken legs and chattered with each other and with the various black people passing by and standing around them. The man fishing was, by comparison, a solitary; to support the impression, he carefully ignored the others, occasionally chuckling or shaking his head in mock-exasperation. His very large head was almost startling to look upon, all the more (for a white person) because of his shiney blackness. Janet didn't realize she was staring at him, at his head, the bludgeon-like force of it, until, smiling easily at her, he asked, "You know me, Miss?"

"No, no, I guess not. I just thought, I . . . you do look familiar to me, that's all."

"You prob'ly seen me around," he said, almost bragging.

"Yes." She noticed that whenever he spoke to her, the others immediately lapsed into silence—but only for as long as he was speaking. When she answered him, they went back to their own conversations, not hearing her. It was as if she said nothing, almost as if she were a creature of his imagination. It made her nervous.

Nevertheless, the two continued talking idly to one another while they fished, with long periods of thoughtful silence between exchanges, and after awhile, she no longer noticed that the older blacks were watching her in attentive silence whenever he spoke to her, switching off and ignoring her altogether whenever she responded. Then, in less than an hour, the afternoon tide turned, and they both finally started catching fish—spots, small, silvery-white fish with a thumbnail-sized black dot over each gill.

"The tide comin' in now," he had explained. "We goin' t' get us a mess of fish now, you wait," he said, and as he spoke, she felt the deliberate tug of a fish on her line. She yanked with her left hand and reeled with her right, swiftly pulling in a small fish that glistened in the sun as she drew it up to the pier and over the rail. The fish she caught, one after another, were only a bit larger than her hand, but as the man explained, they'd be the best little fish she'd ever caught. "You fry up a mess of them little spots in the mo'ning, an' that'll be your best breakfast!" he promised, excitedly grinning at her as he reeled in another for himself, slipping it off the hook and stuffing it into the burlap bag at his feet. She let her own caught fish accumulate inside the tin tackle box she had brought, her father's. She could hear them rattling around inside it, scattering the hooks, sinkers and lures in the darkness. Her heart was pounding, from the work as much as from the excitement; she imagined the large, grey blossoms of sweat that she knew had spread across her back and under her arms. Her arms and legs were feathery and full of light to her, as, one after another, she felt the shudder and the familiar, hard tug of a fish hitting the line, and hooked, felt it pull against the steady draw of the reel. She wanted to laugh out loud, to yell to the man next to her, *Hey! I got another one! and another one! and another one!* as they kept coming with the afternoon tide.

But she said nothing. They both worked steadily now, in silence, grabbing the flopping, hooked fish off their lines, jamming fresh worms onto the hooks, reaching over the rail and casting the lines, underhanded, in long arcs back down into the water, feeling the weighted hooks hit the water, sink a foot or two into it, feeling them get hit again, and then reeling the fish back towards the pier, lifting them up to the pier and the rail again, and again, until her arms began to ache, the muscles of her right hand between thumb and forefinger to cramp, sweat rolling across her face, and still the fish kept on hitting the lines. There was a grim, methodical rhythm to their movements, and they were working together, it seemed, the slender, tanned woman in the blouse and shorts and blue tennis shoes and the black man with the enormous head, a muscular man in a tee shirt and stained khaki trousers and bare feet that were the color of vanilla ice cream at the edges, the color of mahogany on the tops.

And then, as suddenly as it had begun, it was over. Her line drifted slowly to the bottom and lay there, inert, as if tied to a rock. His line, five feet away from hers, did the same. The two of them leaned further out and watched, waiting. But nothing happened. The fish were gone. The tide had moved them closer to the beach, where the school had swirled and dispersed in several silvery clouds, swimming with the current along the beach, away from the pier and parallel to the breaking waves. She watched as the surf-casters scattered up the beach one by one began catching fish, their long poles going up like toll gates as the schools of fish moved rapidly along.

She lay flat on her back in the sand, no blanket or towel beneath her, feeling her skin slowly darken, tiny, golden beads of sweat gradually stringing her mouth along her upper lip and over her skin, crossing her forehead just above her eyebrows, puddling in the gullies below her collarbones and ribcage, between her small breasts, and drifting, sliding in a thin, slick sheet of moisture down the smooth insides of her thighs. It was close to noon, and the sun, a flat, white disc, was now almost directly overhead, casting practically no shadow.

"Mommy, you're really getting red," Laura quietly said. She stood over her mother for a moment, peering down with a serious, almost worried look on her face. She was the older daughter, temperamentally more serious than her sister, her range of emotions normally running from anxiety to grave concern to anger. They had always called her Laura, had never tried giving her a nickname. The other child, even though they'd named her Eva, was called Bootsie, Bunny, Noosh and Pickle—depending on the parent's mood and the expression on the face of the child. Eva's range of emotions seemed normally to run from giddiness to delight to whimsy; even when she was sobbing, her face red and wet with tears, it was close to the whimsy end of the spectrum, just as, when Laura was laughing, it was very close to anxiety. Most people found the two girls attractive and likeable—as much because of their personality differences as for their physical similarities, for the four year old Eva was in appearance a smaller version of the seven year old Laura. And both girls looked exactly like their mother.

This morning the three of them wore deep purple, two-piece bathing suits, and while the mother sunbathed, the daughters, with their pails and shovels, played in the hot sand beside her. The grandmother had driven into the village for groceries and mail, and the grandfather had taken his regular morning walk up the beach to the old Coast Guard station, a three mile walk.

"Look, Mommy, *sharks!*" Laura cried. Janet propped herself up on her elbows and squinted against the hard glare of white sand and mirror-like water. Then she saw them. Porpoises. Their grey backs chopping across the horizon just beneath the surface of the water.

"They're not sharks, they're porpoises, Laura."

"Oh. Are they dangerous?"

"Not really. They're supposed to be very bright and actually friendly."

"Oh," she said, not believing.

Janet lay down on her back again and closed her eyes. She studied the backs of her eyelids, a yellow ochre sheet with a slight, almost translucent scratch, like a thin scar, in front of the lid between her eye and the lid. Every time she tried to look at the scar —which seemed to float across the surface, moving slowly, like a twisted reed floating on still water—it jumped and disappeared off the edge of her circle of vision. It's probably a tiny scratch on the retina, she decided. The only way she could actually see it was if she tried not to look directly at it, but merely looked past it, as if at something else located in the same general region. Even then, however, she would find herself eager to see the line (the scar or scratch or whatever it was), and she would search for it, would catch a glimpse of it, and chasing with her gaze, would see it race ahead of her and out of sight.

She realized that the girls were no longer close beside her, and opening her eyes, sat up and looked around for them. They were gone. A small flock of gulls loped over the water, dipping, dropping, lifting, going on. The porpoises were still looping through the water a few hundred yards from the beach. The beach, however, as far as she could see in both directions, was deserted. She called, "Laura!" Then called again, louder, and stood up, looking back towards the cottage. Where the hell . . . ?

"Listen, Mommy, you're really getting a terrible sunburn!" She opened her eyes and looked into Laura's worried face. Eva was sitting a few yards away, humming to herself while she buried her feet in a knee-deep hole she had dug in the sand. "Did you fall asleep?" Laura asked.

"No." She stood up then, brushing the sand off the backs of her slender legs, shoulders and arms. "C'mon, let's walk up the beach and meet Grandpa," she said cheerfully, reaching a hand to Laura, leaning down and helping Eva pull herself free. The three of them started walking down the beach, towards the Coast Guard station. Offshore, the porpoises cruised alongside, headed in the same direction, and above them, the gulls.

The third night in the cottage, listening to the radio, a top-40 station from Elizabeth City, Janet drank alone until after midnight. She situated herself on the screened porch, gazed out at the ridge of sand that lay between the cottage and the beach, milky-white until almost ten o'clock, when it slowly turned grey, then black, against the deep blue, eastern night sky beyond. She was drinking scotch and water, and each new drink contained less water and proportionately more scotch than the previous one, until she had succeeded in blurring her vision, with her face a heavy plaster mask slipping forward and about to fall into her lap.

She was alone; her mother and father had done their drinking before dinner, as was their habit, and had gone to bed by nine-thirty, which also was a habit. Janet, who had almost forgotten their routines, had been repelled, and a flood of sour memories had swept over her, depressing her, separating her from her own life sufficiently to make her feel, at last, self-righteous sitting there on the porch with the bottle of Teacher's, a pitcher of water, a tub of ice cubes, and a small transistor radio on the floor beside her, pouring and drinking down one glassful of scotch and water after another, letting the sweetly sad songs from that summer's crop swarm over her own self-pitying sense of past and present lives. At one point, she told herself that she was interested in the differences between the way her parents drank and the way she drank —meaning that she was interested in making sure that there were differences.

As the land behind her cooled, the wind blew steadily and strongly, and the sound of the waves crashing in darkness on the packed, wet sand filled all the space that lay behind the sound of the radio. Janet thought in clumsy spirals, about Roger, his years in graduate school, and about their townhouse in Cambridge, the years before that, when they both were in college, when the children were born, her pregnancies, then the years endured while in high school in Connecticut, living at home with her parents, the summers at camps in upstate New York, traveling in the West, then a small girl, visiting her grandparents, here, at Kitty Hawk, where the family had been coming for their summers for as long as she could remember . . . and now here she was again, where she had started, where they had started too, her parents, and she was placing her own daughters right where she had been placed, even to the point of sleeping them in the same room she had used at their age. She felt her chest and throat fill with a hard fist of longing, a knot of emotion attached to no object outside herself. Then, almost as soon as she had become aware of its presence, she felt the knot loosen and quickly unravel, to regather as hatred, clear anger and revulsion for her own life, for the entrapment it offered her. Momentarily satisfied, though, with this object for her emotion and with the longing converted to anger, she flicked off the radio, stood clumsily, slightly off-balance, rocking on the balls of her feet like a losing prize-fighter, and wound her way back into the livingroom, bumping curtly against the maple arm of the couch, grabbing at the light switches, dumping the house finally into darkness, as she made her way down the hall to the stairs and up the stairs to her bedroom, the "guestroom" at the end, moving with pugnacious confidence in spite of the darkness, but, because of her drunkenness, off-balance, inept.

Over on the western side of the Outer Banks, the soundside, the water was shallow and, most of the time, calm. Excellent places for wading lay scattered all along the soundside north of Kitty Hawk, north to where, standing on any slight height of land, one could easily see both the Atlantic and Currituck Sound. The fourth morning at Kitty Hawk, Janet decided to drive over to the sound and take the girls to one of the small inlets where they could wade and even swim safely. They were excited by the prospect, though they didn't quite understand how, only a few miles away, it could be so different. If here by the cottage there was an ocean with huge, dangerous waves and undertows and tides, how could they get into the car and go to the water a few miles away and have it be utterly different, like a shallow lake only with salt water?

Driving fast along the narrow road north of Kitty Hawk, deep sand on both sides, witch grass, sea oats and short brush, with high dunes blocking any possible views of the ocean, Janet slowed suddenly and carefully pulled her father's green Chrysler stationwagon over and picked up a hitchhiker. He was slight and not very tall, an inch or two taller than Janet, probably. About twenty-two or -three, with long blond hair, almost white, that hung straight down his back, he moved with an odd, precise care, as if he were made of glass, that was slightly effeminate and, to Janet, extremely attractive. As he came up beside the car he smiled, showing even white teeth, good-humored blue eyes, a narrow nose. He pitched his backpack into the rear of the car, where the girls were, nodded hello to them and climbed into the front seat next to Janet.

"How far you goin'?" he asked in a soft, confident voice.

"Out beyond Duck, to the sound. Four or five miles, I guess. Will that get you where you want?"

"Yeah," he answered, sliding down in the seat, folding his hands across his flat belly and closing his eyes, obviously enjoying the smooth luxury of the car, the insulating comfort of the air conditioner, as Janet drove the huge vehicle swiftly along the road, floating over bumps, gliding flatly around curves and bends in the road.

"Connecticut plates," the young man said suddenly, as if remembering a name he'd forgotten. "Are you from Connecticut?" He was unshaven, but his cheeks weren't really bearded as much as merely covered with a soft, blond down. He was well-tanned, dressed in levis, patched and torn, faded and as soft-looking as chamois, and a dark green tee shirt. He was barefoot. Sliding a bit further down on the seat, his weight resting on the middle of his back, he placed his feet onto the dashboard in front of him, gingerly, with a grace and care that made it seem natural to Janet.

She explained that she was from Cambridge, that the car was her father's and her parents were the ones who lived in Connecticut. Manchester, outside Hartford. And she was just down here for a while, she and her daughters, visiting them at their cottage. Though she herself hadn't been down here in years, not since her childhood. Because of summer camps and school and all. . . .

"Yeah, right," he said, peering casually around him, taking in the two little girls in the back, who grinned soundlessly at him, the styrofoam floats in the far back of the car, beach towels, a change of clothes for each of them, a bag with sandwiches and cookies in it, a small styrofoam ice chest with ice and a six-pack of Coke inside. "You going swimming in the sound?" he asked.

"Yes, for the kids, y' know?" She started to explain, about the waves, the undertow, the tides, how these presented no problems over on the sound and children their ages could actually swim and enjoy themselves, not just sit there digging in the sand, which was about all they could do over on the sea side, when she realized that she was talking too much, too rapidly, about things that didn't matter. So she asked him, "What about you? Are you staying down here for the summer . . . or what?"

"No. I'm just kind of passing through. Though I may stay on for the summer," he added softly. His accent identified him as a northerner, but that was about all.

"Are you living here . . . in Kitty Hawk, I mean?"

"Naw, I made a camp out on the dunes, a ways beyond where the road ends. It's a fine place, so long as they don't come along and move me out. Nobody's supposed to be, like, camping out there, you know?"

"Do you have a tent?" she asked, curious.

"No. They'd spot that as soon as I pitched it. I just sort of leaned some old boards and stuff together, pieces of wood I found along the beach and in the dunes. Last night, when it rained, I bet I stayed as dry as you did. It's the best place I've had all year. Up north, even in summer, there's no way you can be comfortable, drifting around like this. But like down here, it's easy, at least till winter comes. I work a couple of days every couple of weeks pumping gas at the Gulf station in Manteo, for groceries and stuff, you know? . . . That's where I'm comin' from now, I got my two weeks' groceries an' stuff in my pack . . . and I just spend the rest of my time, you know, out on the dunes, sitting around in my shack, playing a little music, smoking some good dope, fishing on the beach . . . stuff like that."

"Oh," she said, surprised to hear herself saying it sharply, as if he had said something to make her angry.

The road ahead was narrower, and on both sides, dunes and beach beyond dunes, no vegetation but brown grasses scattered sparsely across the sands, and as they rounded a curve, the road ended altogether. There was a paved cul-de-sac at the end where, without much trouble, one could turn a car around, and Janet steered the big Chrysler into this area and parked it, shutting off the motor, opening the door and stepping out quickly.

The young man got out and walked around to the back, where he flopped the tailgate down, pulling his pack out first, then the kids' styrofoam floats, the lunch bag and ice chest, and the towels and clothes. The girls scrambled past him, leaped down from the tailgate and ran for the water. They were already in their bathing suits, and they didn't break stride as they hit the quietly lapping water and raced in, quickly finding themselves twenty or thirty feet from shore, with the water not yet up to their knees. Janet had come around to the back to get their things out of the car, but when she got there the man had already placed them on the ground and was closing the tailgate, lifting it slowly. Smiling gratefully, she came and stood beside him, to help lift the massive, heavy tailgate, brushing his bare arm with hers, then moving tightly towards him, touching his thigh with the side of her own. Lifting the slab of metal together, it slammed shut, and they moved quickly away from the car and from each other. She peered easily into his face, and he answered with a slight smile.

"Want to come up and see my shack?" he asked her. He stood about eight feet away from her, one hand resting on his pack. He clearly was admiring her, making no effort to hide his examination. She was dressed in a two-piece bathing suit, an orange and black flower print, and a long sleeve, denim workshirt, unbuttoned, the sleeves rolled up to her elbows.

"Where is it?" she asked him, tossing her head, slinging a wisp of hair away from her eyes for a second. She leaned over and picked up the two coffin-shaped floats, hating the touch of the things against her hands, their odd weightlessness.

He waved a hand towards the seaside and said, "A couple hundred yards over that way. Just walk over those dunes there and when you get to the beach go along for maybe a hundred yards and cut in toward the dunes again, and then you'll see my shack. It'll probably look like a pile of driftwood or something to you at first, but when you get closer you'll see that it's a pretty fine place to live," he said, showing his excellent teeth again. "I got some good smoke too, if you care for that."

She looked down at the clothes, the paper bag and ice chest, the beach towels, lying in the sand, then back at the bony youth in front of her.

"Well, no . . . I don't think so. I have my daughters here. They haven't had a chance to swim, really, not since we got here, and I promised them this would be it, a whole day of it. But thanks," she said.

He answered, "Sure," lifted his pack onto his back, jabbing his arms through the straps, turned and started off across the pale sand through slowly waving lines of sea oats, leaving deep, drooping tracks behind him.

She stood at the back of the car for a few moments, watching him depart, then turned and dragged the styrofoam floats down to the edge of the water, where her daughters were waiting for her.

"You coming in too, Mamma?" Eva asked her.

"Yeah, Pickle, I'm coming in too."

"What were you talking about, you and that man?" Laura wondered, looking anxious. She stood knee-deep in the tepid water, about twenty feet from shore.

"Nothing much, really. He wanted me to come and see the way he lived, I guess. He's proud of the way he lives. Some people are that way, you know, proud of the way they live. I guess he's one."

"Are you?" Laura asked without hesitation.

"No," her mother answered, just as swiftly. Then she went back to the car for the rest of their gear.

When she woke the next morning, the first thing she knew was that it was raining—a soft, windless, warm rain, falling in a golden half-light, and she couldn't decide if it had just begun or was about to end.

Dressing quickly, shoving a brush through her hair, she walked out to the hall, heard her daughters talking behind the door of their bedroom, saw that the door to her parents' room was still closed, and judging it to be early, probably not seven yet, walked downstairs to the livingroom. Immediately, upon entering the room, she felt the dampness of it. In the mornings here, the livingroom and kitchen seemed strangely inappropriate to her—wet, chilled, smelling of last night's cigarette butts and food—which made her eager to get a pot of coffee made, bacon frying, ashtrays emptied, the new day begun. . . .

As she moved about the small kitchen, from the formica-topped counter to the stove to the refrigerator, she gradually realized that the rain had stopped, but the golden, hazy light had been replaced by a low, overcast sky casting a field of gloomy, pearly light. She stopped work and looked out the window towards the ocean. A gull, as it swept up from the beach, ascending at the ridge between the cottage and the water, seemed to burst out of the ground. She could see that its belly was stained with yellow streaks the color of egg yolk, and at once she knew that the birds she had believed so pure and cleanly white were actually scavengers, carrion-eaters, foul-smelling, filthy creatures that were beautiful only when seen from a distance, only when abstracted from their own reality. Then suddenly the force of the day, the utter redundancy of it, the closure it represented and sustained, hit her, and she knew she'd been staggered by the blow. She was unwilling to believe that her life was going to be this way every day, unwilling to believe it and yet also unable to deny it any longer—a lifetime of waking to damp, smelly couches and chairs, to rooms filled with furniture in a house, to food again, for herself, for her children, to emptying the ashtrays, and smoking cigarettes to fill them up again, of waking to sodden grey skies and stinking birds searching for garbage, and on through the day, more meals, more messes to make and clean up afterwards, until nightfall, when, with pills or alcohol, she would put her body to sleep for eight or ten hours, to begin it all over again the next morning. It wasn't that she believed there was nothing more than this. Rather, she now understood that—no matter what else there was—she would never get away from this; it was as close to her as her own body, and therefore, anything else was little more than worthless. Anything she might successfully add to her life could only come in as background to this repeated series of acts, perceptions, services. She was thirty years old, not old, and yet it was too late to begin anything truly freshly. A new man, a new place to live, a new way of life, a profession even—the newness would be a mockery, a sad, lame reaction to the failure of the old. There had been the last promise, when she had left Roger, of sloughing off her old life, the way a snake sloughs off an old skin, revealing a new, lucid, sharply defined skin beneath it. But the analogy hadn't held.

It occurred to her that she was trapping her own children. The terms of her life had become the terms of their lives now, and thus they too would spend the rest of their lives in relentless, unchanging reaction to patterns she could not stop establishing for them. None of them, not she, not her daughters, were going to get free. Again, she'd been fooled again, but this time, she knew, it was for the last time. She felt a dry bitterness working down her throat, like a wafer eaten at communion. Walking to the bottom of the stairs, she quietly called her daughters down for breakfast.

"Look, it's going to be a lousy day all day, so rather than wait around here hoping the sun will come out, is it okay if I take your car and spend the day with the kids, driving around and taking in the sights?" She lit a cigarette, flicked the match onto the floor, saw it lying there, a thin tail of smoke ascending from one end, and quickly plucked it back, wondering what the hell made her do that? She held the burnt match carefully between her thumb and forefinger while her father tried to answer her first question.

It was difficult for him, mainly because he wanted her to know, on the one hand, that he was eager for her to use his car, that, in fact, he was eager to be able to help her in any way possible (going for his wallet as the thought struck him), but also, he wanted her to know that he and her mother would be forced to endure their day-long absence as a painful event—wanted her to know this, but didn't want that knowledge to coerce her into changing her mind and staying at the cottage or leaving the children here, while she took the car and went sight-seeing alone. After all, he reasoned with himself, they were her children, and right now they must seem extra-precious to her, for, without Roger, she must need to turn to them for even more love and companionship than ever before. He imagined how it would have been for Anne, his wife, if they had gotten divorced that time, years back, when Janet was not much older than Laura was now. Yes, but what would this day be like for him and Anne, with Janet and the children gone? A grey blanket of dread fell across his shoulders as he realized that five minutes after the car pulled away, he and his wife would sit down, each of them holding a book, and they would wait impatiently for the sound of the car returning. After lunch, they would take a walk up the beach (if it didn't rain) walking back quickly so as not to miss them if Janet and the children decided to return to the cottage early, and, because, of course, they would not have come back early, he and Anne would spend the rest of the afternoon in their chairs on the porch, holding their books, he a murder mystery, she a study of open classrooms in ghetto schools. Well, they could drink early, and maybe Anne could think of something special to fix for dinner, blue shell crabs, and could start to work on that early, and he could rake the beach again, digging a pit for the trash he found, burying it, raking over the top of the pit carefully, removing even the marks left by the teeth of the rake. . . .

"*Sure* you can take the car, that's a *fine* idea! Give us a chance to take care of some things around here that need taking care of anyhow. How're you fixed for cash? Need a few dollars?" he asked without looking at her, drawing out his billfold, removing three

twenties, folding them with his second finger and thumb and
shoving them at her in such a way that for her to unfold and count
it would be to appear slightly ungrateful; she could only accept.

Which she did, saying thanks and going directly into the living-
room, switching off the television as she told her daughters to
hurry up and get dressed, they were going out for a ride, to see
some exciting things, the Wright Brothers Memorial, for one
thing, and maybe a shipwreck, and some fishing boats and a lighthouse, and who knows what else. She looked down at her hand,
found that she was still holding onto the burnt match. She threw
it into an ashtray on the endtable next to the couch.

She drove fast, through the village of Kitty Hawk—several rows
of cottages on stilts, a few grocery stores and filling stations, a restaurant, a book store, and the Fish Pier—and south along Highway 158 a few miles, to Kill Devil Hills. The overcast sky had
started breaking into shreds of dirty-grey clouds exposing deep
blue sky behind. Though the day was warm, the sun was still behind clouds, and thus the light was cold, diminishing colors and
softening the edges of things, making it seem cooler than it was.
Switching the air conditioner off, Janet pressed toggles next to
her and lowered the windows opposite and beside her, and surprisingly warm, humid air rushed into the car. In the back, the girls
had taken up their usual posts, peering out the rear window, finding it more satisfying to see where they had been than to seek
vainly for where they were going.

On her right, in the southwest, Kill Devil Hill appeared, a grassy
lump prominent against the flattened landscape of the Outer
Banks, and at the top of the hill, a stone pylon that, from this distance of a mile, resembled a castle tower. "We're almost there,"
she called to the girls. "Look!" She pointed at the hill and the
tower.

"Where?" Laura asked. "Where are we going?"

"There. See that hill and the tower on top? Actually, it's not a
tower. It's a stone memorial to the Wright Brothers," she explained, knowing then why she had never come here before, and
simultaneously, wondering why the hell she was coming here now.

"The Wright Brothers?" Laura said. "Are they the airplane
men?"

Eva saw the hill and the memorial and exclaimed excitedly that it was a castle.

"Yes, they're the men who invented the airplane."

"Oh."

"Mamma, look! A castle! Are we going to the castle? Can we go to the castle?"

"Yes."

"How many brothers were there?"

"Two. Wilbur and Orville."

"Only *two?* I thought there was *twelve*," Laura cried as if she'd been deceived.

"Will there be a king and a queen at the castle?"

"No . . . yes. Sure."

"Oh, boy! Laura, there's going to be a king and a queen at the castle!"

"Stupid! That's not a castle."

"Yes, it is. Let her call it a castle, Laura. It looks like one."

Off the highway now, they drove along the narrow, winding approach to the memorial, passing the field and the low, flat-roofed, glass-walled structure that, she could see from the roadway, housed the various exhibits and the scale model of the aircraft, past the two wooden structures at the northern end of the field where, she quickly read on the large sign posted beside the road, the brothers had housed their device and had worked and slept while preparing it for flight. Janet was surprised to find herself oddly attracted to the place, the hill, round and symmetrical, like an Indian mound, topped with the pylon that even up close looked like a castle, the way, as a child, she had imagined the Tower of London to look, and spreading below it, the flat, grass-covered field with the grey structures, like small garages or barns, at the far end.

Janet parked the Chrysler over on the west side of the hill where there was a small parking lot. The three of them got out and started walking quickly along the asphalt paved pathway that methodically switchbacked to the top. In seconds, the girls had run on ahead, and Janet was alone. The sky was almost clear now, a bright, luminous blue, and the sun was shining down on her face as she climbed. She was sweating and enjoying it, feeling the muscles of her back and legs working hard for the first time in weeks. The closure she had felt a few hours ago could now be recalled only with deliberate effort. She still perceived the entrapment as the prime fact of her life, but merely as if it were a statistic, as impersonal as her shoe size. Ahead of her, the figures of her daughters were darting about the base of the tower, peering up at the top, scurrying around the thing as if looking for an entrance. Then, in a few moments, she, too, arrived at the crest, breathing hard, sweating, and the girls ran to meet her.

"It's a castle all right!" Eva cried happily. "But we can't get in, the door's locked!" She pulled Janet by the hand, to show her that in fact there was an entrance to the tower, the castle—a steel door that was padlocked. "The king and the queen had to go to work, I guess. They aren't home."

"I guess not, Pickle," Janet said, walking slowly around to the other side, sitting on the ground and peering down at the slope the two bicycle mechanics had used for flying their strange machine. Then, as if a wonder were unfolding before her eyes, filling her with awe, she saw a large, clear image of the two men from the midwest, their clumsy wire, wood and cloth aircraft, the sustained passion, the obsession, which was the work, their love for it and for each other. It was like discovering a room in her own house that she never before had suspected even existed, opening a door that she'd never before opened, looking in and seeing an entire room, unused, unknown, altering thoroughly and from then on her view of the entire house.

The image, of course, was of her own making, but that made no difference to her, did not lessen the impact at all. She saw the Wright Brothers as having released into their two lives tremendous energy, saw it proceeding directly, as if from a battery, from the shared obsession and the mad, exclusive love for each other—a positive and a negative post, the one necessitated by the presence of the other. They did not permit themselves (she decided) to live as she had feared she was condemned to live—curled up inside a self that did not really exist, slowly dying inside that shell, no matter how many additional whorls of shell she managed to extrude, each new whorl no more than a dumb reaction to the limits of the previous one, spun by anger or bitterness or despair.

For her, the perception of the image was experienced by her body as much as by her mind, and she felt astonishingly lightened by it, as if she could fly, like a deliberately wonderful bird, leaping from that height of land first up and then out, in a long, powerful glide across the downward slope and then over the field that aproned it, drifting easily, gracefully, slowly down to the ground, coming to rest at the far end of the field, where the two workshops were located, where, she decided, she would go to work, pitching herself into the task of making a machine that could fly, making it out of wires and shreds of cloth and odd remainders of wood and rough pieces of other machinery—the junk of her life so far. Her daughters careened past her, mocking and singing at each other, asserting their differences to each other, and she knew, from the way her face felt, that she would be tireless.

Standing, she turned and waved for the girls to follow, and the three of them descended the hill, holding hands and talking brilliantly.

NAKEDNESS

JOHN UPDIKE

John Updike was born in Shillington, Pennsylvania, in 1932. He is the author of seven novels and five collections of short stories, most of which first appeared in *The New Yorker*. He lives presently in Ipswich, Massachusetts.

"Oh, look," Joan Maple said, in her voice of delight. "We're being invaded!"

Richard Maple lifted his head from the sand.

Another couple, younger, was walking down the beach like a pair of creatures, tawny, maned, their movements made stately by their invisible effort to control self-consciousness. One had to look hard to see that they were naked. A summer's frequentation of the nudist section up the beach, around the point from the bourgeois, bathing-suited section where the Maples lay with their children and their books and their towels and tubes of lotion, had bestowed upon the bodies of these other two the smooth pelt of an even tan, and the sexual signs so large in our interior mythology, the breasts and pubic patches, melted to almost nothing in the middle distance, in the sun. Even the young man's penis seemed incidental. And the young woman appeared a lesser version of the male—the same taut, magnetic stride, the same disturbingly generic arrangement of limbs, abdomen, torso, and skull.

Richard suppressed a grunt. Silence attended the two nudes, pushing out from their advance like wavelets up the packed sand into the costumed people, away from the unnoticing commotion and self-absorbed sparkle of the sea. Their advance could only be meant as, could only be taken as, an affront. In the watching crowds, some faces dropped as if stung. Others gazed steadfastly; for, this strolling nudism being a political gesture, the counter-protest must be a blunt stare. *"Well!"*: a woman's exclamation, from underneath an umbrella, blew down the beach like a sandwich wrapper. One old man, his dwindled legs linked to a barrel chest by boyish trunks of plaid nylon, stood up militantly, helplessly, drowning in this assault, making an uplifted gesture between that of hailing a taxi and shaking a fist. Richard's own feelings, he noticed, were hysterically turbulent: a certain political admiration grappled with an immediate sense of social threat; pleasure in the sight of the female was swept under by hatred for the male, whose ally she was publicly declaring herself to be; pleasure in the sight of the male fought specific focus on that superadded, boneless bit of him, that monkeyish footnote to the godlike thorax; and envy of their youth and boldness and beauty lost itself in an awareness of his own body that washed over him so vividly he involuntarily glanced about for concealment.

His wife, brown and pleased and modern, said, "They must be stoned."

Abruptly, having paraded several hundred yards, the naked couple turned and ran. The girl, especially, became ridiculous, her buttocks outthrust in the ungainly effort of retreat, her flesh jouncing heavily as she raced to keep up with her mate. He was putting space between them; his hair lifted in a slow spume against the sea's electric blue.

Heads turned as at a tennis match; the spectators saw what had made them run—a policeman walking crabwise off the end of the boardwalk. His uniform made him, too, representative of a species. But as he passed, his black shoes treading the sand in measured pursuit, he was seen as also young, his moustache golden beneath the sad-shaped mirrors of his sunglasses, his arms swinging athletic and brown from his short blue sleeves. Beneath his uniform, for all they knew, his skin wore another uninterrupted tan.

"My God," Richard said softly. "He's one of *them*."

"He is a pretty young pig," Joan stated with complacent quickness.

Her finding a phrase she so much liked irritated Richard, who had been groping for some paradox, some wordless sadness. "And you're a beat-up old knee-jerk liberal," he told her.

"My goodness. What have we done to deserve this? It's not as if they came up and tried to undress *you*."

"Maybe that's my complaint," he said, mollifying. For the Maples found themselves much together this vacation. One daughter was living with a man, one son had a job, the other son was at a tennis camp, and their baby, Bean, hated her nickname and, at thirteen, was made so uncomfortable by her parents she contrived daily excuses to avoid being with them. In their reduced family they were too exposed to one another; the child saw them, Richard feared, more clearly than he and Joan saw themselves. He suggested, in further mollification, as in college when they were courting he might have suggested they leave the library and go to a movie, "Let's follow him."

The policeman was a receding blue dot. "Let's," Joan agreed, standing promptly, sand raining from her, the gay alacrity of her acceptance hollow but the lustrous volume of her body, and her gait beside his, which he unthinkingly matched, and the weight of warm sun on his shoulders as they walked, real enough—real enough, Richard thought, for now.

The bathing-suited section thinned behind them. As they turned the point, bare bodies in their vision disengaged themselves from salt and sand. Freckled redheads with slack and milky bellies. Gypsyish girls hard as nuts, standing upright to hold their faces, brazen shields, closer to the sun's arrows. Long blacks emerging from the ocean bleached gray by their nakedness. Sleeping men, their testicles rotten as dropped fruit. A row of buttocks like the scallop on a doily. A bearded man doing yoga on his head, the fork of his legs appearing to implore the sky. Among these apparitions the policeman moved gently, cumbersome in his belt and gun, whispering, nearly touching the naked listeners, who nodded and began, singly and in groups, to put on their clothes. The couple who had trespassed, inviting this counterinvasion, could not be distinguished from the numerous naked others; all were being punished.

Joan went to a trio, two boys and a girl, as they struggled into their worn jeans, their widths of leather and sleeveless vests, their sandals and strange soft hats. She asked them, "Are you being kicked off?"

The boys straightened and gazed at her, her bikini, her pleasant plumpness, her sympathetic smile, and said nothing. The penis of one, Richard noticed, hung heavy a foot from her hand. Joan turned and returned to her husband's side.

"What did they tell you?" he asked.

"Nothing. They just stared at me. Like I was a moonperson."

"There have been two revolutions in the last ten years," he told her. "One, women learned to say 'fuck.' Two, the oppressed learned to despise their sympathizers."

Her body, nearly naked, radiated hurt; he knew he would pay, later, for his words. To soften them, he said, "Or maybe they just resented being approached when they were putting on their pants. It's a touchy moment, for males."

The nudists, paradoxically, brought more clothing to the beach than the bourgeoisie; they distinguished themselves, walking up the beach to the point, by being dressed head to toe, in denim and felt, as if they had strolled straight from the urban core of the counterculture. Now, as the young cop moved among them like a sorrowing angel, they bent and huddled in the obsequious poses of redressing.

"My God," Joan said, "it's like Masaccio's *Expulsion from the Garden.*" And Richard felt her heart in the fatty casing of her body plump up, pleased with this link, satisfied to have demonstrated once again to herself the relevance of a humanistic education to modern experience.

All that afternoon, as, returned from the beach, he pushed a balky lawn mower through the wiry grass around their rented house, Richard thought about nakedness. He thought of Adam and Eve ("Who told thee that thou wast naked?") and of Noah beheld naked by Ham, and of Susanna and the elders. He thought of himself as a child, having a sunbath on the second-story porch with his mother, who had been, in her provincial way, an avant-gardist, a health faddist. From beyond the screen of blankets she had draped on the balustrade the town had called with its many March voices: birds in bushes, children at ball games, the infrequent auto crackling on the pebbles of the street, the rarer commotion of a farm wagon trundling into town, the side boards creaking, the horse hooves clopping, the driver hawking with the abrupt, half-meant impatience of a man freshly awakened. The balusters of the balustrade were boards each jigsawed into an ornamental vase-shape sunlight strained through the blankets and stamped, obliquely foreshortened, along the porch boards. Wasps would come visit, the porch was so warm. An hour seemed forever; his embarrassment penetrated and stretched every minute. His mother's skin was a pale landscape on the rim of his vision; he didn't look at it, any more than he bothered to look at the hills enclosing the town, which he assumed he would never leave.

He thought of Rodin's remark that a woman undressing was like the sun piercing through clouds. The afternoon's gathering cloudiness slid shadows across the lawn, burnishing the wiry grass. He had once loved a woman who had slept beside a mirror. In her bed the first time, he glanced to his right and was startled to see them both, reflected naked. His legs and hers looked prodigiously long, parallel. She must have felt his attention leave her, for she turned her head; duplicated in the mirror, her face appeared beneath the duplicate of his. The mirror was an arm's length from the bed. This other couple lay six feet away. Since it was summer, they were, all four, smooth and tan, with pearly roundnesses where bathing suits had intervened. The other woman smiled, and the man's image followed, smiling in agreement, though within his body Richard was disconcerted, and dizzy with the effort of relating that leggy male nude to the patches and planes of himself seen peripherally, attached to his consciousness like fluttering pink tatters. He asked the woman beneath him if she ever felt disconcerted. She did not. "It's nice," she said. "You wake up in the morning, and there you are." Like the sun piercing through clouds. Yet, in the mirror, what fascinated him was not her body but his own—its length, its glow, its hair, its parallel toes so marvelously removed from its small, startled, sheepish head.

There had been, he remembered, a noise downstairs. Their eyes had widened into one another's, the mirror forgotten. He whispered, "What is it?" Milkmen, mailmen, the dog, the furnace.

She offered, "The wind?"

"It sounded like a door opening."

As they listened again, her breath fanned his mouth. A footstep distinctly betrayed itself beneath them. At the same moment as he tugged to pull the sheets over their heads, she sharply flung them aside. She disengaged herself from him, lifting her leg like the near figure in Renoir's *Bathers*. He was alone in the mirror; the mirror had become a screaming witness to the fact that he was where he should not be (his mother used to say, "Dirt is matter in the wrong place") and that he was in no condition for flight, or to be packaged swiftly.

He had gone onto her sunporch with his bunched clothes clutched to his front.

He squatted to cut the stubborn tufts by the boatshed with the hand clippers, and imperfectly remembered a quotation from one of the Japanese masters of *shungā*, to the effect that the phallus in these pictures was exaggerated because if it were drawn in its natural size, it would be negligible.

She had returned, his mistress, still naked, saying, "Nothing." She had walked naked through her own downstairs, a trespasser from Eden, past chairs and prints and lamps, eclipsing them, unafraid to encounter a burglar, a milkman, a husband; and her nakedness, returning, had been calm and broad as that of Titian's Venus, flooding him from within like some swallowed sun.

He thought of Titian's Venus, wringing her hair with two firm hands. He thought of Manet's Olympia, of Goya's Maja. Of shamelessness. He thought of Edna Pontellier, Kate Chopin's heroine, walking in the last year of that most buttoned-up of centuries down to the Gulf and, before swimming to her death, casting off all her clothes. "How strange and awful it seemed to stand naked under the sky! how delicious!"

He remembered himself a month ago, coming alone to this same house, this house into whose lightless, damp cellar he was easing, step by step, the balky mower, its duty done. He had volunteered to come alone and open up the house, to test it; it was a new rental for them. His wife had assented easily; there was something in her, these days, that also wanted to be alone. Half the stores on the island were not yet open for the summer; he had bought some days' worth of meals, and lived in rooms of an amazing chastity and silence. One morning he had walked through a mile of huckleberry and wild grape to a pond. Its rim of beach was scarcely a stride wide; only the turds and shed feathers of wild swans testified to other presences. The swans, suspended in the sun-irradiated mist upon the pond's surface, seemed gods to him, perfect and infinitely removed. Not a house, not a car, looked down from the hills of sand and scrub that enclosed the pond. Such pure emptiness under the sky seemed an opportunity it would be sacrilegious to waste. Richard took off his clothes, all; he sat on a rough warm rock. The pose of thinker palled. He stood and at the water's edge became a prophet, a Baptist; ripples of light reflected from the water onto his legs. He yearned to do something magnificent, something obscene; he stretched his arms and could not touch the sky. The sun intensified. As mist burned from the surface of the pond, the swans stirred, flapping their wings in aloof, Olympian tumult. For a second, sex dropped from him and he seemed indeed the divinely shaped center of a bowl-shaped Creation; his very skin felt beautiful—no, he felt beauty rippling upon it, as if this emptiness were loving him, licking him. Then, the next second, glancing down, he saw himself to be less than sublimely alone, for dozens of busy ruddy bodies, ticks, were crawling up through the hair of his legs, as happy in his warmth as he in that of the sun.

The sky was even gray now, weathered silver like the shingles on this island. As he went into the house to reward himself with a drink, he remembered, from a forgotten book, an old American farmer boasting that though he had sired eleven children he had never seen his wife's body naked. And from another book, about Africa, the remark, of some West African port, that this was the last city on the coast where a young woman could walk naked down the main street without attracting attention. And from an old *Time* review, years ago, revolutions ago, of the Brigitte Bardot picture that for a few frames displayed her naked from head to toe: *Time* had quipped that though the movie had a naked woman in it, so did most American homes, around eleven o'clock at night.

Eleven o'clock. The Maples have been out to dinner; their lone child is spending the night with a friend. Their bedroom within this house is white and breezy, white even to the bureaus and chairs, and the ceiling so low their shadows seem to rest upon their heads.

Joan stands at the foot of the bed and kicks off her shoes.

Her face, foreshortened in the act of looking down, appears to pout as she undoes the snaps on her skirt and lets the zipper fling into view a white V of slip. She lets her skirt drop, retrieves it with a foot, places it in a drawer.

Then the jersey lifts, decapitating her and gathering her hair into a cloud, a fist, that collapses when her face is again revealed, preoccupied.

A head-toss, profiled.

Headlights from the road caress the house and then forget.

An unexpected sequence: Joan pulls down her underpants in a

quick shimmy before, with two hands, arms crossed, pulling up her slip. Above her waist, the bunched nylon snags; she halts in the pose of Michelangelo's slave, of Munch's madonna, of Ingres' urn-bearer, seen from the front, unbarbered.

The slip unsnags, the snakeskin slides, the process continues.

With a squint of effort she uncouples the snaps at her back and flips the bra toward the hamper in the hall. Toward the bed she says, in her voice of displeasure, "Don't you have something better to do?"

Richard has been lying on the bed half-dressed, watching, holding his applause. He answers, "Nothing."

And he stands and finishes undressing, his shadow whirling about his head. The two of them stand close, as close as at the beach when she had returned from being rejected by the young men, and he had taunted her. They are back on the beach; she is remembering. Again he feels her heart in the fatty casing of her body plump up, pleased. She looks at him, her eyes blue as a morning sea, and smiles. "No," Joan says, in complacent denial. Richard feels thrilled, invaded. This nakedness is new to them.

ALVIRA, LETTIE, AND PIP

JESSIE SCHELL

Jessie Schell was born in Greenville, Mississippi, in 1941. She received both a B.A. in English and an M.F.A. in Writing from the University of North Carolina at Greensboro, and she is now a Lecturer on Creative Writing at the University of North Carolina at Chapel Hill. She has published a novel, *Sudina* (E. P. Dutton), as well as poems and stories in various magazines including *Georgia Review, Southern Poetry Review,* and *Atlantic Young Poets.* One of her poems was selected this year for the Borestone Mountain Poetry Award Volume.

I first began to understand Aunt Lettie during a freshman English course at college. We were studying *Moby Dick* and Dr. Rosenblatt lounged before us on the desktop, her weight on one elbow, spread out like an odalisque with only her mauve lips moving.

"Pip finds God at the bottom of the sea," she said, hitching her slip strap up under the stretched material at her shoulder, "and rises from the ocean mad with his vision."

I was drunk with *Moby Dick,* and at the time, coming directly from Mississippi as I had, I tended to believe intensely, with absolute conviction, whatever words were thrown me at this North Carolina women's college. I felt that I had swum up from the ocean's depths myself, fleeing north to school, where Yankees talked breathlessly fast, where, unweighted with the thick, lush smell of magnolias and cape jasmine, the very air I swallowed was bright and frosty with truth. I had emerged from the watery shadows under Mississippi oaks into this rarefied air, not crazed but visionary, and Dr. Rosenblatt, with her sensuous attitude towards learning, was fleshly proof of the journey.

All I needed to do was remember Miss Cluett from Greenlove High School with her support hose and her tack-on lace collar, with her hair screwed back from her forehead and jabbed together with mother-of-pearl hairpins, her legs eternally amputated beneath the wooden desk she seemed to wear like a great box-skirt. She had taught us books like *The Scarlet Letter* and *Silas Marner* and once had sent me home to my father with a note when she found me reading D. H. Lawrence behind my classroom copy of *Ethan Frome.*

In comparison, Dr. Rosenblatt had a positively sexual relationship with words. She draped herself before us and her hands swam in the air like long white snakes as she spoke about Melville and Conrad, her provocative shoulders shrugging suggestively for punctuation, her voice jaded and weary with knowledge.

But Dr. Rosenblatt has little to do with my discovery about Aunt Lettie, except that she acted as a kind of conduit, her languid musing on *Moby Dick* and Pip left to smolder like hot coals in my head. And it does not matter that it only took me two months to discover that North Carolina was not north at all, only a hilly version of the flat, Delta farmland I thought I was escaping. They grew tobacco in North Carolina instead of cotton, and they allowed a token Negro or two in each graduating class (this was all back in the prehistoric fifties), but otherwise it was the same old story. I did manage to meet the handful of New Yorkers who had been sent south to a girls' college for some inexpensive "finishing," and they made all the difference. And I did get myself worked up enough, thinking I inhaled the heady air of truth, to discover what had always been puzzling me about Aunt Lettie. That is what I want to talk about.

Every family has its black sheep. My father always said it depended on the shade of black, how interesting the family really was. I, for example, was considered my generation's black sheep amongst all my cousins for crossing three states to go to college when the entire football team at Ole Miss was just waiting to be dated. That only shows you how genes get watered down from parent to child if you let yourself get complacent like all my aunts and uncles did, and it supports a theory my father always held about children revolting in every way possible from their parents. Because he and all his brothers, sisters and cousins had married ordinary men and women, husbands and wives as drab as bleached laundry, smooth lumps of quiet flesh that never caused embarrassment or commotion, who never wore anything more fashionable than a drip dry suit, a paisley dress, who never, in short, resembled in any way their generation before them, and that generation was chiefly my great aunt Lettie and my grandmother Alvira.

Alvira we all knew well, for she lived in the same town with her two sons, Harry and my father, Luke. Her daughter Mollie had managed to stretch herself as far away as St. Charles, La., across the river, but Alvira operated from a great yawning brownstone whose grounds had once contained a fruit orchard, a rose garden and even a small stable, but which was now eaten away by concrete parking lots, a Jiffy-Serve drugstore, and even a small luncheonette called DewCumIn—all because she allowed Uncle Harry to manage the family estate.

Harry was the oldest son, and to Alvira, that meant Harry's primal duties were legislated from the start. It did not matter that his brain was vanilla pudding or that Alvira herself had to pay off two cousins from Vicksburg to take his final exams at Ole Miss. She forgot the incident entirely. It had not ever happened. For it was only the exercise of sovereign family tradition that was sacred to Alvira. Form, rules, mandates—Alvira would, in any other family, even in the fifties, be considered a black sheep for her line of thinking, but my father and his generation preferred to call her eccentric, reserving the black sheep title, with all its rattling closet bones, for her sister Aunt Lettie.

Alvira moved among the thick marble busts, the horsehair love seats, the milkglass bric-a-brac of her home like an empress frozen outside time. From her bed, lying underneath the turgid swirl of air from the ceiling fan, she telephoned her family, issuing command invitations, reminding them all of Cousin Josh's birthday next week, "Don't forget to send a card," advising a niece by long distance collect to Little Rock that "Your daughter was here last week with her teeth half chewed out with decay. I've made an appointment with Dr. Hinshaw for next week—What do you *mean* you prefer Dr. Young there. Hinshaw pulled my wisdom teeth ten years ago and he can see as well as you or I."

Sometimes when the phone rang at our house (always during supper), my father would catch Mother's arm as she started to rise from the table.

"Let it ring," he'd say. "I would like to know what food tastes like hot."

"Luke," my mother sighed. "You have to be tolerant with Alvira. Think how your father's illness wears at her."

Father forked a brussels sprout as if he were spearing an enemy.

"She doesn't even care about Pa," I'd mutter indignantly. "It only irritates her. She doesn't want to pay for that nurse she has to have because she won't nurse him herself, and she has to put up with his fishing friends coming in and smelling up the back room."

Alvira and I had never been on good terms. She knew a black sheep when she saw one, and had had me pegged from the day she found me, at the age of eight, sashaying up and down the front walk in Aunt Lettie's red velvet cloak.

"What the devil are you doing? Where did you find that thing?" She yanked me by my elbow into the concealing shade of the hibiscus bush and her quick hands tore at the cloth I had pinned together with a rhinestone brooch from her jewelbox. "Half the town must be driving round the block looking at you," she cried and her cheeks went waxen like the Italian statues in her living room, her eyes as vacant. "Common little thief," she spluttered, jerking my neck forward as she pulled at the brooch's rusted catch.

"I'm not," I said and stamped my foot accidentally on her open-toed sandals. She jumped back from me and her eyes came to life again. "I didn't steal a thing. This old brooch is nothing but cut glass and the cape belongs to Aunt Lettie. I found it in the attic."

She ignored the brooch theft. "There *is* no Aunt Lettie," she thundered instead, then lowered her voice, remembering the shallow protection her grounds afforded her, what with the Dew-CumIn patrons travelling through what used to be a grape arbor. "Lettie is dead," she hissed dramatically and stalked off to the house with the cape tucked under her arm like bedclothes.

I ran the four blocks home that afternoon and sat on the front steps waiting for my father to finish work at the paper. He took me in his arms when he came and shook me until my teeth clicked against each other, making me laugh, and wiped the dirt stains from my cheeks where I had cried rivers.

"Aunt Lettie isn't dead," he said easily. "She's just away, she's not well. Alvira was only being eccentric."

"What's eccentric," I asked, "mean and ugly?"

"No," he said and tickled me under my bony arm until I squirmed with joy.

But I wouldn't forget so easily. "Then what?"

"She has her little ways," he said. "She lives in her own world."

That night at supper, while the phone continued to ring so long that my father gave up spearing brussels sprouts and stared wistfully at the quiet twilight outside the windows, my mother shook her head at me disapprovingly, her soft, placid face ruffled into unfamiliar emotion.

"No, dear," she corrected. "Alvira's just eccentric, you know that. She cares in her own way." She tilted her fork hazily over her plate, taking in my father's black expression. "Go answer the phone," she'd whisper then, like a shy child, and I would throw down my napkin and walk to the phone that fairly jumped with irritation.

"Hello, Alvira," I'd say, powerful in my certainty that it would be she. Then I would hold the phone four inches from my ear to save my hearing and to conserve energy. This way everyone got the message from the horse's mouth and I need not repeat it over my cold food.

Alvira was at her best when she got me on the phone. I think she resented the soft, sighing voices that offered meagre resistance to her latest injunction. She had nothing if not imagination, and she worked at these commands creatively. No wonder the scanty returns provided little pleasure. She tossed boulders into the tranquil lakes of her family's days and seldom witnessed splash or ripple for her effort. On me her imagination and logic were honed to a fine edge. I could almost hear the blood beating in her arteries at the sound of my voice.

"Ah, Antonia," she'd say and I would feel my own pulse quickening behind my ears.

"Tony," I asserted routinely for the hundredth time that month.

"How common. Is your father home?"

I looked towards the table with the phone stretched out from my ear like a conch shell. My father shook his head, no.

"No." I crossed one foot over the other and leaned my head against the wall.

"What are you doing?" The voice airy and light, enjoying the chase.

"Eating supper."

"Without your father? I suppose the poor dear has his supper warmed up and dried out."

Mother's face went blank and helpless.

"As a matter of fact," I said, "he's on a diet. Obesity runs in his family, you know."

There was a short pause while Alvira considered the counter-attack, although it must be said that my remark was misguided, an emblem more of rage than of any icy cunning on my part. At this young age I had only an endless well of sarcasm from which to draw, and by the time I was old enough to know how to win, it was too late to want to try.

"Your grandfather's family was all pudgy, that's quite astute of you, Antonia," she said, rolling the vowels of my name around her tongue like gumdrops. "Now where's Margaret? I want her to pick up a hat for me at Goldsmith's when she's in Memphis next week."

My mother's eyes widened and her head shook "no" at me mutely. Father turned his face towards the disembodied voice crashing out of the receiver, poised for the news.

"Mother's not going to Memphis," I said.

"Yes, she is, dear. And I hope you will not wear that repulsive lip glob when you see Dr. Kremshaw."

"Who is Dr. Kremshaw and if you mean lipstick, I'm thirteen and it's only a Natural, no color at all."

"That's funny," she said. "I saw it quite clearly Wednesday when you were here and it was a most peculiar shade of purple." Then, before I could retort, "Dr. Kremshaw is an orthodontist. He will be fitting braces on your front teeth."

I stared at the receiver, then turned urgently to my father, since my mother seemed to be flattened to the back of her chair, waiting out the conversation the way one sits through a weather disaster report.

Father smiled at me tiredly and said in a normal voice that carried, "Don't worry. We can't afford it."

"We can't afford it," I repeated quickly.

"Who was that speaking? You don't have to afford it. Harry has just closed a deal with a Mexican corporation and he assures me Mama's estate dividends will double. Therefore, I am donating what I can to correct your unfortunate overbite."

I held the phone in front of me like a snake I had caught and strangled the receiver with both hands, but then Father's face pulsed into my vision. He was pale and rigid with disbelief and his curly eyebrows bristled over darkening eyes.

"What Mexican corporation and what collateral?" he distinctly bellowed and gripped the linen tablecloth in his hands.

I repeated his question, the message carried up through my toes like electrical current. I could already feel the steel bands inside my tender upper lip.

"What *is* that voice shouting? It's a Mexican typewriter manufacturer, if you must know, and I *do* think you're precocious for knowing words like collateral. Harry put up some of the land, of course."

"Of course," my father and I said in unison, and then we actually heard what she had said. Mexican typewriters.

"I have to go now, Alvira," I said.

My mother's eyes were closed in a closed face and my father had let go the tablecloth but was heading fast towards the liquor cabinet.

"Next Friday then, dear. Have your poor mother call me later tonight for the details." There was a calculated pause. "About the hat and your teeth."

"Goodbye, Alvira."

"And tell your father. . . ."

"Goodbye, Alvira."

And that was how the rose garden was sold to the UWasheria Laundromat. Alvira transplanted all the roses into family lawns, each rooting turned into a dedication ceremony to her largesse. We got the Queen Juliana (pink) and the Austrian Love Bloom (yellow), and my mother almost had a breakdown nursing them back from the shock of being moved.

It was not simply that Uncle Harry was imbecilic, Father said. It was that everyone in the southwestern United States knew it. But of course, the appointment for my braces fell before Alvira learned that the Mexican government had never heard of the Arríba Typewriter Corporation, and I was dutifully driven to Memphis and to Dr. Kremshaw's hairy fists the following week. Money for the weight of metal in my mouth, for the straight line of tamed and tortured teeth, was simply deducted from my portion of Alvira's will. But, in the end, none of that mattered: not the braces or having to buy my own discomfort. I would gladly endure it all again for the sake of that one Memphis trip.

Mother and I had been to Dr. Kremshaw's and to Goldsmith's for Alvira's hat and were sitting in the coffeeshop of the Peabody Hotel over cokes when it happened. That is to say, I looked up at the ordinary room and beheld the most startling apparition of my life.

I had seen movie stars who came down to Mississippi for location shooting on some film about the decadent South. I had watched the Harlem Globetrotters and their antics in the Atlanta Coliseum. I had even shaken hands with a Russian countess whose bosom was punctured by diamonds, like stickpins in a cushion. (She was a refugee trying to make a career in this country as a medium and Alvira had had her to tea.) I had met Eleanor Roosevelt. But the woman I saw floating through the Peabody Hotel Coffee Shop was more awesome than these.

Flowing through the crush of pinstriped businessmen, of cotton merchants' wives wearing pillbox hats like stoppers on their heads, past truculent children exhausted by department stores, this woman shone iridescent. It was as if a gypsy queen had sailed into the Wednesday Brass Polishing Circle at the Episcopal Church.

She came in with her head poised high on a long swan's neck. Her hair was dyed an unnatural black and glowed in the muted light. The tendrils flicked around her shoulders like tongues. She wore heavy pearl pendants in her ears that dragged at the scruffy lobes and an anklelength black dress of old crushed velvet, with a fuchsia silk scarf thrown over her arms and around that narrow length of neck, Isadora Duncan style. Over one thin wrist hung a gold sequin purse, and on the other hand large knobby rings clustered over each finger—lumps of color: green, gold, crimson.

But more than the dress, more too than the jewels, there was on her face a kind of charmed light. She came into the shop with that delicate head bobbing on its stalk, a white lily, and it was as if she had entered a royal court. If conversation lowered suddenly like a stage curtain, then surged up again to mask her entrance into the sane light of morning, then this she seemed to take as a sign of eloquent deference. She nodded to the faces strained away from her, she touched the top of a child's head who stared wide-eyed, voice plugged with a thumb, at her scarlet mouth. The

mouth itself bloomed in a white field of powder, below eyes that
Cleopatra might have conjured.

"Mother, look," I whispered in awe, and my mother glanced up
from digging in her purse for a tip. Her eyes widened for an instant in confusion, and then a beatific smile washed over her face.
My mother has an ordinary face, her features so regular and symmetrical that I often have trouble remembering her expression
when I'm away. But the smile she wore now transformed her with
delight, and I think I will never forget what she looked like at that
moment.

"It's been such a long time," she sighed.

"What did you say?"

But the pendant earrings swayed closer. All the glittering heaps
of finger rings were rising in a graceful arc of the hands, and the
gypsy's vaguely gracious expression now concentrated itself on
us. I bit into my Coke straw and clutched the glass with trembling
fingers, but the woman swept towards us quickly and was standing with her hands outstretched towards my mother. *My* mother.

"My dear," the woman cried and clasped my mother's hands in
hers. Mother kissed the floured cheek the woman offered and I
caught the sad scent of lilacs as she bent towards us.

"How are you, darling?" Mother asked. I had never heard my
mother use the word 'darling' before but it was sincere and it
jolted me so that I bit through the straw and into my bottom lip.
"How have you been?"

The woman squeezed my mother's hands tightly in hers and
shook them in the air. "The stars have been erratic," she said, tilt-
ing her head back on that long, white neck.

She released Mother's hands, swung the fuchsia scarf around
her shoulders. I was staring at the tiny ribbing wrinkles formed
in her neck and on her hands. Great blue veins lay close under
the surface of her skin, fragile and somehow insubstantial, like
seeing the thin ivory bones in a bird's wing held to the light.

Mother nodded as if she'd made perfect sense, and I began to
squirm in my chair. It was not so much that people had turned
to stare as that I was being totally ignored at my own table. I had
always dreaded meeting Mother's friends on similar trips, suffering introductions and the dreary conversations that followed, but
this was different. And for once, Mother seemed to forget she
knew me at all. I might have been a stranger who occupied the

next seat, even though she absently handed me her change purse to hold when the gypsy approached us.

"I'm sorry to hear that," she said sympathetically now, making a little *tss*king noise with her tongue. "Tell me, how are your investments?"

I noticed now that the gypsy carried a folded newspaper under one arm like a businessman. She whisked it out now, tossing her wild black hair, and lowered herself onto the tip of the seat opposite us.

"My dear, I am delighted you visited me today. My horoscope said this morning that under no circumstances should business be conducted unless a loved one made contact. And I so wanted to sell Sperry-Rand for IBM. You've done me a great service." She fanned her face with the folded paper and a little puff of white rained out.

The talk turned generally then to Dow-Jones averages, common stock, and Merrill-Lynch.

"My, my," was Mother's only comment when the woman leaned back from her precarious perch at the chair's edge to look down her nose between stock quotations.

Then, quite suddenly, the gypsy turned a startled, flaming smile to me as if I had made a sudden noise. Actually, I had sat through the entire conversation in a buzzing trance, hypnotized by the earrings the woman wore. They swung before me, heavy crystallized milkdrops smudged with white face powder where they knocked against her cheek.

"You do resemble your father," she pronounced emphatically, then turned to Mother again. "And how is the lieutenant? Still sailing the high seas and sinking U-boats?"

My mother's smile fixed itself more permanently around her lips. "Oh, yes," she said, "lots of heavy fire."

"Good," the woman said and whacked the table with her newspaper. "Next time you write, you tell him I said 'well done.' " She gathered her paper and golden bag and rose like a dark wave from the sea, her gown and scarf billowing around her. "And when are you expecting, my dear?" she whispered, and bent her white face down on its long neck.

My mother's smile tightened, but she straightened her shoulders inside her linen suit jacket. The little bones in her back stuck out like hidden wings. "Very soon," she said.

"Umm. What will you name it?"

"Antonia," Mother said, and I watched a small pink circle forming itself in the center of her cheek.

The woman threw back her head and closed her eyes, testing
the sound of the name. "Antonia—that's a nice, round sound.
Very good," and she held her jewelled hand out, the stones blinking and winking like stoplights. "So good of you to drop in," she
said, giving us a smile that flashed. "I'm late for the Exchange."
And Mother took the hand gently in her own, then released her
to the humming room.

I held my breath until the tip of fuchsia scarf sailed out the doorway, then I pinched my mother's arm, crinkling the cool linen.
"Sweet Jesus, Mother, who *was* that?"

And, of course, she answered mildly, still smiling sweetly towards the door, "Why, that's just your Aunt Lettie, dear." Then
she looked down at my sweaty palm clutching her sleeve and dis-
entangled my grip. "And don't be profane," she added.

"What do you mean, 'just your Aunt Lettie.' I thought Aunt
Lettie was tucked away in some sanitorium, coughing up blood."

We were driving the long, straight road sliced into cottonfields,
the road I had counted telephone poles on for as many dull trips
as my mind could hold. But there was no time, no need for such
distraction now. The thick green fields blurred past my vision,
red combines and swooping gull-like cotton dusters nervous, irritated movements outside my attention.

"Whatever gave you that idea?" Mother asked absently. Her
hands, as usual, gripped the top of the steering wheel, as though
without the steady pressure of each wrapped finger, the car might
swerve, on its own, into the nearest field. "We never said that."

"You never said anything. You just said Aunt Lettie was away
being ill. What did you expect me to think?"

"I suppose I expected you to find out about Aunt Lettie the
same way you discovered all the family secrets I never knew until
you told me." Her round knuckles whitened as she pressed the
wheel and slid around a tractor. "Usually in front of company, I
might add."

"Well, I didn't. I thought she was lying in a frilly bedjacket in
some mountain hospital, consumptive. I even thought she might
be locked up in an asylum somewhere, a nice one maybe, crazy as
a loon."

Mother smiled into the windshield. "Well, she is, dear. Crazy, I mean. Not locked up."

That night at supper, Father smiled and nodded while Mother told him of the meeting. I had grown angry since the surreal conversation in the car and sat pushing the food around my plate with a fork until Mother finished. Then Father turned to me and said, "You must never tell Alvira who you saw today."

This was too much. I threw down my fork and pushed my chair back from the table. "I'll put it in the *Greenlove Democrat Times* unless somebody tells me what's going on."

"Don't threaten your father," Mother said. "Pass the potatoes around."

I thrust the bowl at her without looking and waited for my father to finish chewing.

"I wonder what hot food tastes like," he mumbled, that old refrain, but turned to me anyway, sighed, and told me the story. Even at that, it wasn't nearly enough. It was like being given a blurred photograph. Locked inside those wavy lines, that mass of grey, was a likeness, a face, something you could outline with the tip of your finger. What I got was watery and pale, teasing with half-light.

It seems Alvira and her older sister Letticia were unusually pretty and popular girls. There were only two years between them, and they entered society together in the Gay Nineties and drove for miles each summer night to dances in plantation halls, in lake mansions, even to Memphis and Jackson to the Grand Mask balls at harvest time.

"But they never got along," Father said, "from what I can gather. They were too close in age, you know, sharing dresses and shoes—whatever girls share—even boys. Neither was prettier or more popular, but it was only because they worked at it with a vengeance, never letting the other catch them resting. One thing and another, there were always spats over flirting with each other's dates, and whose turn it was to wear your great-grandmother's pearls. When Pa came to town to run the paper, they stuck to him like syrup on a fly."

"Pa," I hooted, thinking about the quiet, round man who had never so much as acknowledged Alvira's running commentary as long as I had known him. She got plenty of nods from him and sometimes a grunt, but all I knew of Pa was that he smelled of bream and catfish, that he spent each day from dawn until supper-time out fishing on the river, since his retirement, that he gave me quarters and heavy fifty cent pieces with a wink when Alvira's back was turned. He had never been a verbal man, not only with Alvira, but with his children and grandchildren, though Father assured me he had been eloquent in print. I had looked up some of his old editorials in the musky light of the library basement, and sure enough, this fishy, silent man, with his round smile and his round blue eyes faded the color of old denim, this sweet and al-most invisible Pa had been vividly assertive. His typewriter must have smoked with the fire of his convictions, the words rolling onto the page like thunder—against segregation, against misusing the land, against Hoover. Maybe, I thought now, he had once been charming, dashing, a man to quarrel over, one with a gleam in his eye.

I thought this over while Father was absorbing my outburst, then he went on carefully.

"He took one of them out one night, the other the next. Things must have got awful hot in that house, and your great-grandparents decided it was time the girls began their Grand Tours—people were still doing that then, you know, sailing off their girls to Europe like clockwork, and when the girls got back they all thought they were Queen Victoria. Well, Lettie was the oldest, so she was to go first. They thought it best not to send them both at once, feeling a kind of cooling-off period between them might ease things up a bit.

"She fought it to the bitter end, thinking Alvira would have a corner on the market by the time she returned, but her parents insisted, and Alvira gloated, and Lettie was seen off at the New Orleans dock on June 8th, 1900. She was nineteen."

He paused then and lit a cigarette while my mother took his cold food away and slipped a steaming coffee cup between his hands. And he stirred the silver spoon inside the coffee and stared at the liquid churning there in silence.

"And what? What then?" I prodded him.

Father took a deep drag on the cigarette and rubbed his eyes. "Then a wire came from Calais. It said someone should come and fetch Lettie, she was being kept in a hospital. And Pa and Alvira sailed on the next ship to bring her home."

"For Pete's sake, why? Why?"

"Don't push your father, dear," my mother said.

"Somehow, somewhere, during that crossing, Lettie just—lost her mind," he sighed in a voice still full of wonder at the words.

I felt the air sink out of my lungs, my ribs pushed against my skin as I caught my breath. "But what happened?"

Father shook his head, then shook it again, as if clearing it of sleep. Then as though he were truly waking from a dream, he moved suddenly in his chair and picked up the coffee cup, sipped, sighed again. "No one remembers anything unusual. Only one morning, one night, in the middle of a calm, quiet ocean, Lettie just lost her sanity. As if she dropped it overboard. No one knows why," he said again.

"Eat your apple tart," Mother urged softly.

Later that evening, huddled on the front steps into the sounds of insects beating against the dark air, I thought of Lettie. I saw her ringed fingers dancing before me, heard Alvira insist, "*Lettie is dead.*"

Father came out into the thick night air. "Let's go for a walk," he said and took my hand.

We walked in silence away from the house. I could feel the soft, fat leaves lapping my arms, the pavement still warm under my bare feet, but my mind revolved like a top around the questions in my head.

"Why does Lettie live in Memphis?" I asked him. "Why does Alvira say she's dead? Does she hate her that much still, after everything?" My voice rose helplessly, I could hear the thin, childish sound it made.

"Alvira doesn't hate Lettie, she never did. They're sisters—oh, you should have had a sister. You'd know then."

He was quiet and the insects swelled and throbbed around us. Then he said, "They arranged for her to live at a Home in Memphis and she seemed better there. But she kept running away, and it looked like she would have to be moved to a state hospital to keep her safe. But then Alvira said 'Let her out in the daytime, let her do as she wants—she'll stay then.' And sure enough, the minute they started letting her go her way in the daytime, she calmed down. She always came back at night."

"But why?" I insisted, filled suddenly with anger at Alvira. "Why couldn't she stay at home with Alvira if she could traipse around in broad daylight without harming anyone?" It seemed to me

Alvira was hiding Lettie away like the black sheep she was, wishing her dead to keep the family secret safe from gossip, to preserve the family name in all its traditional rules and outlines, like a neat hopscotch game laid out on the sidewalk for all to witness and marvel over.

But Father said Alvira and Pop wanted to keep Lettie with them—they'd decided to get married by then. Only Lettie got worse at home, ran away more than ever. "It broke Alvira's heart, watching her sister sink back to silence each time she was brought home. Pop had a hard time persuading her Lettie was happier in Memphis. She seemed so much saner there. Not exactly crazy, you know—she was more eccentric in Memphis than crazy."

"Like Alvira," I whispered, and knew that wasn't really true. For an instant I saw Lettie again in the dark air that hung before me. "Only Alvira's nothing like that. Oh, Daddy, you should have *seen* her," reverting to my childhood name. And I couldn't even wipe away the tears that fell down my face and blurred my vision. I couldn't even lift a hand to move the hair they plastered to my cheek.

My father hugged me to him with one arm and let me cry for a minute, then he dug in his pocket and stuck his handkerchief, still pressed and folded crisp from the laundry, into my face. "Wipe up and blow," he said and stopped walking while I did. His arm still hugged me to him as we bumped down the deserted sidewalk.

"Now she wasn't so bad was she? Of course not! You saw her: she's happy, she's got her own interests, she's even quite charming. Like Alvira, only stretched out, exaggerated."

"I guess so," I admitted, and blew my nose hard. "Only when I *think* about it—Daddy, she knew Mama when I was going to be born." I shook my head at the stars swimming into focus again. "How does she know about you at all, much less anticipating me?"

Father smiled up at the lion's blank face which guarded the First National Bank's front door. "Pop took us to meet her during the war," he said. "She was having a particularly clear day and it's stuck in her mind all this time. Your mother was six months pregnant then. But she sees her from time to time now on her trips to Memphis. Lettie seems to favor the Peabody Coffee Shop and Mother sometimes runs into her there, once a year or so."

We were circling the block now and automatically stopped at the Penny Scales outside Knight's Hardware. I stood on the raised scale while Father dropped the coin inside. The ticket popped out of its metal slot with a whirr.

"You will enjoy the fruits of the mind, 102 pounds," I read, forgetting the fortune as soon as I stepped off the rubbery scale to let Father climb up.

His penny clinked inside and the machine sighed again. "Expect a tall, dark stranger to come into your life, 170 pounds." Father held his ticket out. "Let's swap."

"Does Alvira never see her?" I asked as we turned the corner onto Main Street.

"Never," Father said. "She once asked me a few years back if I visited Lettie. 'Only once or twice,' I said. And Alvira said, 'I never got to apologize to her for all those silly quarrels.' And that was all she's ever said to me about the subject."

"Then how do you know all this? Who told you?"

"Pop told me. He wanted to be sure somebody took care of Lettie if anything happened to him."

"It's so confusing," I said. "It's so sad and strange."

"Yes and no," Father answered. "One day you'll understand better, I think." He paused on the sidewalk by a hibiscus bush. "You know, I never will forget meeting Lettie. She was one of the most delightful women I've ever seen and, in her own way, one of the happiest." He looked down at me. "She and Alvira are still very much alike," he said. "You'll see that one day."

"Luke," Alvira called then, and I noticed for the first time where we had stopped. Alvira's tiny figure was tucked into a porch rocker. She swayed back and forth underneath the ceiling fan, her diamond choker blinking like a chain of lightning bugs around her throat.

I followed my father up the front walk and stood before her, noticing too, for the first time, how small she had grown, how large I had become. Her feet barely touched the porch floor, and her quick hawk's eyes glittered inside a delicate face.

"I brought your hat, from Margaret," he said, holding out a roundlidded box I had not seen before either.

"Ah," she breathed and reached out for it with fingers delighted into motion. "How sweet of you." She pulled the hat out of its tissue, all crisp, green feathers, and held it in her hands like a nest. "Go pour yourself a gin and tonic and say hello to Pa," she instructed Father, and he tipped his hand to his forehead in a salute and went inside the vast, dark front rooms behind her.

Alvira looked me over from head to foot, the hat settled into her lap now. "That color is bad for you," she said, shaking her head so the diamonds glistened around her neck. "It turns you pale in the moonlight. And barefoot to boot—where are your manners? How dare your mother let you out of the house that way?"

I stood strangely silent before her and she cocked her head at my pursed lips.

"Well, come and sit down," she said, patting the rocker next to her, "and tell me all about Memphis."

It was only then that I could force myself to speak. "Dr. Krem-shaw has halitosis," I said. And Alvira, rocking in the moonlight, began to smile.

Five years later, scuffing through maple leaves in North Carolina with Dr. Rosenblatt's throaty voice caught in my ears, I began to understand about Aunt Lettie and Alvira and what my father had tried to say that night. Wrenched from that fertile crescent of land, from Alvira's suppertime calls and the astonishing presence of Lettie drifting through city streets only ninety miles away, I could see them both in perspective—small, manageable figures held in the bowl of my mind like a vision glimpsed through the wrong end of a telescope.

Try as I might—Melville, Conrad, Lawrence put to hard use— I saw I could never believe that some dark, evil experience had swallowed Lettie on the waters. What was there, after all, in this small world that could so transform a simple, lovely Southern girl on the calm and glassy seas? I would never know what had actually transpired aboard that ship. But whatever it was, I was convinced it could not have been horrifying—bizarre, perhaps, other-worldly. Private, certainly. But not damaging to the soul or to the heart.

As for Alvira, her patchwork of rules and mandates, her jerking us around like so many puppets, was not only forgiveable but totally understandable: surely, through controlling us as best she could, she was only taking out insurance against the loss of an-other. Her devotion to life's trivia, to dress and tradition, to strict propriety and the right dentist—this was her stronghold against the stray casualties of chance, her levee pushed against whatever dark waters of fear she acknowledged for us all.

It no longer confused me that she should refuse to visit Lettie. I will not say that Lettie, like Pip, saw the face of God. I do not make that connection. But I find in that fictional experience a touchstone, a mark: whatever Lettie read in those green depths, whatever came upon her in the unrimmed night, was beyond what we can bear to see who are left behind. Alvira could not stand to witness it on her sister's face, could not sustain losing that sister to whatever vision it was that claimed her. She castled her instead under the glass bell of her memory, and preferred to call her dead.

There is one more chapter to this story, one last puzzling piece to a puzzle which will never really be finished. I don't even know where this piece fits, or if it does at all.

When Lettie died, my senior year at college, I did not attend the funeral. No one did except my parents and the doctor at her Home. Sweet, silent Pa had died two years before, and Alvira, of course, would not grace any function after the fact. For her, Lettie had died and been buried at sea.

But my father wrote me a letter and told me what happened when a Memphis lawyer drove down to read Lettie's will, for she had one. The lawyer insisted that Alvira be present, and she consented, knitting, my father wrote, through most of the procedure with a condescending smile on her face. It was, he said, as if she were waiting through the ninth performance of a bad play which she had been required, through politeness, to observe.

It seems that Lettie's clear moments had endured throughout her life and had fixed almost entirely on her business dealings. Her stock market conversation with my mother in the Peabody Hotel Coffee Shop had been the one crisp evidence of a mind still functioning, not only in sanity, but shrewdly.

Lettie left Alvira upwards of half a million dollars in stocks and bonds, bequeathing to her parents, long dead, and to my father, the lieutenant, various wildly imagined real-estate holdings such as the Taj Mahal and half of the Vieux Carré. The stocks and bonds—Bell Telephone, U. S. Steel, Standard Oil—these were as real as the ivory bond they were written on. Alvira was a wealthy woman.

Lettie willed Alvira the bloom of her assets, Father wrote she had testified, "because she is my only sister and has never argued with me through the years over anything more trifling than a bauble or a boy."

I telephoned home the night Father's letter arrived. "What did Alvira do? What did she say?"

"She wants to know what Alvira said," my mother repeated to Father, who was trying to begin his supper.

Over the crackling wire I heard his chair scrape, and then the sigh as he took the receiver. But when he spoke, his voice was elastic with delight. It stretched all the way to North Carolina past the feeble Greenlove telephone system without needing to shout.

"Tony?" he asked, "Tony—she just stopped knitting with the yarn still wrapped over her finger and cocked her head at that lawyer. Then she said to no one in particular, 'Lettie always was more tolerant than I,' and started up her needles again."

"What?" I gasped. "That was it?"

"Should there be more?"

The long distance wire sang between us for a moment, humming all the way from Mississippi.

"Of course not," I admitted then, allowing myself at last to be stitched into the embroidered family myth, to become another strengthening thread in that absurdly tangled pattern. "It's only that Alvira's so eccentric," I said.

DEPARTMENT STORE

ANN BAYER

Ann Bayer was born in Cleveland, Ohio, in 1941 and
moved to New York City when she was seventeen. She
has been an editor on *The Saturday Evening Post* and
Life. Her stories and articles have appeared in *Life*, the
Post, *Harper's*, *Mademoiselle*, and *Cosmopolitan*. She is
currently working on her first novel.

My intention was to walk over to Bloomingdale's and browse. It
was a Saturday afternoon and the Lexington Avenue and Fifty-
ninth Street intersection was thronged with Bloomingdale's customers, some leaving and some about to enter. As I approached
the store, I noticed an elderly man in short sleeves standing behind
a card table hawking raffle tickets. "Would you like to help our
little babies?" he cried. "Please help the little babies of the New
York Foundling." Our eyes met and he beckoned to me and said,
"*You* wouldn't let down the little babies, right, girlie?"

"Wrong," I said and walked on.

A few seconds later a spastic selling comic books lurched toward
me waving a sample of his wares. An orange badge with a smiling
face on it was pinned to his collar but his own face, bobbing up
and down, was so sad and imploring that I might have been the
last Captain Marvel fan on earth. I looked away and proceeded
through the revolving doors. Just inside sat a nun collecting alms
for the poor. She was as motionless as Whistler's mother, and her
face, framed by a wimple, was composed. I dropped a quarter into
her black change purse.

Then I worked my way up the stairs to the main floor and
joined the line waiting to get on the escalator. Ahead of me
were two long-haired figures in pea jackets. As they stepped onto
the escalator, the figure on the left said, "I should have known that

my feeling for Ray wouldn't last. How could I lie on my deathbed
and look back and think to myself, I lived my entire life with someone whose name was Ray?"

"Ray's the sort of name gas-station attendants have," said the
right-hand figure. "What about Bruce? Could you ever fall in love
with anybody named Bruce?"

The first one considered a moment. "Bruce isn't as horrible as
Ray." We reached the second floor and transferred to the next
escalator.

"How about Lloyd?"

"Lloyd is what they always call llamas."

"How about Hank?"

"How about Lew?"

"How about *Fred?*"

At the third floor I detached myself and meandered over to
where they were selling casual clothes. I began to sift through a
circular rack of shirts. "I always take the first item I come across,"
a voice said. "Fashion isn't what matters. Style isn't what matters.
All that matter are beauty and truth."

I turned to see a stout woman with an argumentative face. The
stripes on her dress were going in one direction, and the stripes
on her sweater were going in another. Even her hair went in zigzags, though she'd fastened some of it down with a silver barrette
in the shape of a harp.

"Take my advice, young lady, and don't meditate over clothes
when you could be meditating over works of art. Go home and
read Flaubert. You can read *Madame Bovary* in a bathrobe or a
ballgown; it's as good either way."

"I've already read it."

She stiffened. "I guess there will always be some who would
rather stand in front of a clothes rack than in front of a Rem-
brandt."

We were joined by an elegant middle-aged woman wearing a
pants suit and a wide-brimmed hat. She was accompanied by a
large black poodle with a frayed topknot. I put out my hand and
the dog licked it.

"Lulu thinks you're a plate of chopped liver," said the elegant
woman. She lifted out several shirts and frowned at them.

"Go by the price tag," said the stout woman. "Who cares how they look?"

The elegant woman peered out from under her hat. "I care, that's who." She held a shirt at arm's length; it was covered with polka dots and had a removable bow. "I wonder if they have this in a size twelve."

"So what if it's a little tight, a little loose. Why aren't you in Carnegie Hall listening to Brahms?"

"Because I'm in Bloomingdale's looking for something to wear."

The stout woman rolled her eyes heavenward and then turned and walked away. Her heels click-clacked on the floor as if she had swallowed a metronome.

After a few moments a young man with an exhilarated Dalmatian came by. Trailing its leash, the Dalmatian made a beeline for the poodle and sniffed her hindquarters. The poodle wheeled around and glowered.

"Careful, Plato," said the man. "Don't try to make friends when the tail's not waggling." The tail in question had shifted to a down position. The Dalmatian, oblivious, circled back behind the poodle, who responded by curling her upper lip and rumbling. When these measures failed to deter her suitor, the poodle hurled herself at his spotted throat. Both leashes were yanked back simultaneously, and the dogs were left standing on their hind legs, paws churning the air.

"I'm glad that happened, Plato," said the man. "Now you'll remember to always check first and make sure the tail waggles." He pulled the spurned animal away toward the raincoat department.

The elegant woman watched them go with narrowed eyes. "Lulu takes after me. She absolutely refuses to be treated as a sex object."

"Males are all alike," I said. "They're always poking their noses where they don't belong."

She gave me an approving look. "I take it you're in the movement."

"I've been fighting sexism since I was five. I'm the only person I know who ever named her teddy bear Theodora."

"What men do to us," she said. "I've had two husbands. They were both named Leonard and they were both impossible. The moment I married Leonard One, he forgot his table manners. I'd say to him, 'What do you suppose that fork is sitting there for?' And he'd say, 'If I want to eat with my hands, I'll eat with my hands. Who's around to impress?' I'd say, 'I'm around. Why not impress *me* for a change?' '*You*?' he'd say. 'You're only my wife.'"

"Is that ever typical," I said.

"*Wait*. Then I married Leonard Two. By this time I was nearly forty and all I wanted was to have a baby. I begged and pleaded with that man to give me a baby. So one day he came home with a live lobster on a leash and led it around the apartment. 'What's that?' I said. 'It's Ursula,' he said. 'It's our little adopted daughter Ursula.' Then he put a pot of water on the stove and when it was boiling he said, 'Now I'm going to lower Ursula into her bassinet.'"

"That's sick," I said. "Sick but fascinating."

"I've had it with husbands. Since my second divorce I've taken lovers and it's worked out very well."

"The only man I ever wanted to marry," I said, "is John Kenneth Galbraith."

"I'm telling you, the solution is lovers."

"I keep thinking what it must feel like to open your eyes in the morning and there lying beside you on the same sheet is *John Kenneth Galbraith*."

"Buy a dog. Dogs make the best husbands. Believe me, I know. *Lulu* never wakes up with a hangover. She never leaves cigarette burns on the bedspread. She never threatens to walk out or gets surly or throws things. Why, she's so sweet and feminine that sometimes I think if I could just unzipper her, a little pink girl would jump out."

For a second or two we bowed our heads and contemplated this paragon, who had lowered herself on to her side and was closely inspecting her private parts.

"Of course," the woman continued, "I doubt if I'll ever give men up entirely. No matter how old one becomes, the heart beats as violently in the breast; the flesh is as demanding. To me even now the best part of clothes is taking them off." She looked at her watch and gave a cry. "It's after four already. Time for Lulu's dinner. It's Lulu's dinner time. Oh, lucky, lucky Lulu!" The poodle gathered herself from the floor, and they headed for home.

By now I had selected two shirts that I wanted to try on and I went off to locate a saleslady. After circling the area three times, I

eventually found one standing behind a row of marked-down blaz-
ers. Her head was tilted back, and she was putting eyedrops into
her eyes. She had on a black dress and black stockings and shiny
yellow shoes, as if she had just come from a funeral but her feet
had danced on the grave.

"I want to see if these fit me," I said.

The saleslady lowered her head so that the drops spilled down
her cheeks and she blotted them with the inside of her wrist. Then
she led me along a row of dressing rooms to an empty cubicle.
"When you are ready, I am Miss Dexter," she said and drew the
curtain.

I had tried on both shirts and was getting dressed again when
I heard a noise on the other side of the partition. It sounded like
a metal wastebasket clanking against a mirror. This was followed
by a rhythmic thudding on the floorboards. Then a female voice
said, "I've done it with one person, two people, three people, and
a whole bedful of people. I've done it backwards and sideways
and upside down." Her voice was so dispassionate she could have
been reciting the closing averages of the day's most active stocks.
I stood still, one arm partway into a sleeve. "I've done it with vi-
brators," the voice went on. "I've done it with feathers. I've done
it smeared with whipped cream." My reflection gave me a scandal-
ized look. "I've done it in rowboats. I've done it in trailers." Suddenly there was a frenzied rattling of clothes hangers followed
by silence and then more thudding. After a minute the voice re-
sumed. "I've done it under a piano. I've done it in a baptistery. I've
done it in a Holiday Inn. But this is the first time I've ever done
it in a fitting room."

I was still eavesdropping when the curtain was pushed aside and
the saleslady appeared. I pointed in the direction of the voice.
"Somebody's having an affair in there," I whispered.

"That compartment belongs to Miss Henderson's customers,"
said the saleslady. "I am Miss Dexter. Do the shirts fit or don't
they?"

"They fit but I can't decide which makes me look thinner." I
held them up; one was cut like a cowboy shirt, and the other was
printed with swirls of orange. "What so you think?"

"I've given up thinking," replied Miss Dexter.

"In that case," I said, "I better take both." She put the shirts under her arm, and I gave her my charge plate and followed her to where she wrote up her bills.

Another saleslady came over and rested her elbow wearily on top of a display case. "Today I feel one hundred years old," she said.

"That makes two of us," said Miss Dexter, ripping off the ends of the price tags.

"I have angina," said the other saleslady. "I've already had two attacks. Angina's brutal. If I have another attack, I'm through."

"When your number's up, your number's up, period. That's my philosophy."

The other saleslady sighed. "My daughter tells me, 'Ma, you've got fifteen more good years. Have a ball.' Daughter or no daughter, she doesn't care."

Miss Dexter held out a pencil and I signed the sales slip. "Look," she said. "I want to tell you something. Nobody cares."

She thrust the merchandise into a shopping bag and handed it to me.

"Thank you," I said.

"If I die, I'm ready," said Miss Dexter.

It wasn't until I was halfway past budget sportswear that I noticed the commotion. A bottleneck had formed by the escalators; customers descending from the fourth floor were converging with customers ascending from the second. Their attention was focused on a woman standing on a chair strategically placed between the up and down escalators. Even from far away I recognized all those stripes. I moved close enough to hear.

"Go home, everybody!" the woman was shouting, holding her hands to her mouth like a megaphone. "The hour for buying adornments is past."

"But it isn't even five o'clock," someone said.

"What are you people doing in a department store?" the woman demanded. "Don't you know there are books to be read? That there is music to be heard? All that counts are the things of the spirit. Who here has read Aeschylus?"

There was no show of hands.

"It must be some sort of a prophet," said an onlooker.

A few minutes went by while the woman continued to exhort her audience to go off and improve their minds. Then I noticed two men in brown suits filing through the crowd. They positioned themselves on either side of her. "Okay, *out,*" said one. "You can practice your public speaking somewhere else."

The woman glared down at him. "Mister, when was the last time you read Chekhov?"

Her question went unanswered. The man grasped her arm and toppled her from the chair and after that I lost sight of her.

The customers slowly sorted themselves out. It took me a long time to reach the Lexington Avenue doorway and when I did I found that it was raining. Some shoppers were huddled under the marquee waiting for the downpour to let up and I joined them. I was considering whether to go back inside and buy an umbrella when I heard someone talking loudly behind me.

"The first thing I did when I got home yesterday," the voice said, "was rinse out my stockings. Then I went to the kitchen and heated up the chicken that was left over from Tuesday."

I turned around. The speaker was a prim woman in her late forties. Her face was carefully made up, but one eye had blue mascara and the other eye had brown. She was standing all by herself. Her head was turned to the left, and she seemed to be addressing an imaginary friend.

"On Wednesday I opened a can of chicken noodle soup. Thursday night I had dinner in Schrafft's. I ordered their chicken pie."

I looked up at the sky but rain was all I could see.

"What worries me," said the woman, "is what to do about tonight. There's still a breast and a wing in the icebox, but if I eat them now that will make five days of chicken in a row."

SWIMMER IN THE SECRET SEA

WILLIAM KOTZWINKLE

William Kotzwinkle has published the novels *The Fan Man*, *Hermes 3000*, and *Nightbook*, and a collection of short stories, *Elephant Bangs Train*. He has also written several books for children.

"Johnny, my water just broke!"

Laski rose through a sea of dreams, trying to find the surface. The sea was dark, and iridescent creatures came toward him, one of them suddenly exploding into brilliance. Laski woke, sitting up in bed. Diane had her hand on the night-lamp and was staring down at a water-stain spreading on the sheets.

"That's it," he said. "Get ready." The first wave of shock was already over him, speeding his pulse, turning his skin cold, making him shiver.

"I'd better put a napkin on," she said. "I'm getting everything all wet."

He took her arm and helped her to the stairs. She too had begun to tremble, and they were trembling together as they passed the window and saw the forest, covered with snow. The stillness of the woods calmed him, and he paused with her on the landing, drinking in the white nectar of the moon. His trembling subsided some, but hers continued, and he walked with her toward the bathroom. She went stooped over, her arms across her mountainous stomach, where her earthquake had its origin. He helped her onto the toilet seat, then went to the closet and brought a blanket. He wrapped it around her and rubbed his hands up and down her arms, trying to generate some warmth.

She looked up at him, her teeth chattering. He hadn't expected it to be like this, the two of them caught and shaken like rag-dolls. They'd studied the childbirth manuals carefully, and performed the exercises regularly, and he'd thought it would be merely an extension of all that, but there'd been no transition. Suddenly they were being dragged over a bed of rocks. Her eyes were like a child's, astonished and terrified, but her voice was calm and he realized she was prepared, in spite of fear and chattering teeth.

"I can control the water now," she said. "I can keep it from running out."

"I'll get the truck warmed up." He went outside into the snow. Beyond the shadowy tops of the pines the vast sky-bowl glittered, and the half-ton truck sat in the moonlight, covered with brightly sparkling ice. He opened the door and slid in, pulling on the choke and turning the ignition key.

The starter motor whined, caught in the icy hand of the north. "Come on," said Laski softly, appealing to the finer nature of the vehicle, the trusty half-ton which never failed him. He listened for the little cough of life in the whining, and when it came he quickly gunned the motor, bringing the truck completely to life. "You're a good old wagon." As far north as they were, any motor could freeze up, any battery suddenly die, and it was fifteen miles through the thickest forest to the nearest other vehicle. He'd seen fires built under motors, and had heard incredible cursing float out on northern nights, while hours had passed and all ideas had failed and nobody went anywhere. He kept the choke out so the motor ran fast, then turned on the heater and stepped back out into the snow. The truck's exhaust was the only cloud against the brilliant moon, and he went through the swirling vapor, back toward the cabin which sat like a tiny lantern in the great tangled wilderness.

Diane was still shivering in the bathroom, her stomach bulging under her nightgown. He helped her back toward the stairs, and up to the bedroom, where she started to dress, going through all the regular motions but trembling constantly. It seemed to Laski there were two distinct Dianes—one who was shaking like a leaf, and another who was calm and decisive as any old midwife. He felt the same split in himself as he picked up her valise and carried it toward the stairs. His hand was trembling, his heart pounding, but another part of him was calm, unshakeable as an old tree. This calm quiet partner seemed to dwell in some region of the body Laski couldn't identify. His guts were jumping, his brain was racing, his legs were shaking, but somewhere in him there was peace.

He stepped into the snow. The truck was running smoothly now, and he eased off on the choke, until the engine was gently cooking. Turning, he saw Diane through the upstairs window of the cabin, her stomach huge in front of her. She moved slowly and carefully, and he knew that she was going to exactly the clothes she'd planned on, finding them just where she wanted them. His own life was a bundle of clothes flung in all directions, shoes dancing in unlikely places, nothing where he could find it.

He went back in, joining her in the bedroom. "How're you feeling?"

"The contractions have begun."

"What are they like?"

"I can't describe it."

He helped her down the stairs to the door, and looked around the kitchen. She's got everything in place, there's no more to be done here. He locked the door behind him and led her to the truck. She slid inside and he covered her with a blanket.

The truck was warm and moved easily up the snow-packed lane, through the tall pine trees. At the top of the lane he turned onto the narrow road. They'd walked it all winter long and they'd played a game, pretending that the baby had already been born and was swinging along between them like a little trapeze artist holding to their hands, and they'd swung him that way, up and down the road.

The road went past a vast snow-covered field, in which an old wagon appeared, on its own journey, to nowhere, rotting away, its spoked wheels half-buried in the snow.

"I'd feel better if you didn't go so fast."

He slowed down. One minute, ten minutes saved, makes no difference. We know how long the first stages of labor last.

There was ice beneath the snow, and the wheels of the truck did not have perfect traction, but he knew how to play the road, easing through the turns, never using much brake. Both sides of the narrow road had been deeply ditched to carry away the waters of the spring run-off, but now they were covered with snow and it would be a simple matter to slide into the ditch and be there all night. Every winter he'd helped pull travelers out of the ditch, with much swearing, skidding, heaving and hauling. It was great fun; but not tonight.

At the bend in the road stood the one-room schoolhouse, forgotten in the moonlight. He geared down, taking the turn in second, thinking of little boys with caps and knickers on, and little girls in gingham dresses, long ago, coming up the hill toward the schoolhouse. Then he was through the turn, leaving the old ghosts behind him on their endless walk through a buried century.

The road went straight through pines which formed a high wall on both sides. "Old Ben is up," said Laski, nodding toward a ramshackle farm-house in the midst of the trees. Most of the windows were broken out and it was like all the other abandoned farm-houses in the settlement, except for a flickering light inside, from the one room the old lumberjack had sealed off against the elements.

Diane looked toward the light. A hermit herself, she liked old Ben. He had a bad reputation in the village, living as he did, so contrary to the ways of the world. But he could make anything out of wood—fiddles, boats, snow-shoes—and he'd spent a lifetime in the woods. Laski saw a shadow moving in the darkness—old Ben's dog, sniffing around in the snow. Then the truck was into the next turn, near the river that came out of the darkness, its icy skin shining in the moonlight. Laski followed the river until it slipped back into the trees, where it wove a silver thread through the dark branches.

Another clearing appeared, and a small board shack. It was a camp for "Sports," as the backwoods Canadians called the Americans who came to fish and hunt and rough it for a week. Laski remembered a time, a long time ago—his father and he were fishing in Canada, steering a motorboat along on a bright morning over a wide and winding river. Laski had suddenly felt like he was the river and the trees and the sun and the wind.

He touched Diane gently on the shoulder. She was trembling inside her heavy coat, and he knew enough not to ask her how she felt.

The camp for American Sports fell back into darkness. The villagers had thought of Laski and his wife as Sports, with no visible means of support, until it was learned they were artists. Never having had such strange creatures around, except for old Coleman Johns, the mad inventor who had built his own automatic milking machine and promised to make a trip to the moon with a magnet in his pants, the country people left the Laskis alone. There was some talk that Laski, with his thick beard and wire glasses, resembled old Coleman enough to be his twin brother. Whenever Laski drove past the ruined foundation that had once been Coleman's home, he was overtaken by a strange nostalgia, as if he and the mad inventor had shared the same vision of this vast land, which made men build strange objects beneath the moon.

Laski's sculpture was certainly odd. Likenesses of Diane filled the forest, her strangely beautiful face gradually appearing on tree stumps or on rocks. Old dead trees with grey bare branches had become Diane dancing, like a priestess of the wood. Eventually the ceaseless weaving of the weeds had made gowns of green for the statues, bright berry-beads and buttons entwining the arms and legs, marking them as part of the endless dream of the deep pines.

"The contractions are ten minutes apart."

Laski laid a firmer foot on the gas pedal. Baby's in a hurry.

A ghostly light flashed ahead of Laski, leaping out of the darkness of the country graveyard where Coleman Johns lay buried and where Laski's headlights had caught the top of an old tombstone. The truck wheels spun on the turn, the rear-end lashing like a tail before coming straight again. Then darkness claimed the graveyard once more and the road was again lined by heavy forest.

"Maternity?" smiled the receptionist. "Do you have your papers with you?"

Diane took them out of her purse. An orderly came across the waiting room with a wheel-chair and Diane sat down in it, still wearing her shaggy forest coat. Laski looked at the receptionist.

"The orderly will take her up and you can follow in just a few minutes, sir. I have some papers for you to fill out."

Laski touched Diane's hand and she looked at him, smiling but distant, as the orderly turned the chair and wheeled her off.

The receptionist put a form into her typewriter and asked Laski questions about age, address, insurance—lifeless items holding him in his chair.

A drunken young man, face cut and swollen, swaggered into the waiting room. Glassy-eyed, he approached the desk. The receptionist looked up. "If you'll have a seat, please," she said coldly.

The young man leaned on the desk, but the receptionist ignored him, even though he was bleeding from a wound over his eye.

Laski looked into the young man's eyes, expecting hostility. He found a frightened child making brave. The nurses will give him a hard time, thought Laski. Then the doctor will stitch him and he'll be turned back out into the night. But he was once the baby on the way and everybody rallied around him. The great moment was once his.

An older man entered the waiting room and looked around for a moment, until his eye caught the young man's figure. He came over slowly, his walk and manner similar to the young man's.

"What happened?"

"Nothing much," said the young man, striking a confident pose.

"I haven't seen you for a while."

"I've been around."

"You interested in working?"

"Yeah, sure."

"You can go to work tomorrow."

"Oh no," said the young man, shaking his head and touching his bruises. "I can't do anything tomorrow."

The papers were completed. The orderly returned and Laski followed him down the hallway to an elevator. They rode together in silence, to the floor marked *Maternity*. The hall held a couch and two leather chairs. Beyond it was a door marked *Delivery— No Admittance*.

The orderly walked away. Laski sat down. This is where all the fathers wait. He stood, and walked slowly up and down. Now I'm pacing the floor like an expectant father.

The sounds of a floor-waxing machine came along the hallway, somewhere out of sight, whirring, wheels creaking. Laski listened to its approach and then it appeared, pushed along by a uniformed maintenance man. "This is your big night, eh?"

"Yes."

The waxer nodded and waxed on. He's seen it all, thought Laski, seen them come and go, seen them every night—pacing back and forth on his waxed floor.

An elderly nurse came out of the delivery room. Laski looked at her, but she gave him such a blank cold stare all questions dissolved in his throat. He listened to her footsteps going away down the hall, and then he walked over and peered through the porthole window in the delivery-room door.

He paced back again, past the leather chairs. The alcohol-medicine smell of the hospital filled the air. The floor was squared tile; he stepped between the cracks with each foot. His boots were still wet with snow. The dark tips of them looked back at him, worn-down and scarred from the forest.

He reined himself around, came back the other way along the floor. The door swung open again. A young nurse appeared, smiling. "We're just getting your wife ready," she said. "You'll be able to join her in a few minutes."

Diane was sitting up in bed. He went quickly to her, searching her eyes, which showed the same mixture of fear and calm he'd seen all night.

"The baby's upside-down," she said.

The air seemed dreamlike, a dream in which he could make things take any shape he liked. But he was standing in a hospital room and their baby was upside-down. "It'll be all right," he said, touching her folded hands.

"Doctor Barker says he doesn't want you in on a breech birth. I told him I understand, and that I hope he'll change his mind."

Her face suddenly changed as the contraction came on, and she began her breathing as they'd practised it, inhaling rapidly and evenly. She closed her eyes, her brow in wrinkles as she grimaced with pain. He stood powerless, watching the hand within her clenching itself tightly, until her face was one that he had never seen before, a screwed-up mask of desperation which suddenly and slowly relaxed, wrinkles fading, eyes opening, as the contraction subsided.

She looked up at him and smiled. "He must have turned around last week. Remember the bump we felt high on my stomach? That was his head."

"We'll be swinging him down the road soon," said Laski.

Her smile suddenly disappeared as the next contraction came. She went into her rapid breathing and he willed her his strength, trying to make it pass out of his body and enter hers.

The nurse came in as the contraction subsided. "How're we doing?"

"All right."

"Let me have a look." The nurse lifted Diane's gown for a moment, then lowered it. "You're dilating beautifully."

Diane's smile was once again ruined by the return of a contraction.

A young intern entered and stood at the foot of the bed, waiting as the contraction worked toward its peak. He looked at Laski and asked politely, "Would you mind stepping outside a moment while we examine her?"

Laski went out into the hallway. What do they do to her that I can't be there? Does he think I've never seen my wife's body before? . . . Don't send bad vibrations. They're running this show. He walked up and down the hallway, feeling like the odd man out.

The door opened; the intern came into the hallway and nodded at Laski, who went back in and joined the nurse at the foot of the bed.

"You're fully dilated," said the nurse to Diane. "You can start pushing anytime you want."

Diane nodded her head as the next contraction hit. Laski went behind her, lifting her up from the back, as they had practised. He lifted and she hauled back on her knees with her hands, bending her legs and spreading them apart, pressing down within herself. He held her up for the length of the contraction and then slowly let her down.

"Very nice," said the nurse. "Keep up the good work." She smiled at them and left the room.

"Would you wet a wash-cloth and put it on my forehead?"

Laski found a wash-cloth in her bag and wet it in the bathroom sink. He wiped her brow, her cheeks, her neck. "Where's the doctor?"

"He's sleeping in a room down the hall. They'll wake him up when it's time."

"How do you feel?"

"I'm glad to be pushing."

The contraction came and he lifted her again, his face close to hers. The wrinkled brow and tight-closed eyes formed a face he'd never dreamed of. All her beauty was gone, and she seemed like a sexless creature struggling for all it was worth, laboring greatly with the beginning of the world. Their laughter, their little joys, their plans, everything they'd known was swallowed by this labor —a work he suddenly wished they'd never begun, so contorted was she, so unlike the woman he knew. Her face was red, her temples pounding, and she looked now like a middle-aged man taking a shit that was killing him. This is humanity, thought Laski, and he questioned the purpose of a race that seeks to perpetuate itself in agony, but before he had his answer the contraction had passed and he was lowering her back to the pillow.

He took the wash-cloth, wet it again and wiped her perspiring face. "Relax deeply now. Get your energy back. Spread your legs —relax your arms." He talked softly, smoothing out her still-trembling limbs until she finally lay quiet, eyes closed.

The wave came again and carried them out onto the sea of pain, where he wondered again why life ever came into the world. The loveliness of the highway night, when all the stars seemed watching, was now drowned in sweat. The most beautiful face he'd ever seen was looking bulbous, red, and homely.

The tide that drew them out into the troubled waters once again spent itself and they floated slowly back, resting for a minute or so, only to be dragged out again. He held her up while she contracted and pushed inside herself, trying to open the petals of her flowering body. He'd thought that such a miraculous opening would somehow be performed in a more splendid fashion. But she was sweating like a lumberjack's horse after a summer morning of hauling logs.

He lifted her, trying to free the load she was struggling with, but she was straining against the traces, getting nowhere, her eyes like those of a draft-horse—puzzled, frustrated and enslaved. He could see the strain pulsing in her reddened temples, just as he'd seen it in the work-horses when he thought they would surely die of a heart attack, racing as they did through the woods with huge logs behind them, jamming suddenly on a stump, the reins almost snapping and their mighty muscles knotting against the obstacle. Who would choose this, thought Laski, this work, this woe? Life enslaves us, makes us want children, gives us a thousand illusions about love, and all so that it can go forward.

He felt the supremacy of life, its power greater than his will. I just wanted to be with you, Diane, the two of us living easily together and here we are, with your life on the line.

She was coming down the staircase of a brownstone building. She wore a long purple cape with a high collar turned up around her neck. The cape flared out as she touched the sidewalk and he stood rooted and stupid, struggling to speak. She must have felt it, for she turned and looked his way.

Her face contracted again, her eyes closing tightly and her mouth bending into a mask formed by the pain that came on her again. He held her up, feeling the strain in her muscles and the fever in her skin. The short ringlets of hair at her neck were soaked and glistening. A wet spot was spreading across her back.

The intern and the nurse returned while they were out upon the waves, struggling together, pushing together, sweating together to bring the thing to completion, and when the contraction ended, the intern did not ask Laski to leave while he made his examination. "You're showing some progress now."

"You can see the baby," said the nurse.

Laski looked down, and in the shaved and sweating crack he saw something pink and strange, a little patch of flesh he could not comprehend. All he knew were the waves that took them out again, where they were alone in love and sadness that none else could share, alone and clinging to each other in the reality they had long prepared for, for which no preparation was ever enough.

"I've seen you before," he said, stopping her on Broadway.

"Have you?" she said, the slightest touch of flirtation in her voice, just enough to keep him coming toward her, out of his deep embarrassed nature.

Back they drifted, to the green room in the sleeping hospital.

Hardly had they rested when the waves carried them out again, like a nightmare that repeats itself over and over through the night, and over and over again through the years. Back and forth they went and he feared that her strength could not hold. He had no confidence, not in himself, nor in her. He felt like a helpless child, and Diane seemed helpless too, their long struggle getting them nowhere, only repeating itself—contraction, release, contraction again. But the nurse and intern seemed unconcerned by it all, were cheerful and confident. And the doctor is down the hall, sleeping. He's not worried. If there were anything wrong he'd be here.

She dressed by the window of his tiny room, slipping slowly into tight knit slacks and sweater. Her short hair needed no combing or fixing, and she was the most natural thing he'd ever seen, unlike his previous loves, who'd always thrown him out of the room while they dressed and primped or put curlers in their hair.

Her gown was wringing-wet, her hair plastered down, as if the sea had broken over her. She closed her eyes and crow's feet came there, lines he'd never seen before, lines of age, and he knew that ages had passed. "Again," she said, her voice almost a sob now, but not a sob, too tired for tears. And he lifted her up as the tide carried them out again, into the wild uncharted waters.

He held her, his love for her expanding with every tremor of her body. It seemed he'd never loved her before, that all of their past was just a rehearsal for this moment in which he felt resounding inside him all the days of her life, days before he'd known her, days from the frightened child's face he saw before him, and days from the wise woman's ancient life that came calling now to give her unknown strength. All the frustration of Diane's thirty years was present now, and she seemed to be making a wish in the well of time, that everything should finally come out all right, that finally something she was doing would be just as it should be.

"I can't have a baby," she said, "because of the shape of my womb."

"Bullshit."

"He's a Park Avenue gynecologist."

Well, thought Laski, it took us ten years but we finally made one. He lowered her back to the bed, wiping her brow with the washcloth. She smiled, but it was a mask, formed by momentary release from her anguish. In it was none of the flirtation, none of the peace, none of the things he usually saw in her smiles. But he knew she'd made this smile for him, to ease his worry. She's seeing into me too; maybe she sees all the care of my days, as I am seeing hers. He felt them together, then, on a new level, older, wiser, with pain as the binder in their union. We came more than fifty miles tonight; we've crossed the ocean.

Her smile suddenly drew itself up beyond the limits of smiling, becoming a grimace, and he lifted her up. We're not across the ocean yet.

"Gee-yup, Bob!" The great horse pulled, his hooves scraping on the forest floor, sending moss and sticks flying. The tree creaked and swayed and fell and Bob-horse ran with it, dragging branches and all.

"I guess we can get Doctor Barker now," said the intern after examining Diane again. The nurse went out of the room. Laski wiped Diane's brow and the intern stood at the foot of the bed, watching. "You've been pushing for nearly three hours," he said.

"That's too long, isn't it?" she asked.

"It's because the baby's weight is up instead of down," said the intern.

And suddenly they were out again, in the tempest. Laski held her up, pouring himself through his fingertips into her, as she lifted her legs and pushed.

The nurse entered with a tall young man in white uniform. He stood at the foot of the bed with the intern as Laski and Diane held on, out upon the sea, love-blown sailors lost in fathomless depths of time and destiny, coming now slowly back to a room of strangers who seemed eternal too, in a never-ending play. "If you'll just step outside a minute," said Doctor Barker.

Laski went into the hallway and gathered himself together in a single prayer without words, offered to the ocean.

The door swung open. The young doctor stepped out and said, "Things are developing now. We'll be taking her down to the delivery room."

Laski went back to Diane. She was bent up, contracting alone, and he went to her.

"Your baby's on the way now," said the nurse, smiling cheerfully at Laski.

He suddenly remembered the baby, the little swimmer in the secret sea. He's struggling too, struggling to be with us, struggling just as we are.

Laski's heart became an ocean of love, as nine months of memories flooded him, and the baby was real again, real as in the night when Laski felt tiny feet kicking inside Diane. Our baby, our little friend, is being born!

And this, thought Laski, is why we labor, so that love might come into the world.

The contraction passed, and he and Diane were washed back, limp like sea-plants when the waves abandon them on the shore. "It looks very good," said the intern.

The nurse came in, wheeling a stretcher. "All set?"

"Yes," said Diane. They slid her from the bed onto the stretcher and they all walked beside it down the hallway toward the delivery room. Doctor Barker was being put into a white gown. Laski leaned over and kissed Diane.

"Aren't you coming in?" she asked, her voice filled with longing.

The nurse continued wheeling her into the delivery room and
Laski stood in the hall outside. His will, his speech, his guts, were
gone. Barker stepped over to him. "The nurse will give you a cap
and gown and you can watch from behind the table."

Laski's strength came back in a whirlwind as a great smile
crossed his face. We're going all the way together! He stood, watching the doctor and intern wash their hands in a nearby sink, washing them again and again, in slow methodical manner. The nurse
came to him and held up a gown. He slipped his arms into it and
she tied it in back. She gave him a white cap which he fastened
over his ears. Then he and the intern went into the delivery room,
where Diane lay on the central table, her legs in stirrups, her wrists
strapped down.

"You can sit here," said the nurse, setting a stool behind the
table. Another nurse fixed the mirror that was above the table,
so that Laski could see the area of birth.

"A clear picture?"

"Perfect."

One of the nurses then brought a little sponge soaked with sur-
gical soap, and wiped Diane's vaginal area.

"Oh, that feels good."

"Has she had any anaesthetic?" asked the other nurse.

"No."

"Well, now, isn't she wonderful!"

Doctor Barker came and sat on a stool at the other end of the
table. "I'm going to drain your bladder."

He inserted a tube into her urethra and a moment later her
urine ran out of it, into a bucket at Barker's feet.

"I have a contraction," said Diane.

"Go ahead and push."

Laski could not reach her, and she lifted herself, working alone.
When the contraction subsided, Barker said, "I'm going to make
a small cut. First, I'll give you something to numb it." He inserted
a needle at the edge of her vagina, making three injections. Then
he pinched her skin with a tweezers. "Do you feel that?"

"No."

He made an incision, cutting sideways toward her thigh.
"Check the heartbeat."

The nurse laid her stethoscope on Diane's lower belly, and listened, timing the baby's heartbeat with her watch.

"Normal."

"All right—push again." He inserted his finger into Diane's vagina, feeling for the baby. When the finger came out, Laski saw more of the strange pink skin, and a thick dark substance.

"Don't let that worry you," said the nurse to Laski. "The baby's just had a bowel movement."

"Push," said Barker. Diane pushed and Laski could see the baby's rear-end, at the doorway of the world, ass-backwards, thought Laski, but coming!

"All right, dear, push again," said Barker.

She pushed and he put his long fingers into her vagina, moving them around and spreading her lips. Suddenly a foot appeared, followed by a long limp leg. Barker quickly brought the other leg down and Laski looked at it in wonder, at the tiny toenails and the perfectly formed little feet that had been developing all along within her, about which he had dreamed so often, envisioning it in countless ways, and now the first step of those little feet into life had come before his eyes.

"It's a boy!" exclaimed the nurse.

Laski's heart filled with joy. Staring at the entrance-way, he saw the tiny penis and a second later, it squirted a jet of urine.

"I felt him pee on me!" cried Diane, in wonder.

"Push," said Barker. "Push with all you've got."

As she pushed he guided the tiny body out, all but the head, which remained inside. Laski stared in fascination at the dangling little creature, the skin grey and wet—his little son, come at last.

Barker inserted the forceps. "Once again," he said.

Diane pushed and Laski tensed as he watched Barker forcefully pulling with the forceps to release the head. My God, thought Laski, they handle them hard. And suddenly the head popped out and the child was free.

Barker's hands moved with incredible grace and swiftness, turning the baby in the air, holding him up like a red rose. Laski saw a face filled with rage, yet triumphant, the god of time and men, whose closed eyes looked straight into Laski's and said, *See, see, this!*

"Cut the cord!"

The intern severed the cord and Barker carried the child with utmost delicacy in his two hands, moving quickly over to a table by the wall.

"The aspirator," he said, sharply.

The nurse handed him an instrument that looked like an old car horn, a rubber bulb fitted on the end of it. He put it to the baby's face and squeezed.

The child lay perfectly still. Barker worked the pump, then touched the limp wrist, lifting it for a moment and laying it back down. One nurse massaged the feet, and the other handed Barker a length of fine hose which he inserted into the baby's mouth. He breathed into it, and Laski watched his son's chest rise and fall with the breath of the doctor moving inside him.

Barker stopped for a moment, wiped his brow, returned to the blowing-tube. Laski looked on, watching the lungs rise and fall again. The rest of the body lay perfectly still. How long his legs are, thought Laski—just like his mother's.

Barker removed the tube and put his mouth to the baby's, blowing into it with his lips pressed against the tiny mouth. The nurse continued to massage the feet. Laski looked at the clock on the wall: Four-thirty-five.

Barker stepped back, wiped his brow again, and Laski remembered moments from his own life, when he'd worked on things and found them puzzling and unyielding, and he'd wiped his brow that way. Barker put the aspirator back on the still little body and pumped it, a little sighing noise coming from the rubber bulb.

"Is that the baby?" asked Diane.

Laski looked at her, and looked away, drawn back to his little son, to the little arm that rose and fell so limply in Barker's hand.

"Where's the baby?" asked Diane.

"He's over there," said Laski softly.

Barker removed the aspirator and put his mouth to the child's again, blowing in and out gently, evenly. He stepped back, wiped his brow, turned to Laski, and shook his head.

Laski nodded.

It was over.

He turned and sat down on the little stool beside the table. The intern was stitching Diane's opened vagina.

"Does that hurt?"

"No," she said, laughing nervously.

Laski looked at her flat stomach. How can she possibly hold together in the face of this? How do we tell her?

He turned to the table by the wall. The baby had been lowered into a glass case and he was on his side, eyes closed. Laski saw resignation in the little face, the expression of work completely done, like a man who has rolled over to sleep at the end of the day.

"Are you all right?" asked Barker.

"Yes," said Laski.

Barker stepped over to the maternity table and looked down at Diane.

She raised her eyes to his. "I know," she said.

"I'm sorry."

"It's not your fault," she said, a sob breaking from her throat.

"The baby looks perfectly normal," said Barker. "There's no reason why you can't have another child."

Laski listened numbly. He thinks that's what has been at stake —our wish for a child, any child, not this particular child who swung down the road between us. They can't know how special he is. They point to the future. But we're here, forever, now.

The nurse slipped Diane onto the stretcher. "I have a needle for you."

"No," said Diane, still refusing any anaesthetic.

"It's to dry up your milk," said the nurse, gently.

"There are no private rooms," said the other nurse. "We can put you in a semi-private."

"I can go to a ward," said Diane. "I only wanted a private room so I could keep the baby with me."

"It would be better for you in a semi-private. All the other babies will be brought into the ward for feeding, and they'll make you sad."

"I wouldn't mind the babies," said Diane, crying softly. "But I'd probably make all the other mothers feel bad."

They wheeled her through the dimly-lit hallway and Laski walked beside her, to a room with two beds, both of them empty. They helped her into the bed and drew the covers over her.

"May I stay?" asked Laski.

"Yes, certainly," said the nurse. "Do you want to sleep on the other bed?"

"No, I'm not tired."

"If you want to," she said, "just flop down on it." The nurse leaned over to Diane. "These things happen. I'm sure you'll have better luck next time."

Laski looked at the little handbag beside the bed, in which Diane had packed two baby wash-cloths, one pink, one blue, and he saw that it was the blue one he'd been using to mop her brow.

She looked quietly at him and stroked his hair with her hand. He laid his head down on the bed beside her, as the full weight of his own weariness took him. The nurse came in again and said, "Are you sure you won't lie down?"

"All right," he said, and walked over to the other bed.

"Let me slip this sheet over it. "I'm lazy. I don't want to have to make it again."

He crawled onto the top sheet and lay looking at the ceiling. Beneath his head he felt cement blocks. He drifted into a kaleidoscopic sleep so filled with images he could not sort them into any recognizable dream, and they rushed over him like water.

He woke and saw Diane looking at the ceiling. He got up and sat beside her again. The dawn was breaking. Through the window he saw another wing of the hospital, and beyond that the street, on which the grey light was falling. He watched the street as the sunlight fell upon it.

In the hallway the sound of dishes began. "They're bringing breakfast," she said.

The breakfast carts came closer, and an elderly woman entered, carrying a tray. She smiled at Laski. "Well, it's a lovely day, isn't it."

Diane ate cereal and toast and sunlight found the room.

"They'll want me out of here soon," said Laski.

"Yes, the mothers will be feeding their babies."

He saw the sorrow break over her for a moment, like a wave upon a cliff, but the wave washed away and there was the cliff, which sorrow could not drown.

"I'll be back this evening," he said. "Visiting hours are at seven. Is there anything you want?"

"No, just you."

He leaned over and kissed her, her tears going slowly down his cheek.

Laski drove over the bridge and out of town. As he crossed the railroad tracks that ran through the slum on the edge of the city, a delicate film of light came across his eyes, as if a shimmering translucent veil were covering the morning, and he knew that it was his son's spirit, riding with him. And then he saw himself running with his son, through the fields, leaping the old broken fences. They walked to the stream and dove into it, then danced upon it, then ran to the trees, climbing up above the mist.

Laski drove toward home with tears streaming down his face, his spirit racing with his son through time, across the morning of the world, from place to place, in cities and in the lovely valley. The moment of their meeting was endless: they took a boat, and took a train, and saw the sights, and grew up together. It seemed to take years getting to the forest, and as Laski climbed the hills into the abandoned settlement he felt the spirit of his son spreading out all around him. Spreading out as it did, into every tree and cloud, he felt it losing personality, felt it dissolving into something remote, expanded beyond his powers to follow. He's going now, thought Laski. He's grown-up and leaving me. Goodbye, goodbye, he called, looking out to the beautiful eastern sky where the sun was dazzling the trees.

You're free in the wind. You're great with the winds and sun.

Then it was over and Laski was alone again, bouncing along the old winding road through the forest.

Returning to the hospital in the evening, he got lost in the corridors beyond the lobby, none of it familiar to him anymore. He stood looking toward a staircase he could not remember climbing before. A strong voice came at his shoulder. "Where are you headed for?"

"Maternity."

"Follow me," said a powerfully-striding man in boots and ski-sweater. He took the steps as if they were a mountain trail, and Laski kept the pace.

"What did you have?" asked the man, not looking back, keeping his eyes on the trail.

Laski hesitated as fragments of explanations rose in his mind —*the baby died, we had nothing*—but then he felt the spirit of the child again, suddenly surging in his heart, and he said, "A boy."

"Congratulations," said the mountain-man, as they reached the top of the mountain stair-case, at the hall marked

Maternity

"And you?" asked Laski.

"A boy," said the mountaineer, his voice filled with wind and stone and wild joy. He turned off to the left, and Laski went straight ahead, down the hall to Diane's room.

She was in bed, her eyes red, her face pale, the shock of the night still on her. He sat down beside the bed and took her hand.

"Was the doctor in to see you?"

"He said he examined the afterbirth and found that the cord had been connected to the edge of the placenta instead of the middle. It was a weak place and at the last minute the cord tore. The baby bled."

Laski slowly nodded his head and looked toward the window. Through the other lighted rooms of the hospital he saw distant figures moving.

"He'd like to perform an autopsy," said Diane.

"Is it really necessary?"

"It's up to us."

"Do you want to let them?"

"I guess they always do it."

Beyond the windows of the hospital, he could see the sidewalks and the snowy street. In the maternity hallway, at the desk, the nurses were chatting and laughing together.

"He's in the morgue," said Diane.

A nurse entered the room, smiling cheerfully. "Time for your heat-lamp." Then, turning to Laski, "Would you excuse us for a minute?"

Laski stepped out into the hall. The doors of the other rooms were open and he could see women in their beds, visitors beside them. He lowered his eyes toward the floor and followed the sound of the waxing machine and the elevator and the visiting voices, all of it flowing like a stream in which he seemed to be floating. The second-hand on the wall-clock over his head was humming, round and round. The laughter at the nurse's desk continued, and he realized it was New Year's Eve. *In a little room on 91st Street in New York City, in the darkness of a little bed, while the bells rang and the sirens called, he held her.* The waxing machine appeared at the corner, its long whiskers whirring around and around over the tiled floor.

A snowstorm had begun in the city. The night was cold and he was filled with tired thoughts. Twenty-five miles away, out in the woods, the cabin was waiting, empty and cold. A hotel would be warm and bright—a single room, a table with a lamp on it, a bed. I could get some sleep and hang around town tomorrow until visiting time.

The traffic light turned green through the veil of falling snow, and he drove down the main street of town to the street of the hotel, where he parked the truck. The snow was coming harder. He walked along toward the hotel. It's not the best, and that's all I need, just a flop for the night.

His body ached and his eyes were tired. The shops on the street were all closed, the merchandise on display beneath dim night-lights, and he passed by it all on weary legs. The hotel had a single door leading to a cramped little lobby, into which he stepped, looking toward the night-clerk's desk. The clerk, reading a newspaper, did not look up. A television set was going, and two men sat before it, smiling at some flickering image Laski could not see, but he sensed the loneliness of the men and their desperate fight against it, huddled together before the television.

As if turned by a magnet, he went back out through the door into the street. The snow fell on him as he walked back to the truck and climbed into it, driving out of town and over the white highway toward the woods.

He entered the cabin reluctantly, as if it were a cave of ghosts. The stove was low and he stirred it up. When the surface was hot, he slid on a frying pan and cooked himself supper. He ate slowly, staring out the window at the whirling snow. When his meal was finished, he washed the dishes, not hurrying, but working slowly, with concentration, leaving no room for morbid thoughts, ghosts, fears. There was only the hot water, the dish, his hands, the soapy rag.

The stairs to the second floor looked dark and forboding. And what's up there, amidst the baby clothes and crib? There's nothing up there, he said, and walked up the stairs and undressed in the small bedroom. He kept the light on for a few minutes and then, resigning himself to darkness and sleep, switched it off.

Alone in a dark house far out in the woods, with a storm blowing on the outside and the shadow of death on the inside, he crawled beneath the covers. Spectres rose up behind his closed eyes, weird and menacing. He watched his mind play out its age-old fears. Trembling, he fell into dreams, finding himself outside the cabin, walking through the dream-forest. Beside a tree he saw a cloaked and hooded figure. The figure turned and the face beneath the hood was a smiling skull of stone. Death held out his walking stick, and Laski took it in his hand.

Late afternoon sunlight streamed through the hospital window and he sat beside her again. She looked stronger, and the storm was over.

"We have to bury the baby," she said. "They don't want him in the morgue anymore."

"We can bury him in the woods."

"That's what I told the nurse. She said it was highly unusual, but that it would probably be all right. She had a lot of forms. We'll have to have a witness."

"How about the autopsy? Won't the baby be . . ."

"She said they put him back together again."

Doctor Barker came into the room. They both looked at him in silence. He stood, tall and uncomfortable, at the foot of the bed. "The autopsy showed your baby was perfectly normal. There's no reason why what happened should ever happen again."

"Do you think she can go home tomorrow?"

"How do your stitches feel?"

"They burn a little, that's all."

"I suppose you can leave, if you'll feel better at home." He turned to go, then turned back to Diane. "I know it's difficult to lose your first baby when you're thirty."

The last light of day went along the brick wall of the hospital. Laski sat by the window, watching as night came on. Diane, wearing a bathrobe, entered the room. "I told the nurse we'd be taking the baby home tomorrow afternoon."

"I'll build a little box for him tonight."

"Will you be able to dig a hole in the frozen ground?"

A nurse poked her head inside the door. "There are some fluids in the hall if either of you want any."

Laski went out and found a tray of watered fruit-drinks. He poured some orange into two glasses and returned to the room. "Fluids," he said, handing her the thin orange-drink.

The night visiting bell sounded. "I'll be in first thing tomorrow afternoon," he said, kissing her lightly on the lips. Then he went down the green hall, toward the street, the highway, and home.

The steel roof of the cabin was bright in the moonlight as he parked the truck in the drive. He opened the door to the shed, where his lumber was piled. How am I going to do this, he asked himself, looking at the long pile of pine boards, and at his tools. He was overcome by a feeling of dread about making the coffin; he had no wish to build it, or anything, ever again.

He fingered the smoothly-planed surface of the boards; the heavy feeling in him remained, as if he were in a dark cloud, but he grabbed a board and hauled it out of the pile.

Carrying the saw-horses into his studio, he spaced them out evenly. Across them he laid the long clean pine board. Then he brought his tool-box in and set it down. He pulled the metal rule out of its case and stretched it along the wood, imagining the size of the baby's body.

He laid his T-square on the mark, drew a straight line and sawed along it, thinking of the old days when men had always built the caskets of their loved ones, and he saw that it was a good thing to do, that it was a privilege few men had anymore. He marked the next line carefully and sawed a matching piece to form the bottom of the casket.

He joined the two pieces and then cut the sides and ends for the box. The time passed slowly and peacefully. He worked, sanding the edges of the pieces so that they would join well, to form a box that no one would see, but which had to be made perfectly. He drilled holes and counter-sunk them, and screwed on the sides and end-pieces.

Squatting on the floor, sawdust on his knees and a pencil behind his ear, he turned the screws slowly, biting deep into the wood. He sanded along the edge of the box, making another fine cloud of sawdust, which filled his nose with a memorable smell. I built a house for us, with a room for him, and now I'm building his casket. There's no difference in the work. We simply must go along, eyes open, watching our work carefully, without any extra thoughts. Then we flow with the night.

The little box took shape and he resisted feeling proud of it, for pride was something extra. I do it quietly, for no one, not even for him, for he's gone beyond my little box. But he left behind a fragment of himself, which requires a box I can carry through the woods. And the box needs a lid and I've got to find a pair of hinges.

He rummaged in the shed and found an old rusted pair, small and squeaky, but serviceable. Marking the outlines for the hinges, he then chiseled out their shape, so they slid snugly down into the wood. He tried the lid and continued setting the hinges, until the lid finally closed solidly. He worked the lid up and down a few times, enjoying the smooth action of it, until he remembered what it was for, and he saw again that there should be nothing extra in the work.

He put away the saw-horses and his tools, and swept up the dust. Then he sat down in a chair and quietly rocked back and forth, looking at the coffin. A vague dissatisfaction stirred in him, growing slowly more clear and troubling.

If we bury him here, we'll be attached to this land permanently. I can have him cremated at a funeral home, and his ashes will be put in a little metal box and we can carry it around with us when we travel. And when we get to the middle of the ocean some-day, we can throw his ashes there.

That's exactly what we should do. I'll take him to the funeral home tomorrow and they can cremate him in the little coffin.

A feeling of freedom came to Laski—freedom from land and houses and graves. And keeping this thought in his mind, he went upstairs to bed.

When he entered the hospital room, it was into a new atmos-phere—the other bed was now occupied. As he went toward Diane, out of the corner of his eye he saw a young girl lying in the bed he had lain on. Beside her was a young man, and two older women. They pulled a curtain around themselves, and Laski sat down beside Diane.

"She lost her baby," whispered Diane.

Laski glanced toward the closed curtain, behind which soft shad-ows were moving. "I think we should have the baby cremated in town this afternoon."

"But why?"

"If we bury him on the land, it will just be another tie for us, that this is the place where the baby is buried."

Her eyes filled with tears again. "If you think it's best . . ."

"I don't know what's best," he said. "Maybe there isn't any best. But the thought was very strong and I'm trying to flow with it."

"What will you do?"

"I'll go over to the funeral home now and find out if they can do it right away."

He stood and went past the other visitors. Down the hall once more, and down the stairs, his thoughts were racing now—to get it over with, and set them free.

He crossed the parking lot quickly and started the truck. Vaguely remembering the whereabouts of a funeral home, he drove through town. They'll deal with the whole thing, and we won't have to get involved.

Snow-plows were still working, cleaning the streets, and here and there people were shoveling out their sidewalks and driveways. Laski turned a corner and saw the old colonial manor with the black and white name-plate on one of its large old pillars. It was an enormous place, with many windows, and he saw through the front window, down a long hallway that was lined with flowers and muted floor lamps. The parking lot was filled with cars. Three large limousines were heaped with flowers, and a crew of professionally somber men in black were standing beside a fourth limousine hung with grey velvet curtains. The side door opened and the front end of a casket came out, made of dark wood polished to a high gloss and trimmed with silver and gold filigree. Clinging to its shining brass carrying-rails was a crew of professionals, waxed-faced and silent, bearing the huge gaudy coffin toward the hearse, where the back door was opened smartly by a driver who helped to slide the coffin into the richly-curtained interior.

Laski drove on, horrified. What in hell did I almost do?

His hands were trembling on the wheel. Tears in his eyes, he looked down at the little pine box on the seat beside him and laid his hand upon its plain smooth surface.

Circling back through town, he returned to the hospital; once again through the corridors, once again up the stairs, once again past the nurses, and past the people visiting in Diane's room.

"Let's go," he said softly, taking Diane's hand. "We're going home together, and we'll bury him down by the stream."

"But what about the funeral home?"

"Just something I dreamed up to protect myself from the truth of death."

She got up from the bed. "I just have to get dressed," she said, taking her clothes into the bathroom; he sat on the edge of the bed, and heard the voices of the visitors talking to the young girl behind the curtain.

"You mustn't think about it anymore."

"Tomorrow's another day."

"Yes," said the girl. And then again *yes*, softly.

"That's right, dear. You should always look to the future."

"What a pretty nightgown."

"I got it at the K-Mart."

"They'll have the sales there now."

"Everything will be half-price. After New Year's."

Smoke drifted over the curtain. Laski went to the window. The previous day's paper was on the window sill, and glancing at the headlines he saw war, scandal, inflation. We'll bury him by the stream. This moment dies and is followed by another moment, which also dies. Moment to moment I go.

"I'm ready," she said. He picked up her bag and they went to the desk. An elderly nurse spoke to them. "I've told them to have the baby ready for you down at the reception desk. He'll be all wrapped nicely."

Another nurse appeared with a wheel-chair.

"I can walk," said Diane.

"Rules," said the nurse. "You get to ride."

Diane sat in the chair and they went to the elevator. The nurse wheeled her into it and Laski stood beside her as they rode down to the lobby.

The usual crowd was there, reading magazines and staring at the pale yellow walls. The nurse wheeled Diane to the reception room. "The Laski baby," she said.

The receptionist went into the room behind her and returned with an orderly, who carried a small linen bundle.

Diane, still in the wheel-chair, held her arms out, a sob breaking in her throat. The orderly stood puzzled, not knowing what to do. Laski reached out and took the cold little parcel, cradling it in one arm and carrying Diane's suitcase with the other. They went up the exit ramp toward the door. He looked down at Diane and saw her still crying.

"I'll bring the truck to the door," he said, and went out across the parking lot with the baby still in his arms. He could not feel the outline of the body, only the small weight of it in the cold linen wrapping. From a refrigerator, he thought, and he opened the truck and slid inside.

With the baby on his lap, he opened the pine box and laid the linen-shrouded child into it. He closed the lid and latched it shut. The nurse was waiting at the sidewalk as he drove up to the entrance of the hospital. They helped Diane out of the chair and into the front seat of the truck. "You'll have better luck next time," said the nurse. She waved to them, standing for a moment beneath the hospital awning, and then as they pulled away she turned with the empty wheel-chair.

"It's a lovely box," said Diane, her voice calm now.

The box was between them on the seat, and for a moment Laski smelled the sweet perfume of death, or was it the smell of the wood? The delicate odor continued to come to him as they went along the highway, by the fields and the river. The day was unseasonably warm, with wisps of grey mist above the water, and the snow was changing to slush along the shoulder of the road.

"It's just us again," he said.

"Yes," she said, their hands touching on the lid of the pine box.

He wheeled the truck up into the wooded hills, along the old road toward their home. Above an abandoned farm a crow went through the January sky, black wings beating slowly on the grey heights.

Laski turned down the lane to the cabin, and into the drive. He got out and opened the door for her. She stepped into the snow, leaning on him. The sound of melting snow as it dripped off the trees filled the air, and the smell of the trees came strong in the moist warm breeze.

"What a beautiful day," she said, suddenly crying again.

He walked with her slowly up the shoveled path to their door. She leaned on him into the cabin; he had the couch made up for her and settled her on it. Then he stirred the fire and went back out to the car for her bag, and then back again, for the pine box.

He placed the box down on top of the stand, and it remained there in the last light of the afternoon while they sat quietly on the couch.

"I'd better go see old Ben and ask him to come here in the morning." Laski went out again and he saw her watching him through the window.

Ben's collie dog came bounding up to Laski's truck, and Laski got out and petted him, rolling him over on his back and scratching his stomach. He knelt in the snow for a moment, his hand on the dog's belly. In the sky the crow was still calling, circling on the wind, and Laski felt as if he were the crow and the dog and the sky, as if he were transparent and the day was passing through him.

"Come into my castle, friend."

Laski looked up and saw old Ben standing in the doorway of the broken-down farm-house. Ben led him through the labyrinth of broken boards and falling rafters, into the inner-most room of the house, where an old iron stove was glowing with heat and everything was neatly in place—table, chair, water bucket, and a small single bed behind the stove. The hermit sat down on the edge of the bed and tossed a chunk of wood into the fire. "Well, what can we do for you today?" he asked, taking out a package of tobacco.

Laski hesitated, holding his hands out over the heated top of the stove. "The baby died," he said.

Ben stared at the cracked old fire-box of the stove, where tiny sparks were dancing.

"Will you help me bury him?" asked Laski.

"You'll have to get a lot number from the cemetery," said the hermit, trying to roll a cigarette, the tobacco sticking out at both ends.

"I'm burying him in the woods."

Ben hesitated, looking at Laski across the stove. "Do you have a permit?"

"It's ok, Ben. They filled out the papers at the hospital. I put your name in as the witness." He stared back down at the stove. How scared we are, he thought, to even bury our dead unless we have permission from the government. "I'd like to do it first thing in the morning."

"I'll be there," said Ben.

Laski went back through the winding tunnel of debris and out into the snow. The dog jumped up to him, licking his hand, and Laski saw all the sad wisdom of dogs flickering in the collie's dark eyes.

The sun was gone, and they sat quietly, looking toward the box. Finally she said, "I'd like to see him."

"All right," said Laski, his stomach going weak. He had a fleeting image in his mind of the baby he had seen, a powerful face looking at him in the moment of death. What will he look like now, thought Laski, dreading the opening of the box.

He slowly lifted the lid and touched the linen bundle. It was still cool. He felt as though he were in a dream again. "You'd better let me look at him first, in case he's too badly marked." He turned the clean crisp linen back. Beneath it was a faded, dirty piece of sheet, its edges torn and frayed. He unfolded it, expecting to suddenly see the little face, but beneath the sheet were old pieces of rags laid on top of each other, and beneath the old rags was a green plastic garbage bag.

He untwisted the piece of wire that held the garbage bag closed. Slowly pulling down the edge of the bag, he came to the proud little head, now grey and cold. Gently, he rolled down the rest of the garbage bag and looked into the open cavity of his son's chest and stomach.

"They left him open," he said, his hands trembling on the bloody bag.

"It's all right," she said. "I saw."

Laski unfolded the garbage bag until the baby was completely visible, his torso a hollow of skin right to the backbone, holding a little pool of blood, like a cup. Drifting in the blood was a plastic stick, with a number on it.

A fire raged through Laski's body, swelling his chest with blood and burning his throat. "This is death!" he cried, tears bursting from his eyes. "There's nothing strange about it!"

He moved his eyes down the long legs where the little feet were tucked together, one atop the other, and death was upon them, holding them still as stone. He looked again into the open hole in the baby's body, to the framework of the backbone. They took out his lungs and his stomach, took out all his guts. They even took his little heart.

Laski was engulfed again by love for the little boy who lay before him, all cut up. He took the right hand in his own, opening the stiff little fingers and gazing into the tiny cold palm. The fingers held firm against his, with death's unbending grip. How tiny his fingernails are, and so perfect.

He looked at the face of his son and saw that it had undergone a strange transformation. The features had completely matured, the face now that of a man of many years, as if the single moment of life when he was spun upon the doctor's hand had been a lifetime from beginning to end. The triumph and rage, the gain and loss, all this was gone from the face now, and the closed eyelids radiated serenity.

"He's so lovely," said Diane, her tears falling on the exquisite little head, finely sculptured as that of a Grecian statue. "He struggled so hard to be born . . ."

Then the ocean of sorrow took her and she was crying wildly, like a seawind that drives the water into terrible waves. And through the storm the little pine box floated calmly with its strange passenger, the infant who was also an old man.

Laski opened the little eyelid and saw a blackened jewel, gone far into the night. He closed it and put his mouth to the little ear, into which he whispered, "Don't be afraid." Then, looking at the high broad forehead and the noble eyelids, and seeing again so clearly the wisdom they embodied, he knew the being who had come to them and left so quickly didn't need any advice. And he felt much younger than this infant who lay before him, this infant with the head of an age-old sage.

"He never even got to live at all!" cried Diane, howling in the seawind.

Laski touched the little cheek and it sagged beneath his touch, the lifeless flesh like softest putty.

"Oh no, don't," said Diane, her voice suddenly soft, as she gently pushed the flesh of the cheek back into place. Then, bending her head over, she laid a kiss upon the little forehead. "He's just like marble."

Laski slowly brought the garbage bag up around the little body.

"I could look at him forever," said Diane, but she wrapped the bag in the old rags and the dirty sheet, finally pinning closed the clean white linen. Laski lowered the lid of the box, and again it seemed like a dream that could move in any direction he willed. But then he felt reality moving in only one direction. The baby was born and he died and I'm closing the lid of his coffin.

Diane wiped the baby's blood from Laski's face and from her own lips, then went slowly to the couch and lay down. He sat on the floor beside her. There was nothing to say. Neither of them wished to escape the passing of the hours, and they were powerless to change the winding stream of the night; there was nothing to do but sit in the stillness.

He fell into reverie and he fell into fantasy. He was back in the labor room, seeing the baby's skin pushing at her vagina. *He's right there—he's waiting. Get him out of there—don't waste any more time.* But the doctor slept down the hall.

Finally his thoughts faded and there was only the sound of the winter night outside. He felt Diane with him in the deep strange quiet, and holding to it, dwelling in that stillness, he saw life and death merge into one calm and shining sea that had no end.

He woke before dawn and made them breakfast, then carried the pine box into the shed. Through the east windows the first grey light came as he laid the box down and brought hammer and nails. Then slowly and carefully he hammered the lid shut and the pounding of the nails rang out like solemn drumbeats in the winter dawn. As he drove the last nail in, he heard Ben at the shed-door.

Laski opened the door for the old man standing there on snow-shoes, a ragged cigarette in his mouth. "I'll be right with you," said Laski, gathering up his pick and shovel and his own snow-shoes.

"We should dig the hole first," said Ben. "And you can come back for the box."

Laski nodded and walked ahead, over the hard morning crust of snow which crunched beneath their snowshoes. He went into the woods, past the skeleton of an old barn, where a porcupine had made his own beat in the snow, and Laski's path crossed it and went down into the deeper trees.

He followed an old logging trail through the pines and Ben kept close behind him, smoking and coughing in the still morning air. The trail went through alder bushes, and down, to the larger trees, where no lumber had been cut for many years. Laski went on through the old trees to the high bank above the stream. There the bank sloped down, with thin firs growing on its sides. Below was the stream, frozen but still flowing, and the sound of its flowing came up to his ears. He stopped in a square of four small spruce.

They shoveled off the snow, clearing a space of earth in the little square. "The ground doesn't appear to be frozen," said Laski.

"No, it'll be good digging," said Ben, raising the pick. When he'd loosened the dirt, Laski shoveled it and threw it into a pile. The sky remained grey, and the hole took shape and grew deeper, Ben chopping and Laski shoveling out the loosened earth.

"Don't appear to be many roots," said Ben.

"No, it's not bad."

"Has to be wider though," said Ben. He broke more surrounding earth and Laski shoveled it off, so that he was able to climb down into the hole and work at the walls.

"How deep do you want it?" asked Ben.

"So an animal won't dig it up."

"Nothing will touch it," said Ben, but they shoveled deeper until Laski was in up to his waist, throwing the dirt out.

"You go and bring the box back down," said Ben. "I'll get the hole squared up."

Laski climbed out of the hole, put his snowshoes on, and followed the beat back up through the pines. The dampness of the morning brought many smells into the air, of dead wood and leaves, and from time to time he caught a faint trace of the musk of some animal who had passed by. All around in the snow were rabbit tracks, weaving in and out through the trees, and there were also the tracks of a bobcat going in his gracefully curving line deeper into the forest, to the cedar bog, where the deer stayed.

The old barn came into view, and Laski went past it, toward the cabin. At the shed, he removed his snowshoes and stuck them in the snow. He entered the shed and laid the toboggan down on the floor, placing the little coffin on top of it. Then he roped it down.

When it was securely fastened, he went into the cabin. Diane was sitting up on the couch. "Did you find a nice spot?"

"On the high bank above the stream," said Laski. "I'm taking him down there now." He returned to the shed, and carried the loaded sled out into the snow. He put his snowshoes on again, and took the rope in his hands. The load was very light and went smoothly over the crust.

On the slope behind the old barn, the toboggan moved on its own and he ran alongside it, guiding it with the rope through a stand of young spruce. The arms of the little trees touched the box, shedding some needles upon it, and a few tiny cones.

MAGAZINES CONSULTED

American Review—Bantam Books, 666 Fifth Avenue, New York, N.Y. 10019

Antaeus—Ecco Press—1 West 30th Street, New York, N.Y. 10001

Antioch Review—P.O. Box 148, Yellow Springs, Ohio 45387

Aphra—Box 3551, Springtown, Pa. 18081

Appalachian Journal—Box 536, Appalachian State University, Boone, N.C. 28607

Ararat—Armenian General Benevolent Union of America, 628 Second Avenue, New York, N.Y. 10016

Arizona Quarterly—University of Arizona, Tucson, Ariz. 85721

The Ark River Review—348 N. Ohio, Wichita, Kan. 67214

The Atlantic Monthly—8 Arlington Street, Boston, Mass. 02116

Brushfire—c/o English Dept., University of Reno, Reno, Nev. 89507

California Quarterly—100 Sproul Hall, University of California, Davis, Calif. 95616

Canadian Fiction Magazine—595 Irwin Street, Prince George, B.C., Canada

Carleton Miscellany—Carleton College, Northfield, Minn. 55057

Carolina Quarterly—Box 1117, Chapel Hill, N.C. 27515

Colorado Quarterly—Hellums 118, University of Colorado, Boulder, Colo. 80304

The Colorado State Review—360 Liberal Arts, Colorado State University, Fort Collins, Colo. 80521

Commentary—165 East 56th Street, New York, N.Y. 10022

Cosmopolitan—224 West 57th Street, New York, N.Y. 10019

Cutbank—c/o English Dept., University of Montana, Missoula, Mont. 59801

December—P.O. Box 274, Western Springs, Ill. 60558

The Denver Quarterly—Dept. of English, University of Denver, Denver, Colo. 80210

Descant—Dept. of English, TCU Station, Fort Worth, Tex. 76129

dog soldier—323 East Boone, Spokane, Wash. 99202

Epoch—159 Goldwin Smith Hall, Cornell University, Ithaca, N.Y. 14850

Esquire—488 Madison Avenue, New York, N.Y. 10022

The Falcon—Mansfield State College, Mansfield, Pa. 16933

Fantasy and Science Fiction—Box 56, Cornwall, Conn. 06753

The Fault—41186 Alice Avenue, Fremont, Calif. 94538

Fiction—c/o Dept. of English, The City College of New York, New York, 10031

Fiction International—Dept. of English, St. Lawrence University, Canton, N.Y. 13617

The Fiddlehead—Dept. of English, Univ. of New Brunswick, Fredericton, N.B., Canada

The Fisherman's Angle—St. John Fisher College, Rochester, N.Y. 14618

Forum—Ball State University, Muncie, Ind. 47306

Four Quarters—La Salle College, Philadelphia, Pa. 19141

Georgia Review—University of Georgia, Athens, Ga. 30601

The Greensboro Review—University of North Carolina, Greensboro, N.C. 27412

Harper's Magazine—2 Park Avenue, New York, N.Y. 10016

Hawaii Literary Review—Hemenway Hall, University of Hawaii, Honolulu, Haw. 96822

Hudson Review—65 East 55th Street, New York, N.Y. 10022

The Iowa Review—EPB 453, University of Iowa, Iowa City, Iowa 52240

Kansas Quarterly—Dept. of English, Kansas State University, Manhattan, Kan. 66502

Ladies' Home Journal—641 Lexington Avenue, New York, N.Y. 10022

The Literary Review—Fairleigh Dickinson University, Teaneck, N.J. 07666

The Little Magazine—P.O. Box 207, Cathedral Station, New York, N.Y. 10025

Lotus—Department of English, Ohio University, Athens, Ohio 45701

Mademoiselle—350 Madison Avenue, New York, N.Y. 10017

Malahat Review—University of Victoria, Victoria, B.C., Canada

The Massachusetts Review—University of Massachusetts, Amherst, Mass. 01003

McCall's—230 Park Avenue, New York, N.Y. 10017

The Mediterranean Review—Orient, N.Y. 11957

Michigan Quarterly Review—3032 Rackham Bldg., The University of Michigan, Ann Arbor, Mich. 48104

Midstream—515 Park Avenue, New York, N.Y. 10022

Mundus Artium—Dept. of English, Ellis Hall, Box 89, Ohio University, Athens, Ohio 45701

The National Jewish Monthly—1640 Rhode Island Ave., NW, Washington, D.C. 20036

New Directions—333 Sixth Avenue, New York, N.Y. 10014

New Letters—University of Missouri-Kansas City, Kansas City, Mo. 64110

The New Renaissance—9 Heath Road, Arlington, Mass. 02174

The New Yorker—25 West 43rd Street, New York, N.Y. 10036

Nocturne—Box 1320, Johns Hopkins University, Baltimore, Md. 21218

North American Review—University of Northern Iowa, Cedar Falls, Iowa 50613

Northwest Review—129 French Hall, University of Oregon, Eugene, Ore. 97403

The Ohio Journal—164 West 17th Avenue, Columbus, Ohio 43210

Ohio Review—Ellis Hall, Ohio University, Athens, Ohio 45701

Panache—P.O. Box 89, Princeton, N.J. 08540

The Paris Review—45-39—171st Place, Flushing, N.Y. 11358

Partisan Review—Rutgers University, New Brunswick, N.J. 08903

Perspective—Washington University, St. Louis, Mo. 63130

Phylon—223 Chestnut Street, S.W., Atlanta, Ga. 30314

Playboy—919 N. Michigan Avenue, Chicago, Ill. 60611

Prairie Schooner—Andrews Hall, University of Nebraska, Lincoln, Nebr. 68508

Prism International—Dept. of Creative Writing, University of British Columbia, Vancouver 8, B.C., Canada

Quarterly Review of Literature—26 Haslet Avenue, Princeton, N.J. 08540

Quartet—1119 Neal Pickett Drive, College Station, Tex. 77840

Ramparts—2054 University Avenue, Berkeley, Calif. 94704

Redbook—230 Park Avenue, New York, N.Y. 10017

The Remington Review—505 Westfield Avenue, Elizabeth, N.J. 07208

Rolling Stone—625 Third Street, San Francisco, Calif. 94107

Seneca Review—Box 115, Hobart & William Smith Colleges, Geneva, N.Y. 14456

Shenandoah—Box 722, Lexington, Va. 24450

The Sewanee Review—University of the South, Sewanee, Tenn. 37375

The South Carolina Review—Dept. of English, Box 28661, Furman University, Greenville, S.C. 29613

The South Dakota Review—Box 111, University Exchange, Vermillion, S.D. 57069

Southern Review—Drawer D, University Station, Baton Rouge, La. 70803

Southwest Review—Southern Methodist University Press, Dallas, Tex. 75222

Transatlantic Review—Box 3348, Grand Central P.O., New York, N.Y. 10017

Tri-Quarterly—University Hall 101, Northwestern University, Evanston, Ill. 60201

Twigs—Pikeville College, Pikeville, Ky. 41501

Twin Cities Express—127 North Seventh Street, Minneapolis, Minn. 55403

U. S. Catholic—221 West Madison Street, Chicago, Ill. 60606

Vagabond—P.O. Box 879, Ellensburg, Wash. 98926

The Virginia Quarterly Review—University of Virginia, 1 West Range, Charlottesville, Va. 22903

Vogue—350 Madison Avenue, New York, N.Y. 10017

Voyages—Box 4862, Washington, D.C. 20008 (ceased publication)

West Coast Review—Simon Fraser University, Vancouver, B.C., Canada

Western Humanities Review—Bldg. 41, University of Utah, Salt Lake City, Utah 84112

Wind—RFD Route 1, Box 810, Pikeville, Ky. 41501

Woman's Day—1515 Broadway, New York, N.Y. 10036

Works—A.M.S., 56 East 13th Street, New York, N.Y. 10003

Yale Review—26 Hillhouse Avenue, New Haven, Conn. 06520

Stories
Prize   BASEMENT COLLECTION
1975   ASK AT DESK
Prize Stories 1975
The O. Henry awards
7.95

926	JY 25 75
467	AG 11 75

Stories
Prize
1975   BASEMENT COLLECTION
                  ASK AT DESK

Prize stories 1975
The O. Henry awards